C000133810

A.J. Missara remains a mystery to us all.

Dedicated to the people who dare to dream, anything is possible if you believe in yourself.

A.J. Missara

MISANTHROPY

The Dark Matters

AUSTIN MACAULEY PUBLISHERS™

LONDON * CAMBRIDGE * NEW YORK * SHARJAH

Copyright © A.J. Missara 2022

The right of A.J. Missara to be identified as author of this work has been asserted by the author in accordance with sections 77 and 78 of the Copyright, Designs and Patents Act 1988.

All rights reserved. No part of this publication may be reproduced, stored in a retrieval system, or transmitted in any form or by any means, electronic, mechanical, photocopying, recording, or otherwise, without the prior permission of the publishers.

Any person who commits any unauthorised act in relation to this publication may be liable to criminal prosecution and civil claims for damages.

This is a work of fiction. Names, characters, businesses, places, events, locales, and incidents are either the products of the author's imagination or used in a fictitious manner. Any resemblance to actual persons, living or dead, or actual events is purely coincidental.

A CIP catalogue record for this title is available from the British Library.

ISBN 9781398407114 (Paperback)
ISBN 9781398407121 (ePub e-book)

www.austinmacauley.com

First Published 2022
Austin Macauley Publishers Ltd®
1 Canada Square
Canary Wharf
London
E14 5AA

Table of Contents

'…*There comes a point in your life when you need to stop reading other people's books and write your own…*'

— Albert Einstein

Prologue

I'm staring at their hands; their fingers interlock and caress each other. I look up to see my parents, my mother looking lovingly towards my father while he focuses his gaze on the misty road ahead.

The darkness of the night sky fills the atmosphere, with no glimmer of light.

They whisper and giggle in an attempt not to wake us, when all the time, I am awake. I am staring, admiring my beautiful parents and their constant smile and affection towards each other, not knowing, this moment will never come again...

The sudden restlessness of baby Micky by my side throws my mother's gaze towards us.

'Liyana, you're awake,' she whispers in her soft, gentle voice. I give her a warm smile as she leans to the back of the car and puts her palm on my cheek. The impatience of my baby brother breaks the gaze my mother and I share... our final intimate moment.

'Micky baby, we are almost there,' my mother whispers as she takes his hand to console him.

'Less than an hour left, we'll take the back roads to reduce the journey time,' my father states in his firm yet loving voice. His reassurance puts a smile on my mother's face while she strokes little Micky's head as he begins to settle.

The thickness of the mist grows unexpectedly. 'What the...' my father gasps as he releases the acceleration. The sudden uneven surface of the road begins to make me nervous. 'It's okay,' my father affirms as he gently presses on the breaks. 'Don't worry; it's just a little fog...' he offers to reassure us.

Have you ever experienced a sensation where you know within the pit of your stomach that something terrible is about to happen? For me, this was my first encounter with this terrifying feeling.

Micky shrieks unexpectedly. Instinctively I take his hand into mine, hoping that my mother will help my father with the fog-filled road ahead. I look at my brother, noticing our hands begin to tremble. I know something evil is about to happen, and my baby brother can sense it too.

The car slows while the impact from the uneven surface increases, forcing the car to tremor along the road.

Something is wrong; I can see it as I watch my parent's beautiful smiles consumed with fear.

I feel sick from the twisting motion within the pit of my stomach, suddenly, my body paralyses from the sound of my father's GASP.

My mother's unnatural SHRIEK forces shockwaves through our senses. The car loses control as the sound of the breaks screeching can barely be heard over my father's roar. I know understand the fear in the pit of my soul, it is fear for the life of my family and me.

The darkness does not frighten me any longer as I focus on the illuminating glow.

The burning orange eyes surrounding us in the darkness of the shadows terrifies me!

I suddenly wake, the tears having filled my pillow already. That dreadful night has haunted me for all these years,

I pray for the horrific memories to no longer enter my dreams.

'…Remember today, for it is the beginning of always. Today marks the start of a brave new future…'

— Albert Einstein

01. The Start of the Beginning

'Liyana, Nana and Pops are crying,' my brother Micky whispers with a helpless voice through the door.

'Give me a minute, I'll be right down,' I shout out as I stare at my reflection.

My long, dark scraggly hair drape forward as I lean my hands on the basin.

'You're doing the right thing,' I repeat to myself in an attempt to stall the regret I can feel crawling into my conscience.

'You are not selfish; this is the right decision.'

I rinse my hands before combing my fingers through my hair. I pull on the strands as I reach the top of my scalp; the slight pain distracts me from the sickening feeling encroaching my stomach. A sickness now spreading across my senses, breeding from uncertainty and fear that now runs through my body. If only I could be as strong as my father was; so calm and controlled in every decision he had made.

My hazel eyes stare into my reflection, which portrays a slim, young girl. My high cheekbones that I once hated now serve as a daily reminder of the features I have inherited from my mother.

My oval face, small button nose and full lips bring out the perfect blend of my beloved parents.

'What have I done to myself?' I question as I stare at my once tanned skin, which now appears pale and dehydrated. 'Perhaps this can be my fresh start too?' I question.

I am tired of appearing strong on the outside when all the time I can feel myself crumbling away discreetly on the inside. Perhaps this is what I need, to take better care of myself?'

'Liyanaaa…' I hear Micky whisper again in a desperate plea.

I brush aside my inner weakness, forcing myself to become the confident, assertive older sister.

I open the bathroom door to find Micky sitting on his knees. As he raises his glance, I stare down at an innocent young boy. His chestnut coloured fringe frames his eyes. His beautiful piercing grey eyes are full of tears.

Every time I see tears in my little brother's eyes, I cannot help but feel guilty for not taking better care of him. If mom and dad were here, they would never let tears fill his eyes, just as they never allowed tears to fill mine.

As I step out of the bathroom, I bend to my knees and stroke his tears away.

'You know I don't like seeing tears on your face, Micky. It's my job to keep tears away from your eyes; you know that right?'

Micky try's to put on a smile, but the sadness quickly takes over.

'Right now, I'm not doing a good job, am I?' I whisper softly as I lean towards him.

Micky throws his arms around me, squeezing tight around my neck.

'I thought you want to go to Aunty Liz's?' I ask.

'I do, I just don't want to leave Nana and Pops. I don't like it when they cry,' he sobs.

'How about we promise to visit during every holiday, just like we used to with Aunt Liz for the summer…do you think that will make them smile again?'

Micky stops sobbing as he turns his gaze towards me. The faintest smile appears on his soft cheeks from the thought of regular visits.

'Quick, let's tell Nana and Pops now, then we can all celebrate,' I whisper with excitement to encourage his smile even further.

Micky jumps with enthusiasm before running downstairs to share the good news.

I walk down the stairs while listening to the sound of Pops coughing and spluttering from his deteriorating health.

'For his sake, I am doing the right thing,' I reassure myself as I enter through to the lounge.

I find Micky seated on Pops' lap sharing the good news. Nana and Pops force a laugh in a desperate attempt to make positive what can only be described as an unnatural end to our home.

'Liyana, you both always have a home here,' Nana reaffirms as she walks towards me.

Nana takes my face into her palms, as she looks deep into my eyes. 'I don't care what any court order says; we are well enough to take care of our grandchildren. We have great universities here, why won't you stay?'

'Nana, how can I leave Micky when I am the closest thing he has to our parents?' I ask in the hope that she will understand my decision.

Nana quickly wipes the tear from her cheek before whispering, 'You remind me so much of your mother, I am so proud of you.' The mention of my mother always catches me off guard; breaking my heart just that little bit more. I don't think I will ever be able to get over losing them both.

We share an intimate hug while I reassure Nana not to worry; we are only a phone call away.

I say goodbye to Pops while embracing him in my arms. 'You call me if you have any problems Liyana,' Pops looks at me with a stern face as his voice deepens. 'I know what your Aunt Liz can be like, so any problems you call me, I will be straight there! You will always have a home here.' The assertiveness in his demeanour reminds me so much of my father.

'Yes, Pops,' I affirm. I put on a brave, confident smile despite feeling scared and vulnerable deep down.

'Are you sure you cannot stay for a few more weeks Liyana? You could always spend the remaining summer holiday here,' Nana suggests in a final attempt to persuade us to stay a little longer.

'Nana this will be good for us. It will take us time to settle in. Besides, it will be better for Micky to settle before the new school year starts.'

I force a smile and kiss Nana on the cheek before entering our chauffeur-driven vehicle, compliments of my lavish Aunt Liz.

Micky sits beside me, now filled with excitement to start his new adventure, at least that's how we have all sold it to him.

I wish I could feel as excited as he is; I crave to be wanted as much as he is, but deep down I know the truth.

As we sit in the car, the words of Pops play on my mind, '...*I know what your Aunt Liz can be like...*'

From the underlying tone of his voice, I know that Pops understands clearly how Aunt Liz now treats me.

Once upon a time, my Aunt Liz adored me. There is nothing she would not do for me; I remember feeling like the luckiest little girl in the world! I had both, the perfect mother and perfect aunt! But now, I do not think I have either…

Aunt Liz made me feel like a princess, forever calling me her little angel. She would always tell me it was okay that she could never have children because she has a niece like me that she loves just as much as she would her own daughter.

I wish that I could be that same girl again, be the same niece that adored her aunt, just as she adored me.

But since my parents had gone, things have changed.

In a time when I needed my Aunt Liz the most, crying for her comforting embrace, she seemed to grow distant from me.

It broke me even further, the feeling of losing both my parents and my aunt Liz.

No wonder why I have now become a closed book, I think to myself as I shake my head to push out the painful memories.

Aunt Liz was obsessed with Micky; he was just a baby when my parents had disappeared.

She was desperate to claim him and fought hard with Nana and Pops to gain custody.

Her compromise being, they can keep me so long as she gets Micky.

In fact, she never even wanted me, never fought for custody of me – only my little brother.

I know I cried a lot when I was younger, I know that I would have days where I would detract from the world, only to replay the memories of my parents in my mind. I know I didn't handle it well, but I was just a child myself.

Micky was none the wiser of what was happening.

He occasionally used to call Aunt Liz "mama"; she was over the moon, encouraging this as much as possible, till Micky began mimicking my behaviour in calling her Aunt.

Aunt Liz didn't like that, and as a result, didn't like me. She no longer wanted me around, influencing Micky in a way, which didn't suit her.

Micky was the chance she had of raising a child that had no memory of his parents. Aunt Liz would be the closest person Micky would know of a mother.

Me on the other hand, I remember my mother clearly which I imagine did not fit in Aunt Liz's ideal family set up.

I suppose now I am an unwanted reminder, a spare piece to a puzzle that's already complete in Aunt Liz's world.

Though I am now of the age where custody no longer applies to me, I am thankful to Uncle Aidan for having extended the offer to reside with them alongside Micky.

But most of all, I am relieved and thankful that Micky has the love of many; though nothing can quiet substitute the love of your parents; something that he will never know.

For Micky's sake, I didn't want him to miss out on a healthy life. A family set up, after all, Aunt Liz and Uncle Aidan have a gap in their life, which Micky could fill perfectly.

Or should I have taken custody of my brother…? With the inheritance left behind by my parents, I could financially support us both and still be with Nana and Pops.

Am I selfish in not taking this step? Am I selfish in wanting to spend time to find out exactly what happened to my parents rather than taking care of Micky?

Should I not be focusing on the future rather than trying to make sense of the past; a past that is full of pain, anger and unanswered questions.

All these uncertainties accompany me throughout the journey towards what is to be my new home.

As the saying goes, home is where the heart is, and as we drive away from Nana and Pops waving in the distance, it's more evident than ever, my heart is lost, and I know not where I belong.

The journey continues for hours, each passing minute adds to my anxiety. I stare into the thickness of the trees as we pass the deepest of forests. I've travelled this journey on countless occasions, yet the depth of the forest never fails to mesmerise me. I try hard to recall any hidden memories trapped within my subconscious from that dreadful night I last saw my parents. But the darkness of that night shadowed my vision, leaving me unable to recall any part of our trail.

As we approach an hour distance from my aunt's home, I restlessly scour the forests, searching for the dirt trail or back roads that we may have taken that tragic night.

There it is! The smallest of openings within the forest, barely big enough for a car to fit through.

Every time I pass this opening, I cannot help but wonder, perhaps this is the route we took that dreadful night my parents left us? Perhaps this trail is where I should start my journey to find answers?

The car slowly comes to a stop as we approach what is to be our new home. I feel empty as I watch Aunt Liz open the double doors and flutter down the steps of her mansion. There isn't another house in sight as my eyes search around to absorb my new surroundings.

The excitement in Micky's eyes reassures me that this is the right thing for him.

As we exit the vehicle, the warm, loving embrace Aunt Liz shares with Micky comforts my doubt in this decision. Though this did not feel like home for me, I cannot help but smile at the sight of Micky having another chance to be a part of a happy home.

Micky giggles from being swung around by Aunt Liz. Uncle Aidan who runs to take Micky out of Aunt Liz's arms and into his own joins their laughter.

'Liyana!' Aunt Liz calls with a friendly smile. As we wrap our arms around each other, I cannot help but find the embrace somewhat empty; polite, but empty. 'I'm glad you've decided to join us,' she confirms. Though there seems to be sincerity in her voice, the phrase itself makes me feel like an extra part.

I offer a sheepish smile while Uncle Aidan walks towards me, presenting me with a pat on the back as Micky remains in his arms.

'It's good to see you, Liyana. You look more and more like your mother every time I see you,' he claims which brings a proud smile to my face.

As he places his arm around my shoulder, we all walk towards our new home.

The house is warm and inviting. I cannot help but stare at the chandelier hanging from the ceiling of the first floor. The sparkles always bring a smile to my face.

As we walk across the thick wooden flooring, we enter the lounge to the right.

I focus on the bay window, framed with lavish ceiling to floor curtains. A smile naturally appears on my face. This is where I would spend most my time during my visits here; in between the bay window and sofa, hidden away, with the memories of my parents.

The overly large flat screen TV and log fireplace in the centre of the room never interested me as a child, but perhaps now that I am older, I will appreciate it more?

As I take a deep breath in an attempt to embrace this new home, the sweet fragrance of the cluster of burning candles beside the fireplace sooth my nerves.

I walk through to the dining room where the scent lingers on. The solid wood dining table surrounded by eight chairs appears unused.

I walk towards the back of the room and place my hand against the glass of the French patio doors.

I look out to the garden, observing the drastic changes since my last visit.

Once full of trees and shrubs, it is now neatly divided into various quarters. Though at the very far end of the garden, the forest of trees remains.

During our visits many years ago, I use to play a game here, while Aunt Liz would devote all her attention towards Micky.

I would walk into the forest to see how many steps I could take before the fear kicked in, forcing me to run back towards the house.

But each time, I had to take one step further than the last.

I think it is this game, which helped me overcome my phobia of the forests.

I pace towards the patio doors of the kitchen to get a better view of the garden.

I walk in between the smaller dining table to the corner of the kitchen and the breakfast bar beside the kitchen units.

It's hard not to notice the pearl white marble finish of the worktops and kitchen floor against the dark wooden cupboards.

I wish I had a taste for this lavish and glamorous lifestyle, but I think I suit the small townhouse set up with Nana and Pops.

I gaze through the glass-panelled doors, observing the neatly cut bushes that split the garden into three separate quadrants. My eyes focus in on the far-left quadrant, but I cannot make out what is contained within.

'What's behind there?' I whisper as I turn to look at Aunt Liz.

I hear giggles of laughter in the background, but I stood here alone.

They must be with Micky, I think to myself as I turn back towards the garden, not letting the solitude affect me.

A smile appears on my expression at the sight of the oversized curvaceous bench swing towering over the bushes of the far- r i g h t quadrant.

Maybe that will be my new spot, rather than behind the chair in the lounge?

I stare at the quadrant closest to me, which splits the garden in half.

I notice the corrosion of the barbeque on the patio beside the outdoor furniture, all which appears well-used.

Having almost completed a circle around the ground floor, the final room left is the study; where all the laughter seems to be coming from.

This was the smallest room in the house, yet big enough to hold a desk, filling draws, sofa and coffee table.

'Micky, you've made a friend,' I state with a smile as I lean against the doorframe.

'Liyana!' Micky shouts as he jumps to his feet, embracing me with a hug.

The tight hold from Micky is comforting, reassuring me that my decision to stay close to him was undoubtedly the right decision. He has been through enough loss in life without me creating any more holes in his incomplete world.

'Liyana! This is Diesel, Aunt Liz and Uncle Aidan said, Diesel has been looking for me, and he is my friend for life!'

I look down towards the small German Sheppard rolling on the shaggy rug with a white collar around its tiny neck.

'Micky…you are such a lucky boy! Everyone wants a friend for life, and you have now got one,' I say with excitement, to encourage his happy smile even further.

'This was very kind of you,' I whisper to Aunt Liz and Uncle Aidan as they sit on the sofa, cuddling each other at the sight of Micky's excitement. They look at him with pure love, a longing for him to be their own child. Micky would be happy here, he would be well looked after, and this will always remain my highest priority.

'Right, how about we show you your rooms?' Aunt Liz announces with excitement.

As we walk up the stairs to the second floor, I cannot help but gasp at the enormous size of the bedroom. It seems as if it is half the size of the house! The room is filled with toys, furniture, computer consoles, sofa and balcony doors; everything a child could want.

'Micky, this is your room, we hope you like it,' Aunt Liz announces with a look of anticipation in her eyes.

'Wooow… This is AMAZING,' Micky whispers as he gazes in shock. A look of relief passes over Aunt Liz's face.

For a moment, Micky looks confused as he pauses in motion. He hesitates, before finding the courage to ask, 'But whose are all these things, Aunt Liz? There is so much stuff in here.'

'Well, they are all yours, silly! You will never have to go without ever again. Not now, well now that I've become your new mommy!'

I turn to stare at Aunt Liz as her words shatter my heart with the very thought of my mother being replaced.

How can my mom be replaced so quickly? My mom can never be replaced.

Uncle Aidan reads my reaction like a book. He places his hand on Aunt Liz's shoulder disapprovingly while offering me a sympathetic smile.

'I… I… I'm sorry… Was that too soon?' She quivers as she turns to look at her husband.

'My new mommy…' Micky repeats before breaking into a chuckle.

'Aunt Liz you are not my mommy, you are my aunt Liz.' He laughs as he jumps onto his new bed. His innocence is refreshing which quickly lightens the atmosphere.

Desperate to push my weaknesses aside, I take in a deep breath and conjure my strong, assertive demeanour. A side of me that I have found useful, as the years have gone by; a shield to protect the fragile, vulnerable girl that lies within.

'Yes, Micky,' I add as I try hard to control my expression. 'Aunt Eliza is your aunt,' I affirm.

I cannot help but glare at Aunt Liz from her lack of tact! Uncle Aidan gives me a sympathetic smile while Aunt Liz seems to be scowling.

I look over to Micky to make sure he cannot feel the tension in the room. A smile grows on my face as I watch him bouncing on his bed oblivious to the negative emotions.

'Micky, I love your room, Aunt Liz and Uncle Aidan have been extremely generous! They have really tried hard to make this perfect for you,' I state to ensure my appreciation does not go unnoticed.

Micky stops jumping and turns to look at me. The joy on his face suddenly disappears. He seems to be pondering in deep thought when he finally states, 'Liyana, it's only perfect because you are here!' A huge smile takes over his expression as he leaps off his bed, jumping straight into my arms.

'MICKY!' I shout as I struggle to catch hold of him. He laughs uncontrollably and holds on tight, wrapping his arms around me.

The bond I share with my brother is I'm sure the closest relationship any siblings have ever shared. He is my world and from the statement, he has just made, it is clear that I am his. I burst out laughing from joy at the sound of his beautiful, innocent giggle. For a moment, it is just Micky and I. No one else matters and nothing else exists.

'How about your room, Ann,' Aunt Liz states in a direct tone. Oh dear, I am only 'Ann' when Aunt Liz is fed up with me. That didn't take long at all, it's been less than an hour since we arrived and already she is fed up. Perhaps I was a bit harsh I question as I look over towards her. I offer her a sheepish but sincere smile in the hope that she will soften her tone. I cannot blame her really; Aunt Liz becomes Aunt Eliza when I am frustrated with her, perhaps I should have controlled myself better?

We walk back to the first floor where I am presented with a large room. An exceptionally spacious, large bedroom accompanied by a double bed, en-suite, furniture and a beautiful chaise lounge seat. The décor throughout the place is extremely glamorous!

The shaggy rug theme, which seems to run through the house, continues within my room beneath the double 4-poster bed. The white and gold theme throughout the room makes me feel as if I am in a big fluffy cloud. Maybe this is precisely what I need. Perhaps this could become my safe haven.

I could never imagine having such a luxurious room. Style and glamour do not come naturally to me, far from it, in fact, it requires a lot of effort!

I can suddenly feel the guilt begin to consume me.

I turn to face Aunt Liz and Uncle Aidan. 'I'm sorry, Aunt Liz; I didn't mean to be rude earlier. This is really overwhelming for me, and I appreciate everything you are doing I really do… I'm sorry and thank you. This room is beautiful; I can see you have put a lot of thought into everything you are doing for us both.' Aunt Liz's face softens, it is clear I have caught her by surprise.

I've never been ashamed or reserved when it comes to apologising; I'm open to accepting fault where I have made a mistake. Showing my weaknesses and vulnerability, on the other hand, is something I struggle to expose.

Sometimes, I hate the way my natural defence mechanisms keep me so guarded!

I just hope Aunt Liz can hear the sincerity in my voice and genuinely accepts my plea for forgiveness. I wish she could see me for the same fragile, innocent girl that she once knew me as.

'Don't worry kiddo,' Uncle Aidan states as he places his hand on my shoulder to offer a subtle embrace.

'You have gone through more heartache than people do in a lifetime, so it's okay to be defensive. You just give me a shout if you need anything.'

'Thank you, Uncle.'

I stare into his eyes as I see a glimmer of my father in him, my father's confident, assertive ways.

'I appreciate the apology,' Aunt Liz confirms with a hint of harshness in her voice.

'Get some rest now; it's been an emotional day for you.' She forces a smile as they leave the room closing the door behind them.

I sit on the chaise lounge and look around to absorb my new surroundings, my new bedroom – my safe haven. The cloud-like theme makes me feel warm and cosy. Protected almost, as if nothing harmful can reach me in this space of mine.

The laughter from outside distracts me from my thoughts. I walk towards the end of the room, opening the glass doors to the balcony. I am still unable to see what is in the left quadrant of the garden, which is guarded by the shielding hedge.

My eyes focus in on the laughter as I watch Micky rolling around the garden with Diesel as they attempt to play fetch.

The genuine happiness displayed by Micky makes me feel warm and proud. The desperate love and acceptance Aunt Liz and Uncle Aidan seek from Micky make me feel relieved, less afraid for his future and happiness.

The smile emerging on my face becomes uncontrollable. I'm smiling from the heart. Finally, I have the feeling of complete reassurance that I have made the right decision. There is no doubt in my mind!

This was the right move to make for both Micky and me. This is our fresh start.

More so, this is the beginning, a time in which I can finally start to seek answers for what happened to my parents all those years ago...

'…Find the courage to let go, for the past will hold you.
Allow your dreams to unfold, for the future will welcome you…'

— A.J. Missara

02. Unwanted Memories

As we all sit at the dining table, I watch how both Aunt Liz and Uncle Aidan fuss over Micky. Micky, however, is more interested in secretly feeding his dinner to Diesel, who sits under the table beside him.

Our eyes meet as Micky looks around to ensure the coast is clear before discreetly taking another slice of chicken off his plate, dropping it under the table.

We lock our gaze as I give him a stern look with raised eyebrows.

Micky slowly widens his lips, displaying his gap-filled teeth. His baby teeth make him appear a lot younger than he is. Micky's wide grin extends to a hysterical laughter from being caught.

I cannot help but giggle discreetly at the sight of Micky being so happy yet cheeky.

'What's so funny?' Aunt Liz questions in confusion.

'We are just pulling faces at each other, Aunt Liz,' I respond to ensure Micky's cheeky ways go unnoticed.

'No playing games at the dinner table, you should know better than that Liyana, now please stop distracting your brother!' Here we go, I think to myself as Aunt Liz glares at me with a look of disapproval.

'Of course, Aunt Liz. I think Micky would like some more chicken,' I respond softly to ensure the atmosphere remains calm.

'Micky you need to make sure that YOU finish your chicken,' I add softly. He understands the underlying tone of my message as he gently nods his head. I call Diesel over towards me to ensure Micky doesn't sacrifice all his dinner for his love of his new best friend.

'Ann, Micky is doing great with his dinner, he has almost finished which is more than what I can say about you.' Aunt Liz shakes her head in slight frustration as she places more food on Micky's plate.

'My Micky is a growing boy, make sure you tell me if you want anything else,' Aunt Liz requests as she rubs Micky on the head. Her unnaturally thin, tall frame towers over Micky as he eats away oblivious to her tone.

Her short dark hair with blonde highlights is tucked behind her ears while her fringe frames her squinty, brown eyes. Her sharp nose follows down to her thin stretched lips.

I look down at my plate, the words of Pops replay on my mind, *I know what she can be like*. The support from my Pops puts a smile on my slightly saddened expression.

'So, Liyana, have you made your decision about universities,' Uncle Aidan asks.

I look up at him as he offers me an apologetic smile. His dark hair and tanned skin remind me of my father.

'Yes, Uncle, I will be going with my first choice, which is close to here, so I can still be close to Micky,' I affirm with a proud smile!

'You don't have to worry about Micky,' states Aunt Liz. 'He has us now. Besides, why don't you live on the university campus just to experience it? You will enjoy the adult lifestyle! You will never get another chance, you of all people deserve the full experience.'

I put my fork down while my fingertips rub my forehead. The look of exhaustion consumes my expression; I cannot help but release a defeated sigh.

I have lost count of the number of times Aunt Liz has tried hard to persuade me to live out on campus. I hoped we would never have to have the same conversation again after our last altercation on the matter.

I know Aunt Liz means well and I really do feel for her not being able to have children, something she has always desperately wanted. But her lack of tact makes it difficult for me not to react to her obvious desire of not wanting me here.

Here, in this moment, I feel tired of not being wanted yet having to fight, to stay close to my brother.

'Nonsense,' states Uncle Aidan in a stern voice. 'Liyana can have the best of both worlds. This is her home, and she can stay out on campus as and when she pleases with the friends she will make.'

Uncle Aidan gives me a reassuring smile, making it clear that I am still wanted.

Perhaps he can sense my fear of being pushed away?

'Off course this is her home,' Aunt Liz responds as she forces a gentle laugh.

'But if Liyana wants to focus on her life and experience adulthood by living away, we could put all our focus on Micky, to make sure he has everything he could need.'

Uncle Aidan looks to the ground as he shakes his head in disappointment. He tried, but Aunt Liz's dominating character brings the conversation back to the point that she would like to make.

I can feel it begin to happen; the soft, vulnerable Liyana is being protected as my defences start to shield around me, coating me with a layer of confidence.

'Thank you, Aunt Liz,' I calmly state as I plan to bring the conversation to an end.

'Perhaps you are right. It may even be an option for me to spread my wings a little down the line. But right now, Micky is my priority. And I appreciate everything you are doing for him. It makes me really happy to hear your genuine passion for wanting to take care of him; I am grateful for this Aunt... But Micky is all the family I have, so I cannot help but feel protective towards him. I hope you can understand. Once I have reassured myself that Micky will be okay and well looked after without me, perhaps spreading my wings is something I can consider then?'

'Well looked after without you!' Aunt Liz repeats in a mocking tone.

'What would you know about Micky being well looked after, you're just a kid yourself Ann,' Aunt Liz snaps as she starts to clear the table.

'Okaaay...' I reply slowly to control my frustration as my defence mechanism runs in overdrive.

'Either I am a kid where I don't understand what being looked after means, or I am an adult who is ready to move away and live on my own... I can't be both as and when it suits your agenda Eliza!'

'Ladies, let's take this down a notch, we are all on the same team here,' Uncle Aidan interrupts as he moves both his palms in a lowering gesture. I look at Micky to find his beautiful Grey eyes staring right back at me. A slight sheen on his eyes appears from where he hasn't blinked, he must be worrying.

As Uncle Aidan walks away to console his wife who has taken the dishes to the kitchen, I take a 'pea' from my plate and throw it across the table at Micky.

He blinks in confusion from the flying pea before glancing in my direction; a warm smile appears across his face from my unexpected behaviour.

'Ssshh' I gesture as I place my index finger on my pursed lips. Micky giggles quietly as he quickly picks up the pea beside him, putting it in his mouth to keep our mischief discreet.

Uncle Aidan and Aunt Liz re-enter the room with deserts, Victoria Sponge cake with piping hot custard. 'Especially for you, my little boy,' Aunt Liz announces as she places a bowl beside Micky.

She hands a bowl across to me without making eye contact. 'Thank You Aunt,' I state to show my gratitude.

Aunt Liz maintains her loving gaze towards Micky while he eats away his desert.

'You really are a miracle child,' she states. 'An absolute bundle of joy.'

'How am I a miracle, I'm just a boy,' he questions as he looks around the table for answers.

'Well, you were a surprise. No one was expecting you; you surprised us all when you came into our lives.'

'Everyone likes surprises,' Micky states while oblivious to what Aunt Liz is talking about.

But for once I agreed with Aunt Liz. Micky was a surprise hence the big age gap between us. He wasn't planned, yet he is perfect, and without him, I would honestly be alone.

'This has always been your home, Micky. You belonged here all those years ago after that tragic accident!'

An awkward silence fills the room. The desert absorbs Micky's attention; he pays no attention to Aunt Liz.

Uncle Aidan clears his throat to in an attempt to fill the silence as he adds, 'You too, kiddo.'

I force a smile and try to hold back the sadness in my expression.

The mention of that tragic accident which took my parents away never fails to leave me wounded.

But I'm glad Aunt Liz mentions this, as it brings back my focus to one of the reasons I chose to make this move…to finally find some answers.

'Uncle Aidan do you have a map of this area by any chance?'

'Yeah I could do, I'll check the bookshelf in the study. But what do you need a map for,' Uncle Aidan asks with a curious expression?

'Oh, you know, I want to get back into shape before I start University, so was just planning to go for a run. It will be good for me to get to know the area and understand my surroundings.'

'Well you don't need a map for that, we have a great gym in the centre which you could join. It will be easy to get to when you finally get a car,' Aunt Liz responds.

Was that another dig? I question in my mind, *finally get a car?*

'Yes, of course, Aunt Liz,' I confirm in an attempt to get back into her good books.

'Besides, who uses a map these days? Everything is accessible from your mobile!' she adds in a superior tone.

'Technology makes you lazy. Rule 1 of survival camp, never rely on technology,' Uncle Aidan responds in a playful tone while defending my position.

I help to clear the dishes; in the hope that Aunt Liz will not think I am taking liberties. Hopefully, she will see me as a helping hand rather than an unwanted addition.

After rummaging through the bookshelf in the study, I finally manage to locate the map.

As I lay on my luxurious bed, I cannot help but wonder if Aunt Liz had a point? Maybe it will be better for everyone if I did leave and live out on campus? Micky could have a shot at an ordinary family life? Maybe I should start acting my age and just have 'fun' like normal girls my age do?

To the world, I portray myself as a confident, intelligent young woman. Determined and assertive in all decisions I make. But the reality is, I am afraid. I am so scared of the truth that I have no parents or guardian to direct me throughout life. No one to reassure me that I am on the right path or doing the right thing.

I'm not really sure where I belong.

Though my bedroom becomes my sanctuary, this place does not feel like my home. Sometimes, I just feel as if something is missing, the final piece of the puzzle which completes me as a person.

Perhaps once I have the answers to my parent's disappearance, maybe then I will be able to finally move on? Maybe this is the missing piece of the puzzle?

I momentarily stare at the map by my side before getting on my knees to remove the box from under my bed.

I empty the contents onto my bed, laying out the newspaper clippings I have collected throughout the years.

'...Tragic Accident Suspected as a family of four are reported missing...'

'...Car located with 2 Children unharmed six days after tragedy...'

'...Children survive in the forest for six days while the search for their parents continues...'

'...10-Year-Old Child claims parents were taking care of her while stranded in the forests...'

'...Mother and Father still missing...'

'...No signs of parents or bodies after six weeks of searching...'

'...Parents vanish, leaving two young children behind...'

The tears stream down my face as I close my hazel eyes.

My eyes open, I find myself at the scene of the tragedy. A 10-year-old frightened girl, a memory that will haunt me for all my years.

I block my ears to drown out the sound of terrified screams surrounding me.

I feel the blood dripping from my forehead, down towards my cheek, but I am too afraid to remove my hands from my ears to wipe the blood away.

The car shakes as if it is being tossed from side to side.

The shrieks of pain from my parents make my heart pound in my throat; I'm struggling to breathe.

I want to scream, from the terror that possesses me, but I'm too afraid to make a sound, amongst the horror I am living in.

The pit of my stomach churns, as I try hard to open my eyes, yet I cannot stop squeezing them shut, from fear of what I may see surrounding us.

The roaring of an unknown sound amongst the shrieking of my parents makes me tremble in fear. The rocking motion of the car pushes me side to side, but in that moment, one sound out of what feels like hundreds of terrifying torturous screams, stands out from them all; the sound of Micky by my side, screaming in fear.

I find the will to open my eyes, while removing my hands from my ears. Without even realising, I place my bloodstained hands over Micky's ears, to protect him from the nightmare that surrounds us.

I pull my body close to him to block his vision of what is happening around us; his hands grip onto me as if he was terrified, of life itself. His body trembles while we are surrounded by darkness, surrounded by horror.

My only thought is to stay with Micky; I can't leave him alone. The turbulence of the car abruptly stops after a final tousle. I pull my lips towards Micky's ear and whisper, 'Ssshhh, it's okay.'

I need him to hear my voice so that he will know I am by his side, maybe this will give him some comfort.

The shrieks and growls continue, but it seems to be passing us through the forest.

As I manage to control my hysterical breathing, Micky's shrieks soften and gradually resemble a baby's cry. I find the courage to look around me as my eyes dart towards my mother and father.

Their seats are empty while their doors are wide open.

I stare at what looks like splatter of blood on the front windscreen. Whose blood is this?

The sudden feeling of panic rushes through my veins, as reality finally catches up with me. My parents, they are in the forest.

I convince myself that I need to find them; I need to help them, in the desperate hope that everything will be okay if I can just get my parents back into the car. We can all drive off and call the police as soon as we get to Aunt Liz and Uncle Aidan's home.

Micky's grip softens, encouraging me to remove my hands from around his ears.

I lean forward towards the driver's seat to find Mother's handbag still at the foot of the front seat. She wouldn't have gone far; I convince myself. Mom never leaves anywhere without her bag. I'm desperate to believe that they are coming back, that they would never leave Micky and me, all alone, in this nightmare.

I take a deep gulp and clear my dry throat. My palms are sweaty; my knees begin to tremble at the thought of having to leave the car.

Within a fusion of adrenaline and panic, I find the courage to push my door open. I try to rush out only to find myself being yanked back into my seat.

The thud I create from being pulled back, increases the restlessness of Micky, forcing his cry to become louder.

If I don't leave the car now to bring my parents back, I never will. The adrenaline will disappear, and the courage will be lost, forever. 'It's okay, it's okay,' I whisper to Micky as I furiously press the seat belt button to remove the harness around me. Finally, it releases; my heart fills with the hope that I will find my parents outside of the car. I shuffle towards the door when instantly it slams shut!

Micky shrieks as the car vibrates from the slamming of the door.

The adrenaline in my veins is quickly overpowered by the sickness from fear. Suddenly, I do not feel as brave, but I need this nightmare to end and for our parents to be by our sides.

As I look out of the window, all I can see is darkness amongst the thickest of mist surrounding us. There is no sign of any light, any help, anything.

'It's okay, I will be right back, be brave for me, Micky,' I plea as I crawl towards the driver's seat. I continue to whisper reassurance to Micky to distract myself from the thought that I will be entering the forest when suddenly both front doors of the vehicle slam shut!

I burst into tears but am too afraid to scream. I scuffle back to Micky in the back seat and hold him close while I cry inside. The tears flow endlessly, my whimpering cry and Micky's vulnerable snuffling is all I can hear. The rest of the world is silent. No shrieks or growls in the distance; not even the sound of the wind whistling through the trees.

Merely the sound of two terrified, lonely children, trying to console each other while trapped, in a nightmare.

'…Before you ask the brave questions, ensure you have the courage to hear the incomprehensible answers…'

— A.J. Missara

03. My First Journey

I wake to the creaking sound of footsteps coming from across the hall. I look towards the luminous dial of the clock on my bedside table, reflecting a steady glow of 03.12.

I stare at the moonlight shining down upon us. The glass panels of my balcony doors, illuminates my bedroom with a faint glow – the world seems silent.

I must have imagined the footsteps; I convince myself as I force my eyes to close.

The creaking of the floor in the hallway continues. I open my eyes; I see the branches from the tops of the trees in the distance, swaying from side to side. It's an old house full of wooden floorboards; there is bound to be the odd creak here and there.

As I cosy up into my duvet slowly drifting back to sleep, I suddenly hear the sound of my bedroom door handle turning. I feel a spike in my heartbeat as the door pushes open; I am too afraid to turn around. Perhaps it is Aunt Liz checking to see if I am asleep? I feel a force of pressure at the end of the bed. I lay frozen as I feel it move quickly, ruffling the sheets in its motion. I immediately turn to sit up as my heart starts pounding; pulling away the sheets to reveal what is hidden beneath. 'MICKY!' I whisper in a stern voice as the sheets reveal a tiny little body tucking into a ball on my bed. 'What are you doing? You're going to give me a heart attack!'

'I'm sorry, Liyana,' Micky pleads in a vulnerable voice. 'I want to stay next to you. My bedroom is too big and scary in the dark,' he states as he pulls the covers back towards him.

I cosy up in bed while wrapping my arms around my little Micky.

'I've told you before, Micky; while I'm around, you never have to be afraid okay.' I pull him closer towards me while I softly whisper, 'If you're afraid that means I'm not doing a good job.'

'You are Liyanaaa...' Micky confirms in a plea. His innocence brings a natural smile to my face.

I kiss him on his head while whispering, 'I love you' into his ear.

'I love you too, Liyana,' Micky responds.

'You're like my best friend,' Micky whispers before becoming silent. I can sense he is pondering in deep thought.

'No...' he states in a corrective tone. 'Diesel is like my best friend, but you're different to him... I think you're more like my mom...' His beautiful innocence and vulnerability bring tears to my eyes.

As I quietly clear my throat to push back the sound of my emotions, I whisper, 'I will always be whatever you need me to be Micky, you're my world.'

'Liyana...' Micky whispers in a softer tone than usual.

'Why did Mommy and Daddy not come back...? Did we do something wrong?'

My heart breaks as I hear the tones of confusion and guilt within his voice.

'Darling, noo...we did nothing wrong okay,' I whisper as I brush away my tear before shuffling closer towards him. 'Sometimes bad things happen in life, and no one understands why they happen, they just do. And that's why Mom and Dad have gone. But if they could be here, they would be Micky, I promise you! Because you are our baby and they would do anything to be with you. But they left us both together so you will never be alone okay.'

'Well, why does Aunt Liz think she's my new mommy?'

I am caught off guard by his question. Micky's small frame and intact baby teeth make him appear to look a lot younger than what he is. I had no idea he understood what was going on. 'Well, Micky, Aunt Liz doesn't have any children, and by law, she is your legal guardian. That means she has asked the law if she can take care of you forever because she loves you so, so much, and they have said, yes. So, yes, she is your aunt, but maybe she can be like a Mommy to you so that you never have to feel like you have people missing in your life?'

I wait in silence while Micky digests what I have suggested. I begin to feel nervous from what his response may be.

'That's nice of Aunt Liz,' he responds, 'But who's your guardian and why aren't you my guardian, Liyana? I thought you were my guardian.' I giggle and tickle his belly to encourage his laughter. His genuine confusion and pure nature put me at ease. 'I don't need a guardian, Micky, I'm a warrior princess, and by blood, we are bound which makes me your guardian forever! I don't need anyone's permission for that! You are my baby brother, and you are my world. I don't need to ask anyone if that's okay, I will TELL THEM that's okay,' and with that final word I tickle his tummy and we both giggle in the dark.

'I think Aunt Liz might make a good Mommy, so maybe we should try because she really does love you, Micky,' I finally add to try and bring the conversation to an end on a happy note.

'I think she will, Liyana, but it's weird the way she screws her face when she talks to you sometimes. It's like she's had a taste of lemon.'

I can't help but laugh out loud. 'MICKY! When did you become so observant?'

'What's observant…' he asks in his usual curious tone.

'I will tell you in the morning, but right now I think you need your beauty sleep, especially if you want to grow up to become a warrior prince, you need energy for that job you know.'

'Yeah you're right, I'll sleep now. I do need to become a warrior prince, coz then I'm going to be your guardian, just like you are mine.'

Micky kisses my hand as he curls into a tighter ball. 'Goodnight, Liyana.'

'Goodnight my warrior prince,' I add as he slowly dozes off. His final words bring tears back to my eyes.

I don't want him to worry about being my guardian; I want him to have a regular life, playing with friends, getting into trouble, well, only a little trouble.

Not worrying about why I don't have a guardian or who will take care of me. Maybe I should move to campus to show him he doesn't have to worry?

I look at the aluminous dial to see its 3.28. I have a big day planned for tomorrow so enough contemplating for one night; I tell myself as I close my eyes and drift off to sleep.

'Micky you gave me a fright,' I hear a voice in the background shout in a loving yet stern tone.

I turn to the door to find Aunt Liz walking into my room with concern across her expression.

'What's happened, is something wrong with your room, do you not like it?' she asks in a panic.

'He's fine, Aunt Liz,' I reply in a sleepy tone.

'He was just a little afraid last night, so he crawled into bed with me, I'm sure he will be fine once we get a few night lights in the room.'

'Of course,' Aunt Liz confirms. 'Night-lights! I should have known that! How foolish of me.'

'It's okay, Aunt Liz, he doesn't normally need it; it's just that it's a huge room, so a night-light might help. You weren't to know,' I reply in an attempt to keep her spirits up.

'Well, why didn't you come into my room, Micky? You didn't have to disturb your sister.'

I sit up and observe Micky's expression. He appears worried, as if he may have done something wrong. No doubt it's from Aunt Liz's comment on "disturbing me".

'It's honestly fine, Aunt Liz, my room is his room, he could never disturb me so please don't worry unnecessarily,' I quickly add to defuse Micky's worry.

I hold Micky's hand, pulling it towards me as I gently kiss the surface and give him a warm smile.

'Right, okay, well I will leave you to freshen up and join us for breakfast.'

Aunt Liz leaves the room, closing the door behind her.

Micky smiles at me, yet the expression seems absent; perhaps he's still pondering over what Aunt Liz said?

I sit up straight and raise my arms to tense my miniature biceps while whispering 'warrior princess.'

I watch his vacant expression disappear as Micky chuckles at my goofy behaviour.

'C'mon, Micky, breakfast time,' I state as we jump out of bed.

Aunt Liz has cooked a fry up for us all, I've never seen so many options on a table for breakfast. Despite their only being four of us here, the spread laid out could feed the 5,000! 'Wow, Aunt Liz, this looks amazing! Thank you this is so kind of you,' I state to show my appreciation.

'Anything to make this special for Micky! This is his first breakfast in his new home.' Aunt Liz hops around in excitement as she rushes to tuck Micky into his seat.

'It's Liyana's first breakfast here too, Aunt Liz,' Micky responds with a slight frown across his expression.

Micky's reaction catches us all off guard, making Aunt Liz appear a little embarrassed.

'Yes, well of course it is,' she responds as she offers us all a sheepish smile before making her way to the kitchen.

I raise my eyebrows at Micky who gives me a cheeky smile in return.

Micky suddenly raises his arms in the air while tensing his baby biceps, to show off his non-existent muscles, just as I did earlier in the morning.

I can't help but laugh out loud as I walk towards him, brushing my hand in his hair.

In that moment, Aunt Liz walks back towards us; I notice she throws me a glare, as if, well in Micky's words, as if she has had a taste of raw lemon.

Oh great, she probably thinks I am patting Micky on the head for the comment he made to her. I better tread carefully this morning.

We are all seated for breakfast and as I expected, Micky is secretly passing food to Diesel under the table. As there is plenty to go around, I'll turn a blind eye on this occasion.

'So what's your plans for today,' Uncle Aidan asks catching me off guard.

'We could go and get a car for you today. That way you can get used to the car before you start university,' he offers.

'Oh, thank you, Uncle Aidan. That is really thoughtful, but any chance we can do that tomorrow'? I ask in a pleading tone.

'Oh, we didn't realise you had already made plans today Ann,' Aunt Liz adds in a bitter tone.

'No, I haven't, not really. I just thought it would be good for me to get used to the town and explore around, at least that way I will have an idea of my bearings before getting behind a wheel.'

'Well that sounds very sensible,' Uncle Aidan responds.

'Thank you, Uncle, I was just going to head into town, if that's okay.'

'Course it is, kiddo. Just keep your phone on, you call me if there are any problems, don't want you getting lost on your first day,' Uncle Aidan gives me a warm smile as he continues to read his paper.

'Well, Micky, as everyone else seems to have plans already, I thought how about you and I go shopping and maybe meet a few of the neighbours who have children your age too. That way you can make some new friends during the holidays.'

'Okay, but can Diesel come,' Micky asks with excitement.

'Of course, we can bring him along and maybe even take him to the park where you can both run around.'

'How about we all meet for dinner at the Palm in the centre? I'm sure we can all manage our own light lunch in-between,' Aunt Liz suggests.

'Sounds perfect,' I reply with enthusiasm.

'Well, shall I pick you up from where ever you will be Liyana?' Uncle Aidan asks.

'No that's fine, Uncle, I'm sure I will be close by, so I will make my way to the restaurant. What time shall we meet?' I quickly ask to distract the attention from my whereabouts.

'7.00 pm seems sensible, I'll book a table for that time,' Aunt Liz confirms.

'That's good with me, Aunt Liz. Oh, would you mind if I borrow your bicycle for today, just to help me get around?'

'Oh, yes of course, if you would like.' Aunt Liz glances over to Uncle Aidan with a look of confusion.

'Liyana it's really no trouble, I can take you around and show you the places you want to see, why don't we spend the day together that way.' I try to think fast, desperate to be able to spend the day alone.

'Honestly, Uncle Aidan, this will be good for me, after all, I will be going to university soon, so I need to start to learn how to spread my wings somehow.'

'She's absolutely right, Aidan! We should be encouraging her!' I knew that comment would gain me support from Aunt Liz.

'Liyana, help yourself to my bicycle and helmet, it's all in the garage and I think that's a fantastic idea. I'm glad to see you are thinking about your future, even if in the smallest of steps.'

I offer Aunt Liz an exaggerated smile; she can be so predictable at times.

In my room, I open up the map and circle the dirt tracks I can recall from our journey here. This dirt track may be the route we had taken that tragic night.

I feel the nervousness in my stomach at the thought of finally being able to search for my own answers.

I don't know what I'm expecting to find. I'm not hoping to find my parents waiting for me in the forest with open arms, but I think I'm just searching to find some closure. Even if that means finding nothing at all, maybe that will be enough to give me closure, for the mere fact that I have tried.

I enter the destination on my smartphone before throwing the map in my bag along with a few other essentials. I take a deep breath as the realisation sinks in.

My journey begins now.

After riding for hours, I stop to look at the forest ahead of me. I stare into the thickness of the trees, imagining the unparalleled world that lies behind the shades of green.

I continue to ride on as I desperately look through the trees for any hint of a memory.

As suspected, my smartphone loses all reception as I journey deeper towards nowhere.

I take out the map from my bag; a faint smile creeps across my expression as I finally reach the dirt trail. Could this be the treacherous route we had taken that night?

Hesitant about my actions, I stop for a moment to think twice about what I am doing. Am I picking at an old wound that has half heeled? Or could this be the start of some fanatic obsession I develop in desperation for answers?

I quickly dismiss my doubts, I'm here, I may as well just make the most of it.

Besides, I've been cycling for so long I couldn't face another cycle journey back just now.

I slowly ride into the narrow path the trees have left open; creating an arch, which almost feels welcoming. The trees look beautiful, the deeper I ride, the wider the tree trunks seem to appear. I ride on slow to absorb my surroundings. The path becomes narrower which makes me think back to that horrific night. Perhaps the tremors from that car journey were a result of this narrowing path?

I find myself mesmerised by the beauty of this enchanted forest as I ride deeper. The colours are so vibrant with hundreds of shades of greens, browns and yellows. The path narrows significantly before disappearing altogether, now just a worn-in mud path ahead. The colours from the variety of flowers distract me from any rational thought of what to do next.

The sounds of the birds singing in the treetops combined with the sight of the furry wild bunnies hopping around in their groups steal my attention.

It becomes challenging to pedal any further from the uneven surface of the twigs that form the forest bed.

As I approach a fallen tree trunk, I lay my bike against the bark before perching against the side.

I take a few photos just before a wild deer in the distance catches my glance. The alluring atmosphere waiting to be explored, forces me to get on my feet and walk into the wilderness.

I look at the vibrant flowers scattered across the forest floor; white, elegant petals with gentle brushes of pinks, violets and blues. I can't resist but to pluck one from the ground and place it against my nose.

The sweet fragrance brings a smile to my face as I place the flower above my ear.

Perhaps this is what I need. Perhaps this will remove the vivid night terror I have replaying my last encounter in the forest.

The birds up above put a smile on my face from the delightful music they make; I feel a sudden spring in my step as I continue to walk deeper.

I glide through the forest without a care in the world. My heart begins to beat with excitement. This alternate universe I have entered, I can only describe as a reflection of paradise. This has become my enchanted forest, full of warmth and acceptance, a mystical ambiance, which brings to my soul, peace. I continue to walk as I hear the sound of flowing water, snapping me out of my hypnotic state. I rush towards the sound allowing my ears to guide me.

As I reach a flowing stream, I figure it will be sensible to follow the stream to its natural end. Perhaps at the end of the stream, I may find washed up signs of something, of anything, that may link back to that tragic night.

I know the chances are unrealistic, but at least it gives me a direction to head towards, if nothing else.

It seems unnatural to think such a traumatic event took place, in an environment as beautiful and peaceful as this. I continue to walk for what feels like hours, deep in thought about my parents. There must be something I can find which will bring me closure or a step closer to what happened to them. I refocus from the trance on my parents to my current surroundings.

My eyes widen from the realisation that the vibrant colours, the beautiful flowers have long passed. The beauty diminishes; the mystical feel of positivity and harmony can no longer be sensed.

Not even the sound of birds singing in the trees, no sign of any animals for that matter.

Walking at a slow pace, I contemplate whether it will be sensible to turn back? The drastic change in the atmosphere has left me feeling anxious. The positive vibrations, which were flowing through my body, dancing with my soul has changed, leaving me feeling vulnerable and alone.

'It will be a waste of a journey if I don't get to the end of the stream. Besides, I'm warrior princess!' I convince myself as I continue in motion.

I sit beside the flowing stream on another large fallen tree trunk.

I rest my feet from all the walking while sipping on the juice I have in my backpack.

As I look around, the numbers of fallen trees that surround me seem unusual.

The sound of rustling leaves focuses my attention to the right. Out comes a wild rabbit, surprisingly large yet timid.

It slowly walks out of the bush, forcing me to sit as still as a statue, encouraging the rabbit to continue its journey.

I watch as it approaches; I've never been so close to a wild animal before.

I sit starring at its features, its beautiful long hair, a mixture of browns and greys, its big dark eyes and pink triangular nose. It hops on slowly, continually looking at its surroundings.

Suppose you have to be if you're living in the wild, something that I never gave any thought to till now.

The wild rabbit moves slowly, almost as if it is tiptoeing when unexpectedly, its head rises simultaneously as its eyes widen.

It suddenly appears agitated, as if it senses a threat of some kind. I watch with wide eyes as it pushes all its weight onto its hind legs in readiness to leap.

As it lifts through the air, leaping forward, it comes crashing down at the same speed. It's as if it has hit an invisible wall. It rushes back onto its feet before leaping in the opposite direction. Like a mirror replay; it comes crashing down!

The rabbit appears to behave hysterically; my heartbeat rises from not knowing what to do to help it.

I stand on my feet and take a few steps forward only to find myself pause immediately.

The wild behaviour of the rabbit startles me as it jumps in all directions but cannot move any further forward; as if it has become trapped inside an invisible box with no way out.

My eyes glaze over as I see blood gushing out of the rabbit each time it leaps and crashes from this invisible barrier...

Is it having a seizure? Can animals have a seizure? In a panic, I throw my juice on the rabbit, in the hope it will wake from whatever frenzy possesses it. Suddenly, it stops jumping hysterically; it lies on the ground, flat on its back, quivering uncontrollably. I walk closer to the rabbit desperately trying to think of how I can help this poor defenceless creature when to my horror, I witness the stomach of the rabbit opening, while its digestive system seeps out. It continues to quiver uncontrollably while internal organs are oozing out around it. The rabbit comes to a still, lifeless on the ground.

I rush off in the opposite direction trying to make sense of the horror I just witnessed!

Berries! Maybe it ate some poisonous berries?

No, there is no explanation as to why a rabbit would spontaneously explode!

I keep walking not thinking about where I am going; I just need to keep moving, I no longer feel safe.

As I pace along the stream beside me, I find myself stunned by a splash of water. The splashing becomes so intense it begins to soak my clothing.

What on earth could that have been?

Something's not right. The splashing continues further upstream, but only this time, the impact is more substantial; I can feel the vibration in the ground under my feet. The wind picks up, forcing the trees to fill the silence with their rustling leaves.

The speed of the wind seems uneven as I continue with a quick walk while staying alert to my surroundings.

The force of the wind impacts the surrounding trees and bushes; much more than others, it doesn't make sense.

My fast-paced walk emerges into a nervous jog; I need to get away from whatever is in the stream.

The wind breezes towards my direction, I gasp in shock, my ankle feeling trapped, forcing me to stumble before hitting the ground.

I look around for what felt like a log that I tripped over, but there is nothing there.

Feeling consumed by panic, I reach for my backpack to get my phone and call for help. For a moment, I freeze from the realisation that I have left my bag on the bark of the tree next to the mutilated rabbit!

Oh crap! What do I do?

I count to three and jump back onto my feet with all the strength I have. I sprint towards the dead rabbit, enough is enough, I need to get back home. I don't feel safe in this forest. I am a fool for thinking this was sensible!

I attempt to follow the stream back towards my backpack, but as I look up ahead, the wind is incredibly strong in that direction. The trees and bushes are rustling as if they are being hit by a gale. The opposite direction, however, is calm with only a gentle breeze. How is this possible? I feel like I am being forced deeper into the forest...

Forget the Phone! I run in speed and spot the boulders further down the stream, forming a bridge to cross to the safer side.

I jump across the stream, creating distance between me and this unnatural force. So long as I can hear the stream I can find my way back to the bicycle. I continue to run, but it feels like the gale force wind is following me.

Reality hits me. This is NOT right. I AM in DANGER...

Running as fast as I can, I hear the snapping of branches behind me.

I am too afraid to turn around.

It's a storm, a storm heading towards me, I just need to outrun it, I convince myself as I feel the panic kicking in, forcing my knees to tremble.

The speed of the wind picks up around me, forcing branches to fly through the air like missiles.

Suddenly I hear a loud thud! For a moment, the speed of the wind stops, I find myself frozen.

I slowly turn and gasp in shock as I watch a huge tree falling towards me!

I sprint as fast as I can, desperate to escape the path of the tree, it will kill me for sure! As it hits the ground just inches away from me, the vibrations from its ground-breaking impact make me fall to my knees.

I'm struggling to breath; my legs have gone weak as I drag myself forward. I try to lift myself off the ground, but keep tumbling down. Tears from the fear, roll down my face, my vision becomes hazy. I can no longer hear the sound of the stream as the roar of the wind becomes more intense. I manage to stumble back onto my feet, heading in any direction, which looks safe.

I am lost in the forest; falling onto the trunks of the trees to catch my balance as I make my way through this labyrinth.

The vibrant colours that I noticed when I first entered, I can see, further ahead, I am close to safety; I must be heading in the right direction.

My legs feel heavy and bruised from whatever it was that I tripped over. The speed of the wind begins to overpower me, so intense that I can feel it breathing down my neck. I conjure the strength for a final sprint; running as fast as I can, when suddenly I fall and hit the ground. The impact against my head disorientates my vision. The blurry image of the grass and leaves rustling against my body becomes faint. I struggle to focus; it's becoming difficult to breathe. The faint shadows of nothing surround me. The sound of the gale is all I can hear before a sudden beam of light takes over my vision.

I lose my breath, my hearing disappears; all I can see is the brightness of some unnatural light, which soon turns into nothing but darkness.

'…It is the mark of an educated mind to be able to entertain a thought without accepting it…'

— Aristotle

04. The Unexplained

'Liyana! Liyana wake up!' I hear a faint voice in the background as my shoulders are rubbed.

'The doctor, he's on his way!'

I feel a warm palm rubbing my cheek and holding my hands. Visions of me holding my mother's hand as we run through the park, flash before me. Our laughter fills the silence as we run away from my father who has Micky sat on his shoulders chasing after us. As my father catches us, we all fall to the ground on our picnic blanket. I am laying on the grass looking up into the sky with a smile on my face as my mother strokes my cheeks.

The vision becomes a distant memory as my consciousness awakens, I find myself lying on the steps of our porch.

'Liyana are you okay? What's happened? Are you hurt? Can you move?'

As I become aware of my surroundings, I lift myself up off the ground, sitting up on the steps as Uncle Aidan holds me firm in his arms.

My legs feel like lead, unable to move them with ease; I feel the dampness on my face, from the stream of blood that has not yet dried.

'I'm... I'm sorry,' I whisper whilst feeling disorientated.

'How did you get hurt Liyana?' he asks in a stern voice.

'I...n... I don't really know.'

As my vision becomes clear, I see a car pull up; a tall, large man walks towards us.

'C'mon let's get you inside,' Uncle Aidan dictates as he puts his harms under my legs in an attempt to lift me up. Before he can go any further, I press my hands against his arm.

'Honestly, Uncle, I'm fine. Please. I feel awful that you are worrying. I can walk inside, it's really okay.'

'Are you sure, look it's okay, I've got you kiddo,' he confirms in a loving, reassuring voice.

'Honestly, Uncle,' I reaffirm as I go to stand on my own. Uncle Aidan gets to his feet first, and luckily he does as I find myself stumbling as soon as I manage to stand.

'I got you,' he reassures as he wraps his arms around me holding me steady as he walks me through to the lounge.

'She's fine, just a mild concussion, nothing to worry about,' the doctor confirms as he packs away his briefcase.

'Keep an eye on her overnight and if she deteriorates call me immediately. But really Aidan, it's nothing to worry about she'll be fine, the swelling will go down in a few days, she'll be as good as gold.'

'Thanks, Daniel, I really appreciate this,' Uncle Aidan expresses with relief as they both head towards the front door.

As they chat away on the porch, I sit straight, rolling up my jeans to look at the swelling on my ankles.

'What the hell,' I whisper in shock from the redness of the swelling and tenderness of the bruises battling its way through to the surface.

I look across at the clock to see it is 7.30 pm. Oh no! The family dinner!

I go to grab my phone off the coffee table to call Aunt Liz, only realise I don't have my phone.

I look back down at my swollen ankles when it suddenly hits me! There is no way I could have cycled back with ankles this size. I freeze as the sudden shock of reality sinks in; I don't know how I got back home?

Uncle Aidan enters the room; I manage to hobble onto my feet as he rushes towards me.

'Uncle Aidan,' I call out as he reaches me.

I wrap my arms around him, before beginning to sob.

'I'm sorry, I'm so so sorry. I didn't mean to ruin our family dinner! I feel awful; please forgive me.'

'Hey, hey it's okay,' Uncle Aidan reassures as we sit down on the large leather sofa. He takes my hands into his and offers me a sympathetic smile.

'Look, kiddo, what's important to me is knowing that you are okay. Now I still don't understand how you fell and injured yourself?'

Uncle Aidan stares at me as he awaits an answer, but I have no idea on what response to give him.

'Well, perhaps I twisted my ankle which made me lose balance, and that's how I fell, Uncle. That would make sense, but I can't clearly remember.'

'Of course you can't, you have a mild concussion!' he gasps with worry across his expression.

'Uncle I need to phone Aunt Liz, I need to apologise to her, she must be really mad at me for ruining our dinner plans. It's only 7.30, so perhaps we can still make it if we leave now?'

'Liyana, please don't worry about that. I know your aunt Liz can be difficult and tunnel-visioned at times, but she means well. Don't you worry about her I will speak to her and make sure it's all okay! But as the doctor said, right now you need some rest.'

'Okay, but where is Micky? And how did you know to find me?'

'Don't worry about Micky, he's with your aunt, and the two of them are continuing with the dinner plans in our absence. It's okay she's invited a few of her friends and their kids who are Micky's age, so it's worked out okay for them.'

'Oh, I'm glad. Hopefully, she won't be too mad then. But Uncle, how did you know to find me?'

'Well as you weren't picking up your mobile, I thought I would pop home to see if you were here. I had to drop Diesel back anyway and thought that we could drive to the restaurant together. That's when I found you lying on the porch.'

'Oh.'

My expression turns blank. Of course I couldn't answer my mobile, I have left it stranded in the forests, which is where I should be. But just as expected, Uncle Aidan didn't find me in the forest. He didn't look for me there, he found me right here, so how did I get back?

'Liyana, is it your concussion? You've gone silent, you okay?'

I look across to my worrying uncle and offer him a warm smile. 'Thank you for being so good to me, Uncle, I'm absolutely fine. I was just thinking of Micky; I just hope he's not worrying.'

'Liyana, you've been doing the worrying for too long. Please let us take care of you and Micky. He is fine. I've promised Micky that you will be looking after Diesel, which is the only thing that's put a smile on his face since being told dogs weren't allowed in.' We both begin to chuckle, I cannot help but sigh from relief that everything is okay.

I stand in the shower, closing my eyes as each drop washes away the dry blood from my hair. I sit in the shower with my chin resting on my knees as I cup my hands around the top of my head.

'What just happened,' I question myself.

Flashbacks of the events in the forest appear before my eyes; the mutilated rabbit; the splashing of the stream causing vibrations through the ground; the unnatural wind blowing with gale force strength.

Perhaps it was the start of a whirlwind? Maybe that's why the trees came crashing down towards me? That could explain the splashing of the stream and vibrations of the ground?

My eyes catch the redness of my ankles; I stare at the swelling as I notice the deep purples and light greens coming through the surface of my skin.

I try hard to recall my last memories before finding myself on the porch.

I recall a final burst of energy following the collapse of a giant tree in the forest.

I remember falling, not tripping over something, but falling from an invisible force pushing me down, the wind?

As I leave the shower, wrapping a towel around me, I stare into the bathroom mirror.

I lower the towel to uncover my sore back. My eyes focus in disbelief, as I gaze at the redness all up my spine and around my shoulders.

I have NEVER known the strength of the wind physically marking a person!

I take a closer look at the damage on my back, as I move my long, dark hair, to expose the bare skin below my neck and shoulders. The sight of what looks to be some blemish or imprint of an intricate pattern forces me to squint my eyes, focusing my view. My skin is raised ever so slightly, like that of a whale mark as a result of a pet having scratched the skin.

A sudden thud on the bathroom makes me jolt from shock. 'Liyana, are you there? Why weren't you with me at dinner?' I hear an angry voice shout.

'Oh, Micky, give me one minute, I'll be right out.'

I quickly throw on my pyjamas and wrap my hair in a towel. As I open the bathroom door, Micky doesn't give it a second before I find his arms wrapping around my waist.

'You said you would meet us!' he scolds in an angry yet loving tone.

I struggle to walk to the bed with Micky glued to me. My soft instrumental melodies are playing in the background that helps to warm up the atmosphere in my haven.

I pick Micky up and throw him on the bed, which makes him laugh from the bounce. I crawl onto the bed and lay on my back as Micky places his head on my stomach while wrapping his arms around me again.

I place my hand on his head while I stroke his chestnut hair as I stare at the thin white sheets draped around the four posts of my bed.

'Did you enjoy dinner with your friends Micky?'

'Yes but they are mean people because they wouldn't let Diesel in, I never want to go back there!'

'Micky no restaurants let you take dogs. Restaurants are for people only not dogs,' I try to explain while still brushing his hair with my fingertips.

'Well, where do dogs go out to eat?' he asks in a curious tone. I can't help but giggle at his question.

'Micky, dogs only eat at home, they do not understand fine dining, so you don't have to worry about Diesel feeling left out.'

'Well, why weren't you there, Liyana? I wanted to see you.'

'I, I was with Diesel, Micky, but it's okay coz I'm here with you now.'

Micky gives me a tighter squeeze as he talks me through his day.

I giggle as he explains to me the three of them had lunch together in the park.

'So you, Aunt Liz and Diesel had lunch together in the park.'

'No, silly. Me, Aunt Liz and Uncle Aidan.'

I can't help but feel a little surprised, disheartened even. 'Aunt Liz said that it would be the three of us most of the time because you won't be around much. When you go to university, we won't really see you. Is that true Liyana?'

I can feel my patience begin to wear thin with Aunt Liz.

I just hate the way she interferes with negativity in Micky's life and the apparent lack of involvement I will have in it! Surely she can see that he has experienced enough loss in his life already?

'Not really,' I explain to Micky in a soft tone to conceal my frustration.

'I will be busy with homework I imagine, and sometimes I may have sleepovers on the campus with the new friends I make. But I will still be here, my home is where you are Micky, so you don't have to worry okay.'

'Phew! That's good coz I was worrying that I would have to follow you so that you don't forget me.'

My heart breaks a little from the thoughts that must be going through his mind. Micky hums along to the melody of the piano in the background; oblivious to my overwhelming emotions.

My love for my brother was so pure, so strong, the truth is, it's Micky that keeps me strong, that keeps me determined, that keeps me smiling.

A knock on the door abruptly ends our conversation.

'Come on, Micky; your sister has had a long day. Leave her to rest; we can both test your night-lights.'

Micky slowly gets off the bed, as he walks towards Aunt Liz, he softly asks if he could come back after he has tested the night light. She pauses in silence not sure how to say what is really on her mind.

'Micky my room is yours remember, come in whenever you want to!'

Micky runs back and surprises me with a kiss and a cuddle. As Micky leaves to exit the room, I notice Aunt Liz give me an awkward smile before closing the door behind her.

I switch off the bedroom lights; I lay on my bed feeling relaxed yet exhausted. My legs begin to feel stiff from all the cycling and running. My eyes widen as I realise what else I have left behind! Oh damn! Aunt Liz's bike! Oh crap! I've left her bicycle in the forest, on the bark of the tree when the bike trail began to diminish. It's okay, I'll drive down tomorrow maybe to find it. Right now, I just need some sleep.

I walk into the kitchen to find Aunt Liz, Uncle Aidan and Micky sat having breakfast.

'Morning kiddo, how are you feeling today?' Uncle Aidan asks in a jolly tone.

'Good, thanks,' I reply as I examine Aunt Liz to decipher the mood she may be in.

I sit, joining them for breakfast. My body in pain from the battering it took yesterday.

'Ann, I'd appreciate if you could put my bicycle back into the garage in the future, rather than leaving it against the garage door for me to put away!' Aunt Liz hisses without even looking at me, a premeditated comment, no doubt.

Her statement throws me. The bicycle, is here?

A blank expression takes over my face while I try to decipher how this could be possible. My reaction throws Uncle Aidan into a panic.

'Liyana, kiddo what's wrong,' he asks as he gets up from his seat to come closer towards me.

'No, I'm okay, thanks,' I try to reassure.

I look to Aunt Liz; she must be annoyed by the statement I made to Micky last night.

'I'm sorry, Aunt Liz, it won't happen again.'

She glances towards me as she forces a smile while Uncle Aidan sits back down, watching me settle in. He glares at Aunt Liz with a look of disapproval. She seems happy to ignore his expression as she sips away her tea.

'I wanted to wake you Liyana, but Aunt Liz said I am not allowed,' Micky shouts as he screws his face while looking at Aunt Liz.

'Oh, well, no dear, that's not what I meant. I just thought your sister could do with a lie in from her eventful evening, that's all,' she explains with a nervous smile.

'Liyana I will be back at 2.00 pm, how about we get you a car this afternoon?' Uncle Aidan offers with excitement.

'Sounds great, Uncle Aidan, thank you,' I respond with a polite smile.

'Well, Micky, today I have arranged a private tour for you at your new school. You will get to look around the place before you start next week. Would you like that?' Aunt Liz asks sounding desperate for his approval.

'Can Liyana come?' Micky asks with a look of excitement.

'No dear, I'm sorry it's a private tour only. Besides, Liyana will be busy researching on cars.'

'Lizzy!' Uncle Aidan states with a stern look on his face.

'It's important for young children to have their space and be prepared to make their own decisions Aidan!' She snaps back in a defensive tone!

'If you want Micky I can stay here and watch Diesel for you otherwise he will be lonely,' I quickly add, to maintain a calm atmosphere.

Uncle Aidan looks at me with a sympathetic smile.

'I'm such a bad friend, I forgot about Diesel! Thanks, Liyana, you always know what's right,' he compliments as he strokes Diesel sat beside him.

'Perhaps next time the head teacher can arrange for a family visit to the school!' Uncle Aidan scoffs as he puts on his jacket for work.

Aunt Liz refuses to acknowledge Uncle Aidan's statement, as she continues to sip on her tea while scrolling through her tablet.

'See you here at 2.00 pm, kiddo,' Uncle Aidan confirms as he walks past and pats me on the shoulder.

'A word please, Eliza,' he states in a domineering tone as he walks out of the kitchen, entering into the hallway.

Aunt Liz is the head-teacher of the school Micky will be attending. She could have quite easily allowed me to come along, but it's okay. Besides, I need to figure out what on earth is going on with her bicycle!

I have the place to myself as I limp towards the garage, pondering over how the bicycle got back here. I must have cycled back here, I just can't remember. I have never suffered from spells of blackouts in my memory, well not that I remember. But surely that's the point, you can't remember? Perhaps the stress of the move and the weight of finding answers to my parents vanishing are affecting me in more ways than I realise?

I inspect the bicycle, which is accompanied with the helmet. It all looks intact, with no sign of any damage.

Am I losing my mind? I question as I hobble into the garden towards the large swinging bench. I look at the quadrants created by the neatly cut hedges and decide to explore.

I walk through the first quadrant of the patio and garden grass, heading toward the path on the left. Enclosed by a hedge the size of a wall, making it difficult to know what's within this quarter.

My jaw drops as I find myself staring at a Jacuzzi hot tub with a mini bar stand towards the side with a couple of sun loungers to the corner. This is absolutely amazing! I sit on the sun lounger in shock; Aunt Liz really does have impeccable taste!

I shuffle off towards the bench swing, which is in the next quarter, feeling smug from my discovery. As I sit on the bench swing, I'm surprised by how big it is. It is more like a bed swing, large enough to comfortably lay two grown adults. I drag my body onto the far end, putting my feet up comfortably.

As I swing away in the gentle breeze, I try to make sense of what is happening.

Am I now content that I have been to the forest and found nothing? Am I ready to move on without having found any answers as to what happened to my parents all those years ago?

The question itself saddens me. I try to be true to myself, but in all honesty, I don't quite know what I am searching? I don't know what it is I am hoping to find. There is merely a hole in my life, a hole in my world, which I think I am desperately trying to fill. But the hardest thing to understand is knowing what will fill this emptiness.

I sit contemplating for hours as I swing away in the sun, resting my sore ankles with Diesel by my side. I daydream as I lay staring into the clouds scattered across the pale blue sky.

I hear myself giggling. I'm being pushed on a swing, with baby Micky by my side. Behind me, I listen to the laughter of my parents as they swing us both higher, I feel myself heading towards the fluffy clouds. I hear the faint ringing of my father's mobile.

I grow alert as the ringing of the mobile becomes more prominent.

While my eyes remain closed, I begin to frown at the disruption the ringing phone creates, pulling me away from my memories. Suddenly becoming aware of the tone, my eyes flash open in disbelief!

Surely that can't be! That ringing cannot be my phone!

I become startled as Diesel begins to bark as he stares towards the house.

I hobble onto my feet and shuffle as fast as I can in the direction towards the melody of my ringtone.

I pass the patio, entering the house through the doors in the kitchen.

The volume of the ringtone seems to be reducing? I re-enter the patio where the ringing seems to be the loudest.

I look around but cannot see my phone anywhere; it sounds as if it is coming from, above me?

I slowly raise my head to look above; my brows frown as I focus on a large object on my bedroom balcony.

I focus harder when suddenly it hits me, that's my backpack! I shuffle as fast as I can up the stairs to my bedroom.

I open the lock and enter through to my balcony. As I search through the bag, I see all my belongings that I had packed for my journey yesterday.

I finally dig out my mobile at the bottom of the bag and see a call from a withheld number. What is happening? Who returned my bag and who is calling me?

'…An animals eyes have the power to speak a great language…'

— Martin Buber

05. Savage Barrier

'How are you feeling, Liyana,' Uncle Aidan asks over the phone.

'Yes, I'm good, thank you, Uncle, how are you feeling?'

He chuckles as he explains his meeting has finished earlier than expected and he will be home in 30 minutes to collect me. In his voice, he sounds more excited than I, which relieves my worry of putting him out of his way.

As we end the conversation, I focus back on the mysterious appearance of my bag.

I look around the balcony searching for any signs as to how my bag could have ended up here.

It would have been "impossible" for me to place it here during my "blacked out" state, Uncle Aidan found me on the porch!

I take my bag into my room; it all looks intact as I rummage through to see if anything is missing, the bottle of water, map, SOS Pocket knife, heavy-duty torch, it was all there.

I sit on the bed feeling bewildered. It could be plausible to think perhaps I did cycle home, leave the bicycle on the side of the garage, tripping over while heading towards the porch.

Could this explain how I got back safe? How the cycle was here and why I cannot remember the last few hours of getting home. The impact of falling on my head could have erased my short-term memory, I think. I could stretch as far as convincing myself that may have happened. But there is NO rational explanation as to how my bag has appeared on my balcony!

I cannot help but begin to doubt everything; how I got home, a freak gale storm, which now sounds ridiculous, to how the bicycle has returned.

I glance at the clock next to my bed to see I have 10 mins left till Uncle Aidan arrives.

As I strip out of my pyjamas into a pair of jeans, I remember the markings on my shoulder.

I look into the mirrors of my wardrobe to see what remains since yesterday.

The markings are faint, but it's apparent something was there, just too vague to make out what it was.

I take the shirt I was wearing yesterday out of my laundry bin in the bathroom to see if this reveals any further information.

I observe the back of my shirt torn in some places. It's not a clean cut, like a knife or scissors would leave. The material seems too frayed for that, what the hell happened to me?

'So any idea what kind of car you want, kiddo,' Uncle Aidan asks in a chirpy tone.

'Not really sure, Uncle, you can decide.'

'Not sure! Liyana this marks a big occasion for you; the start of your freedom, your independence! We are going to make this a good one,' he states as he grins wide.

It seems Uncle Aidan is more excited than me. 'How's your head today.'

'It's a lot better today,' I reply in a sheepish tone.

'You were out like a light yesterday; I checked on you a couple of times. Thought you fell out of your bed at one point when I heard a thud from your room.'

'Really?' I ask in disbelieve.

'Yeah, I was walking past your room when I heard a thud, I opened the door, and you were fast asleep.'

I begin to feel nervous inside, my heart beating a little harder as I contemplate whether the thud could have been my backpack arriving on my balcony?

'So where did you go yesterday?' Uncle Aidan asks hesitantly.

'Oh, nowhere really, just went for a long cycle ride admiring the views of the trees.'

'Oh, that's a long time to have been out for, looking at trees. But hey, if that's what you're interested in, just be careful around here, particularly around the forests. It's not safe to venture out on your own,' Uncle Aidan responds with a puzzled look on his face.

'Uncle what was your first car?' I quickly ask to distract him while changing the subject. I didn't like lying to anyone let alone my uncle.

Uncle Aidan talks for the rest of the journey about his various cars and from the enthusiasm in his voice, I can see it is bringing out the younger man in him.

'What about this one?' Uncle Aidan suggests as I stand in front of a small blue Audi TT in the showroom.

'Yeah sure,' I reply in an impartial tone.

'Liyana, you have said that about the last three cars I've suggested.'

'I'm sorry, Uncle Aidan, I've never really been good at fashion, trends and everything else that goes with it. How about you just decide for me?'

'Liyana, this is more than some fashion accessory! Today you are choosing your partner in crime!' he shouts as the excitement gets the better of him.

I giggle at his inner child making an appearance and decide to suggest a compromise.

'Okay, if I tell you what I like, you can pick a car for me which matches what I'm into?'

'Go for it!'

As we walk along the showroom, I explain the little things that I like which feels surreal as I've never really been one to talk about "me".

'My favourite colour even though I don't really own anything in this colour, but my favourite colour is red.

'I like cosiness.

'I love my bedroom and the white theme, I think of it as my haven, as if I am in a cloud.'

'Okay, give me more,' Uncle Aidan asks in an eager tone as we continue to stroll around the showroom.

'I wouldn't mind a car with an armrest.

'I think big windows will be good, I love the feel of the wind in my hair when I'm riding a bicycle so guess I'd like it if I was in a car too maybe?'

Uncle Aidan burst into a fit of laughter.

'Okay, what kind of budget did you have in mind?'

'Oh, I've not really thought of that, say maybe £5,000.'

Uncle Aidan looks at me in horror! As he observes my embarrassed reaction, he quickly busts into a hysterical laughter.

'Liyana, there is not a single car here within your price range. We need to up the budget. You still have all your inheritance, so you of all people deserve to splash out! I have chosen the car that meets all your requirements! And here she is!'

As I look over, I see a beautiful, white two-seater BMW Z4; white leather interior with red stitch work detail.

Though the car puts a smile on my face, it's not me. I wish it were, but I didn't feel ready or deserving enough for such a lavish car.

As Uncle Aidan sits in the passenger seat, I head across to the driver's side.

I watch his face light up as I take my seat.

'This is the one, Liyana, exactly how you described!'

'Uncle Aidan, it really is beautiful, but there is one thing I forgot to mention in what I want.'

'Go on,' he encourages almost seeming half-interested as he looks at the gadgets in the car.

'Practical.'

Uncle Aidan scoffs as he states, 'You have been sensible all your life Liyana, what's the harm in just letting loose once in a while?'

As the paperwork completes, I am handed the keys; it feels surreal to think I now own such a luxurious car.

Uncle Aidan was right, the feeling of independence is exhilarating, now that I am driving around in what feels like a beautiful white cloud, my private haven.

As I drive aimlessly, enjoying the thrill of a convertible, I decide to head towards the forest. I'm not planning on another visit inside, but I just need to clear my mind, and if I am driving somewhere, I may as well head towards the only place I am familiar with.

I park up across the road from the dirt track I entered yesterday.

I stare curiously into the forest as I wonder what it could be that has caused me to block out a few hours of my memory.

I find myself staring into the forest, contemplating if I should just take another look, in the safety of my new car?

As I try to persuade myself there is no harm in this; I notice the bushes rustling in the distance. The sudden images of the mutilated bunny, hopping out of the rustling bushes enters my mind.

The movement of the bushes seems somewhat aggressive; I stare deeper within the leaves, trying to see what is creating the disturbance.

Out from the bushes, I see a giant paw placing its claws on the ground. The fur surrounding its paws hold differing shades of beiges and browns.

As the rest of the animal slowly emerges out of the bushes, out appears the largest wild dog I have ever seen!

It was a wild German Sheppard, the size of a Great Dane! I have never seen a dog this size, nor did I realise they could survive in the wild! It approaches slowly, staring into my eyes while bearing its unnaturally large teeth. I can hear its growl from across the road, as I watch the saliva drip from its lower lip. Its hair is overgrown, yet beneath it, I can see a collar; white, just like Diesel.

It continues to growl as it crawls closer towards me.

In a panic, I quickly close the window and drive forward. I stop to look back, at that moment the wild beast begins to run, towards the car, barking in a fit of rage.

It will maul me to death if it jumps into the car! I slam my foot on the accelerator and hear the car raw in speed. My head whiplashes from the sudden thrust of the vehicle, adding to the adrenaline rush, as the wild dog becomes a distant image in the rear-view mirror.

I slow the car as the pace of my heartbeat begins to steady. What on earth was that! Who would keep a savage beast like that as a pet? How on earth did it end up in the wild?

I look up ahead; my eyes focus in on another dirt track through the forest. I bring the car to a stop as I take a closer look through the trees.

To my disbelief, I hear the wild barking of the savage animal as it runs out of the trees and heads straight towards me.

I put my foot down as I head back down the road expecting to lose the animal just as quickly as I did last time, only this time, it manages to keep up.

I add pressure to the accelerator expecting to create a comfortable distance between us, it's no use, it's right there, besides me. My heart is now pounding as I struggle to lose the animal, even at 50 mph.

I take no chances as my finger hovers over the "sport" button, calling out to me.

Without hesitation, I press the button and slam my foot down on the accelerator. The steering becomes firm as I zoom down the roads! Finally, the forest and the beast are now a distant image in my rear-view mirror. I apply pressure on the breaks, slowing my speed to the standard limit.

My heart still pounding, the endorphins from the adrenaline finally kick in. I feel shaken yet alive! My safe haven is my saviour; Thank God I listened to Uncle Aidan about this car!

The house is empty as I walk into the silence. I head towards the garden while grabbing a drink and a couple of painkillers to ease the tension on my ankles. I watch Diesel running around chasing butterflies, while I sit on the patio, digesting my thoughts on the lucky escape from the wild animal.

As I watch Diesel and his gentle, playful approach. I pause for a moment as I notice the shocking similarities between Diesel and the wild beast I had encountered. The colours of their hair, the pattern on their coat, even down to the white collar! How bizarre! Its speed was unnatural; perhaps a Cheetah could run at that speed, but a wild dog!

As I run through the events in my mind, I scoff at my stupid thought! For a moment, I consider if the wild animal was acting as a barrier to stop me from entering the forest?

'Liyana are you home?' I hear a little voice shout. I watch Micky through the patio doors as he runs circles in the house searching for me.

'There you are,' he shouts as he comes running towards me, greeting me with a big hug and a huge smile.

'Soo, tell me all about your school. Was it amazing?' I ask with an enthusiastic smile.

Micky can't hold his excitement and tells me all about his new school and the exclusive tour he received which included sandwiches in the teacher's lounge.

'That's a beautiful car you have chosen, Ann. I'm surprised you have the taste for it, was expecting something a little more simple from you.'

Aunt Liz gives me a genuine smile, though her backhanded compliment was typical of her.

'Thanks, Aunt Liz, Uncle Aidan helped me chose it.'

'Of course he did, that explains a lot.' She states as she walks away in laughter.

The ferocious barking from Diesel grabs my attention as I focus towards the end of the garden.

'Diesel,' Micky cries in panic as he shoots down the garden to save his best friend.

'Micky,' I shout as I run towards him while my heart begins racing away.

I quickly catch up, pulling him aside. He struggles in my grip in a desperate attempt to get to Diesel. I hold Micky's face, turning it towards me as I look into his eyes to grab his attention.

Diesel's unnatural, aggressive behaviour forces all my inner instincts out, my primary focus to ensure Micky remains safe, from whatever threat lies ahead.

'I am here, I will see what's wrong with Diesel, but you MUST stay behind me OKAY?'

As we slowly walk to the right quadrant at the end of the garden, Micky hides behind me, holding onto my shirt.

Diesel's bark becomes less aggressive; I approach, watching him bark towards the trees and bushes at the back of the garden.

I frown as I glance towards the swing bench, I can't understand why it would be swinging away?

'See Micky, it's nothing to worry about, Diesel is fine. But you mustn't run off like that, okay! What if there was a giant snake here or a grizzly bear! You would have been their dinner, and I would have been left all alone. Don't do that again, okay.'

Micky giggles as he runs over to Diesel who is now rolling around on the grass.

He jumps onto the swinging bench and thanks me for saving Diesel.

We swing away staring into the clouds, giggling over silly things.

The moment seems perfect, nothing on our minds other than enjoying the here and now.

'Thanks for saving Diesel, Liyana; you were right, you are a warrior princess, we will always be safe around you.'

We both laugh out loud, and I cannot help but to wrap my arms around him. I pull my phone from my pocket and capture this moment in a photograph, a moment I will cherish forever.

'…Things fall apart so that better things can fall together…'

–   Marilyn Monroe

06. A Fresh Look

I watch the full moon shining down on me as I gaze towards my balcony doors.

The night sky feels peaceful and welcoming. I walk across to open the patio door; greeted by a soft, gentle breeze of the night.

I take in the atmosphere and realise how much I prefer the quiet suburban life; in comparison to the crowded city life we once had with Nana and Pops.

As I admire the glowing white moon illuminating the forests in the horizon, I come to realise, that I have my whole life ahead of me. For once, I feel as if I am in control. The silence of the night reassures me that my life can be as peaceful as this very moment.

The unexpected shimmer of a white reflection catches my eye.

I focus my gaze as I walk towards a small white object, lying on the floor of my balcony.

I bend down to pick it up; a smile grows on my face.

It is a beautiful white flower, similar to that which I had picked up during my dangerous adventure in the forest. A flower that I have never seen before; velvet-like petals, which almost appear to glow from being the purest of whites.

I stand holding the flower, in amazement at its pristine condition.

Not a single petal out of place, no sign of deterioration or lack of hydration; as if it has only just been plucked from the ground.

I smile as I walk back towards my room with the flower against my nose, taking in the beautiful scent.

I place the flower on the bedside table, before switching off the lamp.

I wake to find Micky cuddling up to me. 'What time is it?' I ask in a sleepy tone.

'Sshh,' Micky whispers while half asleep.

From the movement at the foot of my bed, I realise Diesel is also here.

I cuddle up to my baby brother as we both doze off into a deeper sleep.

The sudden barking of Diesel startles us both. As I jump up from his defensive tone, I look to find him growling while he jumps off the bed. He desperately tries to climb against the balcony door while sounding a threatening bark.

'Diesel, quiet boy,' I shout out in a dozy voice. He begins to growl as he stares into the garden.

We all head downstairs for breakfast, Micky asks for cereal, the side effects from days of over-eating no doubt. I open the French doors; Diesel seems eager to run out. I notice Aunt Liz practicing her yoga within the first quadrant of the garden. She's startled, losing balance from Diesel zooming past her, running towards the back of the garden. I chuckle as I put some bread in the toaster and pull together Micky's cereal.

'What on earth are you eating?' asks Aunt Liz is a disapproving tone.

'Food,' Micky responds while he looks at me with a cheeky expression.

I can't help but smile as I look down, continuing to eat my toast. 'A growing boy like you shouldn't be having cereal while you're off school. You need lots of protein and carbs in you,' she mutters as she begins to prepare for a fry up.

'Really, Anna? I would have expected you to know better,' she hisses with her back towards me.

I've grown used to her pretentious outlook and have learned to ignore her holier-than-thou attitude towards me. As much as I wish she would love me like she once did, I accept that those days have long past.

'Micky, I have arranged a day out with your new friend, Maria and her brother, Tommy that we had dinner with,' Aunt Liz announces with a smug expression.

'Ooh, that will be nice,' Micky responds.

'What are your plans today, Ann?' Aunt Liz asks, as if to suggest her plans with Micky do not include me.

'Liyana can come with me,' Micky suggests as he finishes off his cereal.

Aunt Liz forces an unnatural laugher before stating,

'I'm sure Liyana has other things to do than join a bunch of kids. And Micky I'm sure you don't want Diesel to be all on his own for the whole day.'

Great, now I'm a dog sitter in her eyes.

'It's okay, Micky, I have a few things to do today, but we will see each other when you get back.'

I get into my car, heading to the nearest city. It's about time I prepare for university, with the new academic year only being a few days away.

My plan for today, shopping!

I walk around the city; it reminds me of my old life with Nana and Pops, the congestion of people rushing to get to their destinations.

I notice groups of friends laughing out loud, having fun. Maybe they will be at the new university I will be joining shortly?

I wonder what it would feel like to have a group of close, trustworthy friends? Perhaps it would feel like an extension of your family, suddenly the image of Aunt Liz pops into my head, I cannot help but shudder at the thought.

After my shopping for clothes, stationery and everything else that caught my fancy, I sit in a café watching the world go by.

I sip on my coffee and nibble away on my sandwich as I watch the movements of the public walking past.

I watch an elderly couple moving at a slow pace, holding hands as they smile away.

I notice a beautiful, young girl walking with a strut, luscious bouncy hair, with a tall, voluptuous figure. Typically she has a crowd of followers trying to keep up with her erratic pace.

I watch them in amazement as I struggle to understand what it is about this beautiful young woman that makes her "friends" follow her as she unpredictably changes directions. I reflect on myself as I realise, I have always been more recluse and in all honesty, prefer it this way. It's the only way that I have really ever known.

I stare into the beautiful, blossoming trees beyond the busy traffic of people; an unexpected figure catches my eye.

What looks like a tall male figure standing beside the tree, all alone watching the people go by, just like me.

His smart clothing all in white makes him stand out, but the hood across his head makes it difficult to see any of his features.

My eyes zoom into him, trying to understand whom he is, wanting to read the silent words across his expression.

The traffic of people cutting through my gaze, blocks my vision of him.

I manoeuvre my position, eager to catch him in my gaze. As the traffic of people finally passes, I cannot help but sigh. He has gone.

Having finished my lunch, I exit the café, carrying my multiple bags.

Daydreaming of my new life in university brings a smile to my face when suddenly I am brought back to reality as I bump into a stranger.

My bags drop from the sudden halt of my rhythm, forcing my books to scatter across the path.

'I'm so, so sorry,' I plea while bending down to collect my belongings off the ground.

The stranger bends down to help me with my books.

I notice the white linen like trousers and white plimsolls being worn by the stranger; it's the man I was watching besides the tree. As I raise my gaze off from the ground, a passer-by hands me a book, stealing my attention.

I quickly stand as I collect the book from the helpful woman and eagerly turn, to see the mysterious person in white.

I cannot help but frown, my eyes search for him, but he seems to have disappeared, again.

I lay on the sun lounger, soaking up the sun while reading through the course literature. The subject of psychology has always fascinated me. The understanding of how we work and how our inner sub-conscience controls us without our realisation. I feel an element of excitement in my stomach as I eagerly read through the material, looking forward to the possibilities of the future.

I take a sip of my homemade smoothie as I head into the Jacuzzi.

I smile from the feeling of tension evaporating from my body by the power of the jets easing into my muscles.

I glance at Diesel who seems to be dozing off on the sun lounger.

I close my eyes as I lean my head back and enjoy the fading sound of the birds singing in the background.

The warmth of the Jacuzzi makes me oblivious to the cooler night setting in.

I slowly open my eyes; I become mesmerised by the illuminating colours of the sun setting.

The purple and pink swirling amongst the wispy white layers of clouds.

I sip on my drink, dipping lower into the Jacuzzi to keep the chill away from my shoulders.

While enthralled in the atmosphere, I suddenly feel a sense of unease from a glimmer of a shadow, I notice besides me. I look around, but there is nothing there.

A strange feeling takes over my senses; one of perhaps the balance of the atmosphere changing? There's no sense of danger or threat, just a weird sensation, which makes me feel more aware of my surroundings.

Diesel begins to stir, I consider getting out of the Jacuzzi and heading back into the house.

I absorb the glow of the vibrant colours from the sunset for a final moment. I sit up slowly rubbing both my shoulders for warmth.

My eyes widen at the sudden rustling of the shrubs beside me. Diesel ears pick up unexpectedly; he jumps off the sun lounger, growling in my direction.

I cannot help but begin to frown, as I try to make sense of his bizarre reaction. Somewhat defensive yet startled and perhaps even a touch of obedience? His growls are continuously changing, to a whimper, and then back to growls.

The bushes behind me begin to rustle noticeably yet the breeze in the air seems steady. I turn around expecting to find a rodent near the shrubs, but there is nothing visible.

The rustling of the shrubs stops abruptly. Diesel runs off to the end of the garden, barking towards the wall of trees.

I leave the hot tub and gather my books scattered across the sun lounger.

A frown grows on my face as I slowly stand straight and tilt my head while trying to recall my actions.

The frown slowly turns to a smile; a smile I try to control as I gently bite my bottom lip.

My perfectly intact, white mystery flower is sitting beside my books, yet I cannot recall bringing this from my room. I gently pick up my flower and place it within my hair as I tuck the stem behind my ear.

I walk out of the shower, quickly drying off with my towel. The swelling of my ankles seem to have almost healed. I change into my white nightdress, placing the flower back into my damp hair while walking into the balcony. The gentle breeze of the night flows through my hair and gown. I stare up at the sky, watching the twinkling of the stars trying to come through in the setting of the night sky.

Within the silence, I hear nothing but my heartbeat, my slow breathes as I inhale and absorb my peaceful surroundings.

Peaceful, till I hear a gentle whisper, 'You are back…'

'…The most terrible poverty is loneliness and the feeling of being unloved…'

—   Mother Teresa

07. Am I Alone?

My glance zooms to the right from where the whisper came. The pace of my heartbeat picks up with the breeze of the night. My eyes search into the emptiness that surrounds me. The mysterious voice was so clear, yet there is no one here but me.

The sudden knock, followed by the creaking of my bedroom door steels my attention.

'Liyana you're here.' Micky runs towards me, wrapping his arms around my waist before telling me all about his fun-filled day.

I rummage through my bags trying to find the gift I had purchased for Micky during my shopping spree.

'This is for you, Micky,' I whisper as I slowly offer him a wrapped box.

'ME!' he shouts in excitement. I quietly chuckle at his reaction while looking at him with love.

'You're maybe a little too young for this now, but it's something that you can keep forever,' I whisper.

As he opens the box, he pulls out a chain with metal tags. He looks closer at the tags and finds his name engraved at the top. As he curiously lifts the first tag, he gasps in surprise, staring at our image imprinted on the metal, from a photograph I had taken of us a few days back in the garden.

'Liyana, this is us,' he whispers in astonishment.

'Yes, Micky, it's us, I will always be with you now, no matter where you are.'

'This is soo cool!' he whispers with excitement.

'Even in 100 years, we will still be on this tag' he gasps. 'Even in 1000 years,' I answer exaggeratedly.

'Wooowww... I'm going to take you everywhere with me Liyana, even when Aunt Liz doesn't want you to come!'

I laugh out loud at his innocence while I watch him quickly put the chain away into the box, tucking it beneath the pillow.

We both lie on the bed while Micky continues to tell me about his fun-filled day before we eventually fall asleep in amongst the giggles and cuddles.

'Where am I,' I whisper as I walk through the darkness of the forest.

The moonlight shines down on my path, while the glowing trail of the night flowers leads my direction.

The blue velvet night sky holds the sparkles of diamond stars, as they reflect their glitter onto the bed of white flowers scattered across the forest.

'I did not think I would see you again,' I hear a gentle voice whisper. A soft male tone with an accent from a place I do not recognise.

My heartbeat slowly rises with anticipation as my eyes desperately search to see him, but he is lost, or I am lost. I cannot see anyone but me.

There is not an ounce of fear in me, but I am filled with curiosity.

'Where are you?' I whisper as I turn in gentle circles trying to find him.

'I am always here,' he whispers while the sudden breeze of the night picks up, cooling the flush of adrenaline running through me.

My body tenses as I feel a rush of energy flow through my every pour, while I suddenly and uncontrollably gasp. My eyes roll back as I dramatically inhale, while the breeze continues to flow through my gown, through my hair.

A tingle flows through every cell in my body; I reach my hands to comb through my hair, clenching the tip of my scalp to feel the gentle pull.

My eyes widen as the sensation passes, my breathing becomes uncontrollably deep from this mystical embrace.

I am stunned; I freeze from the experience of this sensation, yet my chest vividly rises from the depth of my breathing.

My body feels so light, yet I feel as if I have no energy left to stand from the mystical sensation that has passed through me. I close my eyes as I feel my head gently spin. I desperately try to regain full control of my strength as I slowly feel my legs begin to quiver.

'I... I can't stand,' I whisper as I begin to feel myself falling into the peaceful night.

As my body lies still, the heavenly scent of purity has never been so potent. I feel as if I am in a different world while I lay listening to the melody of the singing birds in the background. I feel the loose strands of hair gently removed from the front of my face,

I become more aware, more conscious as I slowly open my eyes.

I find myself lying in my bed, my cheek brushing against the pillow as I slowly awake. Beneath my nose, a scent that is unexpected; as my consciousness returns, I realise the scent comes from the flower I must have left in my hair last night.

I sit up rubbing my nose while confusion takes over my mind. I scoff at the thought of getting high from the scent of this flower, causing me to have such vivid yet beautifully mystical dreams.

I look around the room to find that I am here alone. It felt so real, as if someone was here with me, brushing my hair away from my face. I shake my head at my somewhat lucid daydreams as I pick up the ruffled flower from my pillow.

As I reach over to place the disfigured petals on my bedside table, I cannot help but frown. I stare at the already laying flower on the bedside table, which is in pristine condition. Where did this one come from? I wonder as I stare at the two flowers side by side.

I walk downstairs and can hear Micky playing with Diesel. I join Uncle Aidan and Aunt Liz at the table as I watch Micky discreetly giving Diesel his food.

'Morning, kiddo,' Uncle Aidan says as he pours me a glass of juice.

'Honestly, Ann, I don't know what you were thinking giving Micky a chain like that! It's hardly appropriate for his age!'

'Relax, Lizzy, it's just a chain,' Uncle Aidan responds with an uninterested tone.

Micky looks up at me with his big, grey puppy eyes, miming sorry while he clasps the tags in his palm. I scrunch my nose as I smile at him, watching him tuck the tags discreetly beneath his T-shirt.

Aunt Liz picks up her mugs and leaves the table while muttering away.

Uncle Aidan throws her a disapproving look as she brushes past.

'I'm just saying, there is no need to throw money down the drain, and what is this? Honestly, Liyana, did you sleep in the garden?' she hisses as she hands me a leaf which she pulls from my hair.

Her rant fades into the background as I stare at the leaf in the palm of my hand.

Flashbacks of my dream appear in my vision, where I was sleeping peacefully amongst the moonflowers blooming in the moonlit velvet night. I recall floating down onto the ground while swept with a sensation, a sensation making me quiver while possessing all the strength I had in me.

'Liyana, Liyana.'

'Yes,' I answer quickly not knowing who is calling my name.

'You alright, kiddo?'

'Yes, I am, good, thank you.'

Uncle Aidan and I talk about my preparations for university, the excitement in his tone feels heart-warming.

'I thought we could have a family dinner tomorrow, just the 4 of us, seeing as though it is your last night of freedom before university starts? Unless you have other plans of course,' asks Uncle Aidan.

His efforts to make me feel a part of the family do not go unnoticed by both Aunt Liz and me.

'That sounds lovely, Uncle, thank you. I would really like that.'

'Well perhaps you would rather go and venture out to make new friends, Liyana, we don't want to hold you back,' states Aunt Liz.

With her back facing towards me, it's difficult to determine if she has made this comment from genuine care or whether it is another attempt to keep me away from her ideal family set up.

'No that's okay, Aunt Liz, but thanks, I wouldn't want to miss it for the world.'

Her silence leaves me unsure as to how she may be feeling towards me.

I spend the weekend reading further on my course literature while preparing for university.

I cherish the last few days with Micky before the start of a whole new chapter of my life.

'Liyana will you be leaving me?' Micky asks in a timid tone, as we both stand on the balcony of his large bedroom.

'Of course not Micky! That day will never come! Why would you even think that?' I ask in a soft loving tone.

'Aunt Liz keeps talking about when you leave and that it will be just her and me, but if you leave you will take me with you right? You won't leave me all alone will you?'

Micky looks up at me with his fearful eyes glistening with tears. I lean down, wrapping Micky in my arms as he rests his head on my shoulder.

'Please don't leave me,' he pleas in a helpless tone.

I kiss his head before brushing my hands through his hair. From the snuffling of his nose, I can sense that he is crying. He's always been similar to me, in trying not to show people when he is hurting. A suffer in silence type.

My blood begins to boil at the thought of Aunt Liz's callous attitude, resorting to my baby Micky in tears!

'Micky, you are my world!' I state in a reassuring tone.

'Aunt Liz loves you too and sometimes, she thinks that I will be going away after university, but what she doesn't understand is that there is this invisible string between you and me. And this magical string will never break between us. It means that you and I can never be apart because our bond will not let us, it ties us together, it keeps us together. So you never have to worry about me leaving you okay!'

'Where is the string?' Micky asks in a curious tone as he looks up at me with his tears falling off his cheeks.

I slowly wipe the tears away before cupping the side of his face in my palm.

'It's between your heart and mine, only people who love each as much as we do have this string. And that's why we can never be apart. Not everyone has this special bond that we do Micky.'

'You're just joking. There is no string,' he huffs as he folds his arms and begins to frown.

'Okay, if you can answer this one question, it means I am making it up. BUT, if you can't answer the question, it means I am telling you the truth – deal?' I ask in a confident tone.

'Okay,' Micky responds curiously.

'Tell me one time, any time that you can remember, where I left you all alone?'

Micky looks to the sky as if he is trying to pluck memories from his mind. After some time he finally looks down with a smile on his face.

'Never' he shouts with joy!

'Exactly,' I whisper in a victorious tone.

He begins to chuckle as he wraps his arms around me with delight while pushing his full weight against me.

My legs have gone numb from squatting for so long; I lose balance as we both fall to the floor. We head downstairs in readiness for our family dinner that Uncle Aidan had suggested.

'Micky, you okay, champ, your eyes seem a little red?' Uncle Aidan asks with concern.

'Me and Liyana were just talking, it's okay, Uncle, she will never leave me,' he states innocently.

Aunt Liz looks up at me from the table before muttering, 'Honestly, Ann; I wish you would just be realistic rather than planting false hope in your brother – it's not fair.'

'Realistic?' I question in a confused tone.

'Well, yes, it's not as if you are going to want to stay here when you could be with your friends and will have your career to focus on.'

Micky looks up at me with his puppy eyes; my frustration builds as I watch the worry grow on his face.

With my priority being Micky, I chose to ignore Aunt Liz only for a moment.

I smile at Micky softly while placing my hand on my heart before pointing at his.

I place my index finger to my lips and whisper, 'Ssh.'

The smile on his face grows into an uncontrollable grin followed with a little giggle.

I look down at Uncle Aidan who is sat at the table opposite Aunt Liz, offering her a disapproving look. They seem to be whispering so quietly, almost as if they are lip reading.

I look down to the table, my internal battle begins; do I address her comment, or let it pass?

Their whispers rise, 'Well forgive me Aidan for just trying to avoid any surprises to Micky later down the line!'

The final straw snaps my patience; I feel the frustration taking over me, I can no longer contain it.

'If there is anything unrealistic about MY outlook on MY future, I'd appreciate it Aunt Eliza if you could discuss this with ME rather than my baby brother!'

In a flash, my eyes lock onto hers, while I stare at her with a blank expression on my face.

I don't want this to become uncomfortable, yet I want to make my point clear.

Aunt Liz stares back at me and to my surprise, after a few moments of silence breaks out into an unnatural laughter, somewhat of a nervous laugh.

'That's enough, Liz,' Uncle Aidan states in a raised voice as he watches her laughing at me.

'Liyana, please, take a seat,' he offers as he pulls out the empty seat beside him.

I glance at Uncle Aidan while forcing a smile and take the seat beside him.

The atmosphere feels tense and uncomfortable. We eat our dinner while making small talk, which seems forced and fake.

Aunt Liz puts all her focus on Micky and seems to be the only one talking, while Uncle Aidan tries to keep me included but seems somewhat annoyed at the situation.

Diesel sat beside Micky suddenly picks his head from off the floor and begins to growl in Aunt Liz's direction.

'What's wrong boy?' Uncle Aidan asks as we all stare towards Diesel.

'It's okay,' Micky says with a mouth full of food. 'Diesel is angry with Aunt Liz coz she's being mean – that's all.' I try hard to conceal my grin as I watch Micky chomping away at his food.

Uncle Aidan chuckles lightly and responds with 'Well, we can't be having that now, can we Diesel?'

'This isn't a laughing matter Aidan!' Aunt Liz scowls.

'There is nothing wrong with being realistic and trying to protect Micky from the reality of life.'

'What reality?' I question as I calmly put my fork down and glare at Aunt Liz.

Diesel continues to bark towards Aunt Liz before jumping up towards her direction.

Aunt Liz becomes startled from Diesel's unanticipated behaviour; you can sense the frustration building up inside her as her face begins to turn red.

'Quiet, Diesel you will get into trouble,' Micky tries to whisper in his desperate attempt to calm Diesel.

'Oh just shut up, you stupid dog! You don't belong here either!' Aunt Liz shouts as she grabs her glass of wine and takes a deep gulp.

Diesel's barking increases from her hostile reaction, when suddenly, the glass in her hand shatters into pieces, leaving her wine dripping all over her dinner.

Aunt Liz screams from the shock and jumps out of her seat. 'For Goodness Sake, Liz! Diesel, out boy, come on!' shouts Uncle Aidan as he ushers Diesel into the back garden.

'This is all her doing!' Aunt Liz screams as she leaves the table taking her plate with her.

Her rant disappears in the background, leaving Micky and I staring at each other.

His eyes are wide in shock, he beings to whisper,

'Liyana, shall we go back to Nana and Pops? Aunt Liz said Diesel doesn't belong here EITHER! So she doesn't want us here AND Diesel!'

Uncle Aidan walks in to hear what Micky has to say.

'No...no, it's okay, Micky, that's not what Aunt Liz meant,' I add quickly hoping that the conversation can end there.

'Oh, don't worry, champ; your Aunt is just a little sensitive! Ignore what she said,' Uncle Aidan requests as he stands beside him and pats him on his head.

Aunt Liz walks in to cuddle Micky as she softly whispers to him, 'I'm sorry, Micky, please don't be upset, Aunt Liz is just trying to protect you.'

'From what?' questions Micky?

'Aunt Liz glares at me while Micky is looking up at her.

Watching Micky sat innocently with both Aunt Liz and Uncle Aidan by his side has never made me feel so unwanted.

The unwelcome stare Aunt Liz offers me, gives me no alternative but to feel as if I should not be there.

I quietly pick up my plate and leave the room.

'No, no, Micky, she will be fast asleep you cannot go in,' I hear a voice whisper outside my door while the pitter-patter of Micky's footsteps pause.

'But, I want to say goodnight,' Micky pleads.

'It's okay, she will know you meant to say it. Where is Diesel? He might still be outside; you need to look after your best friend.'

'Oh no, Diesel!' Micky shouts as he runs back down the stairs. 'At least the stupid mutt comes in useful for something,' Aunt Liz states with smugness in her voice, which soon breaks out into a chuckle.

I lay my head on my pillow feeling consumed by loneliness. Aunt Liz seems adamant about me leaving the house some point soon.

I wish she could just accept me into the family, but deep down, I know this will never happen.

I put my hand under my pillow as I bury my face into the white covers of my pillowcase.

I quietly snuffle, trying to overcome the sense of loneliness consuming me.

I cannot help but feel, there is not a single person in this world that truly understands me; no one that is there to take care of me. But what hurts me the most is the fact that, no one really knows me.

'…Walk with the wise and become wise, for a companion of fools suffers harm…'

—   Proverbs 13.20

08. Late Arriver

The sirens ring as all the anxious students rush to get to their class.

The feeling of apprehension, as a result of unknown territory, raises the rhythm of my heartbeat.

'Heads up!' I hear a voice shout amongst the scattering of students. Just as I turn around, I gasp at the sight of a soccer ball flying towards my head.

Instinctively I drop my books, catching the ball with both hands to avoid it striking my face.

'Wow, great reflexes!' a young man chuckles as he hurries towards me.

I stare at him as he approaches; he's exceptionally tall, broad in comparison to the other students walking past.

'Sorry about that,' he offers as he bends down to collect my books off the ground.

'Oh, it's okay, don't worry about it,' I respond as I offer him back his ball in exchange for my books.

'I'm DeJon,' he responds as he reaches out his hand in a gesture to shake mine.

'Liyana,' I reply as our hands are shaking with a soft rhythm.

'Wow, what an unusual name,' he replies while giving me a generous smile.

'Liyana,' I hear a sharp voice question. 'What kind of name is Liyana?'

I turn to see a beautiful young woman walk towards us followed by a couple of her friends at either side of her.

A face I didn't fail to recognise; the group of girls I had crossed during my shopping spree a few days back.

'Hey, DJ, love your jacket,' she says as she strokes her hand along his shoulders while displaying her immaculate white teeth.

Her clothes are fitted, complimenting her curvaceous figure. The cut of her short crop top beneath her denim jacket leaves little to the imagination.

The loose curls within her dark brown hair entwined with deep orange dip-dyed highlights are unusual yet boast confidence. 'Yeah thanks, Trix,' DeJon responds seeming uninterested. 'Nice meeting you, Liyana and sorry again,' DeJon states as he walks off towards his group of friends waiting along the corridor.

Trix stares back at DeJon as he walks off into the crowd.

He's the tallest of his group and judging from his jacket and soccer ball; I assume he's part of the university soccer team. 'You've blown it, Trixy. He didn't even look back at you,' a young girl beside her states.

'No I haven't! He's just playing hard to get,' Trixy responds with an extremely confident, bordering arrogant tone.

'So, Liyana, what kind of name is that?'

Trixy turns to look at me as she observes my outfit.'

Her pale face is blemish free, her subtle makeup emphasis her beautiful features, full lips and big green eyes.

Her tone of voice sounds somewhat harsh, almost confrontational, leaving me confused as to how to respond. 'It's the kind of name my parents gave me,' I reply in a calm yet confident tone as I stare into her eyes.

I glance at her friends before turning to make my way towards my class.

In the background, I hear a friend of Trixy's giggle, before quickly apologising.

'Out of your league!' I hear Trixy shout out in a condescending tone.

I assume she is talking to me, but have no idea what she's referring to?

A feeling of unease runs through me at the thought of bumping into Trixy and her friends again.

I sit in my class and look around at all the students surrounding me. It seems most of them know each other, from high school perhaps?

'Hi, is this seat taken?' a soft voice asks.

I'm startled by the sudden question and turn to face a lovely, young woman hovering over the seat beside me.

'No, please…feel free,' I respond offering her a warm smile.

A slender, dark woman sits beside me. Her jet-black hair sits below her shoulders, crimped into a sleek style.

Her eyes hold an oriental flick to them, dressed in beautiful, long lashes with thin black eyeliner. Her strawberry shaped face holds the faintest freckles across her cheeks.

'Hi, I'm Nevaeh. I don't think I've seen you around here before, you from out of town?'

'Err, Yes, I've recently moved here, I'm Liyana.'

'C'mon now, class, settle down,' the lecturer interrupts as the last few students rush in.

The introduction to our course begins; I look around the crescent-shaped room at all my fellow classmates.

An element of excitement runs through my body as I realise this is the start of my development, the start of my new life.

The lecturer welcomes us with a powerful opening to our course.

'The human mind holds more connections than the vast amount of stars in the universe! Understanding the potential of the human mind is a challenge far beyond the reach of humanity, yet the mind is a gift that we are all blessed with. A tool that we all possess, how we use it, is what makes us who we are...and who we have the potential to become!

'Ah, fashionably late is not tolerated in my domain!' the lecturer states in a stern tone as the classroom door slowly opens.

A tall, slender young man slowly walks through, seeming somewhat timid, despite the broad frame and steady posture. His hooded white jacket is unusually smart for a student. With the hood draped across his face, it's difficult to make out what he looks like.

His broad shoulders carry him a white bag, which he holds in his grasp, his white trousers complimented with pale plimsolls.

I notice the theme of white makes him appear to have the faintest glow, as he slowly walks past towards the empty seats at the back of the class.

A feeling of familiarity passes my mind, despite being unable to make eye contact nor see his face; other than his jaw, surrounded by faint dark stubble.

I close my eyes and inhale a deep breath; an unfamiliar sensation begins to flow through my body, the feeling of a soft breeze sweeping gently through my hair as the light surrounds me.

'Liyana... Liyana.'

I recall my surroundings, feeling startled as I look towards Nevaeh who is calling my name.

'You okay, girl?' she asks with a look of concern.

'Yeah... Yes. I'm fine.'

Nevaeh focuses back on the lecturer; I cannot help but turn around as my eyes search for the mysterious late arriver.

I cannot see him, though I don't know what he looks like to search for him.

I turn back round to face the lecturer, refocusing my concentration to the class.

'The lecture's over, c'mon lets go,' Nevaeh suggests in a friendly tone.

I collect my books while simultaneously scouring the room on the off chance that I can spot the late arriver, but nothing.

'Let me give you a tour,' she offers as we are walking through the corridor.

The place quickly fills with students as lunchtime commences.

'Here we have the skaters. They are pretty reckless but equally very friendly, though sometimes their sarcasm is overbearing. Here are the typical stereotype of Goths and Emos. Not really sure of the difference between the two, but yeah, as you can see, they love black, pale faces and lots of metal chains!'

I catch the eye of a pale-faced young woman with black hair covering most of her eyes. I'm confused by her expression, as I watch her frowning towards me. She puffs on her cigarette as we walk past making a point not to break her gaze from my direction.

Why do I always attract negative attention? I question myself in pity.

I walk past staring in fascination at the different types of groups that have formed, despite it only being day one of our university life!

I cannot help but wonder where it is that I will fit in, if anywhere at all?

'You gotta love the nerds!' Nevaeh states with a proud smile. A young girl comes running over as we pass a crowd of academic fanatics. She appears short and petite with short bob hair tucked behind her ears.

'Nevaeh,' she shouts in a soft squeaky voice as she greets her with a fond hug.

'Hey, Sammy, been wondering when I'll finally bump into you,' Nevaeh responds with a fond smile.

'This is Liyana – Liyana meet Sammy.'

Sammy looks up at me; here big, blue beady eyes are heart-warming.

She reaches out her tiny palm and welcomes me with a shake of the hand followed by a dazzling smile. The gaps between her teeth were endearing, reminding me of Micky. Sammy was an angelic looking young woman with soft brown hair fringing her face.

'And finally,' states Nevaeh.

'We have the jocks, the envy of many. Always surrounded by the preps. My least favourite of them all!

Too much money to know what to do with, always buying their way through life.'

As we walk past, I notice Trixy and her group of friends who seem to be draping themselves across the athletes.

I recognise DeJon within the crowd who has his head in a book despite being distracted by Trixy. She seems desperate for his attention, while he appears somewhat irritated.

I sit with Sammy and Nevaeh for lunch; they seem to know each other from childhood.

Sammy aspires to be a physicist, while Nevaeh and I share a passion for understanding the human mind and why we work the way we do.

'So which dorm are you in,' Sammy asks in her soft voice. 'Well, I live fairly close by so I'm not actually staying in the dorms,' I respond feeling a little excluded.

'Nah that's cool girl, you can crash at mine anytime you get fed up with the parents and fancy partyin' all night.'

I smile not knowing what to say at the mention of "parents". I chose not to reveal the fact that I live with my aunt and uncle. A small piece of detail no one really needs to know just yet.

Despite the university being huge, it's somewhat of a small community. Everyone seems to know each other, it's the new arrivers like myself that seem to stand out.

I see personal traits of myself within my new friends.

Nevaeh reminds me of a more extreme version of myself. I'm quietly confident, whereas Nevaeh is not as reserved. She seems much more forthright and vocal.

Sammy, on the other hand, is more timid and reserved, gently spoken and very modest yet highly intelligent. Sammy is continually observing people, while analysing her surroundings.

Trixy's laugh can be heard from our table. She seems to be the only person laughing as she brushes her hands across DeJon's shoulders.

He begrudgingly smiles before suddenly closing his book. He rises to his feet before walking away from their table.

I find myself watching Trixy as she initially follows after him, but after a couple of steps, is stood with her mouth wide open; as if she is in shock that DeJon has passed on her advances.

A friend of Trixy's follows behind her quickly, offering a supportive arm across her shoulders. Trixy instantly brushes off the gesture while walking back to take a seat in a sulking manner.

Trixy's glare soon focuses in my direction.

The laughter surrounding me catches my attention as I turn to find Nevaeh laughing with DeJon.

'Hey, it's Leya,' DeJon states as he holds his fist out.

'Liyana,' I respond as I raise my hand and partake in his fist bump gesture.

He begins to chuckle as he repeatedly states, 'my bad.' I subtly turn to Trixy to see her scowling towards us.

'So you're new here right?' DeJon questions.

'Yes. Don't really know many people, though your friend, Trixy has left an impression,' I state in a disapproving tone.

He continues to chuckle.

'That's really polite! That's not the way most girls would phrase it!'

'Yeah, girl, say it how it is, she's a bitch! No need to hold back!' Nevaeh encourages with excitement.

I smile in return as we briefly talk in jest.

His dark brown hair matches his big brown eyes. His clean-shaven complexion reveals strong features across his face, mimicking his strong alpha male presence.

We all stand as we gather our belongings ready for our next class.

Nevaeh and DeJon take me back to their childhood and the pranks they used to play on their neighbours.

We all begin to laugh at the stories they share when suddenly I am jolted forward by an unexpected barge. I cannot help but stumble forward as I drop my books across the table.

'HEY! NOT COOL TRIX!' I hear DeJon shout in an aggressive tone. Sammy quickly helps me to my feet and begins to gather my belongings.

'That girl needs a real good seein' too! What the hell did you see in her anyway!' Nevaeh shouts in frustration.

'Nah, don't go there… I have NO IDEA! But whatever it was, it's gone for sure!' DeJon states with regret.

I look up to see Trixy strutting away, with her friends following behind.

'Don't worry, Liyana, I got you,' Nevaeh states defensively, as she glares at Trixy walking into the crowds.

'C'mon, let's get to our next class,' she continues, trying to defuse the situation.

We sit in class, the lecturer provides a detailed overview of our course, informing us of what we can expect. On the topic of social psychology, I cannot help but think of Trixy.

DeJon seems like a nice enough guy, but perhaps talking to him is what has irritated Trixy? Maybe her psychological reaction towards me is a result of her feeling I have undermined her social status – being a prep.

Maybe I need to stay away from the both of them to avoid trouble?

I look around the class, glancing at all the unfamiliar faces surrounding me.

My eyes search for the late arriver, but it's difficult to know what I'm searching for… Either way, it doesn't appear that he is here.

The topic swiftly moves onto cognitive neuroscience and how the brain enables the mind.

I think back to all the strange encounters I have experienced over the past few weeks, the forest, the flowers and the dreams. I wonder if my mind is somehow creating unrealistic scenarios, for me to feel as if I am ready to move on? Ready to finally put the past behind me and move into my future.

The lecturer informs the class of our first assignment; childhood issues and disorders. Nothing extensive, a short case study of our choice to investigate and provide a hypothesis as to why a child may develop a defence mechanism as a result of a traumatising event.

Following our final class, we gather outside the university towards the car park. Nevaeh and I walk side by side as she informs me about the upcoming party on Friday.

'It's the first party of the year; you have to be there! This will be a big one!' Nevaeh insists with excitement.

'I'm in,' shouts DeJon as he squeezes in between us, putting both his arms around our shoulders.

I didn't realise how tall and broad he was till the weight of his arm weighs me down.

'So you both in,' he asks.

'Sure am, though Liyana here seems tentative.'

'Nah you gotta come, it's the biggest welcome party of the year!' he insists.

'Yo, Romeo,' he shouts out to a crowd beyond us.

'C'mon, meet the team,' he insists as he steers us towards the direction of his friends.

DeJon jumps onto his friends who all begin to stumble and chuckle at his juvenile behaviour.

'Hello, ladies, it's a pleasure to meet you,' a young man in the group states as he takes both Nevaeh's hand and mine, planting a kiss on each.

'Hey, enough of that Romeo, these are my girls, no messin'! DeJon states with a defensive yet playful tone.

'It's all good,' Romeo chuckles as he offers us both a beaming smile, his impeccable teeth glow white. His build is much slimmer in comparison to his friends surrounding him. The dimples across his cheeks accompanied with his boyish young looks make it understandable as to why he may be popular with the ladies.

'Watch this one; he's got a thing for the ladies,' states DeJon as he grabs Romeo in a headlock.

'What a perfectly suited name,' I say in surprise.

'Nah, it's Milo, but most people seem to know me as Romeo, I have no idea why!' he responds proudly as he manages to free his neck from DeJon's lock.

His dark black hair is styled perfectly. His golden skin seems well moisturised; he takes better care of himself and his appearance than I do!

A huge African-American young man walks towards us, wrapping his arms around Nevaeh.

'It's been too long! How you been?' he asks with fondness.

'Aw, was wondering when I'd finally see you! You staying out of trouble these days,' she questions as they both begin to giggle.

'Meet Liyana! Like you were once upon a time, she's new here.'

'Respect, Liyana,' this giant man states as he offers his fist out.

'Respect,' I respond as I partake in his fist bump.

'So how do you two…'

'She saved me,' he quickly states as they both look at each other and laugh out loud.

'A giant like you needs saving?' I question with a smile on my face.

'This was pre-puberty! You know how it is, back in the day, was new in the hood, looking for trouble! And boy did I find trouble!'

Nevaeh bursts out into laughter.

'More like keeping you outta trouble Bazzer!' She states in a patronising tone.

'Exactly! Nevaeh was like the big sister I never had. Clipped me round the ear and made me buckle up – I wasn't as tall back then, and she can be quite scary when she wants to be!'

We all break out into a giggle, which is quickly interrupted by a tall blonde-haired Caucasian man.

'Boys C'mon we're gonna miss the trials!' He says in an energetic yet desperate tone.

'Ah Tucker just give it a rest, that's all you've been saying since lunchtime! We got another…' Bazzer glances at his watch, the look of panic takes over his expression.

'Ah shit, we're gonna miss the trials,' he whispers in shock. We all begin to chuckle as Tucker starts to shake his hands in the air from frustration with Bazzer.

'See you ladies tomorrow,' they shout as they all begin to run through the fields towards the stadium.

Nevaeh and I grab a coffee on campus while we wait for Sammy. She explains how she crossed paths with Bazzer many years ago when they were barely teenagers. He appeared to be heading towards the wrong side of the law when he was new in town.

After she had clipped him around the ear, helping him find his way, he focused all his strength and growing energy into sports. From which he obtained a scholarship and moved up in the world. But he never refused to acknowledge her; always referring to her as his big sister. And that's how Nevaeh knows all the jocks and soccer team and is somewhat untouchable.

She offers more insight to DeJon, explaining his passion isn't sports, though he is extremely good at it. In fact, he's one of the best in the state.

He continues this course but still searches in textbooks for his real passion.

DeJon is somewhat of a lost soul, but it's not all bad, being lost as the captain of the soccer team.

'So…is he your type?' asks Nevaeh in a cheeky tone.

'My type! Err… No. Not that he's not attractive, he's handsome! He's just definitely not my type,' I respond in a panic.

I can feel myself become nervous from the personal intrusion. Very rarely have I been asked about my opinion, or my type. I struggled to tell Uncle Aidan about my ideal car, where would I start with an ideal guy!

Nevaeh begins to giggle at my reaction and questions 'Well who then?'

'Err, no one, I don't really date,' I respond hoping she will drop the conversation.

Nevaeh looks with a disbelieving expression.

'But don't worry,' I quickly add, 'when I see my type, when I see him, I will let you know.'

'He'll be at the party this Friday you know.'

'Who will?' I question in confusion.

'Whoever your type is – so you can show me on Friday,' she insists with a cheeky smile.

I offer a nervous laugh at the realisation that it is unlikely Nevaeh will let me back out from this party!

'…If you're open to new people and new adventures,
Love will come along…'

—   Lily Collins

09. The Harsh Truth

'How was your first day, Anna? Regret not staying on campus?' Aunt Liz questions as she sips on her wine.

As we sit for dinner, Uncle Aidan attempts to lighten the mood with gentler questions.

'Well, we will need to think of some rules around the house, after all, we don't want to set a bad impression for Micky,' snaps Aunt Liz.

She must be bitter from last night's fiasco, and it seems like she is eager for round two, which I am desperate to avoid!

The encounter with Trixy at university is enough conflict for one day.

'What rules and what impressions?' I ask softly to ensure the atmosphere does not become tense.

'Well we can't have you strolling home at all hours in the morning when you're out with your friends! Maybe certain nights of the week you should stay with them?'

I drop my fork onto the table while scoffing.

'Really, Liz, again!' shouts Uncle Aidan in an exasperated tone.

'Well, Micky needs rules and boundaries. We can't have these compromised, it's for his well-being.'

'What about me, will I have a curfew from work events as well?' he snaps.

I feel relieved from Uncle Aidan's desperate attempts to defend me. I look at Micky, his expression full of worry and confusion. 'It's okay, Uncle Aidan,' I whisper in a soft, polite tone to try and defuse the situation.

'Micky, would you like it if Tommy sometimes came round for a sleepover?' I ask with a warm smile.

'That's not your call to make Liyana! How dare you!' Aunt Liz shouts as she slams her cutlery down.

'Please!' I snap back! 'Just give me a minute!' I add in a desperate tone.

'Liyana, whys everyone shouting,' Micky whispers as his lip begins to quiver.

'No no, it's okay. We are just talking about a sleepover that's all. Maybe sometimes Tommy can have a sleepover here. And I might have a sleepover with my friends…what do you think?' Micky looks around the table, examining the negative expressions held by Aunt Liz and Uncle Aidan.

With the atmosphere tense, I force a smile to make him feel more comfortable.

'Sleepovers will be fun right,' I say to try and coax him into agreeing.

He leans his head forward and whispers gently, 'Yes let's have sleepovers, I like Tommy and can show him my room. But shall we have a sleepover at Nana and Pops first? They don't shout like this.'

'Now look what you've done!' Aunt Liz shouts as she slams her hands onto the table before storming out of the room.

Uncle Aidan stares down into his plate with a blank expression on his face.

'I'm sorry, Uncle Aidan,' I whisper in a pleading tone. 'I just want Micky to be comfortable with the idea of sleepovers so that I could agree to whatever rules Aunt Liz wants to impose on me. That was my only intention.'

I cannot help but look guilty for the unexpected U-turn my conversation has taken. I feel awful.

I look up at Uncle Aidan as my eyes begin to slowly fill, I can't seem to do anything right.

'It's okay, kiddo, I know you mean well, you always do! She's just set on a stupid fantasy. Leave her to me.'

Uncle Aidan nods at me with understanding eyes before leaving the table to head to Aunt Liz.

I scurry to clear the table before tucking Micky into bed.

'Why does Aunt Liz want you to have a sleepover Liyana?' Micky asks in a concerned tone as he looks towards me.

I kiss his forehead and explain that he is too young to have sleepovers, but when he is older, he will also be allowed. And that's why Aunt Liz wants me to have sleepovers because I am old enough to look after myself now.

'So you okay with me having sleepovers with my friends, Micky? Because if you don't want me to, I NEVER will,' I ask reassuringly.

'It's okay, Liyana, you can have sleepovers, just promise me you will not go for too long because I will miss you.'

'I promise,' I respond as I wiggle the tip of his nose.

Whilst Micky's fast asleep, I slowly walk downstairs, overhearing Aunt Liz and Uncle Aidan in a heated discussion. 'I just don't understand why she doesn't behave like a normal university student! She shouldn't be here!'

'This is just as much her home as it is Micky's, Liz! You need to stop trying to push her out of our family!'

'She doesn't belong in my family! If it weren't for her, Micky would be calling me Mommy, NOT AUNT! She's the reason Micky will never see me as his Mother!'

The floorboard creeks, both Uncle Aidan and Aunt Liz turn to look at me.

Tears are rolling down my face from the truth that I have always known, finally being spoken out loud.

'Liyana!' Uncle Aidan gasps in shock. 'It's okay…' I whisper as I clear my throat.

Her vicious words reveal the truth, which I have always known. But that doesn't mean it hurts any less to hear you are not wanted.

Her words have struck my exterior shell, which I can feel begin to crumble.

As they pace around the dining table, I walk across and take a seat.

I subtly clear my throat, as I notice my palms beginning to calm from the nerves.

'I'm sorry, Aunt Liz; I didn't mean to undermine you when I asked Micky about sleepovers. I just needed to get Micky to understand the concept before agreeing to any rules or conditions you want to impose upon me.'

'He doesn't need you as much as you think he does, Ann! He needs stability and routine. You cannot offer him these things! He needs a mother! And because of you, he will always be reminded that he is an orphan! You need to grow up and snap out of your selfish little world!'

Uncle Aidan scoffs and throws his hands in the air as he paces up and down. It's clear he is exasperated by this situation and not being able to rein in Aunt Liz.

I try hard to maintain my control when deep down all I want to do is cry. A thousand questions of doubt begin to flood through my mind; am I being selfish? Am I really unwanted in this home?

'What do you want me to do…or not do, from now on?' I ask in a defeated tone as I feel my lips begin to quiver.

'You don't have to be here seven days a week, Liyana. I don't think you should be here seven days a week!'

My heart sinks even more at the realisation that I am slowly being pushed out of Micky's life…the only family I have left. The pain in my breaking heart is visible across my expression; I can no longer control the tears dropping onto my cheeks.

My true emotions are seeping out of the cracks in my once strong demeanour.

Suddenly the lights above us begin to flicker.

Diesel whimpers out loud as he becomes restless from the tense atmosphere.

The faintest buzzing noise fills the silence as we all watch the flickering light above us.

Suddenly the vase on the sideboard flies across the room; it shatters into tiny pieces as it smashes onto the floor.

Aunt Liz screams in shock and Diesel whimpers in fear before running upstairs.

The flickering of the lights instantly stops, Uncle Aidan paces towards me to make sure I am okay.

'What did you do!' he shouts at Aunt Liz in an aggressive tone, which I have never heard from him.

'Enough is enough Liz! You have taken this too far!' He shouts with wide eyes and a stern posture.

'What, how dare you!' She replies with anger.

'I'm not the one throwing things across the room! What if that had hit me!' She snaps back with a fierce tone.

'What!' Uncle Aidan exasperates as he throws his hands up in the air.

The lights begin to flicker on and off once more which brings the room to silence.

'Please!' I whisper in desperation, to which the flickering stops. 'Please don't argue because of me.'

In the calm atmosphere, the sound of my beating heart becomes more apparent. I can feel my voice beginning to shake; I desperately try not to lose control of my emotions.

'I was planning to go out this Friday night.'

Both Aunt Liz and Uncle Aidan throw their glance towards me with a serious expression on their face.

'We have this fresher's party... Maybe we can start off with one night a week? I can stay out, and we can see where we go from there?' I offer in a desperate attempt to keep the peace.

'And I have made loads of friends who are already talking about me staying aro.'

'NO!' Uncle Aidan shouts in a disapproving tone. 'NOT UNDER MY ROOF!'

Uncle Aidan stares at me with big eyes. He has never taken this tone with me before. I almost begin to feel a little frightened. 'Liyana, you are a beautiful young woman, I'm not having you stay out all night just because you are desperate to keep the peace and please you're Aunt!

'Aidan if that's what sh –'

'ENOUGH!' He shouts filled with anger.

'If this is how you are treating my niece... I am thankful you are unable to bear a daughter of your own!'

The sight of Aunt Liz's palm striking Uncle Aidan's face widens my eyes, as I stare in disbelief!

'How dare you!' Aunt Liz shouts before bursting into tears and running out of the room.

Uncle Aidan exasperates from exhaustion as he scrapes back his hair with the tips of his fingers.

I stare at the ground, as I no longer know what to do with myself.

'Liyana, kiddo...get some sleep,' Uncle Aidan whispers with a soft loving tone.

'We will talk about this tomorrow; you have university in the morning, go and rest now.'

'I am so sorry, Uncle,' I manage to whisper before making my way to my room.

The lampshade offers a subtle light throughout my room. I lay in bed, suddenly unable to control my cry, as I rest my face on my pillow. I don't know what I'm doing wrong or what I can do to make things right. Maybe I should have stayed on campus to keep the peace, but my heart can't bear to be apart from Micky.

But surely, me leaving is better than me being here which seems to be creating a hostile atmosphere for everyone?

The sudden flickering of the lampshade steals my attention, distracting me from my self-pity.

I sit up on the bed as I look towards the lamp, which instantly stops flickering.

I rub the tears from my face in an attempt to reinstate my self-confidence whilst inhaling deep.

In that moment, the most beautiful scent catches my senses. For a split second, I forget about Aunt Liz and the ordeal that has been created. I am captivated by this scent, a scent that makes me feel weightless, at peace even.

I lay my head down as I inhale the mysterious fragrance surrounding me; it makes me feel safe, comforted; almost invincible.

Nevaeh, Sammy and I gather in the courtyard before walking into university. Thankfully my eyes are not puffy from my tears last night. The bell rings as we rush to our class.

We walk past DeJon, Bazzer and their friends who gather, in a huddle creating a racket from their roaring laughter.

As expected, Trixy and her friends are surrounding the young men partaking in the laughter.

As we walk past, the huddle slowly parts, I finally notice him. He smiles like an angel; it brings out the soft dimples across his cheeks.

His dark black hair hangs above his thick yet neat eyebrows. His golden skin sparkles in the light, which is in contrast with his snow-white outfit.

A sudden hint of a fragrance, the mysterious scent I've grown familiar with fills the air around me.

The huddle parts, he looks up towards me, for a single moment, our eyes meet in a locking gaze.

My heart skips a beat as I fall in awe of his big grey eyes. The flashes of pale grey within them almost appear as rays of light, surrounded by a dark halo. I feel like I am hypnotised as I struggle to break my gaze.

'Oh. I'm so sorry!' I offer to Sammy as she bumps into me.

I cannot help but feel awkward from the embarrassment of realising I must have frozen in my tracks.

I feel disorientated, my face begins to burns from a hot flush. We head towards our class, I cannot resist but to take a final glance back, only to see Trixy's hands rubbing this strangers arm while he offers her a smile.

I sit in class trying hard to concentrate. I cannot help but recall the eyes I felt lost within. His eyes seem so familiar, yet I have never seen him before.

I look around the class, but he is nowhere to be seen. Is he the late arriver from yesterday's lecture, I wonder?

I recall Trixy and her arms all over this mysterious man, her new playmate no doubt!

Trixy – so beautiful with her fabulous curvaceous figure always on display. No one will really notice me when they have the likes of Trixy parading around them. Besides, I'd much rather blend into the background, than dressing provocatively to gain attention.

I dismiss the trail my thoughts are leading me down and focus on the class.

We sit in the top seats of the outdoor sports stadium during lunch, making the most of the clear blue skies.

We watch the athletes practice for their upcoming trials taking place this afternoon and want to show DeJon and his friends our support.

With no surprise, Trixy and her friends are seated in the front row; I can hear their laughter despite the distance between us.

'Seriously…that girl has no class!' Nevaeh hisses as she glares towards Trixy.

'Each to their own I guess,' I add not wanting to be negative.

'I'm telling you, that girl is gonna create a lot of trouble if she keeps flaunting around the way she does, making out she's God's gift and all,' Nevaeh adds as she takes a bit of her lunch.

'What's her story,' I ask feeling intrigued.

'Usual,' adds Sammy.

'Only child, parents with lots of money. Indulging their only daughter with everything she wants. Trixy now expects to be given everything she wants.'

'Perhaps our assignment for tomorrow on childhood disorders could be on Trixy,' I add with a cheeky grin.

'There you go!' shouts Nevaeh as she bursts out laughing. ' 'New you had it in you girl,' she applauds.

I offer a sheepish smile and rein myself in from university cattiness.

'Yo, Nevaeh,' shouts a man from a distance.

We watch Tucker leaping across the seats to the top of the stadium with ease.

'So you didn't miss the trials then,' Nevaeh asks with a wicked smile.

'Hey, thought you women like your men being punctual,' he responds in jest.

They both share a chuckle while Tucker begins to add,

'Your boy Bazzer seems a little nervous about the trials this afternoon; maybe you could have a word? Big sis n'all.'

'Nervous, how so?' Nevaeh questions with concern.

'Nah jus' the usual. He's not talking much, is skipping lunch, between you and I, I think he's shittin' it!'

Nevaeh slaps Tucker's shoulder as he begins to chuckle. 'That's my baby boy you're talking about. He's got it in the bag! Why is he bottling up?' she questions with confusion.

A whistle blows in the distance to mark the start of a race. 'Nah it's good, thanks for telling me, Tucker. I'll make sure he's okay,' Nevaeh adds as she takes another bite of her lunch.

The shouting and cheering in the distance steals our attention. We look down at the field to find a group of athlete's midway through a race. Though almost at the finish line is the guy in white.

He runs like lightning, despite his broad build, leaving the others far behind.

As he passes the finish line, he looks back at the remaining participants following slowly behind.

He bends his head down towards his knees. Trixy runs over; she wraps him in her arms to offer a congratulatory hug. One that he doesn't seem to reciprocate, she is left hanging onto him.

The remaining athletes finally catch up. Trixy looking somewhat embarrassed finally let's go; she begins to "high five" the others.

Romeo can be seen throwing a tantrum in jest. He came second, but it's apparent he's used to coming first with his smaller frame and fast speed.

'Wow! He was Faasst!' Nevaeh gasps in complete surprise.

'Oh, who Shayth? Yeah, you should see his tackle!' Tucker responds with a proud tone.

Nevaeh, Sammy and I look at each other, we cannot help but burst into a fit of laughter.

'Oh, c'mon, I expect so much better from you three!' Tucker responds as he begins to feel somewhat embarrassed.

'I'm talking about soccer! He was at the trials yesterday, had us all thrown around like skittles!'

'Yeah I bet he did,' Nevaeh adds with a wicked smile.

'You're sick you are!' Tucker hastens to add as we all continue to laugh out loud.

'So, is he new here?' I ask in a casual tone, as I look disinterested while taking a bite of my apple.

'Yeah he came to the trials yesterday, he's new to this area so doesn't know anyone. But he'll definitely make the team. And as you can see...' He says as he looks over to the young man with Trixy loitering around.

'He's caught the eye of the man-eater!'

Nevaeh and Tucker begin to chuckle while my eyes search for him.

'Thank goodness for that,' Nevaeh adds.

'At least DeJon will get a well-deserved break from the psycho.' I watch Shayth sit on the bench with his elbows resting on his knees. He slowly pulls his hood forward; I am unable to see his face.

What an unusual name, Shayth, I wonder.

I watch him while he sits with his hood raised, hiding his features. It is as if he does not want to be seen or is perhaps avoiding attention.

Unlike Romeo who is a few feet ahead, showing off with his summersaults and back flips.

I cannot help but stare at this stranger; there is something so mysterious about him; something more to him, something that I need to know...

'…Knowing yourself is the beginning of all wisdom…'

—   Aristotle

10. Social Identity Theory

The week seems to be racing through; it's Thursday already, almost the weekend!

'I made it!' shouts Bazzer as he comes running across the courtyard, wrapping his arms around Nevaeh.

'I never doubted you would,' Nevaeh responds while kissing his cheek.

'Yeah I know, it still seems surreal at times ya know,' he responds with modesty.

'Congratulations, Bazzer, I'm really pleased for you,' I add with a polite smile.

We both fist bump as we all make casual chitchat.

A roar of laughter distracts my attention; I look across the path to see Tucker and DeJon trying to raise Shayth onto their shoulders, they seem to be failing miserably.

'So who else made it through?' I ask curiously as I notice Shayth wearing the same jacket as the rest of them.

'All who are worthy,' Bazzer responds as he raises his arms out to the world.

Nevaeh quickly hits his arms to lower his ego, forces us to break into a giggle.

We sit in class as we go through childhood traumas and various disorders that could be created by the subconscious mind, as a result of severe circumstances.

The lecturer asks for students to share their case studies and hypothesis with the class.

A fellow student discusses their case study, which captures an experiment carried out whereby an empty box is presented to children. The children are asked to imagine a monster inside the box. Despite the children knowing the box is empty, some were too afraid to go near the empty box.

This case study demonstrates the power of the mind and what it can restrict us from doing despite their being no rational logic.

I'm distracted from the class discussion as a student prepares their presentation of their case study. I watch Nevaeh scribbling notes in her book.

What you wearing to the party? Oh no, the party!

Not sure yet, haven't decided if I'll be going.

Don't worry; you're subconscious mind says you are coming, you just don't realise it yet! She writes.

I look at her and can't help but giggle.

'Attention, please,' states the lecturer in a stern voice.

My ears suddenly pick up on the discussion within the class.

The student presents his work, explaining,

'Her subconscious mind created a defence mechanism whereby she was able to hunt and feed herself and her brother without her conscious mind being aware of it! Unrecognised multiple personality disorder that can be the only explanation as to why she insisted that her parents were still around, providing food outside of the car where she and her brother were stranded.' My body freezes; my heartbeat beings to thump, drowning out all my other senses from its intensity.

My eyes widen, as I look up on the screen to see newspaper clippings on the projector.

My palms become sweaty; my throat dries making it difficult to breathe.

'That's an excellent case study, close to home. Does anyone else have any other views on this scenario?' The lecturer applauds before opening the discussion to the class.

My heart slowly breaks as I realise, I am the subject of a case study, the topic of a child trauma discussion!

'I do,' a voice volunteers in the background.

'Go ahead young man,' the lecturer encourages.

I am frozen, unable to turn to look at who it is that has an opinion about my life!

A past that I have tried so hard to conceal, something that I have wanted to grow stronger from, not be victimised over. 'Maybe there was someone who was helping her? Maybe it's not a case of her subconscious mind creating an alter ego, but perhaps there was another being that was taking care of her and her baby brother – because they could sense the fear in her?'

There was someone there, someone taking care of me, I cry in my mind in the hope that people will believe me.

I manage to find the strength to turn to look at the person with a strange accent who has an opinion on what I went through…it's Shayth!

He is sat at the very back of the class hidden by the shadows. His hood is raised across his head; he is staring down at the table, making it difficult to read his expression. All I can see is his jawline, his white teeth gleaming against his tanned skin. 'Perhaps there would have been some psychological trauma if she was stranded…but she was never alone.'

He slowly looks up, our eyes meet. I cannot help but feel consumed by my emotions as I feel a tear slowly roll down my cheek. Our eyes lock with each other. His deep grey eyes with white flashes of light mesmerise me; for a split second, I forget the pain of what is being presented.

Shayth offers me the faintest sympathetic smile, almost as if he feels my pain, feels my sorrow.

'That's very poetic but doesn't quite fit our theme,' the lecturer ridicules.

'With all due respect, sir, some of what is reality I'm sure we are unable to comprehend. Not everything fits or makes sense…' He states in a soft tone, while continuing to stare towards me.

An overwhelming sensation of shock and humiliation takes over my mind, making me struggle for breath. In a panic, I hastily grab my belongings before running out of the class.

The tears streaming down my face seem uncontrollable; I cannot bear for anyone to see me this way.

I feel sick, I feel weak. I know I am slowly losing control of my emotions.

When did I become a case study? My parents were with me; someone was taking care of me!

I rush through the empty corridor trying to find the closest exit out of the building. My dry throat and racing heart make it harder to breathe.

I'm surrounded by loneliness.

I am alone, the only person in the corridor, I stop and lean against the lockers; I cough to clear my throat and rub the tears from my face.

With my hands in my hair, I begin to take deep breaths, desperate to compose myself and recover from the shock. Suddenly, from nowhere, I hear him call my name.

'Liyana,' he calls, as he appears in my peripheral vision.

I turn to look in his direction; he slowly walks towards me, the faintest white glow surrounds him, I can feel myself losing my focus in his presence.

He comes closer towards me; as he reaches my side, he slowly lowers his hood. For the first time now, I see him clearly. The softest skin on the clearest complexion makes his tanned skin look as smooth as silk. His facial expression looks serious and intense, with his eyebrows slightly lowered from his frowning. My gaze reaches his eyes; my body begins to feel light as our eyes lock onto each other. I look deep into his eyes; I feel enchanted by the rays of light flashing within his beautiful, grey eyes. For a moment, I forget everything.

He towers over me, staring deep at me. He slowly reaches out his hand, which comes close to my face.

I'm lost in his gaze, mesmerised by his presence. The scent of strength and dominance that he carries with him has me hypnotised.

The tips of his fingers slowly brush away the remaining tears on my cheek. His frown deepens as he looks down towards my lips and gently rubs his hand across my neck, into my hair.

He parts his lips as if he has something to tell me. I focus intensely till we both become startled.

'Liyana!' I hear her shout.

Shayth swiftly moves back and walks down the corridor before lifting his hood across his head.

Nevaeh comes running towards me with a look of panic across her face.

'What's wrong? What's happened?' she questions in worry.

'Err, nothing. I just, I don't know, I suddenly felt a little sick, I just needed some fresh air,' I hastily add trying hard not to give anything away.

I look down the corridor. 'He's gone,' I whisper.

'Who's gone? Are you sure you're okay?'

I look back down the long corridor, how did Shayth disappear so quickly? Was he even here with me?

'What's wrong with your eyes? They look, teary.'

I offer a fake smile as an act of distraction.

'I think I need fresh air; my eyes feel really dry!'

Nevaeh suspects nothing as she puts her arm around me as we both head outside.

As we sit in the cafeteria, Sammy informs us of the various subjects including dark matter, which she will be covering in her physics course.

Nevaeh pushes more lunch down me, concerned about my health following this morning's episode.

'He's all yours now Ann,' a voice shouts in the background. I turn to see Trixy approaching me with her friends.

The look of confusion on my face makes it clear; I have no idea what she is talking about.

'DeJon – though he's out of your league! Still, you're welcome to him!'

'So has he agreed to take you out?' a friend of hers asks in excitement.

'Not yet he hasn't, but he will, they always do,' Trixy responds with sheer arrogance.

After looking me up and down with disgust, Trixy walks off with her friends and sits on a table closest to DeJon. Shayth is nowhere to be seen; yet I feel eager to see him once again, almost desperate to see him after our strange encounter in the corridor.

'Err…what's that about you and DeJon?' Nevaeh asks with confusion.

'Nothing, honestly! She saw me talking to him and has hated me ever since,' I respond with sincerity.

'Sounds like she's moved on to the new kid on the block!' Nevaeh states with disinterest in Trixy's affairs.

'So you're coming to the party tomorrow right,' Nevaeh asks with excitement.

'Do I have a choice?' I respond as I smile politely.

I head up to bed early wanting to avoid any confrontation with Aunt Liz.

I lay in bed, reflecting on the past few days. On the one hand, Aunt Liz has made it clear, she does not want me as part of her family. And on the other hand, I am being discussed as a case study for mental disorders in a class I chose to join! I scoff at the odds of these scandalous events happening in the space of a few days!

I recall my moment with Shayth, staring deep into his eyes. He seemed so familiar with me, yet we are strangers not having yet exchanged a conversation.

'Liyana,' I hear a voice whisper.

I look at the door to see shadows of feet on the other side. Micky slowly opens the door not knowing if I am asleep or awake.

As soon as he sees my open eyes, he quickly enters the room and closes the door behind him.

He jumps into bed tucking himself into the sheets, staring at me with his big, grey eyes.

For a moment, Shayth re-enters my mind, such similar rare eyes. No wonder why Shayth's eyes seemed so familiar.

Micky dozes off quickly, from an exhausting week at school no doubt.

I watch him fondly as I think the love we all have for him is what seems to be driving me and Aunt Liz apart.

'Hey, kiddo,' Uncle Aidan whispers as he opens the door slightly. 'Let me take him for you,' he adds as he notices Micky fast asleep by my side.

Uncle Aidan returns to my room; he sits at the end of my bed with a look of sorrow across his face.

I sit up as I realise we are perhaps well overdue a heart to heart.

'Liyana, your aunt, is a good person, she means well.'

Uncle Aidan takes both my hands into his as he shuffles a little closer towards me.

'She's just set on this idea of having her own child. And since IVF didn't work, she sees Micky as her only chance of having a child.'

'I know, Uncle; I just don't know how I can make things better. It's obvious Aunt Liz doesn't want me here, and I honestly do not want to cause any hostility…but I can't leave Micky.'

'No one is expecting you to, Liyana.'

My expression saddens as I try to stay strong and not let my emotions take over.

'Regardless of what anyone wants, you are my only niece and the closest family I have to a daughter. This is your home!'

He puts his hand on the back of my head and looks at me reassuringly.

'I have had a long chat with your aunt; she's finally seeing things from your perspective. Trust me kiddo. It will be okay now.'

He gives me a supportive smile, which I mimic in return.

His smile reminds me so much of my father, the last time I saw him from the back seat of the car as he smiled lovingly towards my mother.

'He would be so proud of you, you know. Just the way I am proud of you!' Uncle Aidan states as he looks towards me endearingly.

'Now what's this about a party tomorrow?' he asks curiously in jest.

The circumstances feel strange, this is the conversation I would typically be having with my father, yet it's heart-warming that Uncle Aidan is taking this upon himself to make sure I am okay and behaving. Perhaps he is trying to offer me a normal life? The thought itself makes me feel a little special that someone is offering me something.

A faint smile appears on my expression; I shake my head while looking down to my palms.

'Okay, I expect you home at some point tomorrow night. I know you will be – but just make sure you are sensible.'

'Thank you, Uncle,' I whisper as I embrace him in my arms.

As Uncle Aidan leaves the room, I sink my head into my palms, feeling overwhelmed with emotions.

I walk outside to the balcony in the hope that the calm night and starry skies will soothe my tensions.

My head feels like it's crammed with so many predicaments I have faced over the last few days.

I can't help but think back about my father's smile, how I was left alone, stranded in the forest.

Shayth's words begin to repeat in my mind, *she was never alone…*

I never felt alone; I knew someone was their taking care of me. Flashbacks of his eyes, his scent, and his mystical presence take over my mind.

The swift breeze flowing through my hair distracts me from my thoughts, bringing me back to reality.

He had disappeared from the corridor so fast; he could not have been there. Must I have imagined the whole encounter? Of course, I imagined it all! How can someone radiate a vibrant glow the way he did? He doesn't even know my name!

I shake my head in disappointment from my overactive imagination and turn to head back to my room.

A flash of white catches my eye on the balcony ground. As I focus my eyes on the object, I smile at the sight of my beautiful mysterious flower.

As I hold the flower in my hands, I am yet again surprised, by its impeccable condition, vibrant with life. The scent I am becoming more and more familiar with fills my senses as I inhale through my nose.

As I stand straight, I look around at the surrounding trees and shrubs on the ground, trying to determine from where this unique flower keeps appearing.

The lamp in the background begins to flicker. I turn to face my room; I notice a misty shadow in my peripheral vision. The moment I focus my eyes towards the shadow, the flickering stops, nothing is there.

The shadow must have been created from the flickering of the light, I convince myself as I head back to my room to stop the eerie feeling taking over my senses.

I take my beautiful flower to bed and absorb the unique fragrance as I fall to sleep.

We sit in our lecture while the theory of social identity is discussed, the concept of human group formation and both acceptance and discriminatory behaviours naturally developing to strengthen the social category of each distinct group.

The group formation can only begin or be related to once one has acknowledged their own personal identity, thus being able to form a view as to which social status and social categorisation they can relate to.

I raise my hand, as I struggle with the concept, which to me seems vague.

'Yes,' the lecturer acknowledges.

'What if there is no desire to conform to social identity thus not falling into any specific category other than one of self-content?'

'Interesting concept,' the lecturer responds as he slowly paces around the room before asking,

'Everyone who forms part of a group, sorority, club, please raise your hands.'

The majority of students raise their hands.

'Great. Now everyone who has been a member, at some point in their life, of a social club, group, etc. please raises your hands.' Even more students raise their hands.

Now, those who have never been part of any form of social group, club, gathering, please raise your hands.

I look around to see not a single hand raised. Despite feeling slightly intimidated, I raise my hand to be true to myself. 'Perhaps the two of you are of the few that are yet to find themselves,' the lecturer responds as he chuckles and continues with the class.

I frown slightly, taking mild offense at the suggestion that I am yet to find myself. Though I may not conform to any typical group, I feel content with who I am. I may be a little lost, but I am okay with it, for now at least.

The words of the lecturer repeat on my mind as I suddenly realise, "the two of you"; I search the class again to see who else dared to raise their hand, I was too slow.

We sit outside for lunch, Sammy relates to my viewpoint of not necessarily conforming to social groups but merely being content with where you are and not necessarily fitting in, or having to hold a label – but just to be free! Whereas Nevaeh has a close group of friends from outside of university, that form part of a Native American group.

'Hello, ladies,' DeJon states as he surprises us from behind.

I turn to see him stood beside us, and accompanied by Shayth! My heartbeat begins to rise; slowing being consumed by a fluttering in my stomach. I glance at Shayth, but he doesn't make eye contact. He is wearing his usual white outfit with his new sports club jacket.

I try to analyse where he is from as he laughs in jest with Romeo and DeJon who seem to be taking the mick out of Nevaeh.

The increased pace of my heartbeat leaves me feeling unsettled, so I think of nothing else but to excuse myself while I pop to the ladies.

As I walk a few feet away with my hand on my forehead, I accidentally bump into, Trixy.

'Watch it,' she shouts, creating a scene.

'Oh...err... I'm sorry,' I offer feeling a little disorientated.

'Why doesn't that surprise me, Anna!' She hisses as she stares over at my friends and looks back towards me.

'First DeJon and now Shayth! You really think you have a chance compared to me?' she challenges in a promiscuous tone. I ignore her comment and proceed to walk past when to my surprise; she grabs my bag forcing me to turn and face her.

'I wouldn't bother coming to the party tonight if I were you, that's if you know what is good for you!'

'Good for me?' I question with a shocked tone.

'Are you threatening me, Trixy?' I ask directly as I stare into her eyes.

My disorientation disappears and is quickly replaced by assertiveness, bordering anger.

Trixy begins to hesitate; she is unable to stutter her words out. 'Yes, I'll be there! And not only that, I look forward to seeing you there! At least that way I may find out what the hell it is you're talking about, given that you're struggling to get your words out!'

Trixy looks shocked and somewhat intimidated. She instantly takes a step back as her lip begins to quiver.

I don't think she has ever had anyone confront her the way I have.

'Let's take it down a notch ladies,' Bazzer states as he comes in between us with Shayth by his side.

I look over to see DeJon is holding Nevaeh back.

'There's nothing to take down, Bazzer, Trixy was just trying to be welcoming,' I reply as I try to defuse the situation.

'Oh, Shayth,' Trixy moans as she wraps her arms around him pressing her body up against his.

'She was awful! She started threatening me about this party tonight; I'm not sure if I should go...' She whimpers like some damsel in distress.

'Oh get over yourself,' I whisper as I roll my eyes with disinterest. I turn to walk away while Sammy links my arm, encouraging me to walk at a faster pace.

I leave the crowd knowing Trixy is being comforted in the arms of Shayth.

She was right; I have no chance compared to her!

'…Sometimes the heart sees what is invisible to the eye…'

–   H. Jackson Brown, Jr

11. The Party

I lower the music as I pull up outside Nevaeh's dorm.

Sammy will be meeting us there with her classmates she gets to know better.

As I wait for Nevaeh to arrive, I think of the various fraternities and sorority clubs that all students have joined, all students, but me.

Tonight is the first Friday of university, where the majority of the initiations or hazing's will commence.

If it's not enough that students need to pass vigorous athletic or mental assessments to qualify for their courses, tonight's the night where wild meets crazy for their acceptance into their chosen clubs.

'Oh, my Gosh,' Nevaeh gasps as she approaches.

'Are you freakin' kiddin' me!' she shouts as she giggles and hastens towards me.

'What is it?' I ask confused.

'You never told me you had a two-seater! Girl put the roof down,' she insists as she admires the interior of the car.

I join her in laughter as she increases the volume of the sound system as we drive away.

We arrive at the party; I manage to park up close as most if not all students plan on getting violently intoxicated. Nevaeh and I walk through to the hall; I notice various social groups gathered in their packs dancing and playing a range drinking games.

As we walk further down, with no surprise, we see Trixy and her friends with the Aphrodite sorority sisters. They all seem to be dressed in very short ivory tunic, fitting the theme of ancient goddesses. I watch as they are all laughing and dancing seductively, enticing the crowd of young males surrounding them, desperate to be chosen by the glamorous girls.

As we reach the bar, we order drinks and join a table with other fellow students of our psychology class. Sammy comes across, greeting us with warm hugs while introducing her friends from her course.

I take off my cream jacket, which reveals a thin, white strappy top. The loose curls in my dark hair cover my shoulders, hovering just above my elbows.

After a couple of drinks and many laughs, Nevaeh and I visit the ladies where we touch up our lipstick.

Surprisingly, I am still able to walk perfectly well in my black heals which brings out my black hair in contrast with my white top and dark blue jeans.

I look at my reflection in the mirror, my smokey eye shadow compliment my nude lip-gloss.

Nevaeh and I walk outside to the beer garden from having received multiple texts from Bazzer, insisting we make our way there.

As we reach the centre of the crowd, we see a handful of the members of our university athlete's team, lined up in a row, being forced to take their tops off as part of their initiation.

With no surprise, Romeo is the first to strip off his top and does so by providing his audience with a sultry dance.

DeJon and Tucker seem keen to get it over with, quickly taking off their tops with no hesitation.

Shayth, he looks confused, almost a little hesitant. Though he is smiling, he seems somewhat unwilling to partake in this childish process of initiation.

I cannot help but stare at him, smiling as he shakes his head, refusing to strip. His dimples seem amplified by the lighting; the look of innocence is all I can notice within him.

'Ladies, a little help PLEAASSSEE!' DeJon invites out aloud which encourages the Aphrodite sorority sisters to runs towards Shayth with excitement.

Shayth looks bewildered as Trixy and her friends who appear like vultures, eagerly tear off his fitted white shirt. It gets shredded to pieces in the process, and his body is finally revealed.

My eyes widen, as I stare at his broad shoulders and impressive traps. He's always been wearing a hooded top, which has disguised the muscular torso he has. As expected, all the athletes are muscular and trim, but there is something about Shayth that stands out from the rest. His golden skin perhaps or his hairless chest and torso with defined muscles throughout.

I focus in on the rustic locket hanging off a black thread around his neck. An unusual pendant or medallion of some kind hangs midway against his chest.

The arm wrestling begins with a single rule that the winner stays on.

As Tucker and DeJon struggle amongst each other, Shayth has no problems; he proceeds to win each arm wrestle with ease. I observe him as he doesn't even flinch, but appears as if he finds the whole process comical.

Tucker and DeJon are by far the stronger guys of the group; perhaps they will provide some worthy competition to Shayth. The crowd cheers while Trixy and her friends are providing entertainment in the form of tabletop dances above the arm wrestlers.

Trixy seems to be taking every opportunity to rub Shayth's body throughout her seductive dance, but to my surprise, he never once makes a single glance towards her.

Why wouldn't he? Surely this is every man's dream, what's wrong with him? Maybe he doesn't like women?

As Shayth arm-wrestles with Bazzer, again, he doesn't flinch in the slightest. It comes across as a breeze to him.

I am overwhelmed by curiosity of Shayth's behaviour.

The final arm wrestle is about to begin between DeJon and Shayth. DeJon holds the reputation of being unbeatable in strength and power.

DeJon works the crowd as he waves his arms and paces in a circle while flexing his biceps, encouraging all to cheer.

Trixy, who is now off the table, rubs against Shayth and raises his arm to encourage further cheers from the crowd.

I watch him as he subtly removes his arm from her grip, taking a step to the side to increase the distance between them.

He doesn't appear competitive or eager to win. It's as if he is having fun, amused by this whole concept.

I slowly walk closer, through the crowd to try and understand Shayth's behaviour.

DeJon takes a seat, and the arm wrestle begins. Again, it seems effortless for Shayth while DeJon is sweating and grunting for more strength.

This final arm wrestle will determine the strongest of the athlete's team and the focus or new target, rather of the Aphrodite sorority sisters.

Shayth smiles playfully at DeJon as he slowly teases him and lowers DeJons hand closer to the candle on the table. The last remaining flame will determine the winner.

DeJon struggles from Shayth's effortless strength, the heat of the flame gets the better of him as he shouts out aloud.

As I take a step closer, I pay close attention to them both; I suddenly find myself stood at the very front of the crowd.

Shayth instantly looks towards me, his eyes lock onto mine. His expression is full of surprise and shock.

'Yeeaahhh,' DeJon roars as he throws Shayth's hand onto the table, stubbing out the flame of the candle.

DeJon lifts his candle, demanding acknowledgment from all that his is the single remaining flame.

Trixy looks torn; she doesn't know who to throw her attention towards, the winner of the tournament that happens to be her old flame or the new arriver who is now second best.

Shayth and I continue to share our gaze. I look deep into his eyes as I try hard to figure out exactly what it is that I find so familiar about him.

My gaze is soon broken as I watch Trixy take his hand before seductively kissing and licking the surface where the candle had been stamped.

The look of disgust takes over my expression as I slowly turn to walk away.

From my peripheral vision, I notice Shayth stand to his feet and reclaim his hand from Trixy's lips.

I walk back into the crowd feeling a little disheartened. I shake my head at my own stupidity of giving Shayth all my discreet attention. Why am I torturing myself? Trixy is the kind of girl who always gets what she wants.

Suddenly my hand is pulled back into the limelight, I find myself in the arms of DeJon! He swings me round in a bear hug; I can't help but laugh. Nevaeh is by his side with Bazzer as they all dance and cheer.

'You not gonna give me a kiss to celebrate my victory,' DeJon asks as he releases me to the ground. The smell of alcohol fills my nose, almost making me want to gag. He has definitely had one too many drinks!

'How about we stick to fist bumps,' I respond with a cheeky smile.

I stick my fist out, DeJon cannot help but laugh out loud and returns the gesture.

I look over to see Shayth walking in DeJon's direction, to congratulate him no doubt, but Trixy and her girls begin to restrain him.

I disappear through the crowds, heading back to the bar to grab another drink.

I find a quiet table hidden behind the crowd of students swaying around the dance floor.

I sit, leaning the tip of my toe against the table edge while I take my hand and brush my hair back from my forehead.

My heartbeat flutters as I recall the locking gaze I shared with Shayth. A complete stranger that I haven't even exchanged words with. Yet, something about him compels me towards him. I cannot make sense of why I am feeling this way; the confusion makes me irritated with myself. A guy has never fascinated me, but there is something about him, something different that I haven't yet managed to figure out.

As I sip on my bottled water, my eyes widen, I am stunned to see Shayth parting through the crowd.

I notice his faded, ripped jeans and his usual hooded top. Only this time, it's sleeveless, displaying his full biceps. Having lost his shirt from the desperate vultures that are the Aphrodite's, his muscular torso and chest display his silky tanned skin.

Trixy dances in circles around Shayth, but his gaze is locked on me. I sit up in shock, my heartbeat now racing as he closes the distance between us. I can feel the hairs on the back of my neck standing from the nervousness in the pit of my stomach.

His eyes are firmly on me; I feel as if I am going to choke on my own heartbeat.

Trixy's grinding isn't enough to break our gaze; he moves her aside while still staring into my eyes, walking closer towards me.

All the time I am thinking, *I know you… I have sensed you*. He is no stranger!

Shayth reaches my table; Trixy grabs his hand, pulling him back towards the dance floor as she glares at me with disgust. I cannot help but break our gazing lock to look at Trixy and her desperate attempts to seduce Shayth to stay in her company. He refuses to look elsewhere other than at me.

As he comes closer, I cannot help but join him again in a deep, meaningful stare. It feels as if he is saying so much to me just from the intensity in his eyes, yet I cannot understand it what it is.

Trixy disappears into the crowds as Shayth takes a seat by my side.

I take my foot off the table; I cannot help but breath deep. Everything slows down, it's as if time itself stops.

In a gentle motion, he takes my hand in his. While staring deep into my eyes, he raises my hand closer to his lips.

His expression looks tense, focused, all on me.

The energy from his body radiates towards me, throwing a sensation of tingles throughout my whole body. I cannot help but take deeper breaths from his intense gaze.

His scent, I know is familiar. It surrounds me; it has surrounded me during many moments when I have felt lost and alone. It's a strong fragrance that can only be described as strength and courage, something that has surrounded me during my vulnerable moments, a mysterious scent filling my senses with euphoria.

He breaks our gaze and looks down to my hand. He closes his eyes, passionately placing his lips against the surface of my hand. I watch him inhale a deep breath before applying pressure to his lips as he firmly kisses my hand as if this had been a long-awaited moment.

He leans in closer, still gripping my palm.

My head begins to spin from the rush of excitement flowing through my body.

With Shayth's body so close to mine, he reaches his hand and strokes the back of my neck, locking his fingers into my hair.

All I can hear is the sound of my heart thumping louder than the music in the background. My deep breaths of air fail to fill my lungs as I sense my head feeling light.

He leans in closer; I eagerly stare into the pigments within his eyes... the flashes of white light embedded within his gleaming, grey eyes.

Time has frozen. I'm lost in his world. The twinkle of lights in his iris has me hypnotised.

He reaches in closer as he slowly parts his lips to whispers the words, 'I am here...'

He leans his forehead against mine, closing his eyes as he begins to frown.

'I have waited so long,' he whispers before he finally releases a gleaming smile that breaks the tension across his expression.

His soft dimples become prominent as he begins to bite his bottom lip from what seems like excitement or disbelief.

'I know you...' I whisper as I am mesmerised by his charisma, by his presence.

'There you are girl!' Nevaeh shouts as she stands in front of us. Shayth pulls back, releasing his hand from my neck. We both sit up straight from shock as we are reluctantly dragged back to reality.

'Aha! So what's goin' on here then?' Bazzer shouts in a playful tone.

'Oh... No. Nothing,' I respond before quickly releasing my hand from Shayth's. I stand to my feet and can feel myself become flustered.

'Excuse me just a minute,' Nevaeh requests of Shayth as she takes my hand and drags me across the room.

We walk into the ladies where I look into the mirror, putting my hands on my temples.

'Well. What's happening? You totally have the hot's for him,' Nevaeh states with excitement.

'Nevaeh...this is going to sound stupid, but I need to ask you something.'

'What?' Her tone changes to become as serious as mine. 'Who was I sat with?'

Nevaeh busts into laughter and I can't help but smile. 'No this is serious,' I plead, 'who was I sat with?'

'Why, you think you're in some daydream? Being chatted up by the hottest guy in university?'

'Which guy,' I ask while I try to keep a straight face to contain my excitement.

'Oh Shayth,' she teases. 'Come...take me!' We both can't help but laugh with joy.

'This is insane, Nevaeh... I can't explain it. I don't know him, but I do!'

At that moment, a cubical door swings open.

Out walks Trixy with a look that could kill. She glares at me with utter hatred, shaking her head as she approaches the sink to wash her hands.

Nevaeh bursts into laughter; taking this opportunity she begins talking out aloud.

'As the saying goes, you win some you lose some. Hash-tag – money can't buy class!'

Trixy looks into the mirror and throws daggers at Nevaeh through the reflection.

'We will see!' she mutters as she walks out of the ladies.

'Nevaeh,' I whisper in disapproval.

She laughs it off before she proceeds with, 'Bitch had it comin'! It's about time someone knocked her off her pedestal.'

Sooo, what's goin' on with you and Shayth? Tell me everything,' she asks in excitement.

'Nothing, Nevaeh. I don't know…we just sat there.'

'What? Well, what did you guys talk about?'

'That's the thing…nothing…we just sat there.'

She looks at me confused; it begins to make me feel confused. 'I know… and it's going to sound crazy, but I swear I know him!'

'Or more like you wanna "get to know" him,' Nevaeh adds as she clicks her tongue followed with a devilish smile and menacing laugh.

'Stop it,' I insist as I begin to blush, before giving into my ecstatic emotions and joining her with a giggle.

We walk over to the bar; I find myself casually searching for him. I see Shayth is sat right where I left him but is accompanied by DeJon, Bazzer, Tucker, Romeo and a few others.

They all seem to be playing some drinking game with shot glasses laid across the table.

Shayth, however, holds a bottle of water in his hand.

Like me, he seems to be the only other sober person in this party.

As we wait for our drinks, I cannot help but smile. For the first time in forever, I feel alive! I feel a sparkle in my own eyes; a sense of fulfilment consumes me.

Shayth and I exchange gazes in and amongst the individuals distracting us in conversations.

I see him smile and laugh amongst his friends, while discreetly watching me in between; I cannot help but do the same.

I feel like a love-struck teenager as we steal secret gazes of each other.

'No I think that's Liyana over there,' I hear a voice in the background.

I turn to see a girl point a guy in my direction.

'Hey, are you the one with the White Z4 parked outside?' he questions with a look of excitement on his face.

'Yes…why?' I ask anxiously.

'There's some crazy chick who is scratching the shit out of your car. I mean she's going proper psycho!' he explains with amusement.

'What?' I whisper in confusion while trying to understand who would do such a thing.

I instantly rush outside with Sammy and Nevaeh following behind.

'Nooo…' I plea as I reach my car.

A small huddle has formed around my vehicle as the students laugh and take pictures.

All the tires have been slashed, and the word "Whore" is etched in throughout the car.

How am I going to take this home and explain this to Uncle Aidan?

The party is well and truly over for me now!

'…We do not meet people by accident. They cross our paths for a reason…'

— Unknown

12. Deja Vu

'Nah, you gotta be kiddin' me! Is that your ride?' DeJon asks in shock.

'Err, it was...' I answer feeling somewhat coy.

The crowd laughs as they watch me besides my car, the words "Whore" scratched all over the exterior.

I feel humiliated; I can't believe Trixy would stoop so low! 'Can't be riding it now,' I mutter as I kick the slashed tyre.

'Don't worry, Liyana, I'll get the car sorted for you,' DeJon offers as he pats me on the shoulder to reassure me everything will be okay.

Shayth and Bazzer appear at the front of the crowd.

Though Bazzer looks slightly amused by the scene, Shayth holds a look of shock before sympathy appears across his expression.

Nevaeh becomes extremely vocal, with profanities and threats directed at Trixy and her friends, who are nowhere to be seen.

'Liyana,' Shayth calls out as he approaches.

'It is okay...allow me...to take you home, wait, just one moment,' he whispers with an eager expression.

Shayth runs off in the distance, at an unusually fast pace.

The guys in the crowd, who have apparently had one too many beverages, share their theatrical version of how a bunch of girls in Greek tunics began to vandalise the car, as they danced around before smashing their bottles across the exterior.

DeJon and Tucker do their best to comfort me while Bazzer alongside Romeo focus their attention on calming Nevaeh down.

I feel so conscious that I am ruining the party for them all. The shock, the total humiliation makes me feel vulnerable, as I watch the students laughing, pointing towards me.

I think I am ready to leave the party; I need to get back to my haven. The feeling of being surrounded by hideous laughter towards my misfortune makes me begin to feel claustrophobic. Nevaeh tries hard to persuade me to stay on, but she eventually gives in, she can see I'm feeling uncomfortable.

'Okay, I'll come with you to drop you off,' she insists once she finally calms her anger.

'No, it's okay, really. You carry on with the party. I'll message you as soon as I am home.'

'Na-ah, girl you think I'm letting you go home by yourself you must be trippin',' Nevaeh shouts as she grabs her bag off the floor.

'Bazzer, please; tell her I'll be fine,' I plead in the hope that he can persuade her.

'Damn right you'll be fine girl,' he responds as he raises his head, staring past us all.

I turn around to see Shayth slowly pull up in a white 2-seated sports car...one that I have never seen before.

As he pulls up beside my car, his lavish unique vehicle makes my car look like an old toy.

The whole crowd begins to silence in awe.

The curves on the car complimented by fine strips of light on the exterior make the vehicle look like a work of art!

He lifts the car door open as he slowly walks out, towards me. 'Nah... I must be trippin'!' DeJon shouts as he runs towards the car, analysing its features.

Romeo runs towards Shayth, breaking his pace towards me. 'Dude, you gotta let me borrow this, the ladies will be drippin'!' He shouts in excitement, before moving on to join DeJon at the car.

The noise increases as everyone begins to rave about the car as they take selfies.

'Seriously, Shayth, where did u get this?' Bazzer asks in disbelief.

'Err...it is a prototype. My Uncle trades in manufacturing,' he replies in an apprehensive tone.

A few women dancing around the car decide to circle Shayth, desperate to entice him to join them.

I notice a woman grab his hand, pulling him towards her as she grinds around him, dancing to the music that can be heard from indoors.

I'm distracted by a prep from the crowd who squeezes in between Nevaeh and me.

'Yep, I know exactly what this is,' he states as he places his arms around our shoulders.

'My cousin has the same car, a new model manufactured by the Japanese.'

Nevaeh and I pay little attention to him as we watch the crowd go crazy over Shayth's vehicle.

'I will be getting the keys to my cousin's car next week if you ladies are interested in going for a ride?' the prep offers, desperate to gain our attention.

I watch Shayth reclaim his hand from the provocative dancers before proceeding to walk towards me.

As he reaches me, he gives me a reassuring smile.

'Excuse me,' he states to the prep as he takes my hand, pulling me away from under the stranger's arm.

I turn my glance back to Nevaeh as I begin to reassure her, 'it's okay; I'll drop you a message as soon as I am home.'

Nevaeh gives me a gleaming smile while holding onto the prep in excitement. She quickly pushes him out of her way as soon as she realises her actions.

I walk slowly, following Shayth's lead as he holds my hand gently with a coy smile across his face.

As we walk past the dancing women, I pay little attention to them as they stop in motion, glaring towards me in a loathing manner.

He lifts the door to the passenger side, like a true gentleman, helping me to my seat.

Shayth closes the door and attempts to walk around to the driver's side before being ambushed by Nevaeh.

'That's my girl, and I want her home with a smile on her face!' She warns while waving her finger around.

'Anything happens to her; you will have to put up with me! And trust me, hell has seen no fury!'

'I can vouch for that! She's one crazy…' Bazzer pauses for a moment, as he looks Nevaeh in the eye before bursting into laughter.

'Yes, ma'am, you have my word,' Shayth responds with a shy expression.

I can't help but smile at her loving concern towards me. Such a beautiful friend I have found in Nevaeh.

I see Sammy in the distance taking photos of me in the car, capturing every moment. She gives me a thumbs up; I return the gesture with a nervous smile.

DeJon and Bazzer make jest with Shayth as he is stood outside the driver's side door.

'I shall see you tomorrow,' Shayth confirms to DeJon and Bazzer, seeming eager to get away.

Shayth sits in the driver's side, pulling down the door. The outside noise is drowned out by silence from within the car. I sit nervously as I watch my fingertips lightly tremor on my thighs. While maintaining control of my breathing, I build the courage to look across to him.

Shayth turns to look at me.

'Hi,' he whispers, as he stares into my eyes, his lips widens as he offers me his naturally beaming smile.

I cannot help but mimic his reaction as I feel my smile naturally coming along. I bite my bottom lip in excitement before whispering, 'Hi.'

He takes the wheel in his hand while looking ahead; his lips are pursed together, almost appearing a little smug.

I cannot help but notice how plump his lips are as I watch him trying hard to conceal his smile.

The engine comes to life, the roar of the car makes the seats vibrate, catching me off guard. I instinctively jolt forward from the shock.

He looks back at me with a smile. Tilting his head towards me, he slowly whispers, 'You have nothing to fear, I am here with you now.'

The crowd seems astonished by the power of the ignition. Shayth puts his arm around the back of my seat, as he reverses to reposition the vehicle.

I'm staring at him the whole time; struggle to take my eyes off him, comforted by the thought that his focus is on the road, he will not notice me admiring him.

His muscular arms are on display as he clutches at the gear stick beside me. His presence makes me feel safe, protected even though there is little I know of him.

As Shayth applies pressure on the accelerator, within seconds the crowd and the party are out of sight. The speed of the car is incredible.

Shayth slows the car to average speed as he looks back and forth at me while trying to focus on the road simultaneously. 'I am called Shayth,' he states while looking towards me.

His accent seems foreign, from a land I do not recognise. I've never heard anyone speak this way.

He sits with one hand on the wheel, the other on the gear stick. The white interior of the car emphasises the glowing tan across his body.

His expression seems to have changed; he comes across as somewhat apprehensive. He stares into the road yet it seems his mind is distracted, maybe he is nervous? But what reason would someone like him have to be nervous about?

'Hi, Shayth, I'm called Liyana,' I respond with a natural smile. Instantly his smile reaches across the sides of his cheeks. In excitement he begins to look back and forth at me again.

He softly chuckles with joy as he shakes his head gently whilst whispering in disbelief, 'I cannot believe this moment has arrived.'

This moment has arrived? I question myself in confusion; what is it that he is referring to? But I soon find myself distracted.

I cannot help but admire the beautiful soft features of his face. An overwhelming expression surfaces across his face as he softly whispers, 'I am here. I am finally here…'

'With me,' I whisper in a soft, gentle voice.

He shouts from excitement 'Hah!' As if he is victorious from some unknown challenge. Shayth begins to laugh out loud in disbelief; shaking his head as if to awake from a daydream.

He looks back at me with a wicked smile as he lowers all the windows before putting his foot on the accelerator. 'Woooooow,' he shouts out to the world as if he is invincible.

My eyes widen from the rush of the speed from his unexpected acceleration. Watching the excitement across his expression, I cannot help but join him, softly giggling from the thrill.

Shayth slows back down to a law-abiding speed before looking across towards me.

I'm sat with my elbow leaning against the window while my fingers are locked in my hair.

My other hand closest to him is placed above my knee.

My heart begins to flutter; the nerves intensify the reality of this moment.

I take in a deep breath, desperate to calm my beating heart when suddenly I realise; I am surrounded by the sweet fragrance I have grown familiar with, the scent of my mysterious flower.

The mystical scent overwhelms me as I close my eyes.

'I know this scent,' I whisper as I close my eyes, tilting my head against the headrest.

The sweet scent makes me feel weightless, surrounded by the feeling of serenity.

I feel the motion of the car slowing down.

My body tenses as I feel Shayth's hand on my thigh. His fingertips brush the surface of my hand before he takes my palm into his.

I open my eyes, I find him staring into me, offering me a warm smile.

Steering with one hand he slowly whispers, 'I have been waiting for this moment.'

He looks at me intensely, which only adds to the erratic rhythm of my heartbeat that I had only just managed to steady. 'There is much I have to tell you, but first…there is something I would like to gift to you,' he whispers in an eager tone.

The nervousness in the pit of my stomach forces my head to spin, as I wait anxiously for what he has to offer.

I feel as if I am losing all control of my senses; I raise my eyebrows as I stare down at my palms, watching them softly tremble in his gentle grip.

'It is okay,' he whispers with a reassuring smile.

'I am no threat to you. You are safe; you are no longer alone.' He slows the car down before pulling over on a quiet road. There is not a house in sight, merely the starry sky above the forest trees.

As the car comes to a still Shayth turns to look at me.

My eyes are locked on his; I watch him observe every feature on my face, every angle of my body.

'If I had, but one wish, I would wish for you to see yourself, in the way that I am able to see you,' he whispers with sincerity in his voice.

'I know you?' I whisper with a questioning tone.

There is something so familiar about him, but I can't explain why.

He leans towards me, taking my hand towards his chest.

I look into his eyes; I cannot help but take in a deep breath as I watch the sparkle of light within his misty grey eyes. I am lost in this moment as we both gaze into each other, moving in closer and closer.

Shayth abruptly flinches. His unexpected motion forces me to gasp in surprise.

He glares into the rear-view mirror, something forces him to become agitated.

As he focuses his gaze on the mirror, his reaction changes to panic!

The engine comes alive as Shayth presses his foot against the accelerator. Both his hands grip the steering wheel as he begins to drive at full speed.

I am stunned by his unexpected reaction, hastily looking towards the back window.

I can see nothing but darkness as we speed through the night. As I stare at my surrounding, it suddenly hits me; I have no idea where I am!

What have I done? I question within myself trying to make sense of his erratic behaviour.

'What's happened?' I shout as the roar of the engine deafens me.

'You MUST remain silent! Do not move!' he demands as he focuses on the road while looking back in the mirrors.

We drive into the thickness of night while swerving through the bends of the road.

The car begins to shudder; I can't tell if it's caused by the speed we are driving, the surface of the road or something pushing against us.

I'm too afraid to look back at the rear window from his demand that I do not move.

I hear the strangest snarling from beside the car, but there is nothing there, simply darkness and trees.

'What's happening? What's wrong?' I scream as the panic finally consumes me. Shayth begins to take sharp bends almost as if he is trying to lose something behind us.

'Be Silent!' He yells as his frown becomes more intense. I watch him struggle to control the vehicle before he begins hitting the steering wheel in frustration.

'You must remain within this vehicle. I need your word!' he shouts above the roaring engine and screeching tyres.

'What?' I shout in confusion.

'Stay in the car!' he yells in a domineering tone.

Suddenly he pulls up the hand-break, forcing the car to spin out of control!

Almost as if in slow motion, I watch Shayth lift the car door, leaping into the darkness as he leaves the vehicle, as he leaves me on my own.

The car spins as I watch him run in lightning speed before leaping into the air, disappearing within the thickness of night. The car continues to spin; I hear the growling of an unnatural kind. I see glimpses of thick smoky shadows in the distance as the vehicle slows.

The car comes to a grinding halt, with me inside clutching hold of the seat.

I am in the middle of nowhere, surrounded by darkness and trees.

The fierce rustling in the trees sounds like I am caught in a hurricane!

Tears begin to stream down my eyes from fright; I cannot keep my hands from shaking!

I lock my eyes on the open driver's side door, petrified of what might come in.

How could he leave me like this, where has he gone!

The snarling in the distance comes closer which I can now clearly hear above the rustling of the trees.

The wind can howl, I convince myself as I try hard to remain in control.

A sudden jolt of the car makes me scream out loud.

I instantly take my seatbelt off, I know what I need to do, I need to run!

I grab my bag and manage to lift the heavy door up. I scream out aloud from the shock of the door slamming shut! Something outside is keeping me in!

The noise in the background becomes quieter as I crawl over to the driver's side, heading for the door that is already open.

In shock, I release another scream as from nowhere Shayth appears at the door.

He is panting as if he has run a mile. His white sleeveless jacket is covered with black stains as if he has been wrestling in a coal mine!

I quickly sit back in my seat as I wipe away my tears, desperately trying to control my breathing and erratic heart rate.

He slams the door shut and drives off as fast as he can.

Shayth makes no eye contact with me nor acknowledges my presence. We drive in silence, his eyes flickering between the road ahead and the rear-view mirror.

My whole body is trembling; I cannot understand why we are breaking all speed limits and driving so recklessly.

'What just happened?' I manage to conjure in a quivering tone. Shayth doesn't answer, nor does he glance towards me. He focuses on the roads with a blank expression on his face. 'Shayth!' I shout, demanding his attention.

'We must get you home. We must get you safe!' he states with a dominant tone. A frown remains on his expression; his whole persona has changed. He seems cold, distracted, maybe even volatile.

I'm left feeling confused, not knowing what to do or say. We drive in silence while I try to console myself.

I stare at him; I watch his hands clenched at the steering wheel. Parts of his body appear bruised, not to mention filthy.

I'm struggling to understand why he would have jumped out of a moving vehicle the way he did?

I cannot comprehend what just happened. The sickness in my stomach begins to ease slowly, alongside the rhythm of my pounding heartbeat as we approach streetlights and houses.

As we pull up outside my house, he finally decides to speak.

'You must get inside,' he demands as he opens his door and walks out of the car.

I take my seatbelt off and turn to find him open the passenger side door.

As I step out of the car, I try hard to control my emotions.

I notice the exterior of the car seems filthy and somewhat damaged, not in its pristine condition when I first entered.

I refuse to make eye contact with him as I step out of the car. I rush past him to get home, to get to safety!

I notice from my peripheral vision, Shayth raising both his hands against his head, as he holds on tight to his hair.

I hear the car doors slam and the engine roar.

As soon as I walk through the front door, closing it firmly, I hear the acceleration of his car as he drives off in speed.

My heart sinks as I press my forehead against the door.

I squeeze my eyes tight, trying to force out the disappointment and fear from what has come of this night. I get out of the shower and lie on my bed, desperately trying to comprehend the dramas from my evening. My phone is bleeping on the bedside table. I find endless messages from Sammy and Nevaeh. I text the group to let them know I am home safe, encouraging them to have fun at the party.

Nevaeh: *Back so soon??*

Nevaeh: *Good!!*

Nevaeh – *Didn't have you down as a dirty stop out* ☺

Liyana – *Me... Far from it* ☺

Sammy – *Will send across the pics, I have taken some amazing shots.*

Liyana – *Thanks Sammy, so thoughtful!*

Nevaeh – *I want all the gory details Miss!*

I sit in silence as I struggle to think of how to respond to this...

Liyana – *you mean all the boring details.*

I try to play it down to get the attention off the situation.

Nevaeh – *Don't even think of holding out on me!!* Nevaeh – *I know he's 'Your' type!*

Nevaeh – *Told you he'd be at the party!*

Sammy - ☺

Liyana – *Lol. Look forward to seeing you both on Monday!* I respond before putting my phone on silent.

I lie in bed, staring up at the ceiling. I feel afraid, I feel vulnerable, I cannot help but curl into a ball, desperate to find some comfort. I barely notice the tears rolling down my face onto my pillow.

In a rush of anger, I feel the frustration with myself, always feeling as if I am crying!

But my tears tonight come from fear within the pit of my stomach of not knowing what the hell just happened.

I'm such a fool! I begin to kick myself for getting into his car! He is a total stranger that I haven't yet had a conversation with! He has women flaunting all around him! Why on earth would I think he would be a gentleman! He is rude, obnoxious, absolutely reckless! I cannot risk falling for someone like him!

'…Your sixth sense is your natural inner Genius…'

— Sonia Choquette

13. Extra Sensory

I open my eyes and find myself terrified in the car; I hear Micky cry in the background. I am the frightened little girl from all those years ago, not knowing what is happening around me.

The sudden uneven surface of the road begins to make me nervous. I look out the window; I find nothing but darkness surrounding us.

I blink my eyes, feeling the tears roll down my cheeks, as I sit still in Shayth's car.

The sudden uneven surface of the road begins to make me nervous. I look out the window; I find nothing but darkness surrounding us.

I'm a frightened young woman not knowing what is happening around me.

The snarling in the background grows closer. My eyes widen. I cannot tell if I am the young girl or the young woman. Evil is upon us; it's happening all over again.

'Hey girl,' Nevaeh calls in a loving tone before wrapping her arms around me.

'It feels like forever since I've last seen you!' she states as she looks at me with fondness.

'I've missed you too!' I respond with a warm smile.

'So Trixy totally denies having anything to do with your car! I know she's lying,' Nevaeh blurts with frustration.

'What? How do you know?' I ask in complete surprise 'I've had a word already; she's such a mouthy bitch!'

'Nevaeh honestly, you really don't have to worry. Please don't stress yourself over this. Besides the cars absolutely fine now, DeJon has done a great job!' I add reassuringly.

'Oh he has…he didn't mention anything earlier,' Nevaeh responds with a puzzled expression.

'He's probably just being modest,' I reassure.

'DeJon – Modest – Please!'

We both begin to laugh as we walk into our lecture.

I notice Shayth sat in the usual place Nevaeh and I are usually seated. Nevaeh nudges my elbow, clicking her tongue with a wicked smile. I smile sheepishly knowing that she is none the wiser of what really happened on Friday night.

I offer her a coy smile not wanting to go into any details, desperately trying hard to play it cool.

How do I avoid sitting next to him!

I pretend to accidentally drop my book, forcing Nevaeh to walk in front of me.

I quickly collect my book, taking a seat next to Nevaeh who is sat beside Shayth.

They exchange pleasantries, before she quizzes him about Friday night.

'Liyana is such a lady, she's not giving anything away – so you can fill me in on what happened Friday night after you left the party.'

He offers her a nervous laugh as he avoids the question. 'C'mon, not you as well! Something must have happened,' she insists in a brash tone.

I cannot help but try to take control of the uncomfortable situation, desperate to avoid any embarrassment on either side.

'Honestly, Nevaeh, nothing happened. Shayth was really kind in offering me a lift home. He dropped me off, and that's it!' Nevaeh looks at me as if the penny has dropped.

'Oh, so you mean, nothing's going on?'

'No. Absolutely Nothing!'

I force a smile to try and make the situation less awkward. The three of us sit uncomfortably, waiting for the class to commence.

'I wonder why we have a dog in the lecture?' I question to break the uncomfortable silence.

'Oh. What, are things that bad? Are you referring to Shayth?' Nevaeh questions in a surprised tone.

My eyes widen, I feel mortified at the suggestion.

'No, Nevaeh! I would never! I mean there is a real dog next to our lecturer!' I gasp from shock as my finger points to the front of the hall.

'Oh sorry, my bad,' she responds feeling embarrassed.

I want the ground to swallow me! The suggestion that I would refer to Shayth as a dog makes me sink into my chair. Yet somehow, for some strange reason, I sense that Shayth is smiling, finding my reaction amusing.

I sit and concentrate on the lecturer as she explains the psychological concept of sensation and perception.

Sensations being the bottom-up process by which our senses like vision, smell, hearing, all receive information and relay outside stimuli.

Perception, on the other hand, is the top-down, direction our brains, organise and interpret the information we have received from our sensation, putting this data into context.

How do we digest the external world – through our senses, into our internal world – our perception.

The lecturer discusses how we allow our perception to be influenced by our past experiences and expectations.

Thresholds are discussed as the lecturer explains the absolute threshold – being the minimum stimulation needed to detect a particular stimulus 50% of the time.

The lecturer pulls out a whistle to provide us with a demonstration.

She explains that as she blows the whistle, the sound will not reach our stimulus. However, the dog will hear it, forcing it to howl. Thus proving the theory that there are sounds in this world that do exist, us humans simply do not have the sensory ability or the mental perception and capability to be able to comprehend all that surrounds us.

As she blows the whistle, the dog starts howling. Nevaeh flinches in her seat from the dog's sudden howl.

I turn to see Shayth holding onto his ears as if some high pitch tone is deafening him.

I cannot understand why Shayth would react in this way. Surely there is no possibility of Shayth hearing the sound of this whistle; it's only meant to be heard by animals that possess extrasensory skills.

The lecturer continues to explain that there are particles that are floating through the air, right in this moment which are colliding against our skin, yet we are unable to feel this, as it does not reach our absolute threshold.

I'm distracted from the nudging of Nevaeh's elbow as she offers me a note.

She places a folded paper on my desk; I know this can only be from Shayth.

I put the note in my book, forcing myself to focus back onto the lecturer as she explains the notion of subliminal threshold.

Though the subject of subliminal messages I find fascinating, I cannot help but think of Shayth and what his note may say.

I have been strong all weekend, I have convinced myself not to give him the benefit of any doubt, but there is something in me calling out for him.

Whether it is my intuition or natural perception, something tells me there is more between Shayth and I.

I get another nudge from Nevaeh as she surprisingly passes across another note.

I internally battle with myself whether to read what it is he has to say, or if I can build the strength to appear uninterested!

I recall how he drove like a maniac, losing control of the car, all while refusing to speak to me!

With my mind made up, I quickly scribble the number "2" on the second note before placing it beneath my book. I force a look of uninterested towards Shayths antics while I try hard to focus on the lecturer.

As Nevaeh sits back, I can sense Shayth leaning forward, looking in my direction. The thought makes me nervous.

I pick up my pen and begin to twiddle it between my fingers to distract myself from Shayth's staring.

My heartbeat picks up a little as I twiddle my fingers faster. Oh sugar! The pen flies out of my hand and hits the back of the neck of the young man sitting in front of me!

Instantly, I cover my mouth with shock while feeling mortified! I can hear Nevaeh discreetly giggling beside me, from my peripheral vision; I see the motion of Shayth's shoulders as if he is also chuckling.

Nevaeh nudges me to give me a final note.

As I slowly take the note from her hand, I glance around in search of a pen; I raise my eyebrows in surprise. I notice the number 3 has already been written on the note.

I frown from the embarrassment that Shayth has read me like a book, knowing precisely what I am writing in his notes!

As the lecture ends, Nevaeh makes small talk with Shayth.

I make the most of their conversation and disappear from the class as fast as I can, desperate to avoid any awkward discussions with him.

As I turn the corner of the corridor, of all people, I bump into, Trixy.

'Watch it,' she shouts without realising it's me.

As soon as her eyes catch me, she begins to look me up and down.

'So, you and Shayth…are you together,' a long blonde-haired girl asks.

'No, not at all,' I respond, as I feel uncomfortable at what all the students may be thinking.

'Hah,' Trixy shouts with delight.

'I knew he'd see sense eventually! Oh and Ann, I told you you'd regret coming to the party!' she states as she struts off with her friends.

'Is she giving you a hard time again,' I hear DeJon shout as he walks down the corridor towards my direction.

'Nah, just living up to the reputation of university bitch,' I state as I walk towards him.

'We've all got our role to play,' I add as I stand by his side. He chuckles as he raises his hand for a fist bump.

We walk along the corridor to the courtyard as I thank him profusely for fixing my car and dropping it off at my house. 'What…' He asks with a confused expression across his face.

'The car, I'm really grateful, thank you,' I add as I begin to mimic his confused expression.

'Well that's why I was looking for you, to talk about fixing your car; I didn't realise it was already fixed. And as much as I would love to take the credit, it wasn't me Liyana.'

'Wait… What?' I question in disbelief.

'Yeah. I'm not sure who it would have been, but it wasn't me… But hey, looks like you have enough of us looking out for you,' he states as he puts his fist on my shoulder to try and lighten the mood.

'DeJon can I ask you something.'

'Sure you can.'

'Shayth, where is he from?'

'Hah, I'm sure you know him better than me, after Friday,' he replies with a cheesy grin on his face!

'Oh no, really. It's really not like that; he just gave me a ride that's all,' I insist, hoping it will stop everyone from jumping to conclusion.

'Oh yeah, that old story is it,' he responds as he chuckles.

I cannot help but begin to blush. As I smile nervously, I notice Shayth in the background, watching DeJon and I. Trixy talks away to Shayth, but his expression seems sad, maybe even a little lost?

'Honestly, DeJon, we are just mates. Besides, Trixy has her eyes set on him,' I state as I casually point towards them. DeJon turns to look back at the two of them, a few yards away from us.

'Oh hell she doesn't. I ain't letting her get her claws into one of mine!' he shouts as he puts his hand on my back, applying pressure which forces me to walk alongside him.

'Where are we going?' I ask nervously as I see us approaching Shayth.

'Yo, Shayth,' DeJon shouts, forcing Trixy to look our way.

I am stood nervously beside DeJon wishing someone would just save me; remove me from this uncomfortable situation.

I'm unable to look at Shayth; I wouldn't know what to say or how to react.

I stare down at the ground as I rub my forehead wishing Nevaeh or Sammy would take me away from here!

'Oh, DeJon, we were just saying how cosy you and Ann looked as you were talking over there. You both make such a cute couple,' Trixy states with her catty attitude.

I wonder if this is the reason why Shayth looked saddened?

'Hah! Funny that Trix! That's exactly what I was saying to Liyana about her and Shayth on Friday night! You do remember, Friday night, don't you?'

The smile instantly disappears from Trixy's face as she glares at DeJon before focusing on me.

'So what do you say, Shayth,' she turns and begins to rub his bare arms.

'Tonight at my place?'

'Yeah, Shayth, Liyana wants a word,' DeJon interrupts as he pushes his hand against my back, forcing me closer to Shayth. DeJon doesn't realise his strength as he almost pushes me to fall onto Shayth, I find myself stumbling.

'You! We need a word!' DeJon shouts at Trixy, before grabbing her by the arm, dragging her to the side of the corridor.

Shayth and I are left there. The voice of DeJon warning Trix to back off from his friends is drowned out by the sound of my heartbeat.

I can feel myself become nervous in his presence, which only adds to my frustration! Why should I feel nervous around someone who is extremely attractive yet extremely rude and barbaric! Not to mention disrespectful and reckless!

'Liyana… I.'

'Please. Don't! It's okay! You don't have to explain! I get it. You gave me a ride home. That's it!'

I blurt out with confidence while looking around the corridor, seeming uninterested.

His body language looks stunned, as he takes a step back. I dare not look at his facial expression, in fear of being hypnotised by the chemistry I feel between us.

'Enjoy the rest of your day, Shayth,' I state with a polite smile as I stare down to the ground.

I didn't want there to be any animosity, yet I need to make it clear that I do not want to be caught up in any of his games.

I slowly turn and walk away, my heart sinks… He doesn't even try to come after me.

I sit with Sammy for lunch; she informs me of the remaining drama I had missed out on from Friday night, having left early. 'So what was the weather like Friday night,' I ask casually.

'The weather,' Sammy repeats with a giggle.

'Liyana, I didn't have you down as one to struggle for conversation where you have to resort to the weather.' She laughs out loud.

I join her in a giggle before explaining.

'I think there was some freak hurricane or tornado at my end of the town but wasn't sure if that affected anyone else.'

'No it was a lovely Friday night – well as far as the weather goes,' Sammy responds.

I had convinced myself over the weekend, the car spinning and snarling in the background was a result of us having encountered a tornado perhaps; how foolish am I!

Sammy begins to worry about the assignment she has received today on the subject of dark matter.

'What's dark matter?' I ask not meaning to sound ignorant.

Sammy begins to explain dark matter is an invisible force that potentially complies with the laws of gravity but does not comply with the laws of electromagnetic radiation.

Sammy begins to giggle at my look of confusion.

'Light. Dark matter doesn't reflect light. It doesn't absorb light. It has rules of its own,' she explains in layman's terms.

Sammy continues to explain that only 5% of the universe is believed to be made up of baryonic matter, which is everything we can physically see, trees, animals, planets, stars, galaxies, etc.

The remaining 95% is made up of dark energy and dark matter – that which we cannot see because it doesn't omit or reflect light.

'But how do we know this dark matter is really there if we can't see it?' I ask feeling intrigued by this whole concept.

'It's like wind, you can't see it, but you can see its effects on other things, you know it's there without having to see it.'

'Yeah or you can smell its effects!' Bazzer adds from behind us with Nevaeh. The sound of Bazzer passing wind fails to impress us!

'I'm telling you! That's been brewed from a dark place!' he laughs out loud.

'Nice!' Nevaeh responds with disinterest to Bazzer's immaturity.

Shayth walks across the courtyard with Romeo and DeJon.

I watch him, as he looks somewhat saddened. He occasionally smiles and laughs as the guys look towards him, but overall he seems down. Even in his walk, a much slower pace, almost as if he is dragging his feet. Not the usual confident strides he takes. 'You like him, don't you?' Sammy whispers to me as she watches me staring at him.

'Oh no, it's nothing like that. We are just friends,' I quickly respond. I look over at Bazzer and Nevaeh who are sharing a deep conversation; thankfully they didn't hear Sammy's question.

'Okaaay,' Sammy responds slowly. 'But that's not what I asked. I get that you two are friends, but you like him don't you?' she repeats in a soft understanding tone.

Sammy is the smartest of us all. Though she's very quiet, there is very little that gets past her.

I offer a sad smile, which answers her question without me having to share a word.

'Hey, do you know where he's from? His skin, his eyes and his accent, I can't put my finger on it, even the way he dresses.'

'I thought exactly the same!' Sammy responds as we both watch him with curiosity.

I spend most of the evening working on assignments and spending time with Micky. Aunt Liz and I are not on comfortable speaking terms, which forces me to spend more time in my bedroom than downstairs. Once Micky has fallen asleep, I prepare my books for tomorrow's lectures.

As I gather my books I notice, one of the notes from Shayth drop out from my bag.

I freeze for a moment as the nerves in my system begin to tingle through my body. The feeling of anxiety mixed with excitement has me hunting through my bag, looking for the remaining notes.

As I line the three notes on my bed, I cup my face in the palms of my hand.

He's not a nice person! He's rude and irresponsible! I know nothing about him!

I tell myself all the reasons as to why I should not feel excited by the thought of Shayth. I just wish my heart would listen to my head.

The butterflies in my stomach can't bear the suspense any longer; I take the first note in my hand…

Forgive me for Friday.
Do not be saddened.
I humbly beg for you to allow me to explain.

Saddened! How would he know I was sad? My heart feels lighter from having read the first note. I am confused as to why he would think I was unhappy? I didn't leave the house the whole weekend because I was so sad! But no one knows that but me!

I slowly open the second note and read.

You sense I am different, for I am not the same as… others.
Allow me to give you all I have, all I am.

My heartbeat begins to dance, sending vibrations throughout my body.

I cannot help but laugh with joy. My smile reaches from ear to ear as I feel a hot flush running through my body.

I bite my bottom lip in an attempt to control my exaggerated smile while holding the note close to my chest.

He is different. He wants to offer me all he has. I cannot help but widen my eyes as I giggle in joy.

Suddenly the light from my lampshade begins to flicker. I sit up straight, instantly the flickering seems to stop.

I need to mention to Uncle Aidan to have the electrical wires looked at; the lights flickering seems to be a regular annoying occurrence.

I reach out for the final note, the one that Shayth had written "3".

As I open the folded paper, it reads…

I know you better than you realise.
I shall continue to wait, till you are merciful. Please, do not be afraid, I am always with you!

'…It's better to walk alone,
than with a crowd going in the wrong direction…'

— Diane Grane

14. Social Experiment

'Sooo, what's going on with you two?' Nevaeh asks with a curious smile.

'Honestly, Nevaeh, we are just friends,' I insist as I feel myself begin to blush.

We look over at Shayth as he bounces the basketball on the courtyard while both Romeo and Tucker try to tackle him. He dodges the ball with ease all while glancing in our direction.

Shayth is not wearing his usual white outfit, but seems to be dressed more in line with other students, ripped jeans, a white top and the team sports jacket.

'So what was in the love letters then?' Nevaeh insists with an inquisitive tone.

'Love letters,' Sammy repeats as she lifts her head out of a physics book. Catching me off guard, I cannot help but stutter.

'Look he's walking over,' Nevaeh informs with excitement as she nudges my shoulder.

I begin to panic as I desperately try to figure out what I should do.

'It's early days yet,' I insist to Nevaeh as I consider leaving the area.

I quickly stand on my feet and grab my bag.

'But like I said, right now, we are just friends,' I add with a confident smile as I walk off in Shayth's direction.

My heartbeat flutters, but I cannot bear the thought of Shayth coming over to speak to me, while I'm in the company of Nevaeh and Sammy; who knows what they would come out with!

He looks straight at me as we both walk casually towards each other.

I clutch the strap of my bag as tight as I can, feel nothing but nervous.

Shayth offers me a gleaming smile, occasionally looking down to the ground as he approaches closer. It almost seems as if he too is nervous!

'Shayth,' a voice shouts from a distance.

Distracting us both from our gaze, we look in the direction of the interrupting voice.

I see Trixy across the courtyard, calling his name, beckoning him to come over.

I begin to frown as I watch her flirtatious body language; I shake my head as she pursing her lips, trying hard to look attractive!

As I stare back at Shayth, my heart melts as he merely raises his hand as a jester of a wave and dismisses her advances.

We stand close to each other; I can smell his masculine scent.

I have so much I want to ask him, but I lose all the words from my mind when I am with him.

How do you know where I live; was it you that had fixed my car; why does your scent seem so familiar; where do I know you from; where are you from, what do you mean you are always with me…all questions I need to ask, yet my voice is weakened by the dryness of my throat.

'Liyana… Hi,' he states as he looks into my eyes and comes across somewhat sheepish.

'Hey,' I offer as I join him in his gaze and begin to feel somewhat lost.

Instantly I look away in an attempt to try and remain focused. 'May we talk, there is much I need to explain,' he whispers while looking shy.

'Yeah, maybe that will help me to understand your obnoxious behaviour from Friday night!' I respond as I raise my head up high, standing my ground. My tone of voice is polite yet assertive.

I'm horrified at myself for being so cold and confrontational! All I want to do is put my arms around him and melt into his eyes, but my defensive personality takes over in an attempt to protect my fragile heart.

He brushes his hand through his hair from nervousness as he looks to the ground. Though a look of disappointment runs through his face, it's soon replaced with a bashful smile. 'Forgive me,' he requests as he raises his head and looks into my eyes.

As I look up at him, my eyes meet his gaze, and as hard as I fight to look away, it's too late. Our gaze is locked together. 'Please, I can explain all' he insists as he takes a step closer towards me, placing his hand on my forearm.

I cannot help but take in a deep breath; I feel my knees go weak. I close my eyes as I take in the scent of his mysterious fragrance that is now surrounding me.

As my eyes open, I find him even closer to me. I look up, examining the intense expression on his faces. His dominating presence leaves me feeling weak; I feel vulnerable as I allow him a moment to stare intensely towards me.

'Sure. Yeah, okay,' I begin to stutter, unable to force the break from his hypnotic gaze.

I pay no attention to the sound of wheels screeching on the ground, till a skater speeds into Shayth!

He surprisingly ricochets off Shayth and falls into me!

In the blink of an eye, Shayth swoops his arms around me, saving me from falling while the skater crashes to the ground. I hold onto his shoulders as he grips firmly against my waist.

He offers me a gleaming smile full of excitement as he holds me in his arms, inches away from the ground.

'Ah! Dude what the hell did you do!' the young student shouts as he stumbles to find his feet.

Shayth pulls me closer towards him, almost taking advantage of the situation.

My arms are wrapped around his neck, he pulls my body up against his, as we both stand straight.

'I have you,' he whispers while looking into my eyes and pursing his lips.

'My arm,' the skater shouts as he manages to stand to his feet. As reality hits us, I re-examine our surroundings, we both stand and part our bodies.

'What you made of dude, you've broken my arm,' the skater shouts in exaggeration.

'Forgive me my friend, but how could you not see us standing here?' Shayth questions in a confused tone. He seems genuinely puzzled as to how this collision happened.

'Are you both in on this? I want double the money now!' the young man insists with an aggressive tone as he walks off holding his arm.

I look up in the direction that the skater walks towards and spot Trixy stood with her friends holding a look of disappointment across her expression.

'You okay, Liyana,' Nevaeh asks as she approaches.

I offer her a reassuring smile as I begin to increase the distance between Shayth and me.

Tucker and DeJon come towards us from another direction, laughing at the skater as they point and chuckle.

'You're made of steel bro,' laughs Tucker as he playfully punches Shayth's arm.

'We should head to class,' Sammy suggests, as she looks at her watch, conscious of time.

'Alright teacher's pet,' DeJon adds in jest as we all walk towards our next class.

I catch glimpses of Shayth as we all walk together. His laughter and smile makes me melt. I've never felt so uplifted with joy as we all laugh together in jest.

The boys ridicule Shayth for his accent and use of language, which they have been giving him tips on.

'You sound less like a Martian; I'm impressed!' DeJon teases as they all burst into laughter.

We all make plans for the upcoming circus and fairground temporarily in town. With Friday being half a day for us all, it's the perfect day to go. Nevaeh, Shayth and I walk down to our lecture.

As I walk between the two, Nevaeh reads my mind and begins to ask Shayth a list of questions.

It's strange; Shayth somehow manages to deviate from answering the questions as he deflects the conversation onto Nevaeh.

As we slowly walk towards class, Shayth's hand brushes onto mine.

A sudden rush flows through my body as I begin to hesitate. Overthinking gets the better of me, as I convince myself that "I" had accidentally rubbed my hand against his, I quickly decide to place my hand on the strap of my bag. At least this way it will avoid me making the same accident.

'But seriously, where are you from?' Nevaeh asks as it seems she has finally realised that Shayth has not yet answered a single question.

We are all handed a leaflet from a student in the corridor, and yet again, the distraction deflects the question posed to Shayth. I release my hand clutching my bag to collect the distributed leaflet of the upcoming fairground.

As I place it in my bag, Nevaeh expresses her excitement about fairground rides.

I suddenly feel the warmth on my hand as I realise Shayth is slowly locking his fingers tips around mine.

For a second, I feel my body freeze from the shock of his affectionate gesture.

'What's wrong with you? You don't like rides?' Nevaeh asks as she turns to look at my stunned expression.

'Oh. No, I do. I just, they make me a little nervous sometimes,' I manage to stutter out amongst my pounding heart.

We walk towards our lecture as Shayth and I tangle our fingertips softly around each other's but are not entirely holding hands.

Each stroke of his fingertips sends a shock throughout my body; I realise I am walking with a smile that reaches from ear to ear.

With my free hand, I tuck my hair behind my ear and subtly look across to Shayth. I notice he is mimicking my expression and seems as genuinely happy – if not more pleased than I am!

As we walk into the lecture hall, a fellow student calls my name for a brief chat. Nevaeh and Shayth continue to walk up the stairs to take their seats as I briefly chat to Nicola about our younger siblings who happen to be in the same class.

As I turn to head up the stairs to towards Shayth and Nevaeh, I notice they are seated and in deep conversation.

A pair of females eagerly sits beside Shayth leaving no room for me.

I head up the stairs and sit a row above, directly behind Nevaeh and Shayth. I watch the pair of females as they excitedly whisper amongst themselves while staring back at Shayth.

Shayth is oblivious to what is happening, as he seems to be focusing on the conversation with Nevaeh.

I sit and smile as I watch him, examining his body language and the little I can make out of his facial expression.

Staring at the side of his face makes his dimples more prominent. His dark, messy hairstyle almost forms a pointed tip at the back of his head.

As the lecture begins, I notice Shayth put the palm of his hand close to the young woman sat beside him, perhaps he doesn't realise I am sat behind him rather than at his side.

As the lecturer presents the course content, I watch Shayth slowly reach his hand across towards the young woman beside him. As he stares directly ahead to the lecturer, his fingertips caress the palm of her hand.

I cannot see his facial expression to understand what reaction he has, but undoubtedly he is unaware that she is not me!

He slowly crawls his fingers across the young woman's hand before holding her palm in his.

I watch the young woman as she nudges her friend sat beside her and points at her hand being held by Shayth.

The friend's jaw drops as I watch the lucky lady begin to blush with a look of excitement!

The two females begin to lip read as Shayth sits staring at the lecturer.

I cannot help but clear my throat to gain their attention.

As the lucky young woman turns back with a beaming smile, her blonde hair sways in the movement, which must have caught Shayth's sight.

He turns to the side and looks at the young woman. The look of shock horror on his facial expression is priceless. I cannot control but to bite my lips to avoid laughing out loud.

She smiles away at Shayth who, for a moment, looks like he has frozen. He turns back to look at me, I watch the discomfort grow across his expression. I offer a sarcastic smile, deliberately holding an expression of annoyance.

As he glances away, I hold in the laughter from the situation he has got himself into.

He offers a quiet nervous laugh as he looks at the young woman who seems to now be clenching his hand.

Shayth looks back at me not knowing what to do. I make the most of the situation as I try hard to keep a straight face and come across as a little irritated, raising my eyebrows at him with a look of disapproval.

I watch the tension grow on his face as he looks up at me with soft puppy eyes.

He slowly moves his hand back onto his knee but to his surprise, the young woman still holds on tight as her fingers are interlocked around his, all while staring at the lecturer with a huge smile across her face.

His body becomes tense as I can sense the unease. He slowly lifts his hand from his thigh, which is entwined with hers, placing their hands on her desk.

With his free hand, he peels her fingertips one at a time, to release his hand from her grip.

As his hand becomes free, the young woman's smile begins to diminish, as she understands his not so subtle message.

Shayth offers her a sympathetic smile as her jaw drops from shock and confusion.

He slowly turns and focuses on the lecturer while she begins to make a scene from her muffled insults before she finally decides to hit her books across Shayth's shoulder. She stands to her feet and storms off, with her friend quickly following.

I watch him sink his head down from humiliation, as the lecturer asks for silence at the back.

I daydream while the lecturer explains the psychological-sociological phenomenon or disorder of imaginary friends and various theories as to what triggers this condition, with potential links to schizophrenia.

After hours of presentations, the lecture finally concludes, we gather our belongings to leave for the day.

Shayth seems somewhat coy as I approach him and Nevaeh outside the lecture hall. We walk along the corridor; it doesn't surprise me that he makes no attempt to hold my hand. As we head towards the exit, we pass Trixy and her friends, who do not fail to notice Shayth.

She offers him a gleaming smile, pouting her lips at him as they make eye contact. He merely raises his hand to her as he walks off with Nevaeh and me by his side.

We hold an in-depth conversation around the psychological state of schizophrenia and toy with the idea that perhaps the individual suffering from this condition are not really suffering, but are the only ones that can see the world for what it is. Maybe the rest of the world is blind to its true reality.

But does the belief of the majority equal the minority being incorrect or somewhat crazy?

'Which pill would you take,' Nevaeh asks, as she appears intrigued by what our answers will be.

'Blue pill or red pill?' she states, encouraging me to give her an answer while I over contemplate the question.

I glance towards Shayth who appears even more eager to hear my answer than Nevaeh.

He stares at me intensely as the look of desperation fills his eyes.

'Red Pill, all the way,' I respond with certainty.

'Damn right girl,' Nevaeh affirms as she offers me a high five. A look of relief seems to spread across Shayth's expression. 'How about you Shayth?' Nevaeh questions.

'The blue pill doesn't exist in my world,' he responds sounding cryptic.

We agree to go for drinks and a bite to eat to continue the conversation on psychological and sociological disorders. Nevaeh insists on looking for DeJon and the others to extend the invite to them.

'I'll meet you guys outside,' I state to Nevaeh and Shayth as I head to the ladies.

My heart is running cartwheels at the thought of spending the evening with Shayth! I cannot believe this is happening, perhaps this evening we will get the chance to talk? Maybe I can understand exactly what happened last Friday and how he managed to fix my car and figure out my address!

I close the cubical door and hear a bunch of women giggling as they walk in.

I know that laugh… it's Trixy and her friends. 'So what's the plan?' a friend of hers asks.

'Well he wants to keep it quiet, he's a VERY private person,' Trixy responds as they all burst into laughter.

Intrigued, I put my ear closer to the door to understand whom they are talking about, surely not DeJon! I thought he had moved on?

'He is so amazing, came round to my house at around 8, took me out in his car. We spent most the night in his car if you know what I mean.'

'I bet you did, how could he possibly resist,' a friend responds as they all oooh and aaah over what Trixy has to say.

'He is soo hot! His body, his lips, his eyes! It's not fair!' another girl responds.

'So why is it so discreet, what's the big secret,' a friend of hers asks in curiosity.

'Something about a social experiment he's focusing his psychology assignment on. I dunno, don't really care! Discreet is cool with me.

I just can't believe that Anna really thinks she has a chance compared to me!'

Trixy laughs with confidence.

'So why is Shayth stringing her along?'

'Something to do with his hypothesis for his assignment, little does she know, she's just the guinea pig!'

They all begin to laugh sympathetically.

'And to think, she really believes she has a chance against me! Dumb bitch lives in a fantasy world!'

They all release a cackling laughter as they leave the restroom throwing statements of pity about me.

I open the doors and walk towards the sink where I rest both my hands as I look up in the mirror.

My eyes shine from the layer of tears they are surrounded in. Be Strong – I tell myself as I feel my heart sinking while shattering into tiny pieces.

She's right. Compared to her, I am nothing.

I never have myself on display the way she carries herself, so how can I expect any hot-blooded man to choose me over Trixy! I scoff at my stupidity as I shake my head in disappointment!

I am just a social experiment! That makes sense as to why he has put his attention on me over Trixy!

I comb my fingers through my hair as I take in a few deep breaths. I search for the strength and courage within my mind, as I fight an internal battle to ensure this does not bring me down.

I am better than this, I am stronger than this, and I don't need Shayth!

'…Life is either a daring adventure or nothing…'

– Helen Keller

15. Fair Grounds

'How you feeling today?' Nevaeh asks with concern.

'Yes, totally better now, thanks. It must have been a 24-hour thing,' I reply convincingly.

'How was dinner?'

'Yeah it was great; Shayth was the butt of all jokes with his evolving accent. But the boys are teaching him how to blend in better!'

I battle with the curiosity in my mind; desperate to hear more of Shayth, of any information he may have shared about his personal life. As hard as it is, I know I need to push him out of my mind.

'It was hilarious! Romeo has taken him up as his apprentice, in teaching him how to get lucky with the ladies!'

I offer a fake smile when all the time I am thinking he knows exactly how to manipulate us women!

'So you're still up for the fairground tonight? I've agreed we'll meet Sammy after lunch.'

'Sure,' I respond as I force a smile.

We reach our seminar; I try hard to hide my expression as I see Shayth, sat at the back of our class, looking eager with a smile on his face.

I glance at him before turning away. This is a social experiment, which will not go his way, I tell myself!

As I follow Nevaeh to take our seats beside him, he looks at me as his smile slowly disappears.

I want to hate him, I want to be mad at him, yet I still can't help but feel curious in wanting to know everything about him.

I raise my glance towards him, the frown naturally appears across my face.

The look of mild exasperation appears on his expression as he takes both hands to his head, tilting his head back while clenching his hair.

'What's happened to you?' Nevaeh asks in jest.

He leans forward, sprawling his arms and chest across the desk with his head resting face down.

'Hey, Shayth, what's up?' Nevaeh asks curiously.

'I cannot keep up,' he begins to mutter as he lifts his head and shakes it side to side.

'What? We've only just started the course. You think this is hard, wait till we get to cognitive neuroscience.'

I stare at him as he genuinely comes across as perplexed. For some reason, I get the feeling he is not referring to the course but may be referring, to me?

'Nevaeh,' he calls.

'Humans are so indecisive – why is this?' he asks in a pleading tone as if he is seeking guidance.

'That's what we are here for. Think, in three years we will have mastered the human mind,' Nevaeh replies in jest.

My heartbeat rises slightly. Is he really referring to me? I question?

'Perhaps if things aren't going your way, you should consider an alternative social experiment!' I snap while staring straight ahead.

I smirk from feeling smug at my witty comment, which subtly lets him know I know, without actually telling him I know!

I glance over to see a look of confused horror across both their faces...oops; suddenly I don't feel so smug as I feel my smirk quickly disappear.

With Nevaeh sitting between us, she looks across to Shayth as he raises his hands above his shoulders as if to gesture he doesn't have a clue.

I simply focus ahead, paying attention to the lecturer.

'Lovers tiff?' Nevaeh whispers to him as she frowns in confusion trying to figure out what exactly I am talking about.

'Settle down now, please,' the lecturer insists as the seminar begins.

The content today covers personality and intelligence.

The lecturer continues to explain the objectives, which are to acquaint students with several leading theories designed to characterise and describe variations in, what people are like – their personality, what people can do – their intelligence.

Nevaeh quietly giggles as Shayth dramatically lifts himself off the table in excitement, as he looks back and forth at the lecturer. Seeming excited, as if his predicaments will be resolved.

The lecturer continues to explain,

Personality and intelligence have often been viewed as distinct domains, which intersect only to a limited degree. Recent research, however, suggests the possibility that both conceptually and empirically, intelligence may be integrated with broader models of personality. This integration may permit a more unified conception of the structure and source of individual differences.

As the presentation continues, Shayth raises his hand while looking somewhat confused.

'Yes, young man,' the lecturer greets welcoming the participation.

Shayth clears his throat before he asks,

'If various studies have taken place on intelligence and personality, surely these studies have all failed – as men are still none the wiser on the mentality of women. So what use is the understanding of intelligence and personality if we cannot save ourselves?'

The class roars into laughter, and the lecturer himself cannot restrain from offering a chuckle.

'Ah, the conundrum of mankind,' the lecturer responds in jest. 'If nothing else, this information may take you a step closer in understanding the opposite sex and why individuals behave in a certain way – But this course will not answer the unsolved mysteries of mankind!'

I cannot help but feel a little embarrassed by Shayth's question. I try to focus on the course yet cannot help but frown.

'Liyana, Liyana,' Shayth shouts out as he tries to catch up with me in the corridor.

'I'm gonna give you two a minute,' Nevaeh insists as she walks towards the courtyard leaving Shayth and me alone in a corridor full of students.

'What fault have I made?' he asks looking worried.

'I don't know what "fault" you have made. Why don't you tell me what "fault" you have made?' I respond trying to seem unbothered by him as we walk at a slow pace.

'But I do not think I have made such faults to justify your hostility,' he quickly responds.

'Hostility! Then why are you asking me for your faults if you have none!'

'Your aura has changed, I can sense the emotions of anger and jealousy within you.'

I stop our slow-paced walk and stand firm as I face him. 'Jealousy? Seriously! What reason do I have to be JEALOUS exactly?'

'I… I know not,' he stutters.

'It is what I sense, but I…no…not…why,' he looks sincere, my heart slightly melts. I look away instantly from his beautiful grey eyes to ensure I do not lose my strong demeanour.

'I have NO reason to be jealous. I just don't have time for stupid games!'

I turn to walk away as I can feel an internal battle within me begging to hear him out.

'Oh, and I hope you enjoyed yourself Monday night!' I add before turning again and marching off!

'What is going on?' Nevaeh questions as I join her and Sammy for lunch.

We sit on the top benches of the sports stadium while the boys practice for their upcoming contests.

'Oh it's nothing, I just wanna maintain being friends and nothing more,' I respond trying to come across as uninterested. Nevaeh scoffs.

'Friends? You were giving him daggers earlier! If looks could kill,' she replies while giggling.

'Why the change of heart, Liyana?' Sammy questions with genuine concern.

'I'm pretty sure Shayth and Trixy have something going on, I don't want to be stuck in the middle. Besides, I'm not really interested,' I say trying to convince myself.

'Nah, don't believe anything from Trixy. She's so manipulative; you have no idea the shit she put our DeJon through,' Nevaeh shares as she glares at Trixy who is at the base of the stadium, watching the players in practice.

We watch the practice trials in and amongst the boys fooling around in jest.

Shayth's body language seems like he is moping, somewhat lost.

We talk about the fairground as Sammy confesses here fear of rides.

'Liyana,' DeJon shouts as we see him jumping over the seats heading towards us.

'Hey, DeJon,' I greet politely as he reaches us.

'Liyana, you gotta give my boy a break,' he insists as he catches his breath.

'He's not focusing and we need him in top form if we want to stand a chance at winning.'

I look at him as I raise my eyebrows.

'Totally selfish I know, but please, you'll be helping us all,' he pleads.

'I don't understand, a break from what?' I question with genuine confusion.

He scoffs as he smiles and shakes his head. 'A break from his bleeding heart.'

The three of them burst into laughter.

I nervously smile with them but can feel myself begin to blush.

I push aside my feelings before responding, 'Hah. So he has one then!'

'Ouch! Girl c'mon. Take one for the team and give the guy a break. He doesn't even know what he's done!

'Anyway, I've told him to man up and fight for what he wants! Just go easy on him, he's fragile.'

'Heads up,' we hear a voice shout out in the distance.

As we all turn to look at the sports ground, we watch Shayth stretch his feet back as the ball approaches him. With a powerful thrust, he kicks the soccer ball with such force, he slightly stumbles once his foot reaches the ground.

The speed of the ball in the air flies so high, to a point where it is no longer visible from the stadium.

Everyone is left in awe.

'Fragile...' I whisper from the shock of his strength.

'Hah! That's my man!' DeJon cheers as he begins to leap over the benches heading down towards his team.

I watch Trixy run over to Shayth as she wraps her arms around him to congratulate him.

'Look, look, see! He is not reciprocating her gesture at all!' Nevaeh points out as Shayth subtly removes her arms from around him as he tries to walk away.

Trixy insists on following him, prolonging whatever conversation they are having.

DeJon reaches them, and from Trixy's body language it appears as if she isn't best pleased with whatever statement he has made to her.

Maybe Nevaeh has a point, I wonder.

Everyone bursts into laughter at Romeo's selection. 'Seriously, is that all there is to you!' Nevaeh comments at his juvenile response.

'Look, it's totally natural in the animal kingdom, if that's the way chimps roll – then call me a chimp. What a better way to greet someone,' he tries to persuade.

'Nah, for me it's a panther. Hiding in the shadows not being sensed. Then pouncing on my prey unexpectedly, like "Don't F**k with me bitch".'

We all burst into laughter.

'Yeah, that's definitely your style Nevaeh,' Bazzer adds with a smile.

'Reminds me of when you pounced on me back in the day, I didn't know what hit me, all I thought was, this girl is crazy, I better do as she says.'

We all laugh as Nevaeh tries to knock the drink out of Bazzer's hand for his cheeky comment.

'For me, without a doubt, I'd be a bear!' DeJon shares with a smug look.

'You kinda look like a bear,' Nevaeh adds, which has us all giggling.

'Think about it, you sleep all winter, miss all the cold and roam around the forests like "who's the daddy".'

'So you wanna be the daddy?' questions Nevaeh.

'I AM the daddy,' DeJon responds as he feathers out his chest and beats on it with his fists.

'DeJon you realise that's the impersonation of a gorilla, not a bear right?' Sammy informs politely.

'Oh shit, yeah…what does a bear do then?'

We all begin to laugh, the atmosphere amongst us is warm, everyone seems to be having fun. I steal a few glances of Shayth, feeling somewhat conflicted on how to behave towards him.

'What about you, Liyana? What would you be?' asks Sammy.

'I'd be a phoenix, constantly rising through the ashes soaring across the skies, free as a bird.'

'Nope, that's a mythical creature, if she's a phoenix then I wanna be wolverine,' Tucker challenges.

'And you, Shayth?' questions Sammy.

'Me? I have never considered this.' He looks in deep thought for a moment.

'Bro c'mon! How many more lessons do you need in talking like a human!' DeJon jests to which everyone bursts into laughter.

Shayth scoffs as he shakes his head in mild embarrassment.

'I would choose to be human. With the ability to speak the dialect as you do. Living in love and harmony with the rest of the world's creations.'

'Love and harmony – you don't follow the media much, do you?' challenges Nevaeh as we all yet again begin to laugh.

As we walk through the fairground, Sammy and Shayth walk side by side, lost in an in-depth conversation. The boys run off in all directions from the excitement of the various attractions.

Nevaeh and I walk ahead; she explains to me that I need to let my guards down and not jump to conclusions, especially when the likes of Trixy have planted the seed.

'Oh come, let's do the shooting game!' Nevaeh insists as she pulls my arm towards the stall.

She hands the rifle to me and asks what prize I am going for. 'The big teddy, I think,' I respond while I stare at the size of the rifle in my hand.

I take my first shot; I am off target by a mile!

'Hah, don't bank on that teddy!' Nevaeh states in jest.

As I turn to look at her, I see Sammy and Shayth standing by her side.

'Oh I wanna have a look at this stall I heard about, Nevaeh come with me,' Sammy insists as she pulls Nevaeh by her arm.

I watch Nevaeh and Sammy walk off, leaving me standing with a rifle in my hands and Shayth by my side.

I turn back around, distracting myself by aiming at the target. The thought of being alone with Shayth makes me feel nervous. I try even harder to concentrate on my target, hoping this will distract my nerves from kicking in.

Already I can feel my hands are no longer as steady as earlier.

I take a deep breath but can smell his dominant fragrance; he must have stepped closer towards me.

My heartbeat spikes in a panic to which I pull the trigger and yet again, miss the target.

I am so crap at this! In frustration, I begin shooting aimlessly managing to hit the target only once.

'Here, let me,' his tender voice offers.

He approaches close, positioning the rifle correctly against my body.

My body has frozen, yet I feel myself clamming up at the thought of his touch.

He puts his hand against mine, as he positions my fingers correctly around the trigger.

He cups his hand under my chin as he tries to position my head correctly for the lens.

I have never been so close to him! My mouth dries up from the shortness of my breath that I am desperately trying to disguise. He leans in close to me as he assesses the angle I have pointed the rifle at. His face is so close to mine, I cannot help but for my mind to lose focus.

My body becomes numb, but my mind is in overdrive! I want to hold him; I never want him to take a step away. Yet at the same time, I want to point the gun at him for playing such a cruel game!

'Now squeeze the trigger,' he whispers gently into my ear as his lip lightly brushes against my earlobe.

In that moment, Shayth places his hand around my waist and offers me a gentle squeeze.

My heartbeat spikes as my whole body pulsates. In a panic, I pull the trigger, the bullet ricochets off the wall panel, inches away from the Stallman.

'I'm so, so sorry,' I offer profusely as I step forward, removing myself from Shayths grip.

'Maybe this one's not for you!' the Stallman remarks as I hand him back the rifle.

'It is harder than it appears,' Shayth comments in a gentle tone.

'Don't be patronising,' I snap as I turn to look at him.

I am clueless as to how to behave or interact with Shayth. My feelings are so conflicting, I wish my defences would ease off, but they seem to be in full flow.

'Actually…' I turn back around, snatching the rifle from the Stallman.

'Let's see how good you are!' I insist as I push the rifle into Shayth's chest.

'Err…we do not have to do this,' he suggests while shaking his head with the rifle in his hands.

'But I would like to! Let's see how much of a pro you are!' I quickly respond as I stand with my arms folded waiting for him to pull the trigger.

He smiles at me nervously while I maintain a stern expression. I wish I could just soften up, but something inside will not let me. I suppose I am just afraid of getting carried away with my thoughts, afraid I will be hurt.

He positions the rifle against his body, takes a final look towards me, offering a beaming smile.

Suddenly his expression changes to a serious tone – *bang, bang, bang*!

I am stunned, as my jaw slightly drops from his impeccable precision!

He glances over towards me with his tilted head and offers me a wink. My expression puts an instant smile on his face as he bites his bottom lip to conceal his smile.

'The teddy for my lady' he announces to the Stallman.

'That's really not necessary,' I snap in frustration.

I cannot bear to continue to be hostile towards him, yet despite my heart yearning for him, I am too afraid to be anything but hostile.

'Great shooting…you really showed me. Enjoy the fairground,' I state while looking to the ground.

I turn and walk away from Shayth, as I brush my hand through my hair, I can't help but feel disappointed at how this evening is turning out.

'Liyana. Wait, hold up,' he shouts out as he paces towards me. Hold up – that's not his general use of language. He must be learning from DeJon and the boys.

My mind goes blank as I struggle to think of what to say. 'Fine! Let's see how good you are at this,' I state as I march toward the "high striker".

I stand on the platform with my arms crossed as I stare at Shayth.

'You…want me to…'

'YES,' I snap.

He takes the hammer in his hands, immediately I regret selecting this game! I stare at his biceps and broad shoulders, instantly realising he will smash this.

Not being able to bear the thought of having embarrassed myself yet again, as he raises his arms with the hammer in his grip, I begin to walk off.

In the background, I hear the chime of the bell, accompanied by a roaring cheer from the crowd over his victory.

I lose myself in the crowds and wander around aimlessly.

I see the hoopla stand with only a couple of people surrounding it. This should be easy for me!

As I collect the hoops from the lady at the stand, I look to my left to see Shayth being handed a prize for having won his game.

He offers me a smile as he reads the look of shock on my face. I instantly put the hoops on the counter and walk in the opposite direction.

What are the chances! I am making such a fool of myself; I think as I shake my head in embarrassment.

As I roam amongst the crowds looking out for Nevaeh and Sammy, hook the duck stall catches my eye.

This is Micky's favourite game! I smile as I walk over thinking about winning my Micky a prize.

I stand at the stall analysing the prizes to be won. My jaw slightly drops from the shock of seeing Shayth standing there, holding up his rod having hooked the tiniest duck, which would have earned him the biggest prize!

How is he doing this!

I scoff as I march off instantly. The frustration of my stupidity is growing, making me doubt my awareness! Perhaps I am unintentionally following him? Of course, I'm not... I'm just wandering aimlessly.

From all the walking, I build up a thirst, which forces me towards the refreshment stall.

'Oh I'm so sorry,' I offer in a hurry as I bump into the person who has just been served.

There staring back at me with a gentle smile I see Shayth, holding two drinks in his hand. I am horrified at the odds! 'Here you go,' he offers with a smug look as he hands me a drink.

I begin to stutter before surprisingly snatching the drink out of his hand.

I shuffle aside, removing myself from the queue before slowly walking off in confusion.

Shayth walks by my side, as I turn to look at him I cannot help myself.

'Why are you following me?' I snap.

The look of playful confidence appears across his expression as he smiles back at me and responds, 'Me following you? Surely it is you that follows me?

'I was at the hoopla stand and guess, who is stood behind me?

'Likewise with the rubber duck stand, there you are again.

I mind my own business getting a couple of drinks, and you follow me all the way here. And tell me this.'

Shayth suddenly puts his hand around my waist and pulls me closer towards him.

'What exactly were you doing in my dreams last night...?'

A sudden rush flows through my body; I cannot help but smile from the thrill of being so close to him and hearing his sweet words.

'Liyana,' he whispers.

'Yes,' I softly answer; I can feel my defences slowly evaporate with every effort he makes in getting closer to me.

'Please do not push me away.'

I look up and see him staring deep into me, with a sincere expression.

I close my eyes and lower my head as I try hard to compose myself and control my weak knees.

I slowly take a step back, removing myself from his grip. I manage to find the courage to look up at him with a playful smile while I respond with...

'I'll try!'

'…Honesty is the first chapter in the book of wisdom…'

–   Thomas Jefferson

16. Heart to Heart

We walk side by side, it's apparent we are both a little nervous. 'Thank you — for the drink,' I offer, in an attempt to break the silence.

'You are welcome,' he responds softly.

I look up at Shayth; he seems a little hesitant; like something is on his mind, stuck in his throat that he can't quite bring out. 'What is it,' I ask softly with a slight look of concern.

'I would like to ask you of something…and I really hope you will agree, but,' he laughs nervously.

'Well, I suppose I am afraid that you will refuse.'

'What is it,' I ask curiously.

'Can we just for tonight, just put everything behind us, and start over? As if we have just met, tonight, here, in this fairground.'

'What, why?' I asked feeling confused.

'It is important to me, that you understand me, for who I am. It feels as if everything is getting in the way. I never thought it could be so complicated…but I just want you to know me for me.'

'Okay, but I have so much that I still don't understand, like last Friday!'

'And I give you my word; you shall have all the answer to all your questions. But tonight, just for tonight, may we please start over?'

'And you promise me answers after tonight?'

'You have my word.'

I look down as I consider his proposal. I can understand where he is coming from, but there is so much I need to know about last week and him and Trixy.

I look up at him as we casually walk along the pier.

The uncertainty in his expression I find endearing, I cannot continue to see him this way.

'In that case,' I respond as I stand to look at him, 'Hi, I'm Liyana,' I say while holding out my hand.

He laughs a nervous laugh, which seems to be full of relief.

He takes my hand, raising it to his lips where he places a gentle kiss.

'It is my absolute pleasure, lady Liyana,' he whispers while looking deep into my eyes.

I turn slowly, continuing to walk with Shayth by my side; only he has not yet released my palm.

I hold up my hand, which is interlocked in his fingers and playfully state.

'I'm sorry, sir, I have only just met you, this is a little too forward for me.'

He offers a soft nervous laugh as he releases my hand.

'Of course, my lady,' he responds as he bows his head subtly. 'Soo...do you come here often,' he asks as he bites his lip.

I cannot help but giggle.

I decide to embrace this moment, joining him in this genuine desire of wanting a clean slate, if only for tonight.

'No actually, it's my first time. I'm new to this area so haven't really ventured out much.'

'As am I, I have relocated to university, thus do not know the area or the people. Two lost souls, coming together.'

A faint smile appears across my expression from his poetic outlook.

'Where are you from?' I ask feeling relieved that I can really get to know him.

'Well, a small town up north from here, but I am quite the traveller, still seeking a place I can truly call home.'

His expression seems down as his eyes lose the sparkle in them.

'Well, that explains the accent I suppose,' I add in an attempt to lighten the mood.

'So do you have a big family,' I ask curiously.

'Yes. The town that I am from — we are all like one big family there. Everyone takes care of each other,' he responds with excitement.

'Does it not get lonely now that you have come here, leaving your family behind?' I ask, wanting to know more about him.

'Err, not really, I see them very often, they are just a flash away,' he adds casually.

'And is your girlfriend not wanting you to go back home?' I try to keep a straight face, so my eagerness to hear his response does not show.

He chuckles lightly; I can sense his eyes are on me, watching my expression.

'No, she does not.'

He pauses in his speech, leaving me confused. I hold a straight face, despite alarm bells ringing within me. Any moment now, I feel as if my heart will take the hit.

'She does not exist…There is no girlfriend.'

I feel the weight lifted from my shoulders as if I can finally breathe again.

'We are raised somewhat traditional in my, town.'

I look up at him, watching him stare ahead with a smile on his face. The sparkle is back in his eyes; it naturally makes me smile.

'That is the reason why I am here though.'

He pauses as he smiles while biting his lip, looking slightly nervous.

'There was something in my heart telling me to come here. Maybe here I will find what I've never known existed…'

He looks at me intensely; the depth of sincerity on his expression makes me freeze.

'So what are your plans for when you graduate,' he asks in an attempt to dilute the tense atmosphere.

My mind goes blank as I am still stuck on his statement of being somewhat "traditional". What does he mean by this? Focusing back to the present moment, my mind scrambles to gather my thoughts.

'Err; I'm not really sure, to be honest. I've not thought that far. It depends on what my little brother wants to do.'

'Why is it you always put him first? Even before you? I've not seen that from a sibling.'

'Well if I don't, who will? Besides, he is my world,' I respond with a proud smile.

'But what do you mean "always" put him first? I've not mentioned Micky to you before, have I?

'Oh, No. No, you have not.' He seems a little anxious. 'I just figured you were always this way with him.' Suddenly, with the thought of Micky, it finally hits me.

'His eyes! I mean your eyes… I mean you have his eyes.'

Shayth smiles at my excitement, 'You like my eyes?'

'I love your eyes!'

Instantly I realise what I have said; I desperately try hard to backtrack. I become a stuttering mess before blurting out,

'I mean, the colour of your eyes is like Micky's. That's why I, err, love your eyes, because they remind me of his eyes. So really, I love his eyes and not yours!'

Shayth chuckles lightly while I desperately think of how I can distract us both from my love comment.

'So it was pretty impressive to see all your winnings back there.'

'What can I say, I have many talents,' he responds playfully.

'Hmm…there seems to be an awful lot of things you can do, why not tell me something you can't do?' I ask to bring him down a few pegs.

A wicked smile appears on my face at the thought of being able to ask him anything.

'Err. I cannot live in the ocean.'

'What, who can? Next, you'll be telling me you can't fly through the air!'

A huge grin spreads across his face, which leaves me confused. 'Are you afraid of heights?'

'No.'

'The ocean?'

'No.'

'Spiders?'

'No.'

'Snakes?'

'Definitely not!'

'Err…dancing?'

'Nope.'

'Love?'

Shayth pauses for a moment till he finally responds 'Perhaps…'

'I don't understand, you are either afraid, or you're not,' I question wanting to know more.

He hesitates for a moment before finally opening up.

'Well, does the idea not frighten you, the thought of loving another with all your soul? Suddenly the world revolves around them. What would you do if you were ever to lose the one you love? It would be as if the whole world itself has stopped spinning.'

'Wow, that's very deep,' I whisper as his profound response takes me back.

'But at least now I know you're not invincible,' I add with a cheeky tone to soften the mood.

'What about you, you would love to be a bird, to be able to fly?' he asks with a smile on his face.

'Who wouldn't, to be free...to be able just to pick up and go, that is a fantasy I would love to live, even if in my dreams.'

He purses his lips as he hides a smile.

'I shall take you flying very soon,' he whispers.

'Sweeping me off my feet doesn't count as flying,' I reply confidently.

'Is that what I am doing?' he questions with a flirtatious expression.

'That's what you are trying to do,' I reply with a cheeky smile. We both share a giggle as we have completed a full lap at the fairground.

'I'm kidding. It's been really nice finally getting to know you,' I add to encourage the friendly banter.

We both stand nervously in an emptying fairground with our hands full of winnings. He looks as if he wants to say something yet he hesitates.

'Liyana, will you allow me to take you home?'

'Oh, I don't know... I don't think that's a good idea Shayth. Not after...'

'Please, I give you my word. There will be no detours! There will be no – events.'

I look at him with reservation, feeling unwilling to agree. 'Please, please, please,' he whispers as he bops his head from side to side.

'Okay, but Shayth, I mean it. Any of what happened last week and I will Never Ever be speaking to you again!'

'Understood my lady, loud and clear. Thank you, thank you, thank you,' he repeats profusely.

As we drive in his car, I feel a little apprehensive from memories of the last time we were here.

'Trust in me, you are safe,' he states as if he had read my mind I smile at his warm expression.

'So...do you offer many girls a ride in this car?'

He scoffs at my cheeky tone.

'Never. You are the only lady permitted.'

'Oh please! Like I am going to believe that!' I snap instantaneously.

'I do not understand, why would you not believe?' he questions with a look of confusion.

'What, are you for real?' I ask with a bitter tone.

'Yes, I am for real!' he affirms in a confident tone.

I see nothing but innocence and sincerity in his expressions.

I scoff at the thought that he is joking, but his expression says otherwise.

'Are you serious?' I whisper.

He smiles gently as he states.

'Much about me will surprise you…perhaps a conversation for another day.'

He slowly pulls up in my drive. 'You know where I live.'

'Yes, I do.'

He puts the car in park; we sit there in silence.

'Do… Do I know you,' I ask.

He stares at me with serious eyes as he slowly whispers, 'Do you feel that you know me?'

The atmosphere becomes tense as we both stare at each other. 'There's just something so familiar, like…it's as if I have been around you, but I just can't recall.'

A soft smile appears on his face.

'I am so relieved you feel this way,' he whispers before leaning forward, placing his palm on the back of my neck.

'I need to see you again,' he insists, as he looks deep into my eyes.

My mind refuses for this to be true, yet my heart is yearning to melt in his arms and see him again.

'I can't, not unless I get to ask you one question,' I insist.

'If it is the only way to see you again, I will answer your question.' He looks somewhat nervous yet eager to please me.

'Monday night, where were you?' I manage to ask.

He looks at me in shock as he leans back, releasing his palm from the back of my neck.

His reaction says it all.

'So it's true,' I whisper as I force a smile, desperately trying hard to remain strong.

I feel like I've been hit in the face with the unwanted truth that my heart and mind were not ready to hear.

'So you had a great time I'm guessing,' I add as my tone becomes sarcastic with a hint of anger.

'How do you know…did you sense me?' he questions I scoff at the thought of my stupidity.

'Yes… I did,' he continues to whisper. 'In all honesty, it was one of the greatest moments I have been longing for! A memory I shall cherish for all my years,' he insists as he takes my hand into his.

'Hah. 10/10 for honesty!' I shout as I begin to feel myself becoming irritated.

I slowly remove my hand from Shayth's palm as the worry on his face begins to grow.

'So much for traditional,' I whisper under my breath.

I can feel it happening inside me; my defences are building a wall around me, stopping me from breaking.

'Look Shayth, I'm not that kind of girl okay!' I try hard to tame my frustration and be as gracious as I can be, given the situation. 'You two may be okay with this non-exclusive way of life, but deep down I'm old fashioned at heart. I just think it's best we stay friends – at most, if that!'

Shayth shakes his head, furrowing his brows in disbelief.

'What are you saying,' he whispers as the look of confusion takes over his expression.

'My Liyana, your aura is showing to me your feelings, yet you speak an alternate language. I do not understand,' he pleas.

'My aura?' I shout with exasperation.

'I can sense how happy you are around me – but you insist on holding yourself back; encouraging yourself to become hostile, why?' he pleads trying to understand my point of view.

'I don't really know what you're talking about; I just think it's easier this way.

'And it looks like the freedom from your "traditional" lifestyle clearly has the better of you!

'Like I said, I'm old-fashioned.

If you and Trixy are cool with it, that's your business! Me on the other hand, I'm not interested in you, or your social experiment!' I blurt out in an attempt to defend my position.

'Trixy! What does Trixy have to do with this?' he asks looking even more puzzled.

'That's where you were, Monday night! With Trixy!' I shout with frustration.

Shayth looks away from me as he begins to smile which soon breaks into light laughter.

'This explains everything. How did you learn of this? Who has informed you?' he whispers with an amused tone.

'You did,' I shout! 'When you told me it was a moment you will cherish for all your stupid years!'

Shayth begins to chuckle even more as he leans in my direction, trying to take my hand again.

'Why would you think this is even funny?' I snap feeling frustrated as I pull away my hand from his.

'You have learned this from Trixy, is that not correct?' he asks softly while gently reaching for my hand, taking it towards his chest.

'Okay, I may have heard it from Trixy, but you have just validated it!' I snap as I try to make sense of what it is he finds amusing. 'Listen, lady Liyana, I shall share something with you which may be difficult for you to accept, but in time you shall have all the answers you seek,' he insists as he tries hard to ease my frustration.

'Go on,' I state in a stern voice.

'Monday night, I was not with Trixy. I was with you; you simply did not notice my presence. You have never noticed my presence.

'And that is why I am here. To be noticed, by you.'

I cannot help but frown, despite my heartbeat fluttering, pulsating my body; I was at home all of Monday night, certainly not with Shayth! But he wants to be noticed by me?

'Look at me,' he asks as he puts both of his palms on my face forcing me to look his direction.

'I know how this must sound, I know you are in doubt. But please, I ask you to trust in me! I will explain when the time is right.'

'You're mad! I would know if I was with you Monday night!' I whisper as I try not to lose myself in his eyes.

Shayth suddenly looks over my shoulder while releasing his palms from my cheeks. I glance over; the porch light has been switched on. Aunt Liz is watching no doubt.

'Allow me to prove it to you,' he whispers.

I turn to look at him, feeling confused as to what to think. 'Tomorrow night, after you have tucked Micky in, 9 pm, talk to me. Tell me something, tell me anything! When I see you on Monday, I shall discreetly repeat to you what you have shared.' I am baffled by his bizarre request, yet a part of me is desperate to trust in him.

I don't know if I should be listening to the sensible side of me that is flashing alarm bells or simply just give in to my desire.

He looks so sincere but is making no sense at all.

As he holds my face with his gentle palms, he whispers, 'Trixy is not the one I want; I would not be here if she was.'

I look into his eyes, mesmerised by the sparkling lights of his grey iris.

Am I dreaming? Eyes cannot sparkle in this way…

I look down, not knowing how I should feel, without realising, I whisper the words,

'Okay.'

I feel his soft, tender lips on my forehead as he gives me a gentle kiss.

I slowly lower his hands from my face; my voice feels soft, as if it will struggle to be heard.

'I should go now; they will be watching me from inside,' I manage to whisper.

I position my body towards the door as I manoeuvre to get out. I suddenly hesitate for a moment.

I sit and turn to look at him; he is staring right at me, with one hand on the steering wheel, the other arm around the back of my seat.

I begin to feel nervous; I go back to open the door. I hesitate again, sitting back to look at him.

What am I supposed to do? Do I just walk out of the car? Do I offer him a kiss? I'm not kissing his lips! But do I place a kiss on his cheek? Or his hand? No, not his hand, that's what gentlemen offer to ladies. Why am I making the simplest of things so complicated? Just get out of the car, I tell myself.

Shayth's smile widens as he puts his head down before chuckling softly.

'Allow me to make this easier for you,' he whispers.

He takes my hand and looks me in the eyes while raising my hand to his soft full lips. He places a firm kiss on the surface.

As he closes his eyes, I take a final deep breath of the masculine scent I am surrounded in.

Once his eyes open, he releases my hands and pushes open his car door.

Within moments, I find him on the passenger side, opening the door, extending out his hand to assist me out of the shallow seats.

'Thank you,' I whisper as I feel a hot flush running through me. He smiles softly.

'Do not forget these.'

He walks over to his boot and hands me the super-sized teddy along with all the other prizes he had won today.

'These are your winnings,' I state in hesitation as he brings them towards me.

'You are the lady, I have won these for,' he whispers with a dazzling smile.

I am left speechless not knowing how to respond. I struggle but manage to grip them all.

'You will speak to me tomorrow night?' He insists as we slowly part from each other.

'Err... Yes. Okay,' I confirm as my heart becomes desperate to see him again.

'Thank you,' he whispers in a soft tone.

I offer a coy smile as I whisper, 'Bye,' before turning to head towards the house.

My heart is pounding. Though he makes no sense at all, I cannot help but trust him.

He is no stranger; I believe that in my heart, yet I know nothing about him, despite feeling as if I have known him for so long.

The one question I cannot seem to answer in my mind to explain my behaviour – Is this curiosity, lust or is this love?

'…And he found you lost and guided you…'

—   Quran 93.71

17. Labyrinth

'What is all this in aid of?'

Aunt Liz stands at the table observing the various options laid for breakfast.

'Oh wow, Liyana you didn't have to go through all this trouble,' Uncle Aidan comments while looking excited.

'I wanted to. Just to say thank you, really,' I reply as I walk towards them with a spring in my step.

'Oh, and the young man who dropped you off last night has nothing to do with this?' Aunt Liz questions with a wicked smile.

'Man? What man?' Uncle Aidan questions in surprise.

'Oh no, nothing. He is just a friend from university,' I insist trying hard to discourage the conversation.

'That's what they all say!' Aunt Liz adds as she pulls back a chair and takes a seat.

'Dropped you off, but your cars outside?' Uncle Aidan states with confusion.

What – my car is outside? How did that happen? How is Shayth doing this?

'Oh yes, a friend dropped it off,' I hesitantly reply, not knowing what else to say.

'It's great that you're being sensible when you're drinking by not driving, but just be careful who you give your keys to Liyana,' Uncle Aidan mildly lectures.

My expression is blank, I wasn't drinking and have never given my keys to anyone, but sharing this information will only encourage more questions from them.

'Yes, Uncle Aidan, I am sorry. I'll be more careful,' I respond in agreement.

'Liyana!!' Micky comes running towards me, leaping onto my lap, wrapping his arms around me.

'Did you have a sleepover last night? I waited for you.'

'Oh, I'm sorry, Micky! Not a sleep over, no, but when I got home you were fast asleep.'

'This is what I was talking about,' Aunt Liz mutters under her breath.

I turn to look at her as she sips on her cup of tea looking somewhat smug.

'Liyana, are all those gifts for me!' Micky asks in excitement. 'ALL for you! That's where I was yesterday evening, busy winning everything for you.'

'I've never had a teddy so big!' he shouts with excitement.

'It had your name on it the moment I saw it,' I say while brushing my hand through his hair.

I look at his eyes, which amplifies my smile. So similar to Shayth's, minus the streaks of bright white within his iris.

'So will you be telling me about this guy or do I need to get the rifle out,' Uncle Aidan states with a stern tone yet a smile on his expression that he tries to hide.

'Oh, he is just a friend from university. We have a few classes together. Nothing more.'

I try to come across blasé while hiding the excitement in my voice.

'That's a very unusual car this "friend" of yours has,' Aunt Liz comments.

'It's Japanese, I think. A new model maybe?' I reply trying to sound casual.

'What's this friend's name?' Uncle Aidan asks while munching on his breakfast.

'Shayth.'

'Shayth. That's unusual. Where is he from?' he quizzes.

'Err, not from around here, just further up north.'

'Well that narrows it down,' Aunt Liz adds with sarcasm.

'Uncle Aidan what do you have planned for today,' I ask desperately trying to change the subject.

'I thought perhaps we could all go trekking today. There's a couple of good spots around this area so why not make the most of the weather?' he suggests with enthusiasm.

'Yay! Can we bring Diesel,' shouts Micky with a mouth full of food?

'Of course, champ! It wouldn't be a family day out without Diesel!'

'Is it safe?' I ask with a hesitant tone while recalling the dangers of the forests.

'Course it is, kiddo. You're with an expert! So long as you stay on the tracks! Otherwise, there's no coming back!'

'Hah! An expert! You've not been trekking since you were just a few years older than Ann,' Aunt Liz teases.

'Hey, once you've acquired the skill, you never lose it!' he states as he quietly grins to himself.

It's nice to watch Aunt Liz and Uncle Aidan being playful. Perhaps this trek will be good for us all. Good for me, to try and bond with Aunt Liz again after our altercation a few weeks back.

'Can we do this EVERY weekend?' Micky asks in excitement as he walks with a big stick and a small rucksack he'd packed himself.

'Sure can champ. You're quite the adventurer aren't you!' Uncle Aidan responds.

'I want to be an explorer,' Micky replies with a serious expression. We cannot help but begin to giggle at how adorable he is.

I watch Aunt Liz and Uncle Aidan ahead of me with their arms around each other as they watch Micky run off with Diesel. I cannot help but smile, I could not have wished for anyone to love Micky as much as they do.

I look at the forest; suddenly recalling my chilling encounter here.

Yet it appears so peaceful, being surrounded by nothing but nature.

The beauty of the forest enthrals me, as I walk in awe.

I listen to the birds singing in the treetops; watch the wild squirrels scurrying with their treasures, the butterflies dancing amongst the flowers.

'Liyana, Liyana!!' I hear a voice shout in the distance.

My lips part in confusion as I turn to see I have walked off the track, leaving the others at some distance.

I jog towards them; amongst the rustling of the bushes I run past, I notice a pair of wild rabbits. The vivid memory of the rabbit being mutilated before my eyes forces me to pick up my pace.

'Kiddo you need to stay with us! These forests can be dangerous,' Uncle Aidan warns as I finally reach them.

'Sorry, Uncle, I got carried away with the views.'

'Ann, stay close to us, what would Micky do if you became the next missing person!' Aunt Liz shouts.

'I'm sorry. It won't happen again.'

I'm left confused by Aunt Liz's statement, "become the next missing person", is she referring to my parents?

I begin to feel restless as we continue on our trek.

The number of families and groups of friends we pass along our journey surprises me.

I didn't realise this place would be so popular.

'Do many people get lost in these forests,' I ask as I try hard not to sound hurt from the memories of my parents.

'All the time!' Uncle Aidan states with certainty.

'It's somewhat of a labyrinth stroke Bermuda triangle if you go off the tracks!' he confirms.

'Oh just the thought of it makes me shiver,' adds Aunt Liz.

'Can you remember the young boy! God knows how he survived!' she continues to say as she puts her arm around Uncles Aidan's waist to be comforted.

'What happened?' I ask as my eyes shoot over to Micky further ahead, making sure he's okay.

'It's surprising how many people go missing here, Liyana! Far too many people! And only a handful ever returns! Very few missing bodies are found, maybe an arm here, a leg there, never a full body which is easily identifiable.'

I feel a sickness grown in the pit of my stomach.

'And what of the missing boy that survived?' I ask while I still keep my focus firmly on Micky.

'Well of the few that have turned up, they all pretty much say the same thing. They were lost in the woods, got caught up in a storm. And once they've regained consciousness from having been hit by falling branches, they find themselves at the edge of the forest or the middle of the road. But they are always injured, some quite seriously!'

'He was such an adorable little child,' adds Aunt Liz.

'Maybe about 10 or 11 years of age, broken bones, chunks of his flesh missing. But somehow he survived.'

'Why would people come here if it's so dangerous,' I ask feeling a little vulnerable.

'It's like with anything, kiddo, from swimming in the ocean to crossing a road. Why would someone cross a road if they know that's where cars drive, and they could get hit?

'If you follow the tracks and are in a group you are in no danger, it's only going off the trail where you might get lost, and who knows what lies within these forests.'

I feel a cold shiver run through my body as I recall my last encounter here, and all those years ago with my parents. 'What's the longest period someone has been missing before being found? I mean, has...Has it been years?' I ask in desperation.

I cannot control my voice from shake as feel my emotions getting the better of me.

'Oh God no! A week or two at most,' Aunt Liz laughs.

I can feel Uncle Aidan's eyes on me; I am too afraid to look up at him.

I continue to look down to the ground as I try and get a grip on my oversensitive emotions!

He walks closer towards me; I think he knew exactly why I had asked that question.

I feel his arm around my shoulder as he squeezes his hand tight and pulls me close towards him.

I raise my glance from the ground and a sudden shock spreads through my body, for a split second it feels as if time stands still.

'Micky,' I whisper. 'Where is he?'

'Micky!' I scream out aloud while running towards the horizon desperately searching for him!

'Micky,' I hear Uncle Aidan shout as he paces up behind me.

'Micky!!!' I scream again as the tears fall down my face while I run erratically!

Micky suddenly steps out from behind a tree with Diesel.

'I'm sorry, I think he needed a poop,' Micky responds looking panicked.

I fall to my knees, wrapping my arms around him while not being able to control my sobbing heart.

'Micky! You cannot do that again!' I sob as I try to calm my emotions.

'You can never wander off like this! What would I do if something happened to you?' I whisper as Uncle Aidan reaches us.

I release him from my grip, quickly wiping the tears from my cheeks.

'Am I in trouble? I'm sorry, Liyana,' Micky whispers as he keeps his eyes on me while Uncle Aidan holds him in a bear hug.

'Nah, champ, you're not in trouble. We just got worried we had lost you that's all.'

'Micky my love, what were you doing!' Aunt Liz shouts as she finally reaches us, pulling him from Uncle Aidan to hold him tight.

'I won't do it again, I'm sorry, Diesel just needed a poop, and I didn't want him to get lost!'

Micky begins to cry softly which then turns into a wail of a cry as he sobs sorry to us all.

Our reaction has terrified him, yet he has no idea why we have reacted in this way.

I watch as they both comfort Micky from his sobbing. The sight of their love reassures me that Micky would be well looked after and very much still loved if anything were to ever happen to me.

He would never be alone from the love that Aunt Liz in particularly has for him.

As Aunt Liz and Uncle Aidan release Micky from their grip, he looks towards me and hesitates as he takes a few steps forward. He holds onto the pendant around his neck, the tag with the engraving of him and I.

He looks frightened. I've never screamed in front of him the way I just have.

'It's okay, I'm sorry for shouting,' I offer softly to remove the fear from his expression.

At that moment, he runs towards me wrapping his arms around me, sobbing even more.

'It's okay,' I say as I stroke his hair.

As he catches his breath from his tears, he states with a defensive tone.

'I don't like Diesel anymore!'

I clear the dishes, and we all sit to watch a family movie together.

Micky cuddles up to me on the sofa; I find myself staring more at him than the TV.

Everyone seems exhausted from the long trek, and Micky quickly dozes off in my arms.

Uncle Aidan carries him to bed; I sit with him for a short while wondering if any person has ever loved their sibling as much as I love Micky.

I lie on my bed, absorbing the calm ambiance in my safe haven. I cuddle up to the small teddy on my bed that Shayth had won for me.

Shayth! I stare at the clock beside my bed; it's 20.26! I instantly jump out of bed, running to the shower. My heartbeat rises as the water drips onto my body.

What did he mean to speak to him at 21.00? Is he going to come here? Is he expecting me to invite him in, are we going out?

I haven't thought this through at all!

I jump out of the shower with just the towel wrapped around me and open my wardrobe to find something to wear.

How do I dress for an occasion that I don't know of?

I pull out my jeans, nope. Dress, nope. Joggers? Definitely Not! Okay, I'm having a wardrobe issue; maybe it's easier if I start off with my hair and makeup?

I sit at the dressing table as I contemplate the look to go for; dramatic evening look? Nope. Nude, contoured look? Nope!

What have I got myself into!

After drying my hair, I put on my subtle everyday makeup, with a tad of colour on my lips.

I try to remain calm as I look back into my wardrobe.

I try on the dress; it looks like we are going out on a date; it's no good.

I put on the jeans with a pair of heals; am I trying too hard to look casual? Nope, no good!

I put my nightdress on and hang the towel to dry.

I look into my wardrobe a final time, nope; I can't decide anything! I close the doors, taking in a deep breath from defeat! The anxiety soon disappears as the atmosphere lightens from a familiar scent.

I know that smell; I look towards the balcony doors, which are slightly ajar and notice my beautiful, mysterious flower.

I look over the balcony to see if Shayth is there, but nothing. Where does this flower keep coming from? I look above towards the roof to see if maybe a bird has set its nest above, but there is nothing in sight.

A thought runs through my mind. I begin to scoff at myself for even thinking Shayth could be here bringing me the flower.

I take a look at the night sky; the stars are sparkling beautifully in the distance. It reminds me of his eyes, the thought of his eyes begin to make me feel excited.

Though there is a chilling breeze tonight, I feel a layer of warmth wrapped around me. I close my eyes as I indulge in the moment.

The wind swirls the fragrance of the flower around me; I lose myself in a daydream full of warmth.

As I come to my senses, I rush inside towards the clock, having felt as if I have lost the sense of time.

It is 21.34; he's not here, he's not coming.

I sit at the edge of my bed with my head in my hands.

I feel like such a fool! I try hard to recall our conversation.

He never once actually said he would see me or that he would come over to the house.

I sit here while I try hard to recall precisely what he had said. 'Tell me something, tell me anything! And when I see you on Monday, I will repeat to you what you had said.'

'You will speak to me tomorrow night?'

What is he talking about? What is he asking me to do? How can I speak to him if he is not here?

In frustration, I stand up straight, wiping off the colour from my lips.

I sit at the dressing table, staring into the mirror as I shake my head in disappointment.

'Tell me something, and I will repeat this to you when I see you,' I say out loud.

Does Shayth want me to talk to him right now, even though he's not here? To then repeat my words back to me, which in his strange head will prove that he was not with Trixy, but with me?

Ok, here goes nothing!

'Hi...'

'I'm looking into the mirror and talking to myself. This is a sign of madness, have I gone mad?' The look of worry grows on my face.

'What am I doing?'

I sink my head down as I breathe out in a sulk.

What have I got to lose, I convince myself. If I make a fool of myself, there is no one here but me, so I may as well just say something!

I look up in the mirror as I feel more in control at the realisation that if I am a fool, no one will know but me!

'Shayth…

'Something's not quite right with this. Either you've gone mad, or I have gone mad! To be honest, I think it is me; I think I have gone mad.

'But it is okay, no one knows yet, just me! What do I say, what do I say,'

I stare at myself in the mirror, taking in a deep breath as I convince myself to open my heart a little.

'I feel like I know you, yet I feel like we are worlds apart. There is something so familiar, so comforting when I am with you, yet I feel like I don't know you at all!

'I know, I am making no sense, just goes to prove that I have gone mad I suppose.

'I wish I could open up to you, I really do.

'You were right. I do hold back! It's just the way I am used to being now.

'But if I could let myself go… I'd wish I could let myself go, with you…

'I don't know if you can hear me?

Of course you can't hear me! You're not here with me to be able to hear me!

'But if I'm not going mad and you can miraculously hear me, then you can prove it to me!

'You can prove it to me…by…err…okay, I got it!' A grin appears on my face at the thought.

'You can prove it to me by coming to university on Monday and be wearing a pink headband!'

I feel somewhat smug as I smile wide. I bite my bottom lip to control my little giggle.

The lampshade begins to flicker erratically. 'Not again!' I sigh.

I put on my nightgown and head downstairs.

'Uncle Aidan, please could you get the electrical wires looked at? The lamp in my rooms keeps flickering every day; it's like a disco in my room right now.'

He chuckles lightly, 'Yeah I've noticed that around the house a few times too. Don't worry, will get it looked at tomorrow.'

'Thanks, Uncle, goodnight.'

'Night, kiddo.'

'...Look at situations from all angles and you will become more open...'

– Dalai Lama

18. Ethereal Body

'So you two looked very cosy at the fairgrounds,' Nevaeh gives me a wicked smile, I cannot help but laugh.

'I suppose you and Sammy had something to do with it! It was nice, just to get to know him you know.'

'Oh yeah, so how "well" did you get to know him.'

'You have a dirty mind Nevaeh,' I say as we both start to giggle.

'Oh please, tell me you haven't thought about it.'

'Thought about what?' I question as I click my tongue while winking, throwing us into a burst of laughter.

'What's going on there?' Nevaeh questions as she looks over my shoulder.

We stare at the small huddle behind us from which comes a roar of laughter. As the students part from the corridor, out walks Shayth. He is being pointed at and ridiculed, but it appears he doesn't seem to care from the smile he wears proudly across his face.

His white plimsolls are complemented by his pale blue denim jeans.

His white top hangs just over the buttons of his jeans.

A few of them wear the same sports team jacket in the crowd. He stares at me, offering me his dazzling smile as he approaches closer towards me.

My jaw drops, I can't believe my eyes.

'What the hell is he doing?' Nevaeh gasps in shock.

Shayth ducks his head repeatedly to avoid the likes of DeJon and Bazzer trying to take off the pink headband on his head.

'He's gay!'

Nevaeh looks at me in shock as panic takes over her reaction.

She begins to whisper, 'He's gay; he's gay! You need to backtrack, Liyana and move on; he's gay! Oh my gosh, I feel like I'm in the twilight zone!'

'Oh… Hi, Shayth, nice err, nice headband, it suits you,' Nevaeh offers in a polite yet nervous tone as Shayth reaches us.

'I doubt that, but thank you,' he replies as he fist bumps her before turning to look at me.

He gets up close, placing his hand on my waist as he pulls me softly towards him.

This feels like a dream! Is this really happening? I question myself, as I look to the ground.

Shayth cups my chin between his fingers, which raises my head, closing my dropped jaw.

'Is this what you wanted,' he questions with a smile while looking straight into my eyes.

My mind is in overdrive. Everyone is watching us, pointing and laughing, while all I can think of is the rush flowing through my body.

He laughs gently while slowly swaying my waist.

'Take it off,' I manage to whisper, as I shake my head in disapproval; I look noticeably embarrassed.

'Whys that? Is this not what you asked of me?' he questions in a teasing manner.

My smile widens as I gasp from shock; the adrenaline fills my body with excitement.

'Please. Please, please take it off,' I whisper again as I stare into his eyes, biting my lip from the awkwardness of knowing everyone's eyes are on us.

'You are blushing. You are almost as pink as this headband,' he whispers with a wicked smile.

I feel my body burning as I look down in the hope that he will see less of my blushing cheeks.

He comes in closer as his lips brush against my ear. He softly whispers, 'Anything for you, my lady Liyana.'

He takes off the baby pink headband, forcing his friends around him to break into a cheer before laughing out loud.

I sit in between Nevaeh and Shayth in class, trying hard to wipe away the constant smile on my face.

The lecturer covers old ground of some fundamental psychological theories on sleep stages studied in high school. This makes it easy not to concentrate but daydream about Shayth besides me.

I feel his arm brush against mine as he reaches over, scribbling on my notebook.

Now do you believe me?

I smile as I can feel my body become nervous.

How did you know?

Shayth ignores my written question and underlines his first question,

Now do you believe me?

I scoff quietly.

Yes.

I proceed to mimic his actions, underlining my first question,

How did you know?

I was with you, in some shape or form.

Not Possible!!!

I then begin to repeatedly underline*!!!*

I hear him scoff at my exaggerated underlining. To my surprise, he raises his hand.

'Yes young man,' welcomes the lecturer.

'Sir, at what stage of the sleep cycle, can one experience astral projection?'

'It's a fascinating concept but not one really covered within the syllabus of our course. But I'm more than happy to provide a high-level overview because it really is quite remarkable.'

'Please,' Shayth insists as his demeanour becomes more focused. As I look at him with curiosity, he points at the lecturer, almost suggesting that the lecturer's overview may perhaps answer my question.

'Well, like I said, it's a remarkable concept which generally takes place within REM. Bearing in mind, someone who is sleep deprived can fall within REM sleep in a matter of minutes and not the typical 90-minute cycle.

This notion suggests one can leave their physical body in a spiritual form and in some instances, carry out this act in a conscious manner, allowing them to control the journey of their spiritual body. The astral body is what does the travelling when the person's physical body is sound asleep.

'The astral body is sometimes referred to as the ethereal body.'

'So if such an ability exists, where does our ethereal body or astral body go?' asks a curious student at the front of the class.

'Well, the scholars suggest the ethereal body visits the astral plane which is within our universe, only an alternate reality which vibrates at a different frequency to our physical world.

'There are many that claim they can teach individuals various techniques to be able to astral project. Not that I can recommend any!

'Some of you may have even experienced astral projections yourselves.

'Raise your hand if you have ever had a falling sensation in your sleep that vibrates your whole body just as you become conscious?'

I look across the room observing the number of individuals that have raised their hands. I glance over at Shayth who has a slight smile on his expression. Is this what he is trying to tell me? Did he bring his ethereal body to my room while watching me have a conversation?

'Good, quite a few of you I see,' the lecturer continues.

'Well, it's suggested that the sensation of falling is a result of your physical body sending calling vibrations to your ethereal body, which in turn comes back at speed to re-join your conscious mind.

'Thus the falling sensation is your ethereal body falling back into your physical body. The sudden jerk is when the two bodies collide.'

'Is this concept of astral projection real?' I ask.

'It depends on who you ask. If you're asking me is it a proven fact, then the answer is no. But perhaps I can link this question to our syllabus content on observation and perception.

'So if a tree falls in a forest and no one is around to hear it, does it make a sound? Can we assume the unobserved world functions the same as the observed world?

'Back to Astral Projection, can we assume the various frequencies, which makes up our universe, which is a proven fact, is designed to inhibit multiple frequencies of our conscious and subconscious?

'Because we do not know it's happening, does this mean it is not happening?'

For the remainder of the class, I contemplate the concept of astral projection and ethereal body not knowing whether to believe this concept or not.

'So what's going on with you two then,' Nevaeh asks abruptly as the three of us and Sammy sit in the refectory for lunch.

'Nevaeh! Nothing!' I insist as I feel myself begin to blush.

'Okay, well if it's nothing, Shayth you are sitting far too close to her and Liyana you have gone as bright as a beetroot!'

I hang my head down in shame while I hear Nevaeh giggling away.

'Please, I need all the help I can get! To make sure she doesn't push me away again,' Shayth adds as he nudges his shoulder against mine. We all sip on our drinks whilst I silently wish for the conversation to move on.

'LI-YA-NA,' shouts DeJon as he approaches our table.

I'm relieved to see him! I am sure his presence will change the subject of our conversation!

I look up at DeJon, forcing a smile.

'You're looking a bit flush their girl, what's going on under the table?' he adds with a huge grin on his face as he chuckles softly.

Shayth releases his hand from his drink and raises them high to which all burst out laughing.

'Not you too,' I whisper sounding like a victim.

'Nah you're good. And I owe you – for taking it easy.'

He points at his forehead and offers me a salute. I look at Shayth who seems oblivious to why DeJon is thanking me – thank goodness!

DeJon, Romeo, Tucker and Bazzer grab the empty chairs and join us at our table.

'So who's up for the party next Friday?' Bazzer asks.

'You'll be alright, Tucker. You won't need a mask, just come as you are,' Romeo adds while tucker begins to play fight with him.

'Another party!' I whisper feeling unsure of my attendance.

'Hell yeah! We're students, that's what we do!' Bazzer insists as he responds to DeJon's high five.

'Hmm, I thought students were here to study,' Sammy states quietly as she munches on her sandwich.

'If I were the next Einstein like you Sammy, I'd agree with you, but seeing as though I'm not; I'm in with the boys,' Romeo responds as he flashes her a gleaming smile accompanied with a wink.

'Hey, Liyana, you can come as bridezilla,' Bazzer announces which creates a raw of laughter.

I can feel myself burning from embarrassment, and to make it worse, I can feel Shayth's eyes on me.

I offer the group a sheepish smile in an attempt to avoid feeling even more awkward.

Shayth puts his shoulder against mine. Suddenly, I feel his warm hand on my thigh under the table. I am caught off guard from his gesture; my natural instinct forces my knees to jump, hitting the table with a loud thud!

'Oh, I'm sorry,' I offer as everyone leans back with surprise.

I give a coy smile as I rack my brains as to how I am going to cover this up.

'I've had a great idea! Bridezilla is just so cliché, I think I can do one better,' I affirm as I pick up my bags and lean over the table as I face the group.

'I'll be coming as Lizzie Borden!'

I offer a sarcastic smile as I walk off with confidence.

I hear Sammy giggle while the boys ask each other, 'Who's Lizzy Borden?'

I knew Sammy would get the joke. 'So you're in?' shouts Tucker.

'I'm In!' I respond as I raise my hand whilst walking away.

I feel the nerves easing as I walk away, I have no idea where I am walking too!

As I head out to the courtyard, I notice Trixy talking to a group of girls dressed in gothic attire. They are looking intensely at something in Trixy's hand.

Desperate to go unnoticed, I pick up my pace to avoid any altercation with her.

'Liyana,' I hear Shayth call out from behind me.

My body begins to tense; I focus my mind on staying strong, staying in control.

'Hey.'

'Hi,' I respond as he reaches my side.

'I am sorry, I did not mean to make you uncomfortable,' he offers in a sincere tone.

'No, it's okay, just caught me off guard that's all.' I stop in our tracks, turning to look at him.

As nervous as I am, I focus hard on maintaining strength in my knees.

'I need answers, Shayth,' I whisper as I look up to him.

He stares at me with an understanding expression, offering me his heart-melting smile.

'Is that what it was, your ethereal body?' I ask in a quiet tone.

'What do you think of that concept?' he responds playfully while tilting his head to the side.

'I, I don't know,' I stutter as I turn and begin to walk.

'I've never come across this notion before. To hear about it in the lecture to think that I know someone who has done this, with ME... I don't know; it's all a little surreal.

'But No, it's crazy. I can't believe it.

'Wait...at what point were you in my room last night?'

The look of horror takes over my expression, as I recall myself constantly dressing and undressing from not knowing what to wear.

'What does this matter if you do not believe?' he replies with a wicked smile.

I'm silenced, not knowing how to respond. I can't understand how he would know about the headband without having been there.

'Did you, did you see me, as in, my wardrobe malfunctioning episode?'

I dare not look at him; I can feel myself become nervous as my stomach begins to carry out summersaults.

'My favourite is the long, blue dress,' he whispers as he tilts his head closer towards me.

I pause in my tracks as I stare at him, my eyes widen as my jaw drops to take a deep breath.

'Be careful,' he whispers while grinning profusely.

'Your aura is spiking! If you continue in this manner, your head-rush will intensify; you will pass out.'

He puts both his arms around my waist, offering some support to my quivering limbs.

I stare into his eyes, gasping as I see the flashes of white within his deep grey eyes, it's magical; it's out of this world.

An electrifying sensation runs through my body as the tips of Shayth's fingers rub against the skin of my waist.

My vision becomes blurred as my body goes limp. 'It's too late,' I manage to whisper.

I hear the melody of birds singing above me.

My body feels as light as a feather, as if I am floating through the air.

I open my eyes slowly. I see the tops of a tree with birds fluttering amongst the leaves.

I lean forward on my elbows; I'm lying at the end of the university field.

Shayth appears from behind the tree. In his hand, he holds a few drinks, chocolate bars and cakes.

'What happened,' I manage to blurt out as I begin to sit up straight.

'Your body went into overdrive, and I am pretty sure you have had no lunch so are lacking sustenance.

'Please, have a drink. You need to increase your energy.' Shayth insists as he sits beside me, handing me a drink and chocolate bars.

I sip on the drink as I try to recall my last memories. I look over at Shayth, and surprisingly I'm not nervous in the slightest. The shock of passing out has made me feel somewhat blank to emotion, perhaps as a result of still feeling disorientated.

'How did you do that?' I ask directly as I turn to look at him sitting beside me.

It's strange; he almost comes across as a little nervous. 'Your eyes, you looked at me! I saw them.'

He scoffs at my adamant tone.

'You can stare at them now,' he offers in a flirtatious tone as he leans towards me and smiles.

His gesture throws me off track; I cannot help but scoff.

I turn away to take another sip of my drink and focus on making the most of my disorientation.

'I saw them, they sparkled! And you keep talking about aura. Who talks about aura! Who can see aura? And then...' I gasp in shock as I recall what happened.

I stare to look at him and watch him sit up straight in panic. 'You touched me!'

'I...err, I am sorry. I did not mean any offense. I, I wanted to hold you, so you would not fall.'

I look back and forth as he sits there panicking.

'No, No. That's not what I meant,' I respond while shaking my head.

I look to the ground, placing my hand on my forehead before combing my fingers against my scalp.

'Something happened when you touched me.' I look straight at him with a confronting expression.

'Like something went through me...'

I realise what I have actually said. I pause in shock.

'I sound ridiculous,' I mutter as I shake my head in confusion. 'Am I weird,' I ask as I look up at him feeling confused.

'Far from it,' he whisper's, as he looks sincere. 'You are pure.'

His response makes me feel even more confused.

'What does that even mean? Why would you say that? People don't talk like that.'

I start talking out aloud, as if all the filters have somehow been removed.

'Something's happening, and I don't know what. I know you; I know, I know you! I've just never known anyone like you. And I don't know why I know you. I just know…that I do… know you…'

I put my face in the palms of my hands. 'I think I've gone mad,' I whisper in a sulk.

'I'm not mad!' I shout as I raise my head, becoming fuelled with a dose of self-confidence.

'You're mad! You think you can project your ethereal body which is crazy!'

Shayth chuckles at my random behaviour as he stares at my lost expression.

'Okay. You are right. I am crazy! But…

If you do not believe that I have the ability to project my ethereal body, then this would mean you were talking to yourself in the mirror!

Surely that would make you, a little crazier than I?'

He looks at me intensely while still holding a glimmer of a smile.

He places something in my hand. I look down to see the pink headband.

'You're right,' I whisper.

'I've gone crazy; I'm mad,' I insist, as I begin to pity myself.

'How about, we both, be crazy…together?' he whispers as he pulls my hand closer towards him.

'You do not have to feel alone,' he insists sincerely, 'I am here now.'

I pause for a moment, almost instantly, I decide.

'If we are both crazy, I need to know what I am getting into. I need to know everything!'

'…For it was not into my ear you whispered, but into my heart
It was not my lips you kissed, but my soul…'

– Judy Garland

19. Heaven on Earth

As the day finally ends, we all head out from our class as we leave the building.

I see Romeo stood with Tucker, Bazzer and DeJon. Romeo, with his back to Shayth, extends his arms, wrapping them around his back while wiggling his whole body, providing a comical impression of a couple making out.

I wish I wasn't so prudish, but the sight of Romeo with everyone laughing around him makes me cringe inside, I dare not look up at Shayth besides me who is no doubt finding this amusing.

'How is the assignment on dark matter,' I ask Sammy desperately trying to distract my thoughts, so I don't look obviously uncomfortable.

'It's almost complete, I just need to document my conclusion on a feasible suggestion on what dark matter may be.

'Vibrations,' suggests Shayth.

'How about, vibrations of alternate frequencies? Maybe you can suggest in your conclusion that it's part of the universe that inhabits ethereal body's alternate entities?'

Shayth nudges my shoulder; I cannot help but smile. 'Ethereal bodies? I've never heard of this,' Sammy responds.

'That's quite a cool theory,' I add feeling impressed with Shayth's witty thinking.

Nevaeh expands on the theory of astral projection to Sammy who begins writing notes as we walk to exit the site.

As we all say goodbye, Shayth walks me to the car park.

Shayth looks agitated as we approach my car.

As I stand at the driver's side door, I ask politely,

'I never see your car here, would you like me to give you a ride home?'

He paces around as he rubs the back of his neck before surprisingly blurting out, 'No! But perhaps I could take you out tonight?'

'Oh,' I respond feeling caught off guard. The look of shock takes over my expression; instantly my heartbeat raises its rhythm. 'Not for long if you are busy, I can pick you up after dinner? If you would like?'

He subtly bites his lip while puckering. He frowns as he looks down at the ground anticipating my response.

I cannot help but smile as I watch him feeling overwhelmed which makes a change. His reaction lifts a sense of confidence in me.

'Yes, I would like that,' I respond softly.

Shayth looks up at me in delight, his smile extends to a soft laughter.

I lower the windows as I slowly reverse the car. He walks over, leaning into the window. 'Maybe you could wear the blue dress,' he asks with a wicked smile.

'I'll see you at 20.30?' I stutter as I feel myself begin to blush.

'It cannot come soon enough,' he whispers before standing straight and walking back with his hands cradling the back of his head.

School night, Micky will be in bed by 19.30. That gives me an hour to get ready after I have tucked him in.

I get out from the shower and head downstairs. Micky is in the garden playing with Diesel.

'Uncle Aidan, Aunt Liz, I was hoping to go out tonight if that's okay. I won't be back late, just be gone a few hours.'

'Sure, kiddo you don't need to ask, go and enjoy,' Uncle Aidan confirms with reassurance.

'Oh, anything to do with Shayth?' Aunt Liz pries Uncle Aidan lifts his head and becomes alert.

'I take that back, don't enjoy,' he adds as he walks over towards me.

'Right, so, Shayth,' he states.

'We are just going to catch up on some work maybe,' I add feeling uncomfortable as I have no idea what we are actually doing.

'Okay, well just make sure you call me if you want me to pick you up or anything.'

'Honestly, Uncle, please, don't worry. He is a genuinely nice person.'

'You're a smart girl, Liyana, you always have been. Make sure you don't change. For anyone! Including Shayth!'

I tuck Micky into bed, kissing him goodnight before heading into my room.

I could barely eat dinner from the excitement of going out with Shayth tonight.

I apply my makeup, having decided to go for a soft smoky-eyed look with light pink lipstick. I put lose curls in my hair for a soft, natural look.

I pull out the blue dress from the wardrobe; it quite unusual, which is what attracted me to buy it in the first place.

The multiple chiffon panels of various shades of blue almost touch the ground.

The strappy shoulders with the balcony cut expose my tanned shoulders.

I stand on the balcony to cool myself from the hot flush running through me. The swift wind makes each of the panels of my dress float above my knees. The night has set; I take a moment and stare at the stars desperate to twinkle in the darkening night.

'Wow. That's a sophisticated dress for someone who's catching up on some work.'

Aunt Liz catches me off guard as she walks up behind me in the downstairs corridor.

Uncle Aidan peers his head from his seat before walking towards us with a genuine smile on his face.

'You look beautiful. And long dresses, I can handle! It's the short ones I don't like!'

'Oh, err, thanks,' I respond feeling a little shy.

'I know what these young, hot-blooded students are like! Have fun kiddo, but remember, not too much fun!'

'Please don't worry, and thank you,' I reply while offering a sheepish smile.

As I close the door behind me, I see Shayth standing beside his car, his back towards me. He turns to face me at the sound of the front door closing. He stands tall and strong watching me walk down the path towards him.

Shayth is wearing a similar style smart-hooded blazer, which hangs midway to his thighs. Glowing white with fine blue stitch-work, accompanied by subtle studs.

Complemented with similar white smart trousers, yet the material seems incredibly soft and comfortable.

He holds one hand behind his back, the other against his stomach.

His smile grows wider with each step I take towards him.

I focus on my footsteps trying hard not to let my knees tremble from the rush of excitement running through me.

As I approach closer, I hear him clear his throat, which makes it difficult to hold back the smile on my face.

'Hi,' I offer as I stand in front of him looking him in the eyes.

'My lady,' he barely manages to whisper as he takes a deep breath.

He appears even more nervous than I, which puts me slightly at ease.

'These are for you,' he whispers as he brings out his hand from behind him. To my surprise he is holding a bouquet of my beautiful, white mysterious flowers, the flowers that carry the scent of heaven.

I gasp in surprise as my eyes light up from the number of flowers within the bouquet.

'You look mesmerising,' he whispers as he watches me inhale the flowers.

'Allow me,' he offers as he lifts the car door.

We sit in his car as he drives with a smile that seems to be ever growing.

I lean my head back as I stare at him; he puckers his lips, to hide his smile, no doubt.

The music playing in the car is a soft melody of instruments I cannot quite recognise, yet beautiful to the ear.

My heart flutters inside as I feel, what can only be described as...alive! A thrill of excitement runs through my veins as I realise this is only just the beginning of what could be.

As my nervous breathing begins to deepen, the sweet fragrance I have become so familiar with of my mystical flowers surrounds me, putting me at ease.

I glance at Shayth trying to understand my feelings. How can I feel so connected to someone I have recently met? It feels as if I have always known him. Is this what people mean when they say – when you find the "one" you just know? He has come into my life, yet something in my heart tells me he can never and will never leave my life. Is he the one?

I am a closed book, constantly refusing to share information about my life, my thoughts, my feelings. Yet I feel as if he knows me perhaps better than I know myself?

I don't have to try with Shayth, I can just be me, without the worry of what he will think or say. Is this love?

How would you know what love is if you have never been in love?

As I continuously glance over towards him, I feel nothing but warmth and serenity. Whatever this is, I never want it to end.

We have been silent throughout the car journey, but it's not been uncomfortable or awkward. We have perhaps both just cherished the moment.

The darkness of night has crept in fast with little visibility through the windows.

Curious as to where we are going, I lean forward and focus in on the path ahead. 'We are almost there,' he whispers in a gentle tone.

I sit back into my seat, I notice that the surface of the road changes from a smooth drive to somewhat uneven.

A sudden streak of fear runs through me, a phobia of driving on an uneven surface perhaps.

As I begin to feel agitated, I feel the warmth of Shayth's hand on mine.

'Do not worry. You are safe. I will always keep you safe,' he whispers as he gives my hand a gentle squeeze.

Comforted by his protection, my anxiety eases as he slowly brings the car to a stop.

He lifts open the passenger door and offers me his hand as I delicately exit the vehicle.

'Where are we,' I ask as I look around to find trees surrounding us.

I should be nervous; I should be afraid. There is no sign of any home, no visibility of any light. I am in the middle of a forest, yet I feel completely at ease with his presence alone.

'I want to share something special with you,' he whispers as he takes my hand and guides me through the trees.

I follow Shayth's lead along a narrow footpath with minimal visibility around us.

As we walk deeper into the forests, the stars seem to shine brighter.

I see a spotlight ahead, which we seem to be heading towards. As I focus on the ground to mind each step, we come to a sudden stop. Shayth steps aside from my view; I look up, I am mesmerised by the sight.

I gasp at the unbelievable view that surrounds me.

I cannot help but cover my lips with my hands as I take a few steps further.

I part my hands as I place each palm against my cheeks.

'Is this real?' I whisper as I feel lost in a mystical dream.

'I wanted to share with you a part of my world,' Shayth whispers as he stands beside me watching me fall in love with the world.

I stare into the waters, which are calm and motionless.

The reflection of the moon in the clear sky creates an illusion of a spotlight within the waters.

A garland of trees frames the perfectly round lake, As I look around me, I feel as if I am in a parallel world. Above me is the same sight as beneath me.

The calm waters reflect every faint cloud, mimicking each twinkle of the hundreds of the stars above. This truly is heaven on earth.

'Do you trust me,' Shayth asks softly.

I cannot help but smile as I look across to him. Shayth takes both my hands as he asks me again, 'Do you trust me?'

'More than myself,' I whisper. I have let go of all my guards. I just want to feel free, if only for tonight. I don't want my defensive personality to protect me from Shayth. I want to live free in this moment without a care of what may come next.

We both stare for a moment as our smiles widen.

He bends down as he places an arm under my knees before sweeping me off my feet.

I wrap my arms around his shoulders in shock from the unexpected gesture.

He walks closer to the lake. A small streak of panic begins to flow through me.

'Shayth, I can't,' I whisper nervously.

'Trust in me,' he interrupts in a soft tone as he continues to walk towards the lake.

Not knowing what to expect, I fill with anxiety. I think of nothing else but to trust him as I wrap my arms around him tight, burying my head in his neck.

He seems to have stopped walking, but it feels as if we are still in motion, ever so slightly.

A moment later, he slowly lowers my feet to the ground while I maintain my grip on him.

I am surprised by the hard surface my feet are placed upon.

I slowly loosen my grasp around Shayth, as I feel somewhat foolish for thinking he was walking into the lake.

As I am stood firmly on my feet, I release my grip and lower my hands from his shoulders.

I look up into his eyes as I slowly lower my hands to my sides. He has the most beautiful smile on his face with a look of excitement.

'You trust me?' he asks again softly.

'Yes,' I whisper breaking a smile as I nod my head.

'Turn around,' he whispers.

I turn around and gasp in Shock!

I begin to step back, suddenly feeling his hands around my waist as I step into him. I grasp onto his hands and squeeze them tight.

'It's okay,' he whispers with his lips against my ear. 'I am here with you.'

I cannot control but to breathe out aloud. I look down to the ground and am stunned at what Shayth has done.

We are floating upon a thick glass panel through the lake amongst the night sky.

I have never before, experienced anything so captivating. I find the courage to walk further along the glass.

As I walk away from Shayth, I cannot help but extend my arms to maintain my balance, despite the floating panel being large enough to hold 20 people.

I struggle to hold my emotions and begin to laugh from excitement as I walk further along the panel.

It feels like I am walking into the night, into the sky. I feel like I am surrounded by stars, as each gem twinkles within the night sky and within the reflection of the lake.

The breeze of the wind picks up slowly as my hair and panelled dress flows through the air.

I cannot help but to twirl in the excitement from the magical sensation flowing through my body.

The sensation of freedom, the excitement of living in a dream I could never imagine. A dream I never knew existed.

Shayth takes my hand and raises it above my head as he encourages me to continue twirling.

He pulls me closer towards him as my hands fall on his shoulders. He places his hands around my waist.

I cannot help but smile as I find him looking at me intensely. 'Welcome to my world,' he whispers while offering me a gentle smile.

'This is magical. This is a dream,' I whisper as I begin to feel my heartbeat rise.

'You are always in my dreams,' he whispers as he continues to look into me.

I lower my gaze, looking to the glass panel from nervousness as to what may happen next.

Shayth cups my chin with his fingers as he gently tilts my head higher, which forces me to look at him.

I attempt to glance at his eyes but find I cannot look away. The streaks of white within his iris become prominent; his eyes begin to sparkle in the night. I gasp at the sight of his flashing eyes glittering with the stars.

His intense gaze and sparkling eyes have me captivated. As he gently holds my chin, he lowers his gaze.

He looks at my lips and glances back into my eyes.

As he tilts his head closer towards me, I cannot help but to wrap my arms further around him, bringing him closer towards me.

He moves in closer as he lowers his gaze. I join him as I stare at our lips.

I close my eyes in anticipation; I feel a gentle brush of his soft lips against mine.

For a moment I feel my body go numb as I no longer feel his lips but feel hypnotised in some trance from an electric pulse running through me.

The brush of his soft lips comes again, but this time more pronounced.

As he pulls away, I keep my eyes closed and find myself wrapping my hand around his neck, slowly pulling him closer towards me.

He pulls me in by the waist, gripping me tighter while his lips lock onto mine. We share a passionate kiss while floating throughout the night.

Our moulding lips linger against each other avidly as we try hard to pull apart but struggle to stop the caressing of our lips against each other.

We slowly pull away; I lower my head down. 'Do not open your eyes,' he whispers, 'not just yet.'

My eyes remain closed as I focus on my breathing; it feels lighter than usual.

'Your aura is spiking; your head rush will pass in a few moments,' he whispers while brushing his hand through my hair.

'Can you feel that?' I whisper softly.

I stoke my fingers along my neck to the tip of my chest.

'I can feel it,' I whisper as I am hypnotised by the tingling sensation within my body; it vibrates through all my senses.

I lean my head on his shoulder before we gently sway in a soft dance.

'I have never felt freedom like this before,' I whisper as I wrap my hands further around him.

'I will give you the world,' he responds in a soft, gentle tone.

As I raise my eyes to look at Shayth, I find him staring intensely towards me.

He takes my hand before taking a few steps back. He gently pulls my hand, which adjusts my posture.

Shayth extends his free arm and offers me a wicked smile. I understand his gesture.

I spin into his arms, and we both laugh out loud while we begin to dance away under the night sky, yet above the reflection of the night sky.

We steel soft, gentle kisses throughout our dance.

As our heart rate begins to rise, the tempo of our dancing increases along with the intensity of our kisses.

We hold hands, as we stand apart. Shayth pulls me forward, immediately releasing my hand. I spin into his arms as he instantly raises my thigh and leans forward.

My hands are almost touching the glass panel as I find myself breathing heavily.

For a moment I am lost from the reality of what is up and down, what is high and low, for it feels as if I am floating within the night skies of a parallel world.

The wind blows softly through my hair as the blood rushes to my head.

Shayth lifts me forward slowly. The tip of his nose glides up my neck as I reach close to him.

As my eyes finally reach his, he offers me a gleaming smile while the light within his eyes glow. He shares soft and gentle kiss when suddenly, he becomes distracted.

We have reached the end of the lake; Shayth focuses his attention on the trees.

His soft loving expression turns to one of intense curiosity.

I turn to look in the direction he is glaring. I cannot see anything beyond the thickness of the trees.

'It is okay. Do not be afraid. He is a friend,' he clarifies in a protective tone.

I stare at him somewhat confused and turn back in the direction he stares; a figure walks out from within the trees.

A young man, wearing similar clothes to Shayth appears from the darkness; the off-white sleeveless fitted jacket hangs above his knees with similar toned soft trousers.

'Shayth,' the young man shouts.

'We need to go! Argyle is asking after you; he suspects something!'

'…You know someone is very special to you when days just don't seem right without them…'

– John Cena

20. Absence Makes the Heart Grow

I glance at the empty seat beside me.

Despite trying hard to concentrate on the lecture, I cannot help but scan the hall to see if he may be here.

We sit in the cafeteria for lunch.

'It's an amazing concept. The theory of dark matter combined with ethereal bodies and alternate frequencies of various vibrations within the atmosphere will surely get me the points I need,' Sammy briefs in excitement.

Sammy and Nevaeh talk about the course content while I am distracted, desperately searching for Shayth.

'Earth to Liyana,' I hear in the background.

'Sorry, what?'

Sammy and Nevaeh's expression startles me, it seems they may have been calling me for some time.

'Where you at girl?' Nevaeh asks with curiosity.

'Liyana's looking out for him,' Sammy responds with a cheeky smile.

'Ooh! Of course, the abnormally handsome Shayth with his strange sexy accent and questionable taste of hair accessories!' Nevaeh adds as she has a quick glance around the room.

'So you still adamant that you two are just friends?' Nevaeh questions with a friendly yet sarcastic tone.

'Ladies,' Romeo announces as he joins us at the table with DeJon and Tucker.

'Where's Bazzer?' asks Nevaeh.

'He's practicing in the stadium. That guy is like a machine!' responds DeJon as he tucks into his lunch.

Perhaps Shayth is with Bazzer, I wonder, but why then would he not have been in our class?

I look down as I ponder the possibility of Shayth being at the stadium.

'So what have you done with him?' asks DeJon in a flippant tone.

'She's butchered his ass, Lizzie Froden style!' Romeo adds with a cheeky tone.

'It's Broden you fool,' DeJon teases in a superior manner.

'Borden…you fool,' Sammy confirms in a polite tone, to which we all break out into a laughter.

'He's probably with Bazzer practicing,' I add trying to come across as blasé.

'Nah he's not been with us at all,' confirms Tucker.

'Then maybe he's at the back of the trunk, Lizzie Borden style,' I add with a mocking expression.

'You mean the back seat of your car?' Romeo responds while smooching aloud and rolling his shoulders.

'No back seats in Liyana's car Romeo,' Sammy corrects.

'Damn girl! Why do you always have to be so smart!' Romeo shouts as we all smile and laugh away.

They all talk about next week's party and the crazy outfits they plan to wear. I half-heartedly join the conversation, when at the back of my mind I cannot help but wonder where is he?

'The electricians been round,' Uncle Aidan confirms as we are sat around the dinner table.

'A few loose wires in the circuit board, nothing else. That should have sorted the flickering now,' he adds reassuringly.

'That's great, thanks, Uncle,' I respond with an appreciative tone.

'So how was your date,' Aunt Liz asks abruptly.

'It was nice, thanks,' I reply not knowing what more to say.

'So will we get to meet this young man anytime soon,' she continues to pry.

'I…err…' I hesitate, unsure how to answer the question.

'Leave the young girl alone,' Uncle Aidan responds in my defence.

'What's a date,' Micky asks with curiosity.

'It's something you will find out about in another ten years, Micky!' Uncle Aidan states.

As I tuck Micky into bed, he suddenly asks me, 'Liyana what's a date?'

I hesitate not knowing how to answer the question.

'It's when you make a special friend, and you like them a lot, sooo, you spend time with them to get to know them more.'

'Oh,' he respond's while he looks deep in thought.

'Diesel's my best friend, can I take him on a date?' I cannot help but laugh, so innocent and adorable.

'Noo, Micky,' I respond as I giggle.

'When you are big, I'll explain better okay, but right now, my little warrior, you need some sleep.'

I kiss him goodnight before leaving his room.

I lay in bed as I wonder where Shayth has been.

I hold onto the teddy he had won for me as I lie on my back and look towards the balcony, watching the full moon appear from behind the clouds.

I cannot help but smile as I reminisce about my magical night dancing amongst the stars.

While deep in thought, I am distracted by the flickering of the light within the lamp.

In frustration, I switch the lamp off, my room now lit from the moonlight shining down through the glass balcony doors.

A strange sensation fills the room. I feel as if Shayth may be thinking of me, maybe calling for me. After what feels like hours of daydreaming of my magical night, I pull the bed sheets towards me.

I burrow into my sheets as I continue to dream about my mysterious Shayth. The memories send light impulses through my body, which maintain the smile on my face as I sleep.

I become half-conscious from a deep sleep when I feel a sudden chill across my body. As I pull the bed sheets further around my body, I begin to struggle.

I pull slightly harder, yet the sheet seems caught.

In a semi-conscious state, I tug at the sheet to wrap it around me.

My eyes suddenly open at the sound of a thud! Diesel? I sit up and turn to the side but notice nothing unusual.

My heartbeat paces in fear as I rush to switch on the lampshade. The room illuminates but reveals nothing out of place.

I switch the light off and lay back down, I try not to think too much of it, but the truth is, sometimes, this house gives me the creeps!

Time has never passed so slow! I return home from university feeling deflated, not seeing Shayth today makes me feel empty. I spend the evening helping Micky with his reading before retiring to bed.

I stand on the balcony watching the stars, reminiscing the feeling of floating within them.

I frown as I worry about the sudden disappearance of Shayth. I hope he is okay.

A chilling breeze flows through the air, which forces my hair to sweep my face.

As I tuck my hair behind my ear, I cup my face with the palm of my hand. Yearning to hear from him, I slowly whisper the words, 'where are you?'

'Right here,' I hear the faint whisper respond.

I stand up straight and widen my eyes as the wind continues to blow.

Did I really hear that? Or was it just the whistling of the wind playing tricks on my wishful mind.

I shake my head, deciding to head back into my room.

I suddenly pause in my tracks from the light tapping sound coming from behind me.

I turn to look at the balcony and notice a couple of stones rolling on the surface.

Another stone appears from nowhere. 'Liyana,' I hear a whisper.

My heart beats faster as a sudden flash of excitement takes over my emotions.

I gasp as I see my Shayth stood at the bottom of the garden. He stares up at me with a gleaming smile.

I watch him grip the top of his hair with his fingers while biting his bottom lip.

He looks delighted to see me, which fills my heart with love and excitement!

He holds out a single flower; my flower, as he bends down on one knee and opens up his arms.

I cover my mouth with both my hands at his adorable gesture. 'I am here,' he whispers.

The shock of seeing Shayth dries up my throat leaving me unable to respond.

He takes a few steps back and leaps onto the side of the house, climbing up the ivy wall screens.

'Careful,' I whisper in fear that he may fall.

Reaching the top of the balcony, he jumps over, now standing in front of me, tall and strong.

I stare up at him with confusion across my face. How did he just do that?

'Hi,' he whispers as he hands me the single flower.

'Hi,' I manage to whisper as I desperately try to control my nerves.

I slowly reach out my hand and hold the flower, which is still in his grip. Shayth instantly grabs my hand, forcefully pulling me towards him.

I fall into his arms; he holds me tight as he begins to gently rub his face against the side of my hair.

His arms are wrapped around me; I cannot help but squeeze him tight!

I have missed his scent. I have missed his warmth.

We sway for a few moments in the silent night as it feels that we have been apart forever.

'Where have you been?' I whisper in a lonely tone.

'I am sorry, I have missed you more,' he responds as he kisses the top of my head.

There's a knock on the door!

'Hide!' I whisper as I pace into the room drawing the net curtains behind me.

I rush towards the door when Uncle Aidan pops his head through.

'Hey, kiddo. I didn't wake you did I?'

'No, no, not at all! I've just come out the bathroom,' I insist. I sit at the end of my bed, forcing a full yawn.

'Just wanted to make sure everything's okay, you were very quiet at dinner.'

'Yeah I'm fine, Uncle, I was thinking about my assignment grades I'm waiting to receive that's all.'

'Oh okay. Shayth.' My heartbeat thumps as I turn behind me! Shayth is not in sight.

'Everything's okay with you and Shayth, yeah?'

'Yeah of course, Uncle, he's a good friend, he's a nice guy.'

The look of concern remains on his face, which makes me feel helpless.

'Uncle, please don't worry, I will let you know tomorrow what grade I receive for my assignment. I want to make you proud.'

'You already do, kiddo.'

He gives me a warm smile, he seems slightly more relaxed. 'Goodnight, kiddo,' he says as he closes the door behind him.

The doors firmly closed, I turn behind me to see Shayth step into the room from behind the net curtains.

I sit further on the bed and wrap my arms around my shins. He joins me as he sits at the end of the bed.

'Where have you been?' I ask in a soft tone as I look down to my lap.

'I am sorry,' he offers as he shuffles closer towards me.

'I have had a few family predicaments that required my attention.'

'Wow,' he states in a shocked tone.

I raise my eyes to look at him. His grin widens as he continues to whisper,

'I had no idea you would miss me this much!'

'I didn't,' I respond in a soft yet defensive tone. A frown grows across my expression; I can feel myself putting my guards up, not wanting him to know how I feel.

He laughs softly as he approaches closer towards me, taking my hand in his.

He softly kisses the surface of my hand.

'I have missed you more,' he whispers as a look of sincerity fills his expression.

'Was everything okay? With Argyle?' I question from recalling the last moments we were together.

His smile widens.

'You know Argyle do you?' he jests. 'Everything is fine; I just need a day or two to settle the situation,' he continues.

'So you won't be coming to university tomorrow,' I ask unintentionally sounding disappointed.

He kisses my hand again as he confirms, 'I shall try.'

'That's better,' he whispers as he looks at me and smiles.

'Your heartbeat has calmed now; your aura is in a comfortable state.'

A look of confusion grows on my face.

'You see auras?' I question with an intrigued yet somewhat doubtful tone.

'You find me strange?' he questions confidently.

'Yes! Very, very strange!' I cannot help but smile.

'But…you like strange?' he questions as a frown grows on his face.

'Not particularly,' I respond as I tilt my head and look to the side.

He tugs on my hand, which jolts my position; I cannot help but giggle.

I bite my lower lip in an attempt to control my smile.

'Tell me about my aura, what is it that you see?' I question with genuine curiosity.

'It's rare,' he confirms as he slightly squints his eyes and grins profusely while shaking his head.

'I have never really seen it this way on a human. Not to this extent. Not this intense.

''It's a glow of white with hints of pale blue swirling around.'

'So what does this tell you?' I ask wanting to know more.

He looks down and smiles.

He shuffles closer as he releases his hand from mine.

He places his hand a few inches away from my face and waves his hand in motion as if he is touching an invisible shield surrounding me.

The strong, vibrant white represents purity and truth. This is how I recognise you're innocence; you're chaste.

And the pale blue associates your current emotion of caring, loving and sensitivity.

Occasionally comes in a twinkle of yellow, showing me your optimism and playfulness.'

'So you can sense my emotions?' I ask softly.

'Yes. When I am close to you, you do not have to be in my sight for me to sense your emotions. The vibrations of your aura flow towards me where I can sense how you are feeling.'

The thought that Shayth knows how I feel perhaps better than I do, makes me feel nervous.

'Here we go,' he whispers with excitement as he chuckles and takes my hand back into his.

'What colour?' I frown.

'Flashes of oranges and bright reds! No more yellow or blue.' I take both my hands and cover my face wanting to hide.

'How is this possible,' I questions as my tone suggests I am having a mild sulk.

'Come here,' he whispers as he takes both my hands into his.

'There is more to this world than humans realise.

Continually being taught to think logically and be rational which forces you to ignore your senses. Your senses, your instincts, they are a gift. A gift which will tell you more than using your mind alone.

Your minds are powerful, and your senses exist to support the extraordinary capabilities of your mind. Yet you have been taught to allow logic to take precedence over all.

That's better,' he chuckles.

'The flashes of red have disappeared, you must feel more in control now.'

I offer him a smile, but my mind is intrigued by his constant distance and referral to humans in the third person.

'Why do you do that?' I ask with a slight frown.

'Do what?'

'Your constant referral to humans?

Choosing any species in the world, I come out with phoenix, your response is human.

And just now; you referred to humans in the third person, as if you're not one?'

'What does it take to be human?' Shayth asks as he looks eager to hear my response.

'A heart? A mind? A soul? Someone's intentions?' he rolls off his tongue.

'Yes, all of the above,' I confirm as I nod in agreement.

'These are all things that I possess. Let's just say I am more spiritual than the average human.'

'That explains your approach with auras,' I affirm.

'Exactly,' he agrees.

We share a moment in silence as we stare at each other with an innocent smile.

'I need to know more, what made you more spiritual?' I ask trying to understand him.

'It is the way of my people. We see things as energy and vibrations.'

'Your people,' I repeat in confusion.

'Yes, within my community shall we say.'

'Like a cult,' I question with a hint of apprehension.

'No! Not in the way you are thinking. We have specific beliefs, a particular way of life, just like you do. We are merely taught to follow our senses and trust our instincts.

'We are more mindful of our surroundings and are tuned with the frequency of various vibrations we are surrounded in. Like your aura for example.'

'How did you know where I live Shayth?'

'I...err...'

Shayth hesitates, as he seems unsure how to answer the question.

'I have passed you before, and I could not help but notice you.'

'Oh. I had no idea,' I respond.

It feels unbelievable to think that someone like Shayth would notice someone like me, more to the point, how could I have not noticed him!

'It must have been dark,' I state. 'Your car stands out, so I am surprised I didn't see you.'

'Yes, it was. And this area is quite secluded so seeing people around does stand out,' he affirms.

'So you live close by to here?' I ask.

'Not quite, I was just passing through.'

' Where do you live?'

He scoffs.

'Beyond the forests. You are very keen to understand me are you not?' he questions with a smile.

'Yes, yes I am.

'Is that how you know of the lake? You live close by to there?' I question desperately wanting to know more.

'Yes. It's a huge forest, but I know where the safe areas are,' he elaborates.

'So that's not a public lake then?' I question, wanting to understand how well he knows the forest.

'It would not appear so natural and untouched if the general public were aware of its existence.

'But it is for the best; the forest is dangerous if you do not know where you are going,' he affirms.

'Yes, I've heard,' I whisper as I recall my past experiences.

'You must promise me you will never venture into the forests, Liyana. It is not a safe place for you.'

A sudden look of fear takes over his expression.

'Let me ease you into my world, into my reality. I am afraid that it will become too much for you to be able to accept...' he pauses for a moment before confessing.

'I am afraid, afraid I will terrify you.'

A look of sadness overtakes his expression, which he quickly seems to dismiss before continuing to state,

'In the meantime, I want you to understand me for who I am.'

'That is all I am interested in, who you are,' I respond with a supportive smile which seems to relieve his tension.

'Will you close your eyes,' he requests of me.

Without hesitating I close my eyes whilst feeling at ease. 'Now just think about how you feel. Clear your mind of everything and try to feel your emotions, your energy.'

'Ok,' I whisper as a sense of tranquillity fills me.

'How do you feel when I am with you,' he asks.

'Comforted,' I respond with a genuine smile.

'How do you feel when I leave you?'

'Incomplete.'

He kisses my hand on my response. 'What would life be like with me?'

'Euphoria,' I whisper with a wide smile.

'What would life be like without me?'

'Lonely.'

'Are you afraid of me?'

'No.'

'Do you ever think you will ever become afraid of me?'

'Never!'

I open my eyes whilst a frown grows on my face from the odd question,

'Would you want me to be afraid of you?' I ask in confusion.

'It would shatter my world if that day was to come.'

He approaches me as he holds me in his arms and we share a warm, intimate embrace.

We talk all night, yet the time passes as if it is only a few brief moments.

'I must leave you now,' he whispers as he stands to his feet. I climb out of bed, following him to the balcony.

'Will I see you tomorrow?' I ask as he climbs over the edge of the balcony.

'I am unsure; I will try,' he responds as he looks slightly disappointed.

I cannot help but look down whilst the natural smile disappears from my face.

I crouch down between the pillars of the balcony rails in an attempt to be closer to him.

Shayth takes a moment to look at me before slowly whispering, 'How can I keep away?'

In that moment, he pulls up and presses his lips against mine catching me off guard.

As our lips part, he gently rubs the side of my face before climbing down and jumping to the ground.

As I watch Shayth run off towards the trees, my heart saddens.

'Goodnight my sweet prince.'

'…Do not be misled, bad company corrupts good character…'

— 1 Corinthians 15:33

21. Forked Tongues

I eagerly await Shayth's presence as I sit in our seminar studying mind and behaviour.

We explore the nature versus nurture debate whereby we consider the extent to which particular aspects of behaviour are inherited or acquired.

I cannot help but consider the views of Shayth and our lack of appreciation of intuition over logical rationale.

I ponder over whether this is a result of nature or nurture. Either way, I would welcome the opportunity to explore a spiritual awakening, which seems to be fundamental to Shayth's way of life.

'I'll catch up with you in a bit, just need to check a few books in at the library,' I confirm to Nevaeh and Sammy as we part our paths.

'Okay, see you in the cafeteria,' Nevaeh confirms as they walk away.

I return a couple of books to the library and take a browse within the spirituality section at the far back of the hall.

I glide my fingers across the row of books containing insight on aura and extra sensory perceptions.

'Beyond your body – beginners guide to the aura.'

In hope for further insight into the hidden meanings behind auras, I remove this book from the shelf. I cannot control my smile as I find a pair of grey eyes staring at me from the adjacent aisle.

His dazzling smile melts my heart as I feel a sudden rush of excitement awakens my senses.

Trying hard to contain my smile, I casually walk along the aisle to the far end of the library.

I feel Shayth staring at me as he follows alongside.

The rhythm of my heartbeat rises with every step I take closer to the end, where I know we will meet.

As we both reach the end of our aisles, he swiftly takes my hand as he holds me up against the back wall.

'You're here,' I whisper as my breathing deepens.

His glowing eyes stare at me as he slowly tilts his head towards mine.

My heart races as I feel the faintest of vibrations flowing through my body; the energy Shayth is releasing towards me.

I cannot control but to close my eyes and tilt my head back.

'What is this,' I manage to whisper, feeling overwhelmed by the sensation.

He places his hand on the back of my neck as he locks his fingertips into my hair.

The gentle press of his lips against my neck sends a shock through my body, making my heavy breathing intensify.

I drop my books as I begin to lose control of my body.

At that moment, Shayth takes my hands into his and reaches them against the wall.

I am lost in a trance from the soft vibrations running through my body, yet feel an uplifting shock when Shayth's lips mould against mine.

The intensity of the vibrating pulses flows through Shayth into me.

For only a moment, it feels like our lips are locked together when suddenly the books shelved around us begin to vibrate as they fall off the shelves and onto the floor.

I instantly become alert from the scattering of books surrounding us; Shayth pulls away while stepping apart from me.

Shayth appears shocked in amusement, which forces a smile on my face as we both scoff.

'What is this!' whispers the librarian in an aggressive tone. 'I, I'm so sorry,' I offer as I begin to feel myself blushing.

Shayth grabs my hand as he moves swiftly towards the exit.

'There you are my man!' shouts DeJon as we enter the corridor outside of the library.

I instantly release my hands from Shayth's, before tucking my hair behind my ears. I place my fingers on my lips, worrying that I may look a little flustered.

'Ah! What's this then?' Romeo asks with a wicked smile while pointing at my lipstick on Shayth.

Shayth offers a light chuckle before rubbing his fingers against his lips.

'Liyana!! I never thought you had it in you!' Romeo states in a teasing tone.

He was well aware of my prudish outlook, yet cannot help but tease me for entertainment.

Shayth chuckles as he puts his arm around me in a loving yet protective manner.

No doubt Shayth is sensing the flashes of red in my aura becoming more prominent.

'Have fun gents,' I state in a confident tone as I begin to walk away adding, 'I'm off to meet Nevaeh and Sammy.'

Shayth takes a few steps forward as if to follow me when Tucker holds him back.

'You're not going anywhere, we have practice!' he insists. Shayth looks lost as I look back at him with a sympathetic smile.

'I cannot broth,' he insists before being interrupted by DeJon.

'No chance! You missed it yesterday, not today as well.'

Shayth looks back at me once again with obvious disappointment across his face.

I give him a warm smile as I wave goodbye.

Typically, Romeo stands between us, turning his back to me before wrapping his arms around him and wriggling his whole body mimicking a couple who may be kissing and caressing.

At that moment, I cannot help but to roll my eyes, walking off as fast as I can.

I leave behind a roar of laughter as I rush to find Nevaeh and Sammy in the cafeteria.

I walk along the corridor outside of the cafeteria where I notice a large gathering of students, focusing on a flyer they all seem to have.

I notice the wide-eyed expression of the students; their glare seems one of shock, making me feel uncomfortable.

A few students begin to point in my direction, looking back and forth at their flyer.

'There she is.'

'Is that her.'

'Is she crazy.' I hear whispered by the students around me.

As the gathering of students passes, I see Trixy with her friends handing out flyers with an expression of excitement.

They seem to be trying to target everyone heading towards the cafeteria for lunch.

'And here she is! Our very own celebrity!' Trixy announces as she sees me along the corridor.

She skips over to me with a gleaming smile looking very proud. I look around to see everyone pointing and staring. Some even laughing at me, but I have no idea what I have done?

Shayth, the social experiment? Was Trixy telling the truth? Was Shayth playing a wicked game with me?

My heart begins to panic while my mind jumps to all types of irrational conclusions.

Not being able to bear the suspense, I stop a group of students who are walking past me, taking their leaflet from their hand.

My heart sinks at the sight. I cannot help but lower my jaw as I gasp while the tears slowly fill my eyes.

A collage of me…my past, my parents, the forests.

'Girl survived in forest for six days.'

'10-year-old claims missing parents took care of her.'

'Child disorder.'

'Mental health stability.'

'Increase in university attacks by dysfunctional students.'

'Ann, I need to tell you something,' Trixy states with a serious expression as she grabs my arm.

I am stunned as I look up to her in shock from what is happening.

'Your parents! I don't think they want to be found!'

I instantly focus onto her words and can no longer hear the laughter from the crowd surrounding me.

'The woods, you know there is a small group of gypos that live in the woods… I swear I've seen your parents there! They left you to become hobos!'

My heart goes into overdrive as the adrenaline kicks in. My parents!

I begin to take a few steps back as I feel the tears uncontrollably dripping from my face. The vision of my parents laughing, holding me, caring for me, flashes before my eyes.

'The gypos of the greenlake! I can't believe your parents abandoned you to become forest loving freaks! I've seen it myself!'

With no hesitation, I run out of the university site and frantically get into my car. The car screeches as I reverse out of the site.

Is any of this true? I'm desperate for any reason to believe they may be okay. Desperate for any chance of hope; to see them again, to believe I am not alone.

They were the ones taking care of me! Everyone doubting me but I knew I was being looked after in the forest! It must be them!

My vision becomes blurred from the tears streaming from my eyes. But I need to find my parents! I am such a fool for not searching for them sooner!

I drive recklessly to get to the forests, desperate to find my parents.

The humiliation of all the students knowing my past, laughing at my pain, makes me desperate to run away, run away and be in comforting arms of anyone that will accept me!

Uncle Aidan had even said lots of people go missing in the woods! They probably lost themselves and are unable to find their way back! It's entirely plausible for people to choose to live in forests! Perhaps my parents were saved and remain lost deep in the forests?

The children that re-appear from the forests that Uncle Aiden spoke of, they must have been returned by the help of the forest residents! The wild, savage dog! That must belong to them.

My parents might be with them! They may be injured, having lost limbs, which is why they have been unable to make their way back home?

A thousand questions and scenarios run through my mind as I drive as fast as I can to get to my parents, desperate to hold them again. I just want answers; I just want closure from thinking "what if".

Having underestimated my speed, I face the trees as I slam the breaks hard, forcing the car to spin out of control.

Just inches away from the trees ahead, the car finally comes to a stop before I throw the door open and I run into the forest.

I run as fast as I can, calling out, 'Mom,' while the tears fly off my cheeks.

'Dad! I'm here!' I call out as I run further into the depths.

I dodge the branches and the bushes, occasionally stumbling from the uneven surface of the forest bed.

The birds begin to fly out of their nests; the wild animals run frantically from the disruption I am causing.

I run uncontrollably leaping through the air to avoid the obstacles in my path.

My adrenaline rush begins to wear as my breathing becomes difficult with my chest tightening for air.

I keep moving, keep journeying deeper into the forests, but my reflexes become strained, I find myself tumbling down a steep bank.

My hands and knees now covered in mud, with a graze on my head from scraping the rocks.

I lift myself off from the ground and find myself struggling to breathe.

In this moment of loneliness when I look at my surroundings, I cannot help but to release a wail of a cry.

'Why did you leave me?' I cry out, longing for my parents.

I wail as the tears stream down my cheeks and cannot help but bury my face in my knees, wrapping my arms around them in an attempt to console myself.

Why can't I find you? Why won't you come to me? I would do anything just to hold them again, only to see them again, thoughts of pity run through my mind while I struggle to control my weeping.

I need to keep searching before the sun goes down, I tell myself, giving me the motivation to stand and continue my search.

I walk further as I brush the tears from my face.

I search desperately for any trace of people, but there seems to be nothing!

I turn not knowing which way I should walk, which direction I have come from, it all looks the same.

I walk in a direction which I think takes me deeper into the forest. Suddenly I recall my last encounter here as I watch the aggressive rustling of a nearby bush. A streak of fear runs through me but the desperation to find my parents force my legs to keep moving. I run through the forest as reality finally hits me, I am never going to see my parents.

I halt in my tracks as the unnatural silence deep within the forest forces me to become aware of the eerie atmosphere.

There are no birds in the trees, no flowers on the ground. I walk slowly as the fear within my stomach begins to grow. I nervously ask myself, 'What have I done?'

I can hear the breaking of twigs with every step I take.

The trees cling to their leaves while the flowers have withered away.

The daylight seems dimmed from the thousands of trees blocking the sun rays.

The sound of my heavy breathing fills my ears for there is nothing else to hear.

I freeze for a moment as I focus in on a threatening sound becoming more apparent.

The deep panting sound and slow crackling of twigs comes from behind me.

As fear runs through my body, I slowly turn and am petrified at the sight of a huge, black dog-like creature stood yards behind me.

Its black, long scruffy hair has noticeably large bugs crawling within it.

Its exaggerated nozzle bares multiple rows of misaligned teeth with unnaturally long canines. Scars are visible from across its face where the dirty black fur has not grown.

Its claws would be able to lacerate even the sturdiest to mere ribbons of flesh and bone.

But something that seems so familiar, the orange eyes buried within the filthy black fur!

A haze of dark mist surrounds the wild creature, making it difficult to tell whether this is a part of its thick hair, the insects that burrow into its fur, or something else.

It bares its teeth with an aggressive growl before baring its forked tongue towards me.

As it tilts its head forward, its ears are twisted within its curled horns similar to that of a wild sheep; this is like no animal I have ever seen, this is a beast!

Its paw brushes the surface of the ground as saliva thick with mucus drips from the gaps within its teeth.

The mutated wild beast growls, as it bears all its twisted, broken teeth and I know, at this moment, I have no choice but to run, my life depends on it!

The adrenaline through my body created from the fear for my life keeps me moving as fast as I can. I leap in the air as I jump over hurdles of logs and obstacles lying on the forest bed.

I can feel the wild animal close as we both tumble from the muddy patches.

I scramble back to my feet as I keep running! I look back to see the wild animal struggling onto its paws, yet the moment it sees me getting away, it leaps across the glutinous mud.

The aggressive sound of its barking and growling catches up with me.

The large trees offer a barrier between the savage animal, and me, yet as its speed increases, the barrier will render useless.

The sight of an enormous tree with fairly low branches becomes my target as I run as fast I can towards it, leaping with all the strength in my legs to reach the first branch.

I clamber through the tree as I hear the wild dog growling ferociously.

With a threatening leap, it reaches the branch of the tree!

I climb as high as I can, reaching towards a branch, which shockingly snaps as it cannot hold my weight.

I struggle to hold my balance as I find myself falling abruptly onto another lower branch! The fall takes me inches away from the savage creature!

With the broken branch in my hand that's formed a sharp edge, I use this as a weapon as I watch the jaws of the vile animal come closer towards me!

As it leaps in the air to attach its canines to my throat, I take all the strength I have to thrust the sharp branch into its face!

The moment the branch connects; the shock of my strength pushes the beast to fall off the tree hitting the ground!

I watch the beast fall away from me, its eyes filled with fury as the distance increases between us before it finally crashes to the ground. I desperately continue to climb, praying the beast will be too injured to pursue its meal.

Suddenly the branch within my grip begins to vibrate. The branch in my hand slithers out of my grasp!

I turn to look while grabbing for another branch and am faced directly with an enormous serpent with its hood flared in an attack. The head of the serpent is almost double the size of mine, bearing its fangs while flittering its forked tongue.

The glimmer of a sinister smile feels as if the serpent can taste my fear, as if it is playing with its meal!

It strikes, pushing me out of the tree from my imbalanced dodge.

I hit the forest floor hard! The wild dog is not in sight. My arm feels injured, but I cannot lose my focus in this battle for survival. I hold my arm as I run aimlessly in any direction to safety.

I turn back to see the serpent slithering and hanging off the branches as it tries to reach the ground, to pursue me.

Ahead of me, the aggressive rustling of the bushes makes me fear for what is coming next.

As I turn to avoid the deathly bush, my peripheral vision catches a wild creature jumping out towards me!

The mutated animal can only be described as comparable to a steroid induced porcupine, combined with a centipede!

Its two front arms as big as gorilla's ooze out strength as it thumps the ground while running towards me. Spikes cover its arms as they grow thicker and wider reaching the tip of its back.

Its smaller teeth are bared which are sharper and shorter than that of the wild dog!

There are no hind legs! The inbred animal narrows down from its wide shoulder blades to mimic the structure of a giant centipede, accompanied by its deathly spikes!

The giant spiked creature and serpent chase from behind. As I take a glance, the one thing they have in common…a mist of black smoke following them accompanied with the glowing orange-red eyes.

My legs become heavy; my chest feels tight.

I struggle to breathe as the tears begin to fill my eyes. I know my strength to continue is quickly diminishing.

I run through a small stream in the forest. The cold water splashing across me cools my overheated body. But the rocks are difficult to keep balance on as I find myself falling across the inclined bank.

I try crawling to my feet; my body has no strength to lift my weight.

I turn to look back and see the demonic creatures across the stream, heading towards me, bearing their teeth with an evil smile of victory.

I have no energy left…my fate will be ceased. I begin to hyperventilate with every step and slither the wild animals take towards me.

I desperately scramble my hands into the muddy banks, in search of any item that can be used as a weapon.

It is no use, my energy rendered; I stare into their darkness waiting to be mauled alive.

An outburst of wind circles us, instantly the wild savages appear to look defensive.

Falling within the stream that separates me from my death stands a tall figure, glowing white.

Easily mistaken for my guardian angel, the wings of this creature are drawn wide. The dragon-like wings appear somewhat scaly textured with its span creating a wall between me and my predators.

The scales gleam in the reflection of the sunrays desperate to pierce through the clouds and treetops.

'She's mine!' I hear a growling voice shout in a threatening manner.

I begin to lose my focus. The hyperventilation draws my final ounces of energy. My vision becomes clouded as I struggle to watch the winged creature wrestle with the savage beasts.

I shriek as I feel my legs twisted within the coils of the serpent; it drags me towards a burrow.

The scaly white glow intervenes while battling amongst the hisses of the serpents flickering tongue.

I don't know what injuries I have... I don't know if I am dying. I hear the whisper of my name as I am held in comforting arms. I know that scent; it always surrounds me when I am lost.

With the final ounce of strength left in me, I struggle to open my eyes. Holding me tight, I see Shayth. With a fearful look in his eyes, he shields us both with his scaled wings.

Wait, this can't be! Shayth...has wings?

'…You never know how strong you are until being strong is the only choice you have…'

— Bob Marley

22. Forbidden Entry

'I love you, Liyana,' the sound of laughter surrounds me.

I open my eyes and stare at my parents as Micky crawls around on the grass coming closer towards us.

My parents sit beside me as they cuddle each other while holding my hand. A filter of sepia clouds my vision, making everything around me glow in a hazy light.

I can feel something pulling me away from my memories; I hear the calling of my name in the distance.

'Liyana!' The shaking accompanied by splashes of fresh water across my face startles my senses as I open my eyes wide and gasp for air.

'I thought I had lost you!' Shayth whispers as he holds me tighter in his arms.

'Where am I,' I babble while trying to refocus my bearings.

'You are safe,' he responds as he kisses my forehead.

Wrapped in his arms, I look around and see the sun setting amongst the treetops at the bottom of the valley.

I find myself at the edge of a steep hilltop while my eyes scan our surroundings.

I squeeze a tight hold of Shayth.

I feel safe, yet afraid of what is lurking within the trees beneath us.

As my vision focuses close, I notice the scaly wings extended from Shayth's back.

I gasp in shock while releasing my arms from around his neck, pushing him away.

The look of fear fills his expression as I increase the space between us.

My hyperventilating returns with a vengeance as I recall the horrific encounter deep within the forests.

'Liyana… Please,' he insists as he shuffles towards me.

'Stop!' I shout as I scramble to get on my feet.

'Get away from me!' I hastily add as I stumble around trying to find my balance.

I attempt to walk down the hill not knowing where I am going. I stumble, moments from falling flat on the steep hillside; suddenly my arms are halted forward.

I look at the upside-down trees as my head hovers inches above the ground. My feet are on the floor, my wrists being held by Shayth.

I tilt my head forward to reduce the rush of blood flow to my brain; I find Shayth watching me with a look of sorrow and disappointment.

He pulls me forward in a steady manner and releases my wrists when I reach a sturdy posture.

'Liyana, please, I mean you no harm,' he begs with desperation in his eyes.

'What are you?' I shout while my voice quivers.

Shayth looks down in disappointment as if his world is crumbling to an end.

His typical white attire is covered in stains from the battle with the unknown creatures.

His clothes are torn with grazes across his arms and face. His hair is damp, with his fringe handing over his eyebrows.

I watch him frown before he finally raises his head, 'I shall tell you everything.'

I don't know if I want to know. I don't know if I am ready to know. But one thing that I know for sure, Shayth is no ordinary human, maybe not human at all!

We sit in silence as I try to get my head around the riddles he has offered me.

'So you are like a human, you just have different strengths and abilities.'

'Yes,' he responds in an assertive tone.

'And these abilities are what allow you to see people and their aura.'

'Yes,' he affirms.

'But you're not human…you're just like a human, without being a human.'

'Yes,' he continues in a less confident tone.

'What does that even mean Shayth? What am I supposed to make of that?' My tone becomes defensive from the confusion of not having straight answers.

'What does it take to be human?' he snaps.

He begins to pace up and down as he combs his hair with his fingers.

'A heart? A mind? A soul? Intentions?' he rolls off.

'Yes, all of the above,' I confirm as I begin to frown.

I recall this very conversation when he entered my bedroom last night.

'I have all these things! Yet you cannot accept me, for all I want to be is human!'

'Humans…don't have wings, Shayth,' I whisper as tears fill my eyes.

It is heart-breaking to see him vulnerable and desperate for acceptance.

'Liyana, please,' he insists as he approaches me and holds my face in his hands.

'Are you afraid of me?' he asks with deep, fearful eyes.

'No,' I whisper as the tears finally drip onto my cheeks.

I see his eyes begin to well slightly from gratitude of my response.

'Do you feel safe around me?'

'Yes,' I cry as I hold his hands against my face.

'Then please, let me ease you into my world!' he insists as he looks desperate for my acceptance.

'I may not be human, but I am here for you. I always have been.' He rests his forehead against mine, wiping away my tears before releasing his hands. As he takes a step back he stares down to the ground; he begins to pace around me.

'Your instinct come from your sub-conscious. Yet you are taught to be rational and analyse and assess every situation thus ignoring your intuition.

'Trust your instinct, Liyana, trust your sub-conscious. Trust your soul! If you feel safe around me, then believe that I am right for you.'

'I live here, with humans. But my reality you cannot see.'

I look at him confused, not being able to keep up with his riddles.

'I am from a parallel dimension,' he states as he stands tall and strong.

'The creatures that were attacking you, they are of my dimension.'

I scoff at the wild suggestion.

'This is not some fairy tale, Liyana, of vampires and werewolves! This is reality. Written in the scriptures long before you and I were created!'

'Scriptures?'

'Spirits?' I whisper as I frown from confusion.

'Not in the way you recognise, not in the way modern society has manipulated people into believing.

'But yes, you could call me a spirit that lives by your side and sees into your soul.'

'Ethereal body,' I gasp as the link suddenly hits me.

'Yes, I live through my ethereal body in a parallel dimension. If it's possible for a physical body to transcend into an ethereal state, thus entering a new domain, is it not possible for the beings within this spiritual realm to join the parallels of your reality? Transforming their ethereal bodies to that of a physical form?

'We can see you in our ethereal state, but you cannot see us.'

I clench the hair on my scalp with my fingers in the shock of Shayth's revelation.

A sense of relief flows through me from finally grasping hold of the truth.

'You feel at ease?' Shayth questions with a confused expression.

'How can you be a spirit if I can hold you? If I can touch you; if I can kiss you?' I ask with bewilderment as I struggle to understand through the modern-day teachings of spirits.

'Is truth easier to live with, or is living in ignorance bliss?' Shayth questions as he tilts his head eager to hear my views.

'Truth,' I respond with a stern tone.

'No matter how difficult it may be to hear, the truth is what I need to know!'

'Let me ease you into the truth,' he insists as he takes my hand in his.

'We communicate at a different frequency that is why you cannot hear us. We survive in a different dimension, which is why you cannot see us.'

I recall the exercise in class where the dog whistle was blown. No student was affected; we could not hear the sounds, other than Shayth. This explains his theory of noise and levels of different frequencies that humans are not embraced with. 'We are made of a consistency lighter than that of the human race. Our density is far lighter. This is what allows us to take different forms. To be seen or unseen.'

'Dark matter? What Sammy was talking about?'

'Yes, we form the energy that humanity recognises as dark matter. Our density of energy vibrates at a frequency that cannot be detected by light, which is why you are blind to my world.'

Though a part of me is afraid of learning this truth, the sense of relief remains stronger, though somewhat surreal.

'This can't be real!' I snap as I begin to pace around with my hands in my hair.

'This doesn't happen, not to people like me! This isn't real,' I mutter as my breathing becomes uncontrolled from feeling overwhelmed.

'Liyana, you need to control your breathing, your aura, your head will begin to spin.'

I feel the spin slowing invading my mind as I sit on a log and take in deep breathes.

I take a moment to digest all that I have heard, but there is more I need to know.

'Where do you live?' I ask feeling intrigued by this whole unnatural concept.

'I, err…' he begins to stutter not knowing how to answer the question.

'The truth, Shayth!' I shout forcing him to look in my direction.

'I mentioned that I am from up north, my family lives up north from here.'

'Yes you did, but that doesn't narrow it down! Which town? Which state?

Shayth scoffs before biting his lips. He points up as he whispers, 'North.'

I look at his pointing gesture and observe the treetops above us.

'In the trees?' I whisper with a tone of disbelief.

'What we see now, this isn't the reality of my world. This is not what I see when I am in my ethereal state.'

'Well, what do you see?' I ask intrusively.

'See the trunks of these trees,' he states as he pats the tree trunk close to us.

'These form the roots of the trees in my world!' He smiles with a glimmer of excitement in his eyes.

'It's a mystical place beyond the imagination of what has been created in this world of mankind.'

A faint smile breaks from my lips as I am captivated by his words describing a magical world.

'You would love my world, Liyana,' he continues as he breaks from his daydream to look at me.

'It is a beautiful world, from the nature of our beings to the kindness of our animals. Even down to the flowers we have, vibrant colours and glows.

'Though not everything lives within our sacred laws...' Shayth pauses as a look of concern grows across his expression.

'What is it?' As I ask the question, the answer suddenly hits me.

'The creatures,' I whisper as a hint of fear comes over me.

'Yes. We have different species within our dimension. They live within the roots of our world as they have been banished from our society.'

'Why? Why would you banish someone?'

'They are the miscreant entities of our world. We had given them opportunities to be a part of our society. But they are evil in their nature, refusing to abide by our scared laws.'

'So what do they live by?'

'They have their own code, their own way of life.'

'And they live here!' I gasp as the fear becomes visible in my expression.

'This is why I insisted last night for you not to come to the forest! This is why I appeared in the shape of Diesel all those weeks ago, to keep you out of here!'

'I, I'm sorry,' I whisper before the reality of what Shayth has just shared sinks in.

'Wait! You appeared as Diesel all those weeks ago?'

Shayth's eyes widen as he becomes nervous from my reaction.

'So what...you can shape shift?'

'Err... Yes, to any living being.'

I scoff at the unbelievable revelation.

'And what you thought you would just scare the hell out of me as an overgrown DOG! Chasing me down the road!!!'

'Err...it was to keep you safe; to keep you alive.'

I shake my head in disbelief, as Shayth grows more restless from my disapproval.

'Liyana please, try to understand, I could not bear to see anything happen to you again!' he insists as he puts his palm on my arm to try and sooth my discontent.

'So what, is this the real you or have you shape shifted in this way to appeal to me?'

'I…err…' Shayth hesitates in answering my question.

'I don't know you, do I?' I whisper, feeling overwhelmed with loneliness and dishonesty.

'No, please Liyana, please do not think this way,' he insists as worry grows on his expression.

Shayth covers his face with the palm of his hands, which he then swipes across his head.

'This is very difficult,' he whispers under his breath.

'You have seen me in my natural form!' he insists.

'I… I was passing out Shayth.'

'I will show you if it is that important to you. It really is not that much more different to how I am now…' Shayth pauses for a moment as he looks down to the ground and steps away from me.

'Perhaps just a little taller, maybe a lot taller, somewhat scalier, with the wings.

'But this IS me! And yes, you do know me!'

Shayth stares towards me as he closes the distance between us. 'Please do not doubt everything we have gone through, everything you have grown to know of me, everything you find endearing about me.

'I wanted you to spend time with me, for who I am…not what I am. I wanted you to love me for me… Not be intrigued or, afraid of me.'

Shayth kicks the ground as he shakes his head while pacing around.

I watch him become agitated and once again notice the grazes across his body. Grazes he would have endured from saving me.

I stand to my feet as I rip a piece of cloth from my already shredded shirt.

I walk over towards him and dab at the grazes to remove the grains of dirt from him.

'This explains your strength and speed in sports,' I jest to try and remove the disappointed expression across his face.

He offers me a warm smile as he takes my hands in his.

'So why didn't you win the arm wrestle?' I ask in a teasing tone as we both smile.

'I would have if I did not sense your aura coming closer towards me.'

'So your failure is down to my existence,' I mock as we both smile.

'Your existence is the reason for mine.'

My calm heartbeat begins to flutter. Despite hearing and seeing everything today, I cannot help but feel even more drawn to him.

'How long have you been watching me for Shayth?' I ask with a soft tone.

'A while...' he responds trying to avoid the question.

My eyes glare into his; I am sure he can sense from my aura that the answer is not good enough.

'When you came to the forest weeks ago and were attacked by these animals. Since saving you that day, I have struggled to keep away.'

'I have never been attacked. This is the first time I have seen these creatures,' I clarify.

'Yes...the first time you have seen them in their visible form. But this is the fourth time they have attacked you!' he insists with certainty.

I suddenly have flashbacks as I recall the mutilated rabbit and what I perceived to be an unnatural gale.

'Why?' I gasp in shock.

'Why would they attack me?' I face the ground as the shock sends vibrations of fear through me.

'It is okay; you are safe, I will always keep you safe,' Shayth insists as he sits me back down and joins me.

'Over 200,000 humans go missing every year, over 600 people a day!'

He frowns as his tone changes from one of concern for me to one of concern for humanity.

'These creatures, they feed on the souls of humans in the name of sacrifice for the evil they worship.

'They dwell in secluded areas and await the victims that cross their path.'

My throat dries at the thought of being hunted by an invisible entity, a creature that intends to feed on me, preying on me, when I am none the wiser that it watches me, that it approaches me.

'When else have they attacked me?' I manage to whisper in my quivering voice.

'When I was driving you home from the party, they came out unexpectedly. No doubt they too could sense your pure aura.'

I sit back in shock! Being targeted with no idea that I am in grave danger. Had it not been for Shayth, I would have been their sacrifice.

'That explains your behaviour, why you jumped out of a moving vehicle,' I whisper in disbelief.

'The National Park, Lake Superior, The Bennington Triangle, these are just a few places where the largest group of beasts dwell, that is still actively visited by humans. The highest disappearances of humankind take place here.'

'Wait, is that where they live?'

'It is where they temporarily dwell to increase their sacrifice from the volume of humans that can be taken. But this is not their natural dwelling.'

'I don't understand. Why not just go to a shopping mall or into the city centre if all they want his human sacrifice? They would find hundreds of people there.'

Shayth scoffs as he glares at the ground. He slowly turns to look at me.

'Light. That particular species are afraid of artificial light! And the frequency of sound in the human world. The fear to stay away from groups of mankind has been drilled into them from generations ago, to the point where it is engrained in their makeup. Human frequencies and auras are what they fear, dependent on the purity of the human.'

'So why aren't you afraid?' I ask eagerly.

'I am a different species. Our species are the ones who reside in the skies, the trees. Hence – the wings. We are the most advanced species whereby we understand and study mankind and how we should best live our lives to ensure we co-exist in harmony. We keep the order between our dimension and yours.'

'Wait, what did you say earlier?' I blurt out as my mind struggles to keep up.

'You said this is the fourth time they have attacked me,' I state as I try to recall all incidence.

'This is the fourth time, you driving me home was the third time, the mutilated rabbit in the forest was the second.... What am I missing? When was the first time?'

I look at Shayth intensely, eager to hear of the first occasion, I was unknowingly attacked.

When was my first blind encounter with the demonic beasts?

'Liyana, I do not know how to tell you this.' Shayth becomes tense as his expression fills with sorrow.

'I need to know, Shayth!' I demand, feeling myself becoming agitated.

'It wasn't when...it...wasn't...' I can't bring the words out of my mouth as I feel my throat dry and a sickness building in my stomach.

'My parents?' I manage to choke out as tears fill my eyes.

'I am truly sorry. I did all I could to save them,' he reveals as he takes my hands and pulls me towards him.

My parents, they were attacked?

For a moment I freeze, my eyes widen before the tears begin to stream down my cheeks in my frozen state.

I bury my head into Shayth's chest as he squeezes me tight, comforting me from my weeping heart.

Flashbacks of that tragic night flash before my eyes as I sit trembling in the car fighting hard with my fear, praying for courage to be able to exit the vehicle and enter the forests.

I recall the doors slamming shut during my attempts to leave the car.

Snuffling away during sunrise while Micky slept by my side. The feeling of loneliness consuming me till the strangest fragrance filled my surroundings. I recall the moments when the strangest sensation would absorb into my soul, making me feel safe and comforted.

The words of Shayth replay in my mind over and over, *'Perhaps there would have been some psychological trauma if she was stranded...but she was never alone.'*

'So you were there, the whole time? It was you the one who stopped me from leaving the vehicle? You were the one taking care of me?' I repeat while my mind tries to digest the information.

'I never thought I would see you again after you had left,' he whispers.

'I searched for you, but you had left your Aunts, and I knew not how to find you.'

Shayth offers me a kiss on my forehead, as he seems to reminisce about his attempts to find me.

'You were only a young child when I had saved you. I could not believe my eyes when all these years later when I was convinced you had disappeared, somewhere safe, somewhere loved, you suddenly appeared. A beautiful, young woman with such a majestic aura, such a pure soul, I never thought I would see you again.'

De'Ja Vu suddenly hits me as I recall hearing these words from Shayth in my dreams. Before I knew he even existed.

'Wait, have you said this to me before? In my dreams? I never thought I would see you again...' I pause for a moment before shaking my head.

'I sound crazy! This is crazy,' I whisper in disbelief.

'Yes, you are right. When I first entered your dreams, desperate to be noticed by you, these are the words I had whispered to you.' Shayth offers me a coy smile while looking somewhat reserved.

I sigh heavily as I try hard to understand all of what Shayth is capable of.

'So you can fly, you can shape-shift; you have incredible strength and speed, not to mention looks! And now, you can enter my dreams.'

'Yes,' he whispers in a prolonged tone.

'What more of your sacred laws? What else is there that you must or must not do?'

'The highest order of our sacred laws forbids us to enter the domain of mankind.'

Shayth frowns while watching my expression turn to that of confusion.

'So what is the consequence of someone who breaks this sacred law?' I ask as my heart rate begins to increase.

The sense of worry grows within me. Shayth looks up at me and offers me a warm smile.

'It is okay; I will be okay,' he whispers as he takes my hand into his and kisses the surface.

'We must not enter the domain of mankind. We must avoid artificial light, as it is a symbol of mankind's dwellings.'

'Why did you come here? Why would you break your sacred rules?' I ask as I look deep into his eyes wanting to understand his motives for breaking the law that govern his species.

He pauses for a moment, as he looks to the ground before raising his eyes to meet mine.

'Is there anything anyone, human or not, could possibly want more, than to just be noticed?' he asks with sincerity and vulnerability in his expression.

'I came here to be noticed...to be noticed by you...' his voice softens as he looks deep into my eyes.

'I wanted you to see me, to smile with me...to laugh with me. Being in your presence makes me feel, alive. All I want is for you to know I exist...for you to exist...with me.'

I gasp feeling overwhelmed by his motives for breaking is sacred laws governing his species and risking the consequence. It is all, for me.

'…One of the basic rules of the universe is that nothing is perfect. Perfection simply doesn't exist…'

— Stephen Hawking

23. My Omega

As each drop of water penetrates my skin, I wash away the remains of the grime and dirt masking my body.

I sit in the shower with my head resting on my knees trying to make sense of what has become of my world.

I look around my light, airy bathroom, scented with fresh fragrance, yet cannot help but wonder, is there more surrounding me than what my feeble eyes can see.

I lay in bed trying to get my head around the unknown, the unseen.

Tears drop from my eyes as I cannot comprehend the complexity of our parallel dimension, or perhaps I just don't want to. Maybe I don't want to believe that we could be preyed upon in a way that I could never imagine in my wildest nightmares.

I cannot bear to think of the trauma my parents must have suffered at the hands of the evil creatures lurking within the shadows.

I scoff at my stupidity. I now have the answers I have been searching for. I now know the fate of my parents. Yet I am not filled with closure, only more pain, more sorrow.

The worst of it is; there is no one I can share this with. Not Micky, not my aunt and uncle, it is a burden I must bear alone.

I recall Shayth's touch. Shayth's smile, his gentle, caring approach towards me. This mystical world on the lakes which he opened my eyes too. Perhaps it's not all bad? Maybe it's not all evil? I think about Shayth's world, which he describes, with the trunks of our trees forming the roots of his.

What a huge and magical dimension it must be.

I text Nevaeh and Sammy in response to their numerous missed calls. No doubt they have heard about the altercation between Trixy and me!

Trixy…how malicious must she be to mock the disappearance of my parents?

I just need some time. I don't know how I feel, let alone how I should feel.

I think I feel broken at the thought of the possibilities of my parent's return being taken away from me. My hopes and prayers have been ripped to shreds.

I don't understand how I feel for Shayth. From all this time, I have known him, or he has known me rather, he surely knows the depth of my desire in searching for answers of my parents. He could have revealed the brutal truth much sooner.

What do I even know of him? Do I even know him?

I need time, time to let my mind absorb the realities of life, the reality of the fate of my parents. The reality of what Shayth really is and what this means for him and I.

'Hey! We were worried about you!' Sammy states as she offers me a warm, inviting hug.

'Seriously, Liyana, you pick up your phone when I'm calling you! I've been so worried!' Nevaeh shouts as she squeezes me tight.

'It's okay, I'm sorry. I just needed a bit of time alone,' I respond trying to bring the conversation to an end.

We walk into the building; I observe the stares from the students we pass.

'We need to talk, why didn't you tell me!' Nevaeh questions as we walk towards our class.

'What can I say, I'm somewhat of a closed book,' I respond sheepishly.

'Well at lunchtime we are going to talk about everything!' she insists.

I see him stood in the corridor. They are all stood together, DeJon, Tucker, Bazzer, Rome and Shayth.

They all laugh out loud while DeJon brushes his hand on Shayth's head.

I freeze in my motion as he glances towards me, sensing my aura, no doubt.

His body stiffens as he stares at me.

The smile disappears from his expression as he stares at me intensely.

He lowers his head while a frown appears on his face.

Shayth proceeds to take a few steps towards me, but I cannot maintain the gaze we momentarily shared.

I don't know what to do; I don't know how I feel.

'I need to grab a drink,' I call out to Nevaeh as I make my way to the cafeteria.

I sit on the seat with my drink and cannot help but feel lost.

I watch the students that surround me, laughing and jesting without a care in the world.

Nevaeh takes a seat by my side and begins to talk about our course.

Her voice begins to drown out as I watch Shayth and DeJon walk into the cafeteria.

I can't... I can't speak to him. I don't know if I am afraid or if I am angry or if I feel betrayed.

I watch Shayth with a frown on his face as he proceeds to walk towards me.

Yet when DeJon looks towards him, he replaces his frown with a smile.

Tucker and Romeo join Nevaeh and I at the table, which gives me an excuse to break the gaze between Shayth and me.

As Shayth approaches the table, I can sense him stood behind me.

It's so hard, trying to pretend everything is okay. I laugh and jest with my friends while Shayth does the same. Yet between us, we both know that things are far, from okay.

'What is it?' I ask Tucker opposite me as he and Romeo giggle while staring at Tucker's phone.

'Come have a look,' Tucker offers as they continue to giggle at the screen.

Desperate to increase the distance between Shayth and me, I stand to my feet.

I can feel him staring at me as I stand inches away from him. He reaches out his hand, as if to stroke my arm.

I just don't know how to be around him anymore. Instantly, without making eye contact, I pass him as I walk around to the other side of our table.

Uninterested in what Tucker has on his phone, I see Sammy enter the cafeteria and decide to walk towards her.

'How long can I avoid Shayth for,' I question to myself.

As Sammy and I walk back towards the table, I watch Shayth as he approaches us.

He looks broken; as if he is being tortured.

'Hey, Sammy, your assignment on dark matter. How is it going? Did you need to ask Shayth anything about his suggested theory?' I quickly ask desperately to start a conversation between the two of them.

'Oh yeah, actually! Hi, Shayth,' Sammy replies as Shayth reaches us.

'I'll leave you two to it,' I respond before Sammy begins to ask Shayth questions on the theory.

I notice in my peripheral vision, Shayth staring towards me, as I slowly increase the distance between us. We walk through the doors to our lecture hall; I can feel a nervous sickness building within my stomach.

I feel lost and confused as I stare at the ground as we walk up the stairs, towards empty seats at the back of the hall.

I raise my head and find Shayth sitting to the back of the class looking nervous and agitated.

'Hey, there's Shayth!' Nevaeh whispers as we walk towards his seat.

I sit beside him and offer a, 'Hey,' desperate to avoid Nevaeh from jumping to any conclusions.

'Hi,' he responds in a soft yet down tone.

The lecture promptly begins on social psychology and the conditioning of the human mind with the conscious mind working desperately for acceptance.

Thus society plays a significant role in how we portray ourselves and what we believe to be acceptable.

Even more so, society can influence our very own likes and dislikes through the desires of the subconscious mind of acceptance and inclusion.

'Media,' the lecturer states as he presents a slideshow of attractive males and females to which the whole class creates an uproar. 'Heavily influence initial attraction or also referred to as physical attraction.

'Social attraction, on the other hand, involves being attracted to someone based on his or her personality.

'And finally, the task attraction, which includes being attracted to someone based on his or her abilities.'

As the class sits in silence, I think of what it is that I am attracted to about Shayth? He has intrigued me from the moment I noticed him stood beside a tree while I was sipping on my coffee. Yes, he is obviously attractive to look at with his unusual tanned skin and grey eyes, but the bond between him and I go deeper than physical attraction.

I wonder if he is thinking of me.

I make no eye contact with him as I try hard to appear to be focused on the lecture.

Equally, he makes no pass to grasp my attention. Though the atmosphere between us seems tense, I cannot help but still feel a little nervous from sitting next to him.

My stern expression easily masks my excitement to be close to him, but what does my aura say I wonder.

The lecturer provides detail on the transcript of mate selection theories, which makes me feel awkward, being sat next to Shayth.

Attraction is based on a person's unconscious image of the ideal mate formed by their perceptions of the meaning of specific characteristics.

What characteristics is it that I possess which attracted Shayth towards me? To an obsessive point whereby he is prepared to sacrifice his own world?

I ask myself would I ever be prepared to sacrifice my world for someone I wanted to be with?

I think of the qualities I find endearing about him.

His soft, gentle approach. Only really speaking when he is being spoken to, thus not a fan of the limelight.

His genuine smile. Constantly dressed in simple clothing rather than mimicking the rest of the fashion fanatics in university.

The lecturer slowly moves onto the male characteristics of alpha, beta and omega.

Alpha is the leader, the stand-up guy that others look to for motivation. A dominant character that possesses a hint of jealousy.

Shayth certainly doesn't fit in this category. DeJon however with his constant drive of being the fastest, the best and is the leader of the sports academy, DeJon makes the perfect alpha male.

Shayth, though he is a warrior from what I have seen, doesn't fit the remaining traits of alpha. He is more of an introvert than the extrovert, characteristics the alpha male possess.

Beta males don't like to associate with a lot of masculine men, as they believe the way these alpha males act is wrong, but are taught the beta traits make the ideal man.

I assess Shayth to this category but conclude he doesn't fall within this either!

He is just as muscular if not more than his friends and doesn't seem to judge any particular way of being.

The lecturer continues to explain the omega males are the polar opposite of the alpha male yet hold similarities.

Quietly confident, intelligent like the betas, yet holds the charisma and strength of the alpha.

However, unlike the alpha, they do not hold the wolf pack mentality and are entirely their own person, unafraid of solitude.

I cannot help but smile. Shayth risks a life of solitude by breaking his sacred law to enter our world, merely to be in my presence. He is quietly confident while acting as my protector in the background. My protector, my warrior.

I focus on my peripheral vision where I can see Shayth looking uninterested in the class, somewhat distracted perhaps.

I hate the thought of him being down when he has done so much to try and protect me. When he has concealed his whole world from me, simply to be around me.

My heart begins to melt at the realisation of everything he has sacrificed for me. Every effort he has made for me.

I slowly move my hand to hold his while staring at the lecturer ahead of us.

As my hand touches his fingers, I can feel a rush of excitement going through me.

For a moment he remains still, I cannot sense what his expression may be.

Before my mind has the opportunity to jump to any conclusion, I feel a tight grasp on my hand, instantly drawing a smile on my face.

I glance over to Shayth as he gives me a warm smile. I watch him take a deep sigh, from relief no doubt.

We walk out of the class hand in hand, haven't yet exchanged any words.

'Na ah!' states Nevaeh as we enter the corridor.

'She's mine for lunch! We have a lot to catch up on!' she insists to Shayth as she observes us holding hands.

He offers a light chuckle as he still holds onto my hand.

'Now you need to find, DeJon! He was looking everywhere for you!' Nevaeh insists as she stands between us, forcing us to release our hands.

He offers a coy smile as he softly speaks, 'I will see you after university?'

'Sure,' I respond with a sheepish smile.

As he walks away, my heart is saddened at the thought that I have no further lessons with him today. The possibility of seeing him after university fills me with hope, but I am left feeling lost as to when or where.

As we walk down the corridor, I watch the Aphrodite approaching us.

Trixy stares at me as she laughs away with her friends.

I can sense the feeling of anger growing within me from her malicious, arrogant attitude!

'She's got a nerve!' hisses Nevaeh, as she too must be feeling a fraction of the hatred that I am.

'Liyana!' Trixy shouts as she approaches us.

'Did you find your dead parents then?' she hisses before laughing out loud with her friends!

'Surprised you made it out of the forest alive! Was hoping you would disappear just as they did!' she adds with a wicked smirk.

How dare she! I am fuelled by hatred as I watch her turn to her friends in fits of laughter with no care in the world of how much their venomous words and cruel actions can hurt others. There is not an ounce of remorse in her, which enrages me even more!

As she turns to look at me I cannot control the rage growing within the pit of my stomach, I raise my hand and smash my fist into her face with all the power I have in me!

For a brief moment, her emerald green eyes widen before they squeeze themselves shut as my fist slams her down.

'Liyana!' Nevaeh cheers as she bursts into laughter and pats me on the back.

'Don't even think about it!' Nevaeh shouts to an Aphrodite who takes a step towards me.

'C'mon girl, the trash has been dealt with!' Nevaeh shouts for all to hear as a small group gathers around us.

We walk off as the crowd parts, leaving Trixy bleeding on the floor with her friends surrounding her.

'Where the hell did you learn to swing like that?' Nevaeh shouts full of adrenaline.

I force a nervous smile when all the time I am thinking about how much my hand hurts as I rub my knuckles.

We meet Sammy in the courtyard and Nevaeh dramatically explains the commotion in the corridor.

'Are you okay?' Sammy asks with concern.

'I'm good,' I respond forcing a smile.

'Liyana, why didn't you tell us?' Nevaeh questions. Her tone changes while sorrow grows on her face.

I look down not knowing how to respond. I've never spoken to friends about what happened or my personal life for that matter.

'I, I don't really talk about these things. I've never really told anyone things about me,' I respond sheepishly.

'That's why you ran out of the class right? The child disorder presentations?' Nevaeh questions having dotted the lines.

I force a smile as I nod, not knowing what to say.

I am comforted by the loving care both Sammy and Nevaeh offer me and am incredibly grateful for their friendship.

But deep down, I want the conversation to finish, as the memories are too saddening to bear, even more so now, from the knowledge, my parents were victims of the beasts from the parallel dimension.

Though my appetite has disappeared, I force food down to avoid any attention. It's drama free at the dinner table, as we all partake in a polite conversation.

I settle into my room after dinner but my mind is in overdrive. There is so much I want to know; so much I need to know!

I sit on my bed with paper and pen as I begin to gather all my thoughts.

1. *What are you called?*
2. *What are you made of?*
3. *Why me? What's wrong with my aura?*
4. *Who is Argyle?*
5. *Can your creation die?*
6. *Do your creation marry?*
7. *How can I tell if I am being watched?*

8. *How do I protect myself?*
9. *Do the flowers come from your dimension?*
10. *Does your car come from your dimension?*
11. *I want to know what your world looks like.*
12. *What's the consequence you will face for taking mankind's form?*
13. *What do you want from me...?*

I hear a tapping from outside. *The rain must be coming in*; I think to myself as I focus on what other questions I need to ask. The lampshade begins to flicker, which distracts me from my task.

As I look up from my pad, I gasp from the sight of Shayth stood on my balcony!

'What are you doing?' I ask in shock as I open my balcony doors.

'I, I wanted to see you,' he whispers in an insecure tone.

'I'm sorry, I didn't mean to snap!' I add hastily.

'You just scared me,' I continue as I gesture him to come in.

We both sit at the edge of my bed, he watches me tuck my hair behind my ear.

'Something is wrong,' he whispers.

I look up at him and watch him analyse the surroundings of my body.

'Something has happened, your hand!' he exclaims, as the swelling is visible.

'Oh, it's nothing,' I add as he takes my hand into his.

'Trixy?' he questions with a concerned tone.

I nod feeling a little ashamed. 'You mustn't let people manipulate you to bring out the worst in you.'

'Easier said than done,' I scoff feeling a little sorry for myself.

'Rage is such a dangerous emotion! It can possess even the purest of us.'

He takes my hand to his lips and places a gentle kiss on the surface as he stares into my eyes.

I gasp and release a heavy sigh of relief as I feel a weight has been lifted off my shoulders. At that moment, we both lean forward to wrap our arms around each other!

I squeeze hold of Shayth tight as I forget for a moment who or what he is and focus on simply how he makes me feel.

'I thought you would hate me,' he whispers as he kisses the top of my head.

'I did not think you would want to see me,' he reveals in a sincere and disheartened tone.

'I thought that too!' I scoff as I hold him even tighter.

'But it didn't feel the same... I didn't feel the same, without you,' I confess.

He releases a gentle chuckle of joy while the smile on my face widens.

The lampshade begins to flicker again, which distracts my attention from Shayth as I release him from my arms.

'I'm sorry, I need to get that looked at,' I add as I walk over to the lampshade.

'It is me,' he confesses.

'I am sorry, I shall control my emotion better,' he adds.

I glance over at him while frowning, feeling totally confused. 'I don't understand, what do you mean? What's you?'

He begins to scoff nervously.

'My, my vibrations interfere with the energy within the light if I do not control my emotions.'

I'm baffled by his claims as we have had electrical issues in this house for weeks now.

'Soo, how often have you tampered with the lights here?' I ask curiously as I take a few steps towards him.

Shayth clears his throat as he sits twitching his thumbs, looking visibly uncomfortable. I stop in my tracks eagerly waiting for his response.

'I...err... A few times.'

I scoff not knowing how to react. Should I be flattered or offended?

'And the flowers?' I ask inquisitively.

'I wanted to give you a gift. The flowers, they always made you smile,' he responds sheepishly.

As I stand in shock with my body frozen; within seconds I cannot help but laugh.

'I can't believe you have been doing this!' I whisper as I walk towards him and hold him in my arms.

'As flattered and creeped out as I am, we need to make some ground rules!'

'...I have a dream, that we will not be judged by the colour of our skin, but by the content of our character...'

–   Martin Luther King

24. Stereotype Mind Trap

'Firstly, no more being here without me knowing you are here!' Shayth looks at me while raising his eyebrows, like a young schoolboy in shock from being told off by his teacher.

'We either agree times – or if you decide you cannot resist being apart from me then, just as you have done today, you can wait in the balcony till you get my attention!'

'Agreed!' he affirms as he offers me a cheeky salute with a dazzling smile.

'What is the next rule?' he asks eagerly as he sits at the edge of the bed.

'Well, I, err,' I slowly pace around the room trying hard to appear dominant, but it's no use.'

'That's it, no more rules,' I declare while offering a confident smile.

Shayth stands to his feet and takes a step towards me.

'So what rule must I follow if I want to hold you,' he asks, as he approaches closer, looking straight into my eyes.

His question catches me off guard; I cannot help but look around the room, trying hard to fight the butterflies in my stomach.

'Oh, err, yes! You need to make sure that... I...umm...'

I have no idea what I am saying or how to respond to this question! The butterflies within my stomach are carrying out summersault, making it harder to maintain a steady breath. 'That I'm in a good mood!' I hastily add trying to recover my confident demeanour.

'You need to make sure that I am in a good mood!' I repeat.

I stand tall and confident, trying hard to appear dominant so that he cannot sense my melting heart.

'Sooo, are you in a good mood now?' he asks as he ducks his head slightly.

I take a deep breath as I cannot help but join him in an intense gaze.

'Well, I'm not mad right now,' I whisper as he stands inches away from me.

'Or am I?' I ask as I tilt my head back to maintain our locked eyes as he towers over me.

I slowly stroke my hands along his arms and reach towards his shoulders while he pulls me closer by the waist.

My breathing becomes shaky and shallow as I close my eyes to become lost in this moment.

His warm lips rub softly against mine.

My hands work around his body as I feel each crevasse, each line along his perfect physique. Our kiss becomes fiery as I claw my fingers through his hair.

His body begins to vibrate with strong pulses echoing into my soul. Our breathing intensifies as we momentarily part for air, before pushing our lips against each other once again.

His hand rubs tightly against my waist; I feel his warm touch against my skin.

Something is happening to me. As my breathing becomes uncontrollable, his hand rubs against my bearskin.

A sensation of energy flows through my body, rendering all my senses numb. My knees begin to tremble as I feel myself lose every ounce of strength while I slowly fall into a dreamlike abyss. I try to open my eyes; I see nothing but darkness. The pulsing vibration has consumed me. I can no longer stand, I can no longer see. My strength consumed by Shayth's energy leaves me peacefully unconscious.

'I am with you,' I hear his gentle whisper as I search for him. I am surrounded by a field of my beautiful, mysterious flowers.

The velvet sky is enhanced, by the sparkles of the stars, far more vivid than I have ever seen.

'Where am I,' I whisper as I walk amongst the cool breeze of night, yearning to see him.

I can smell his scent; I know he is close to me.

A sensation of energy flows through my body; I can feel every cell of mine awakened by this strange phenomenon.

'Shayth,' I whisper as my breathing becomes heavy.

The vibration of energy presses against my skin, with my whole body feeling the pulse of the energy.

The cooling breeze against my sensitive skin adds to the intensity of the energy I am absorbed by.

'Breath,' I hear him whisper as I desperately take deep breaths from the sensation flowing through me.

I can feel him around me, his hands around my waist, his body pressing against me, his lips on my neck.

I can't see him.

The sensation intensifies, as I can no longer keep strength in my limbs.

My body falls weak while my knees begin to tremble. I can feel his energy pulsating within me. With all I have left, all I can do is take a deep breath.

My senses slowly awaken as I notice the shadows from a flickering light. I release a comforting sound as I slowly stretch my shoulders while lying on my bed. I gently run my hand along my face as I slowly wake from a rejuvenating sleep.

A smile grows on my face, from the feeling of serenity. I slowly open my eyes, my vision focuses on the shadows on the wall created by the flickering of the candles. Why are the candles lit I wonder?

I turn to my side; Shayth is sat beside me, reading through my notes.

'What just happened?' I blurt as my eyes widen from reality kicking in!

'Liyana! I am so very sorry!' Shayth insists as he puts the pad down and leans towards me offering me my glass of water!

I sit up rubbing my head in confusion.

'What, just...happened!' I ask feeling disorientated from the mystical experience that I faintly recall!

'I, I made you pass out,' he responds while trying to restrain the smile on his face.

His eyes are alive; his expression looks mischievous!

'How is that possible?' I question as I sit up and observe the candles while sipping on the glass of water.

'Where was I?' I add not knowing if I was dreaming. 'Wait, were you with me?' I question as I turn to look at him.

'Yes. I accompanied you in your dream,' he whispers, appearing unsure as to how I may react.

'Astral projection,' I whisper as a faint smile appears on my expression.

Shayth bites his lips together looking somewhat amused. 'Rule Number 2! I must control my energy when I am with you!' he states in a playful tone.

'Err, yes! Yes, you must!' I respond as if it was my suggestion. 'Why are the candles lit?' I ask looking confused as I place the glass of water down.

'Well,' Shayth clears his throat as if he is unsure as to how to explain this to me.

'When my energy, my emotion intensifies, it reacts with the energy in this world. In your case, it stimulates all the cells within your body, giving you an overwhelming sensation.'

'To the point where I pass out?' I slowly whisper Shayth offers me a cheeky smile.

'As for your lamp, my energy has, err, the lights blown.'

I scoff, as I fall into a state of total relaxation from the stimulation of all my cells no doubt.

'My very own drug dealer,' I whisper as I sink my head into my pillow, looking towards the ceiling feeling invigorated.

'It is I the one who is on a high,' he whispers as he hovers his head above me.

I pull him towards me as we both embrace in a warm, loving cuddle.

Cautious of what this may lead to, I lift my body weight and press against Shayth, tilting him onto his back.

'That's enough prince charming,' I whisper as I hover over him while stroking his soft, dark hair.

'We have a lot to get through!'

He raises his eyebrows as I offer a smile full of excitement. The interrogation begins!

'Firstly, why do your eyes occasionally glow?'

'The same reason your eyes are hazel. We are just born this way. The energy that flows through us is visible from within our eyes.'

'So everyone has the same eyes as you?'

'Not quite, all our eyes glow, but in different shades.'

'That's why the beasts have orange eyes that glow?' I whisper.

'Yes, they are enraged with hate and vengeance. It thickens their souls. Thus they mostly have orange and red eyes which reflects their evil, devious nature.'

I take a deep breath as I shake away the memories of the evil creatures preying on me.

'Okay, so what would we call you?'

'What do you mean?' he asks as he tilts his head in confusion.

'As in you refer to us as humans or mankind. What would we humans call you?'

Shayth scoffs, as he looks somewhat cautious as to how to answer this question.

'Liyana, before I answer this, I need you to remember that not everything is as it seems.'

I cannot help but frown from confusion, as I try to understand what could be the reason for Shayth feeling the need to make this statement.

'Sometimes a perception or a stereotype is created, which is unfair and does not reflect reality. Yet for the untrained mind, the stereotype forms their judgment, their opinion on people or subjects.'

Shayth sighs, as he seems reluctant to answer my question.

'I know you are different, I'll try to keep an open mind,' I whisper to offer him some comfort.

'We are called many things, but what I am…is…a *jinn*.'

He pauses for a moment, as he watches my reaction. The frown deepens across my expression as I struggle to comprehend if Shayth means what I think he does.

He inhales deep before continuing to proceed. 'The Abrahamic religions refer to us as, *jinns*.

Some call us *shedim*. And others call us spirit or, demon.'

A cold shiver runs through my spine as I inhale to take a deep breath.

My eyes open wide as my heartbeat becomes noticeably heavy, to which Shayth removes his hand from mine.

This can't be happening, my Shayth, he's a *jinn*, a demon!

My hands begin to shake simultaneously as my eyes begin to fill. You can hear it in my heavy breathing, which becomes more rapid as I begin to lose control of my emotions.

I close both my eyes as the tears drop onto my cheeks.

I cover my face with both my hands knowing full well that I am slowly losing control; I cannot overcome my weeping.

My world comes crashing down as the fear consumes me. Evil, demonic spirits that take pleasure in destruction and conflicting horrific pain, terrifying every soul it touches. Their darkness and malevolent desires, this is all I know of demons, of *jinns*.

'Liyana,' Shayth whispers, but I cannot bring my eyes to look at him.

I weep in my hands silently with my shoulders visibly shaking from the depth of my cry.

'Please! Do not think of me from what I am called, think of me from how I make you feel,' he pleas in a desperate attempt to gain acceptance of what he is.

I cannot help but cry into my hands, desperately trying hard to console myself.

'I'm sorry...' I whisper as I wipe my tears and part my hands while still holding onto my cheeks.

'Liyana...listen to me,' he whispers as he puts both his hands on my shoulders.

'How would you feel in a life without me,' he asks with big eyes.

'Lonely,' I whisper amongst the teary breathing.

'What would life be like with me?'

'Euphoria,' I offer a faint smile as I recall our conversation from last night.

'Are you afraid of me?'

My eyes fill again as I pause from worry as to how to answer this question.

'Not of who you are,' I whisper.

'But of what you are...'

His expression changes to one of anguish and hopelessness. Shayth sighs as he looks away from me. His eyes glimmer from a shine as the tears begin to reach the surface.

He stands to his feet and takes a step away as he brushes his hand through his hair.

'I... I am sorry,' he whispers in a shaken voice.

'I, I know not what I was thinking... I should not have...'

He walks closer to the balcony doors as he shakes his head side to side, in disbelief, in disappointment.

He grips the door handle before looking down to the ground as he whispers, 'I have been so foolish, I am truly sorry.'

At that moment my heart stops; I have no choice but to run to him.

I feel compelled towards him.

I wrap my arms around his neck as he stands there in shock. I weep on his neck as my lips brush against his skin, but he seems distant.

He offers a supportive hand on my back but seems reluctant to comfort me any further. As if he is forcing his emotions to remain in control.

At that moment, I realise… I am not crying for fear of him but in fear of losing him.

'What would life be like without me?' I sob as I squeeze him tight.

'Forsaken,' he whispers in a shaky voice.

'What would you do to be with me?' I cry.

'I would leave my world for you,' he scoffs as he slowly releases the door handle, placing his arm around my shoulders.

'Then don't ever let me go!' I cry. I feel his embrace tighten as he wraps his arms around me further, burying his head against my neck.

'Come with me,' he whispers while looking into my eyes.

As I look into his shimmering grey eyes, I feel safe. A sensation of warmth flows through me when I am close to him.

He's not a monster; he's not evil! He's *my* Shayth, my protector, my world.

I take his hand as we both stand on the balcony.

He brushes my hair behind my ears while wiping away the final drops of tears remaining on my cheeks.

'Do not let go,' he whispers as he holds me tight in his arms.

I embrace his body, his warmth, closing my eyes while the realisation of how much he means to me finally becomes apparent.

I bury my face in his neck, as I come to accept, though he is a *jinn*, a demon, he is all I want.

I focus on exactly how he makes me feel, safe, secure and complete; this is the only thing that matters.

'I can't be without you,' I whisper as I appreciate each second of being close to him. His masculine scent, his caring nature, his sacrificing outlook.

'Do not open your eyes,' he whispers as he tucks his feet under mine. I hold him tight as I feel us gently sway while a sudden chill from the night breeze sweeps in.

'Are you ready?' he whispers in a warm, soft tone.

I rub my nose against his cheeks feeling disheartened as I recall the sadness on his face that I had created.

He means so much to me; I could never put him through the pain that I saw in his eyes, from my fear of him.

'Open your eyes,' he whispers.

I can tell from his tone, he is smiling. The thought of him smiling puts a soft smile on my face as I squeeze him tight, from delight that he is no longer saddened.

I take a deep breath of his unique fragrance as I lift my head from his neck, slowly opening my eyes.

The stars look brighter than usual, larger than usual.

I stare in awe as I take a moment to appreciate their twinkling beauty.

We slowly spin around; how is he creating this illusion? How is he doing this?

I loosen my grip to look around and within that moment clutch hold of Shayth with dear life!

'HOW!' I gasp in shock.

My breathing accelerates from fear and excitement as the adrenaline rushes through my body.

'You thought I was joking when I said I would take you flying,' he teases.

'How is this possible?' I gasp as I laugh nervously at the sky.

'My world is not full of evil,' he whispers in a pleading tone. 'There is beauty, beyond any imagination.

'Let me show you,' he whispers with a warm, inviting smile.

I am mesmerised by the beauty of the peaceful night as we hover far above the trees. The streetlights become a faint glow in the distance.

He extends his wings as a wispy glow of white and blue surrounds him; it's his aura, his energy.

I pull away to see the illuminating lights are flowing all around his body!

'This is magical,' I whisper as I look into his eyes, which are sparkling with different shades of pale greys and whites with a hint of blue.

'If you could see what I see, you would know that your aura, your glow shines far brighter than mine!'

I smile in disbelief. How can this beauty exist?

'Hold onto me,' he requests as he gently lifts my body and places me on his back.

I immediately hold onto his shoulders and firmly press my body up against him, my arms around his neck with my cheek against his.

'I will never let you go!' he affirms as he takes a sudden sweep into the sky leaving me inhaling deep from the dramatic change in motion.

My body lies between his wings, which he extends to its full span.

They glisten in the moonlight from the scaly texture of each feather-like fragment as the wispy glow surrounds them.

We fly above the mountains and swarm in close to the waterfalls; each falling water droplet glimmer in the moonlight. As we glide further along we reach the sea, which holds gentle ripples from the breeze.

Shayth can sense my excitement at watching the calm ocean as he dives closer.

I watch our reflection against the smooth waters and notice a gleaming smile on Shayth's face.

I cannot help but feel alive! To feel free! I release a hand from around his shoulders and hover it above the ocean.

I lower my hand as it touches the fresh, dark waters.

My hand flows through the tip of the sea as it creates a faint splash leaving a trail of our presence rippling through the ocean.

I laugh out loud at the unimaginable beauty of this moment. As I pull my hand back from the glistening waters, Shayth takes my hand into his as he presses his lips against them.

We glide through the calm skies and twirl amongst the twinkling lights, watching the birds fly beneath us while knowing that no force can come in-between us.

'…The only limits in our life are those we impose on ourselves…'

–   Bob Proctor

25. Spectrums of Life

The days seem a blur as I lay in my bed and make the most of a lie in.

I smile up at the ceiling as I think of my Shayth and everything he has tried to do for me. The way he is always there for me. The way he has protected me. When all the time, I never knew it was him; I never knew he existed.

Surely there can be no evil in a person who does all they can to keep you safe, regardless of what the typical stereotype may suggest. It makes me think of how brainwashed and ignorant I may be in other aspects of my life.

The thought itself makes me frown; I feel blind to the world. It feels as if I have a veil cloaking my eyes from the realities of life; a veil created by mankind. No longer able to appreciate things for what they are, but allowing society and media to dictate how I view the world.

It saddens me to think what I have learned to fear is a result of societies stereotypical views rather than any factual substance.

'Pleeaaasee, Aunt Liz,' I hear Micky plea. 'I just want to check if she's awake.' I can hear Aunt Liz respond to Micky, but her voice is too faint for me to make out clearly.

No doubt she is instructing Micky not to come to me!

I instantly jump out of bed, wrapping my gown around me as I head downstairs.

'Liyana!' Micky shouts with excitement as I see him stood in the middle of the staircase. Aunt Liz walks away from the bottom of the stairs the moment she notices me approaching.

Micky and I share cuddles and head downstairs.

'Will you come with me to get my Halloween costume? I want to be a pirate!' Micky asks in excitement.

Aunt Liz puts her spoon down onto her bowl of fruits with a look of discontent.

'I thought we were going to go together,' Aunt Liz snaps.

'Yeah but Liyana can come too,' Micky insists with a worried expression on his face.

Uncle Aidan glares at Aunt Liz who refuses to make eye contact with anyone on the table.

'Oh. I actually have a few things to catch up on, Micky, but I thought maybe tomorrow we could spend the whole day together? We could all have a barbeque maybe and a cinema night?'

'Sounds fantastic,' Uncle Aidan adds as he offers me a warm smile.

Regardless of how tactful I try to be, to please Aunt Liz discreetly or rather avoid her from becoming even more furious, Uncle Aidan seems to always see right through me.

I sit on my bed as I search the Internet for Halloween costume ideas; witch, that will do!

Knock, knock! I look up at the balcony to see Shayth standing there with my beautiful majestic flower.

'What are you doing here?' I whisper with the widest grin on my expression as I run to the balcony.

Panic runs through me as I pull him into my room and look out into the garden; Uncle Aidan is still sat there with a book not having noticed a thing.

'Are you mad!' I snap from the shock of almost getting caught. 'My uncle could have seen you!' I whisper as he walks towards me.

'I was just following your rules,' he responds with a cheeky smile.

He hands the flower to me and holds me in his arms with a gentle squeeze.

'I have missed you,' he whispers as he pulls away from our tight embrace.

My heart begins to flutter; I can feel a hot flush working its way through my body.

'I can see,' I respond with a cheeky smile as I start to inhale the scent of my mystical flower.

'What are these called?' I ask, forcing my hot flush to cool away as I distract myself from Shayth's loving affection.

'Missara; it's the most opulent graceful flower in my dimension. It reminds me of you.'

'It's beautiful,' I whisper as I tuck my hair behind my ear, feeling nervous and not knowing where to look.

'I need to go away for a few days,' he states in a soft but serious tone.

Instantly I look up at him; my eyes are wide open.

He smirks at my reaction; no doubt he can sense something from my aura.

'It's just for a few days, a few family matters I need to attend to.' He offers me a warm smile as he puts his hands on my arms.

'Is everything okay? They don't know, do they? That you have broken the sacred law?'

He chuckles as the panic grows on my face.

'Do not worry; they know not,' he responds reassuringly.

'And your friend? No one knows he has broken the rules to help you?'

'Who, Khallum? He knows what he is doing. He will not get caught.'

We pause for a moment as we hold onto each other's hands. 'Will you be in lectures on Monday?' I ask with hopeful eyes.

'Unlikely,' he confirms as he shakes his head.

The look of disappointment is evident from my facial expression.

'But, I would like to come and see you Monday night, if that is permitted?'

My frown suddenly turns into a sheepish smile.

'Suppose I have to let you, otherwise who knows what you will do in despair,' I respond with a cheeky smile.

'Liyana!' Uncle Aidan shouts from the base of the stairs.

'You need to go!' I whisper in panic as the footsteps of Uncle Aidan become louder.

I walk towards the balcony forcing Shayth to walk backward; he smiles away at my panicked reaction.

I turn to look back at the door as Uncle Aidan calls my name again.

'Before I go,' Shayth whispers.

I turn to look at him as he places a gentle kiss on my lips.

For a split moment, I think of nothing but the warmth of his touch as his lips brush against mine!

Knock, knock. 'Liyana,' Uncle Aidan calls as he opens my bedroom door.

I gasp as I turn to look at him. My heart pounds from the fear of what Uncle Aidan will say! How will I even explain this to him! 'Uncle!' I gasp.

'You okay, kiddo? You look like you've seen a ghost!' I turn to the balcony, Shayth is nowhere in sight!

'Oh. You just made me jump that's all.'

I help Uncle Aidan with the gardening and the weekend soon disappears as we spend family time on Sunday where I can focus my attention on my beautiful little Micky.

We sit in the cafeteria during lunch; Nevaeh is full of excitement while explaining to us the Halloween costume she had purchased over the weekend.

I glance across the cafeteria and notice Trixy walk in with her Aphrodite friends following behind.

She doesn't look her usual glamorous self. More gaunt and plain than usual.

Her hair is dull and lifeless, not holding the usual bouncy curls she usually has styled in.

Her friends seem to carry a constant frown on their face as they look somewhat distant to Trixy; almost coming across as timid. As they take a seat, I watch her closest friend put a comforting arm around Trixy whilst pushing forward her lunch tray.

In a fit of rage, Trixy pushes the tray across the table, forcing her friends around her to jump from fear.

Perhaps the paleness in her face is from the thickness of multiple layers of makeup she has applied to camouflage any bruising I wonder. Maybe an ego dent hence her effortless look today.

The day drags slowly as I await the company of Shayth in the evening.

I sit in bed as I catch up on my assignments.

My heart flutters at the tapping sound on my balcony.

I look up to be greeted with a warm smile from Shayth as he leans his head against the glass.

He stares at me with gentle eyes, seeming as if he may have been there for some time.

I blink my eyes, instantly he is sat beside me!

I gasp in shock, feeling stunned by his unnatural abilities that my mind struggles to comprehend.

'I am sorry. I did not mean to startle you,' Shayth whispers softly with a brash smile on his face.

'I have a lot to get used to!' I whisper as I shake my head in disbelief.

'How were your family matters?' I ask with a hint of nervousness.

He chuckles at my fearful facial expression.

'Do not worry,' he whispers as he glides his fingers across my cheeks.

'Everything is fine, nothing to be concerned over.'

He takes my hand as he places a gentle kiss on the surface.

I hear footsteps along the corridor. Perhaps Aunt Liz or Uncle Aidan going to their bedroom.

'Let's go from here,' I whisper as I stare at the door.

'Where would you like me to take you? There are so many beautiful sites you would love!'

I cannot help but giggle at his offer.

'Nowhere, prince charming! Meet me on the swing bench in the garden.'

I grab a fleece blanket as I head out of my room, leaving Shayth looking confused.

I tiptoe downstairs and quietly enter the garden.

I find Shayth sitting patiently on the bench shaking his head in confusion with a curious smile as I approach him.

I sit on the bench beside him and offer him half my blanket.

'What is this in aid of?' he asks while lowering his eyebrows.

'To keep us warm when the night's breeze sets in,' I whisper as I lean further back on the seat to get comfy.

He offers a faint chuckle as he pulls himself back onto the bench coming closer towards me.

'I am your blanket,' he whispers as he tilts his head to look at me.

'I am made of energy, of fire. My job is to keep you warm,' he whispers as the tip of his nose caresses my cheek.

I scoff at the very thought.

'I don't understand? What do you mean?'

Shayth leans back as he stares into the sky admiring the glimmer of the stars above.

'Our creator had made mankind out of clay, angels out of light, and *jinns* from the smokeless flames of fire.'

He smiles as he turns to look at me.

'I cannot sense any fear in you; you are taking this well,' he mocks as he takes my hand in his.

I scoff, as even I am surprised. But I have realised, the one who has been protecting me in the darkness, who's broken their sacred rules for my attention, is never one I have to be fearful of.

'So you believe in God?' I ask intrusively.

'We believe in a higher power. In my world, we have seen so much. We are able to do so much. And the beauty that exists, the way we are all in harmony with each creation, belief in a higher power, our creator, the almighty, this forms part of our sacred laws.'

A sense of comfort flows through me as I realise we may have more in common than what I had initially anticipated, far from the stereotypical views of *jinns* and their satanic rituals and beliefs.

'So how is it possible that we have not known of your existence? This parallel dimension?' I ask in surprise.

'This is written in the holy scriptures and even validating by science to some extent.

'Like with most truths, it is hidden from the vast majority. How do you think the world would react to the news that entities of another dimension surround them?'

I scoff at the stupidity of my question.

'Whoever reveals this, would be deemed by the world as crazy! And those that believe it would drive themselves crazy from fear.'

Shayth Chuckles as he holds me closer. 'Take the concept of matter,' he continues. 'We are dark matter; you are baryonic matter. Baryonic matter makes up 5% of the universe. Dark matter makes up 26% of our universe.'

'What's the remaining 69%?' I ask in confusion.

Shayth scoffs. 'Dark energy, but we will talk more about that when you have dark matter under control.'

I offer him a smile as I feel like a student, a novice.

'Mankind, trees, plant, stars, solar system, galaxies, everything you can see, this is matter. Baryonic matter.

'Dark matter is the unseen creation of this world, of this universe. Unseen, making you unable to sense or see its impacts, you are unaware of its existence.

'Like I have been, all this time, all those weeks when you did not notice me.

'Look around you, can you see everything here?'

'Yes,' I respond wearily as I'm sure my answer is wrong.

'What about the dust particles, the oxygen, the carbon, gravity even? Can you see these?'

'No.'

'But you know it exists?'

'Yes,' I offer confidently.

'Not all mass and matter are visible,' he continues in his teachings.

'It's estimated that what you can see, is only 0.005% of what exists, 0.005% of the electromagnetic spectrum.

'Humans are virtually blind in what can be seen, compared to what there is to see.

'Visible light is only a small frequency of the full spectrum that is visible to you; this is not the end of the spectrum.

This explains the parallel dimension that I exist in. It's on a spectrum which the human eyes cannot envision.'

Shayth pauses for a moment while he looks deep in thought.

'The ordinary mind will believe what is simple and easy to understand. This is the way society has trained your minds.

'It is a proven fact; things exist that you cannot see.

'Mankind believes this in the most basic form; air, wind, gravity, particle, microscopic bugs even.

'But put a religious connotation to it, and the human mind refuses to believe that things that cannot be seen actually exist, be it dimensions or spirits. Mankind will then demand visual proof of this to validate its existence.

'Mankind argues that there is no rational or logical to believe in another life form co-habiting the earth as it cannot be seen, yet it is never questioned how can it be reasonable to believe in dark matter which cannot be seen.

'Mankind refuse the belief of my world only because it cannot be seen.'

'Hypocrisy,' I whisper as I snuggle into the blanket from the chill breezing in.

'Here let me,' he whispers as he squeezes my hand gently. A force of heat flows around us, shielding me from the wind.

'Wow,' I whisper. 'I could get used to this.'

Shayth scoffs as I tuck in towards him.

'I am your very own thermostat,' he jests.

'I always thought when spirits are around, the atmosphere freezes, like a sudden cold chill.'

'Yes, that can happen,' he affirms.

'We are creations made of energy, fire – a form of energy. Thus we can absorb the existing energy in an atmosphere or provide the atmosphere with our energy, our heat.'

'So why would you absorb the energy from an atmosphere?' I question eagerly.

'For strength.'

'Strength?'

'It is like a recharge of our batteries. But to be honest, it's never a good sign. If you enter a room and suddenly all the heat is drained out, it's more than likely that an entity is present who has sucked out the heat energy for its own gain. That's unless you've opened a window of course.'

I am stunned at this thought as I try to recall if I have ever experienced such a phenomenon.

'There was a joke in my statement,' Shayth whispers as he nudges my shoulder.

I scoff at my slow response and proceed to put my arm around him.

'So how do you do it?'

He looks at me with raised eyebrows. 'How do you appear, disappear?'

'We have the capability to transform from one spectrum of mass to the other. So if you think at one end of the spectrum is matter, and the other end is dark matter, we can transfer our energy to the varying levels of the spectrum.'

I look deep into him as all this information consumes me. 'Take water for example; imagine water had its own conscience whereby it could control its own temperature.'

'Okay,' I respond feeling confused on where this is going.

'Now frozen water becomes a solid form, in freezing temperatures.'

'Yeah,' I agree while being none the wiser of where this is going. Shayth smiles as he watches the confusion grow on my expression.

'Now, anything less than freezing and the water appears in a liquid form right?'

'Yes,' I respond in a more assertive tone.

'Good. Now, what happens when you heat the water to a boiling point? The same water that was once in a solid and liquid form?'

'It evaporates,' I whisper.

'Exactly. Here you have a compound that can transform into solid, liquid and gas molecules.

'We are the same. We can transform our energy from one spectrum to be unseen, to another spectrum, to be seen, thus having a physical form.

'We will simply shift into the colour spectrum of light-waves that is visible to mankind and increase the density of our matter.

'And it is the same concept with our tone, our voice.

'We have the capacity to project the energy of our voice to a frequency which you can hear or not.'

Shayth pauses for a moment, as he appears to recall a memory. 'The ability to transform matter into energy and back into matter…the cusp of Einstein's famous relativity equation, E=MC Squared.

'Energy and matter are related, he knew of our dimension and our abilities to execute this. We are the very basis that inspired his equation. Equally, he knew that mankind was not ready to be introduced to our dimension just yet.'

I absorb all the information that Shayth has shared.

Though I feel much more enlightened to the nature of his species, I know I have only hit the tip of the iceberg.

'So what about the darker side of your dimension,' I ask hesitantly.

'What do you mean?' he whispers softly as he strokes the top of my hair while we swing below the stars.

'Well, the typical stereotype of demonic spirits and their evil ways; is there any aspect of truth behind this? Especially from the creatures that I encountered?'

The thought of the evil beasts sends a chill down my spine; I hold onto Shayth a little tighter.

'Are you sure you want to talk about the darker side, lady Liyana? As I said, I want to ease you into my world; I do not want you to be afraid.'

'No it's okay, I'm ready,' I affirm, though my heart begins to beat faster as the fear slowly creeps in.

'…Do not be overcome by evil, but overcome evil with good…'

–   Romans 12:21

26. The Dark Side

'Think of felidae, the biological family of cats.

'This ranges from Lions, tigers, panthers, leopards all the way through to jungle cats, wild cats and domestic cats.'

I nod as I pay careful attention and follow his line of thought. 'These are all various species but are still part of the same biological family. Some are wild animals that would devour you alive, whereas others you would welcome into your home and consider as part of the family – two very extreme spectrums.

'Yes,' I agree as I sit eagerly to hear more.

'Well, we are very similar to that concept, just far more extreme!'

Rather than staring at the sky, Shayth stares into me, as if to monitor my reaction from what he is about to share.

'There are many types of species within our race.

'All of the species are capable of transforming into visible matter and dark matter.

'We are all able to see the dimension of mankind and the aura of humans.

'We all live, and we all die.

'These are the 3 points that each species has in common.

'Now within the species, we have two major groups, similar to the felidae where you have the wild cannibalistic cats and the friendly household cats.

'I am a *jinn* or a spirit as some may call us. We reflect the advanced civilised species.

'Then we have the *shayateens*, demons, or *shedims* as others call them. These are the wild animals, the cannibals you want to avoid.'

I gulp as the fear crouches deep into my mind.

'Within the realm of the *jinns*, we uphold our sacred laws and govern the remaining species to ensure they live within the boundaries set by these laws, sentinels of the dimensions if you will.

'We are the most intellectual in our species and hold the most self-control. Something we have learned to master over the centuries.

'We are able to fly, and our fire or energy reflects that of a blue, pure flame.

'The *shayateens*, the demons come in three main sects.

'Those that primarily shapeshift, those that travel, known as the dwellers, and those that wreak havoc, the most powerful and maleficent of them all.

'The shapeshifts are limited to what each demon can shapeshift into, dependent on the strength and skill they have.

'They primarily shift into wild dogs and serpent like creatures. Some are able to fly but only a few.

'The travellers or dwellers you will be more familiar with as poltergeists.

'As for the most powerful, there is only a handful of these that exist at any one time. They are known as *ifreets*.

'Their fire, their energy reflects that of the orange and red flames, uncontrolled and raging.'

I can't help but imagine the uncontrollable rage which must be experienced by their most powerful, the *ifreets*.

'What do mankind associate with the *ifreets*?' I reluctantly ask, not sure I want to know the answer.

'*Ifreets*, like I said, are very rare. Their power is extreme and challenging for even them to control at times.

'*Ifreets* tend to have little interaction with mankind. But in terms of association, *ifreets* are what causes the rare phenomenon that mankind refers to as SHC.'

'I don't know what that is,' I confess as I try to control my raising heartbeat.

'SHC – Spontaneous Human Combustion. Combustion of a living body without an apparent external source of ignition.'

'When humans randomly burst into flames?' I barely manage to whisper.

'Yes, their abilities have no limits,' he affirms.

'Are all *ifreets* evil?' I whisper as I am captivated by this extraordinary world that exists alongside mankind.

'Most are, though not all. We have one who has this power amongst our species, Argyle.

'Argyle, so is he a *jinn* or a *shayateen*, an *ifreet*?'

'*Jinns* are those who have vowed to protect the parallel dimensions, those that dedicate their lives to ensure peaceful cohabitation, upholding our sacred laws. There are many *shayateens*, many demons that were once evil, but have changed their world, changed their ways to now become protectors of the realms, protectors of the innocent.'

'So Argyle, he used to be evil?'

'I have never known Argyle to be evil, but yes, at some point of his existence, he was not righteous as he is now.'

'Is Argyle the most powerful in your realm?'

'Yes, he is! He is the marshal, the general, the admiral in my world.

'He is capable of traveling at the speed of light. These are the most powerful of us all. They have the ability to transform matter into energy and back into matter.

'But as I said, only a handful – if that exists at any one time.

'In the time of Solomon and Sheba from the biblical and Hebrew scriptures, only one *jinn* existed at that time who was able to transport Sheba's thrown into King Solomon's palace at the blink of an eye.'

I stare at him blank from confusion.

'But I thought all in your dimension could transform from dark matter to matter.'

He looks at me with a loving smile.

'Yes. We can transform ourselves from dark matter to matter, but transforming a manmade object of baryonic matter into dark matter and traveling at the speed of light to then transform the object back into mankind's existence is not something any of us can do other than *ifreets*.'

'So you can transform objects from your world into mine?'

'Yes.'

'Like the missara flower and your car!'

'Exactly.'

'But you cannot transfer something from my world into yours?'

'No, I do not have the physical strength to do so. There are very few that can.'

'So your cars not Japanese?'

Shayth begins to laugh as he offers me a cuddle.

'You know, I cannot recall ever stating it was Japanese.'

281

I scoff at my stupidity of thinking his vehicle was manufactured here; it's so unique, it all makes sense now.

'So why do you all have different abilities and strengths?'

I question as I try to get my head around the varying levels of abilities they possess.

'We have abilities which seem to you to be supernatural. Flickering of lights, the opening of doors.

'We are not all-powerful supernatural incredible beings, lady Liyana.

'When you see an animal has abilities that you do not possess, for instance, when you look at birds flying through the sky or fish swimming the depths of the sea, you are not surprised, nor do these things terrify you.

'In the same instance, you should not be surprised there are other creations out there that are able to carry out actions, which you are incapable of.'

I sigh, my mind feeling overwhelmed from the depth of our discussion. I cannot help but feel frightened from the abilities of this parallel world; it could destroy me without me even knowing I am under attack.

'Let me try and find an analogy which may comfort you,' Shayth adds as he can sense my discomfort.

'Birds can fly just as I can.

'Certain animals are able to change their colour and their shape to some degree; this doesn't terrify you, you do not fall into paranoia. Such as a chameleon, or the mimic octopus.

'Just as there are humans that are able to lift 20 kg while others can lift 100 kg. Some are far more intelligent than others. Some humans can run as fast as animals whereas others would struggle with a brisk walk.

'We are merely another creation with different abilities. We can manipulate matter and have the advantage of being unseen. But this does not give us the warrant to be feared. We do not deserve to be feared.

'But when we are feared, that is when the miscreant *shayateen's* confidence is enhanced. They feed off fear, the energy that fear gives off; it offers strength to the *shayateen*. Do not give them more respect than they deserve.

'You see a plate or a vase flying across the room – you throw one back across the room.

'Do not show any reverence.

'Only our creator deserves to be feared, not his creations.'

'How can people not know this?' I whisper as I try to apprehend this information.

Shayth scoffs lightly as he rubs his hand against my shoulder. 'This isn't a new modern day notion,' he whispers as he tries to comfort me.

'The Gnostics who had ancient scriptures and accounts from 100 AD referred to non-human energetic forces they called Archons; made from luminous fire existing in an unseen realm.

'Through to the realm of the Zulus in Africa, who talk about the Chitauri in similar terms.

'Even in ancient Egyptian times, why do you think the pharaohs kept statues of human bodies with animal heads? *Jinns* and *shayateens* were openly cohabitating with the Egyptians. Working side by side with them in many instances, like the creation of the pyramids; without the strength and abilities of the *jinns*, the structures could never be assembled.

'To more recent times of the early 1960s, an American anthropologist, Carlos Castaneda, authored books detailing the unseen forces described as the flyers.

'The first recorded demonic possessions took place in 1500; to more recent years, right here in the 21st century.

'There is a lot of awareness out there, though the subject is somewhat controversial.'

I stare at the tops of the trees as I watch the wind pushing against the branches.

I cannot help but think of what *shayateens* may be lurking behind the trees beside us, watching us, conspiring against us.

'Can we go back inside,' I whisper in a timid tone.

'Have I shared too much?' Shayth asks with a concerned expression.

'No! No, not at all...' I pause as I take a deep breath.

'I need to know this; I need to understand your world, just the way you understand mine.'

I wrap up in the blankets and cuddle onto Shayth who lies by my side on top of the sheets.

'Do you all live in the trees?' I ask as I stare at the treetops from the comfort of my own safe home.

'No,' he responds with a smirk.

'Uninhabited places primarily. The forests do inhabit a significant amount of us, but we also live in the desserts, canyons, mountains, even the seas.

'So there is nowhere that is safe?' I whisper as for the first time I feel so minute and insignificant.

'You are always safe, Liyana,' Shayth whispers in a reassuring tone. You do not understand the strength you have, the strength I see in you. And besides, I am always here to protect you! You are mine now.'

'If I'm so strong, why would the *shayateens*, the demons attack me?' I whisper as my voice begins to shake.

'I, I do not know,' he whispers suddenly not sounding so sure. 'There has been increased activity in this area, and I am not sure why. But look, it took three *shayateens*, three demons to face you! One would not be capable of defeating your strength alone, so they rely on your fear to overpower you.'

'I don't feel strong, Shayth,' I whisper in confession as I'm daunted by this new revelation.

'It is not a physical strength I am referring to. It's the strength of your mind, of your soul, your sub-conscience, your grace.'

'How do I make it stronger?' I desperately ask.

'Your way of life, maintain your purity. The way you love others, the way you help others. The way you never wish harm to others and constantly seek to do good. And above all, the sacrifices you constantly make for your loved ones around you, without even realising you do.'

I squeeze Shayth tight as his comforting words lift my spirit. 'Why do they hate us? These *shayateens*, these demons! Why do they want to harm us?'

'It's the oldest battle of existence...' he whispers as he begins to frown.

'But how do they chose who to target? What are we doing wrong?' I question, as I cannot understand why we would be hunted.

'They are attracted to people dependent on their aura which is a reflection of their mindset and their emotions.'

Shayth sighs as I watch the look of discomfort fill his expression.

'We, amongst the *jinns* have our sacred rules that we live to which foremost is to preserve the peaceful co-existence of our planet.

'The rebellious spirits within our dimension that form the race of the *shayateens*, the demons live differently to the way we do. They follow a different set of laws, a conflicting and hostile code, which promotes the dwelling and manifestation of the human race. Corruption to scale down and eventually diminish any pure soul.'

I hold onto Shayth tight as I bury my face in his chest from fear of being a target.

'So if I have a pure soul, I will always be a target…'

'Liyana, you must believe me,' he whispers in a stern tone.

'It is not as simple as you think it is…' Shayth pauses for a moment as I loosen my grip on him.

'The *shayateens*, the demons cannot dwell within a pure soul. They need to entice it first to become corrupt. The more corrupt you become, the easier it becomes for the demonic forces to manipulate your physical form.

They are attracted to people dependent on their aura – their mindset. The purer your aura then, the stronger you. They will not be able to overrule your inner conscious, your spiritual soul.

'When humans are weak, their aura reflects this. When they have ill desires and an evil streak within them, auras reflect this.

'Could you possess me?'

I whisper as I look into him.

He offers me a loving smile as he gently bites his bottom lip.

'No,' he whispers.

'If I tried, your spirit, your aura will drain my energy. It would be like me fighting with an invisible force, which is your aura – I would always be defeated.

'This is why I say; never fear them for they are not worthy of being feared. With a pure soul and clean heart, no evil force can defeat you. However, if fear overcomes you, this is what weakens your aura and gives the *shayateen* strength. This is why you must never fear them, this way, your aura will always repel them.'

'So what attracts them? As in what qualities would encourage them to dwell within a human body.'

'It is difficult,' he sighs.

'They will try to target the purest of souls for they are the gold prize within the demonic realm.

'But equally a gold medal does not come easily. This is why it is not very common to see this type of dwelling and why it may take more than one *shayateen* to break the pure soul.

'What is more common is the influence, manipulation of a person who is weak souled, that the *shayateens*, the demons will find easier to manipulate.'

'What would make someone weak souled?'

I stare up at Shayth with a serious expression as I eagerly wait to hear more.

'The desire to see people fail or for them to not outdo you. Excessive arrogance, with little appreciation or gratitude, constant laziness and negativity, backbiting and hypocrisy. Love for possessions rather than love for life, for nature, for the less fortunate.'

I begin to think of all the faces I know in university to ensure they do not possess the majority of these traits.

'An egotistical outlook, constant manipulation of others, materialism, jealousy, anger, superiority...' Shayth pauses for a moment.

'Superiority and materialism comes from evil.

'Satan thought himself better than Adam, as he was made of fire and Adam was made of clay.

''Superiority enraged the reasoning of his disobedience and dislike of mankind.'

He scoffs as he shakes his head.

'Yet mankind has taken this a step further and judge their superiority against other races within their species! Based on their colour, their origin, their social class. But were you not all made from the same substance? Your bodies will decay in the ground no different to each other.

'Materialism feeds pride which feeds superiority, which feeds greed. This is a vicious cycle as it creates arrogance and disobedience in acceptance that we are all equal. We all have our place in this world; it does not belong to a particular race or species, it was gifted to us all.'

We both sit in silence as I contemplate over everything Shayth has shared.

'Evil is not an easy force to conquer. We all have it in us; it's simply a question of whether we will let it manifest within us or whether we will have the courage not to allow it to control us.'

I think hard as I reflect upon my life and picture the laughter of my family until the darkness had taken them away.

'How would you know if someone is being influenced? If a *shayateen*, a demon dwells within?' I ask as I prepare my mind to stay strong to hear of the effects of this evil and disguised battle.

'It rarely happens overnight. As evil a person may be, there is always goodness hiding within them, somewhere!

It's a phenomenon that can take days, if not months, depending on the individual's strength and awareness of what is happening.'

'So you are aware of demonic influences happening – when it happens?' I ask in surprise.

'You are aware that something is happening to you that you are changing. But in most instances, people do not know why they are changing or the reality of what is actually happening.'

'So what would someone experience? What would the symptoms be?'

'If I explain this to you, you must promise me you will not jump to irrational conclusions and begin to analyse every aspect and behaviour of individuals you pass,' he jests as he shakes me gently by the shoulder.

'I'll try,' I whisper as I force a faint smile on my expression.

'Okay. The symptoms are shared with many other illnesses and problems in life, which make it very difficult to diagnose.

'There is no guarantee that a *shayateen*, a demon touches everyone who displays these symptoms.

'Let me give you an example to make sure you do not take this out of context.'

Shayth sits up and looks towards me.

I mimic his movement as I sit up straight and focus on his words.

'Let's say you visit a doctor and explain you have a headache; there could be a hundred reasons for this!

'You may be dehydrated; you may need glasses, you may not have slept the night before, you may be stressed, you may have a brain tumour! Such an array of possibilities, from the most insignificant matter to the most extreme severe condition.

'Accompanied by other symptoms, the doctor can diagnose you accordingly.'

I nod paying careful attention to every word.

'Never look at a single symptom in isolation as you will worry yourself to death. When a person displays the majority of these symptoms, then is the time to consider the possibility of a demonic presence, a demonic influence.'

I brace myself as I eagerly await Shayth's knowledge.

'Sudden rapid changes in personality, like extreme mood swings or drastic changes in interests.

'Bodily sensations such as extreme heat with the sense of burning or coldness even with constant shivers.

'Severe and repeating nightmares, which seem so vivid and real, you, are almost convinced they happened.

'Sleep problems such as sleep paralysis, sleepwalking, hallucinations, particularly of clouds and figures that you sense are not human.

'A liking to be in places of filth and isolation.

'Crawling sensations such as ants all over your body, thus constantly scratching at your skin to the point where you are tearing into your flesh.

'Hearing voices that others cannot, voices on a different frequency; the voices of the *shayateen*.

'Sudden displays of emotions in the most inappropriate of times; for instance, when everyone is crying, and the subject appears laughing in extreme pleasure.

'Extreme increase in physical strength, speaking in tongues with no experience.

A change in facial structure or voice – when their entire face completely twists to the point where you can no longer see the person in the way they usually are.'

I cover my face with the palm of my hands and slowly part them while resting my fingertips against my temples.

'This is insane,' I whisper in disbelief.

Shayth takes me in his arms as he holds my hand for comfort. 'Like I said, you are not in a frequency range that they can manipulate. Your frequency range is visible from your aura that you radiate.

'When you reach a frequency of love, peace and integrity, you become a challenge to the darker forces who want to destroy your frequency as it overpowers them when they come close to you.'

Shayth pauses for a moment as he focuses on an abrasion on my knuckles, from my altercation with Trixy.

'If we respond with anger, aggression and fear, we are playing within their field of frequency, which can be manipulated by them without us even realising. We enter their playground.

'It's essential that you never lose yourself from who you really are.'

'Why isn't this public knowledge?' I whisper as a sense of remorse runs through me.

'You would be surprised!

'More people know of our existence than you realise. Some chose not to believe this truth, while others chose to manipulate this truth.'

Shayth pauses or a moment and then shakes his head as he scoffs.

'The irony here,' he whispers.

'Is that we are dark matter, yet it is humans that are kept in the dark...'

'…The enemy is fear. We think it is hate but it is fear…'

–   Gandhi

27. Psychological Disorder

As I walk towards the building, I watch the behaviour of all the students in the courtyard, some jumping around, some laughing, some being aggressive.

I feel as if the rose-tinted glasses have been removed from my eyes; for the first time, I am able to see life for what it really is; I am no longer walking blind.

I watch the behaviour of the students and feel much more alert to what surrounds me.

Are they behaving in this way from their choice, or because their strings are being pulled; because they are being influenced; manipulated by the unseen.

As the crowds part, I find him standing there, wearing a smile as he shakes his head.

Shayth had warned me not to get carried away in analysing the behaviour of everyone that crosses my path.

I break a smile as I approach him and cannot help but feel as if I am free.

As if I have been released from unseen shackles, released from a veil, which blinded me to the realities of life.

I feel as if I see life, for what it really is, rather than some poetic fantasy that society has led me to believe.

But most importantly, I see Shayth, for what he really is.

A caring, loving person, a *jinn*, who would literally sacrifice his world for me!

'Name three behaviours that enable a minority to influence a majority?'

A number of hands are raised in the lecture before a student is selected.

'Behavioural style – appearing to be unbiased.'

'Well done!' the lecturer applauds as he scans the room to select another student.

'Style of thinking – the minority simply encouraging the majority to think about the minority issue.'

'Excellent! And a final behaviour.'

'Identification,' states another student. 'Hearing a message from someone you consider similar to yourself. Whether this is age, race or gender for example.'

'Now, who can give me one problem associated with alpha bias? Yes, you young sir.'

'There is a misrepresentation of behaviour; researchers/theorists overestimate/exaggerate gender differences.'

'And for beta bias?' the lecturer asks the same student.

'Simply that they are underestimated.'

'Good! That was the warm-up. Now for more interesting matters, psychological disorders!

Who can tell me what disorder involves extreme swings of mood from elation to depression?'

'Bipolar,' shouts Nevaeh besides me.

'Great. Now according to the biological preparedness hypothesis, which phobias would you expect to be most common.'

'Ophidophobia,' shouts Shayth besides me.

'And that is?' the lecturer encourages.

'Fear of snakes,' Shayth responds.

The topic of snake phobia forces me to recall flashbacks of the snake-like demon I had encountered in the forest.

Perhaps I may develop Ophidophobia, I wonder.

'Now what about hallucinations and delusions; what are these symptoms of?'

'Schizophrenia,' I state in a quieter voice compared to the rest of the volunteers.

'What was that?' asks the lecturer.

I clear my voice as I proceed to respond.

'Schizophrenia – a mental disorder involving a breakdown in the relation between thought, emotion and behaviour. Leading to faulty perceptions, inappropriate actions. A sense of mental fragmentation forcing one into fantasy and delusion while withdrawing from reality.'

'10 out of 10!' compliments the lecturer.

'A couple more, what label did Emil Kraepelin give to schizophrenia because he believed it resulted from premature deterioration of the brain?'

'Dementia Praecox,' a young lady in the front row answers.'

'Perfect! Now for the final question, one of the most serious side effects of neuroleptics is a continuous involuntary movement disorder, particular movements of the face and mouth. This disorder is known as?'

'Akathesis,' answers a young student in the room.

'Close but no! Akathesis is the movement disorder characterised by a feeling of inner restlessness with the compelling need to continuously be in motion, fidgeting, rocking back and forth, crossing and uncrossing of legs, etc. Anyone else?'

The lecturer is quiet, as no one seems to know the answer. Shayth suddenly raises his voice.

'Tardive Dyskinesia,' he states softly.

'Well done young man!' the lecturer complements before the students begin to pack their belonging for lunch.

Nevaeh and I sit outside in the stadium as we wait for Sammy to join us. We watch DeJon and the team practice for their upcoming tournaments. They seem to be laughing as Romeo rolls around on the floor from having missed in his attempt in kicking the ball. 'Nevaeh, can I ask you something strange?'

'Course hun, they are the questions I love the most!' she responds with a welcoming smile.

'When you attend your tribal festivals, what do you talk about?' She laughs as she shakes her head!

'You said it was something strange! I was expecting something more than that,' she jests.

'We have so many festivals! Spring festival, Green Corn festivals, Winter festival! Amongst all the singing and dancing, we always revisit the teachings and customs of the tribe. We always partake in the water purification ritual and a fast. You can come with me next time,' she suggests.

'Sure, that's really kind, thank you,' I confirm.

I smile nervously as I feel hesitant to ask the next question, but am desperate to understand a different viewpoint.

'So what about evil and demons? What are the tribal teachings on that aspect?'

'Hah! Is Halloween getting the better of you,' she jokes.

'The Cherokees, we have a belief system, which includes spiritual beings known as the little people. Though it's against our beliefs to talk about them or any encounters with them, particularly at nightfall when they are mostly about.'

'Oh, I'm so sorry, I didn't mean to make you break the belief in talking about them.'

Nevaeh cannot control her fit of laughter as she points at my serious facial expression.

'It's cool, it's just old folklore!' she insists.

'Oh, okay,' I respond feeling relieved that I can proceed with more questions.

'So why do you call them people?'

'I suppose it is because we believe that they inhabit the world with us and are not quiet animals as they can be very intellectual, they are aware of their conscious mind. There are some good and some bad so very much like us, but not quite.

'Even though the beings are different from people and animals, we do not consider them as "supernatural" but are very much part of the real world, just unseen by our mortal eyes.

'But the little people should be dealt with carefully mind, like if you suspect one is near you or approaching you, never make eye contact or acknowledge its presence as they can be malevolent, that's part of our teachings.'

'So have you ever seen the little people?'

'No, I haven't. I think my gran has, but I haven't. They cannot be seen by humans unless they wish it.

They supposedly reside in rocky shelters, caves in the mountains or laurel thicket.'

'So does the idea not scare you?' I ask softly while a frown grows on my expression.

'Nah girl! There's no point in fearing them when I can use that energy in fighting them!'

She gives me a wink as she clicks her tongue.

I admire her strength; her confident approach to life, always so sure and courageous.

'What does Cherokee mean?'

'It's kinda strange, I think it means principal people or people of the mountains. I suppose that's what makes us neighbours to the little people,' she jests.

'But my Halloween costume is one of the feared beings within my tribe… The Raven Mocker! It's the most feared Cherokee witch! I need to hide it from my parents; they'll go mad if they see me imitating what they all fear!'

Nevaeh bursts into laughter and I offer a faint giggle.

Her expression turns serious as she stares into the distance. 'What's going on,' she whispers as her eyes squint ahead staring in the direction of DeJon and the team.

I look towards the same direction and see Trixy in some altercation with… Shayth!

Shayth is slowly walking back with his hands up as he guards himself while she aggressively shoves into him.

'My Shayth,' I whisper as I instinctively jump to my feet and run towards him!

DeJon grabs Trixy's arm, pulling her away from Shayth with force.

She looks different, ill perhaps. She seems to have really let herself go since we had our altercation.

Her hair a mess, her skin seems grazed with rashes throughout her paleness. Even down to her outfits, which were usually well coordinated, now seem a mishmash of colours and styles in a desperate attempt to be noticed.

Trixy and DeJon exchange p r o f a n i t i e s b efore she unexpectedly throws him to the ground!

I hear the gasp from the crowd around them.

'Shayth!' I shout as he helps DeJon to his feet.

Trixy walks off with her friends unwillingly following far behind.

'Are you okay?' I ask as I put a hand on his shoulder and the other across his cheek.

'I am fine,' he whispers as he offers me a loving smile and puts his hand on top of mine.

'Yeah I'm the one that just got thrown across the stadium, but don't worry, I'm fine too!' DeJon jests, which forces our attention towards him.

'DeJon I'm so sorry. I don't know what happened!' I state as I watch him dust off his clothes.

'Yeah, me neither! What was that bro?' DeJon asks confusingly as he looks to Tucker.

'You almost got your ass kicked by a girl bro!' Tucker teases.

'That wasn't Trix!' DeJon responds in disbelief while his ego seems dented.

'No, it was not,' Shayth whispers in agreement as he stares into the direction in which she disappeared.

The week flies by, and it's the penultimate day before the big Halloween party. I walk into the building and find Shayth stood in the corridor as the boys huddle together in fits of laughter. He senses me walk through and focuses his gaze on me while he continues to speak to his friends.

Shayth taps DeJon on the shoulder, before proceeding to walk towards me. I hold a smile on my face, which mimics his expression as we slowly close the gap between us.

'Hi,' I offer with a sheepish smile.

'Hi,' he responds as he slowly places his hands on my waist.

'People will see us,' I whisper as I place a hand on his shoulder and look in his eyes.

He flashes a glimmer of light from his misty grey eyes. I gasp at the beauty combined with his rebellious behaviour.

I cannot help but laugh, and he joins me in the gesture while he tilts his forehead against mine.

'So it's official then? Or are you still going to insist that you are just friends?' Nevaeh taunts as she surprises me from behind.

I instantly remove my hand from Shayth's shoulder and take a few steps back as I focus on composing myself and paying attention to my surroundings rather than to Shayth.

'Good Morning, Nevaeh,' Shayth greets as the cheeky grin remains on his face.

'Hey, Nevaeh,' I offer with a sheepish smile as we make eye contact.

She links my arm while Shayth wraps his arm around my waist. We make our way to our seminar as we all bear a smile on our expression.

'What took so long? Everything okay?' Nevaeh asks Sammy as she joins us at the table for lunch.

'I'm sorry, I didn't mean to be late again,' Sammy responds with a look of concern on her face.

I have never seen Sammy look so restless. She is always the calm and balanced person of our group.

'What wrong, Sammy? It's not like to you be frowning,' I ask as I mimic her expression.

'Well, I've been with Courtney, trying to console her.'

'Why what's up with her?' Nevaeh asks as she takes a bite of her sandwich.

'She's really worried about Trixy. Trixy is developing some kind of OCD.'

'Well, where is she?' I ask as I look around the cafeteria to see if she is here.

'She left her dorm in the early hours of this morning and hasn't been back.'

'She's probably in the bed of her next victim, responding to a booty call!' Nevaeh adds with a hint of anger.

'No it's more than that…' Sammy responds; her concern changes to a look of confusion.

'Bianca who shares the same room as Trixy said she was freaking out in her sleep. Some kind of sleep paralysis or sleepwalking, I'm not really sure.'

'Well, where is Bianca now?' I ask as I take another glance around the cafeteria.

'Her parents collected her, first thing this morning! I'm guessing they have had some kind of falling out.'

'Doesn't surprise me! There's only so much that anyone can tolerate of that bitch!' Nevaeh hisses.

'I don't know, Courtney, she's hiding something. I just don't know what,' Sammy responds as she looks deep in thought.

As I walk towards my car at the end of another day, I find Shayth leaning against the bonnet. We share a brief smile before I am unexpectedly startled!

'Oh no, you don't!' DeJon shouts as he puts his arm around my shoulder and follows me to my car.

'DeJon! Hey,' I respond in surprise.

'You've got a good one there Liyana,' he states as he discreetly points to Shayth.

'He's a top guy! You both look good together! But right now, we need him more than you do!'

I look up at DeJon in confusion as the faintest smile appears on my face.

'Yo, Shayth, my man! Where do you think you're going?' he asks in a stern voice.

Shayth steps away from the car as his expression reflects that of someone who has just been caught.

'I was just here to say goodbye to Liyana,' he responds with a brash smile.

'Yeah, that's what I thought!' DeJon responds feeling smug. 'We're gonna raid the stores to see what we can conjure up for this Friday!' DeJon informs as he removes his arm from around my shoulders and places it over Shayth.

'I shall be with you, allow me five minutes brothers,' Shayth requests to DeJon.

'Cool,' DeJon manoeuvres and takes a step to walk away. He pauses before placing his hand on Shayth's shoulder.

'Shayth, I'm really pleased for you bro!' DeJon glances back at me and gestures a perfect sign with his hand, before jogging off shouting after Romeo in the distance.

Shayth smiles as he looks at the ground while rubbing the back of his neck.

I notice a few groups in the distance staring in our direction, which includes a handful of the Aphrodite Sorority.

'So, shopping,' I state as we both look to each other and cannot help but laugh.

'It will be an experience; I'm sure you are going to love it,' I offer in a supportive tone.

'Would rather be with you,' Shayth whispers as he approaches closer to me while placing his hands on my waist.

'People are watching,' I whisper as I feel myself begin to blush.

'Let them,' he responds as he looks into my eyes.

I look to the ground, as the courtyard seems to get busier with more and more students staring.

Shayth cups my chin in his fingers as he raises my glance to his. 'You are mine now,' he whispers in his hypnotic voice.

'It is you and I. No one else,' he adds as he tilts his head forward. I can feel my heartbeat begin to spike as his lips brush against mine.

'LIYANA!' The call of my name shocks my senses back to reality, forcing me to lean away from Shayth.

Shayth and I glance towards the direction in which my name was called.

Just as I expected! Romeo has his back to us as he wiggles his whole body imitating a couple caressing each other.

'I should go... I...' I whisper as I feel my face burning with embarrassment.

Shayth puts his hand up to Romeo, whose laughter can be heard, despite our distance.

I roll down the window as I reverse slowly.

'May I see you tonight?' Shayth asks as he leans through the window.

'I'll wait for you,' I whisper with a sheepish smile.

My eyes widen as I notice Romeo in the background with his imitations becoming more dramatic and explicit!

'Shayth I need to go!' I request with urgency.

Shayth takes a step back and glances over to Romeo at which point I drive off to preserve my prudish sanity.

I cannot help but smile as I see Romeo run behind Shayth, jumping onto his back, they all seem to be laughing. I look at my clock, displaying a time of 22.40. I lie in bed with the lampshade on and stare towards the moonlight from the balcony doors.

'Where are you My Shayth,' I whisper.

I rest my eyes as I wait for his arrival. Who knows what influence DeJon and the gang are having over him.

I hear the faintest tapping on the glass doors.

While still in a sleepy state, I can feel the natural smile grow on my face, from the thought that my Shayth has come to see me. I wipe my hand on my face and glance at the clock. 03.14.

A frown spreads across my face; he has never arrived this late. But the thought of seeing him alone quickly banishes the negative thought.

I begin to yawn as I slowly walk across the room to open the door for him.

The lamp flickers before it switches off completely.

I scoff as I realise he has struggled to maintain his energy in a calm state. His excitement from being here must have blown the light.

I bite my lower lip as I approach closer to the glass door.

His silhouette appears different, shorter as if he is crouching perhaps.

I stop in my tracks as my body senses the cold chill in the atmosphere. The chill is emphasised by the sight of my breath, forming small steam particles within the darkness.

The moonlight breaks through the cracks in the cloud-filled skies; I see the dark, scraggly hair cloaking the face of an unknown creature.

Its dirty white cloth like tunic is covered in blood and earth.

It breathes heavily as the motion of its shoulders rising and falling appears dramatic.

I begin to mimic its reaction as my heartbeat becomes uncontrollable from fear! The sound of its growl begins to vibrate the glass door as it slowly raises its tilted head.

Time almost stands still; I watch the figure crouch before leaping towards the glass.

This is not my Shayth; this is something else, something evil!

'…Don't think of Satan as a harmless cartoon character with a red suit and pitchfork. He is very clever and powerful, and his unchanging purpose is to defeat Gods plan at every turn – including his plans for your life…'

–   Billy Graham

28. Trick or Treat

'You okay, Liyana? You seem a little distant,' Sammy asks with concern.

'Oh, yeah. I'm good. Just didn't sleep well last night. That's all.'

'Well you need to make sure you're recharged for the party tonight, coz it's gonna be WILLLD!' Nevaeh states with enthusiasm.

'Hey, have either of you seen Shayth today?' I ask trying to sound casual.

'That guy seriously needs to get a phone!' Nevaeh adds without answering my question.

'Maybe he's here now,' Sammy suggests as she spots DeJon, Tucker and Bazzer walking through the cafeteria.

'Hello, ladies!' Romeo announces as he surprises us while poking his head between Nevaeh and me.

He cheekily pecks Nevaeh on the cheek before sitting across the table from us.

Nevaeh glares at him with an unimpressed expression.

He smiles at her while blowing her a kiss, which he knows will infuriate her!

Nevaeh leans her head back while she raises her eyebrows. She places her apple on the table, and Romeo instantly retracts as he raises his hands. 'Chillax, chillax, girl. I'm just practicing my groove for tonight,' he pleads.

'NOT on me, you don't!' Nevaeh states as she offers Romeo sarcastic smile and proceeds to pick up her apple and take a bite.

DeJon and the crew join us at our table, as they all seem excited about their outfits for tonight.

'Liyana where is Shayth?' DeJon asks as he lowers his eyebrows.

'Oh, I was gonna ask you the same thing!' I respond in surprise.

'Nah, we haven't seen him since last night!' DeJon confirms as he looks around the cafeteria.

'Was that before or after you shit your pants?' Tucker questions with a wicked smile!

'Whatever, bro, your pants were stained just as much as mine!' DeJon replies as he shakes his head!

'I thought you guys were shopping last night, not having some weird shitting contest?' Nevaeh asks with confusion.

'Trust me! No one wants to follow through!' Tucker affirms as he shudders his shoulders.

'What happened?' Sammy asks as she focuses past the shit references.

'Some fucked up people playing some fucked-up pranks!' Bazzer adds as he rests his forehead on the tips of his fingers.

'Sounds like you've been trick or treating,' Nevaeh responds with a soft giggle at her own joke.

'Seriously, Nevaeh! I've never been so scared in my life!' DeJon confesses.

'Hah! You're letting the side down! Tucker comments in an attempt to tease the alpha.

'I didn't see you hanging around! Weren't you the one that was screaming, Tucker?' DeJon retaliates as he joins Bazzer in a high five.

I scan the room, but there is still no sign of Shayth.

'So what happened to Shayth?' I casually ask trying not to sound concerned about his whereabouts.

'We kinda got split up as we were all running. He's a fast runner! He must have lapped us all. One minute he was with us, the next minute he was gone!'

I look at the ground as I wonder if Shayth altered his energy to disappear from the men. But then why would he not have come to me last night?

'So what exactly happened?' Nevaeh demands to know.

DeJon shakes his head as he looks down to the table, before raising his glance to us.

'We went for a bite to eat which ended with a few drinks, so we were all pretty merry!' He begins with a fairly relaxed expression.

'I'm telling you we should never have taken that detour!' Bazzer adds as he recalls his memories.

DeJon sighs as he nods his head in agreement with Tucker. 'So…for whatever reason we decided to take a detour. A more scenic route if you will.

So we are all walking through the grand park...' he pauses for a moment as he smirks from acknowledging their mistakes.

'Yeah, that's when I left their sorry asses! And I'm so thankful I did!' Romeo adds with a smug smile.

'Well, it seemed like a good idea at the time you know. It was a fairly warm night. Clear skies. We were all pretty relaxed.'

'Sounds romantic!' Nevaeh adds with a smirk.

'Far from it, Nevaeh!' Bazzer responds with wide eyes!

'So anyway!' DeJon continues. 'We are walking along the park, being loud and obnoxious, what you'd typically expect from us lads! So then...as we turn the corner we see this girl...she's like, slithering around on the ground, in the distance.'

'So which one of you is the snake charmer?' Nevaeh asks in a teasing manner.

'Seriously, Nevaeh... I've never seen anything like this!' Bazzer adds with a serious tone.

'It was fucked up! She was twisting and turning in a way that I never knew was possible!'

'Bearing in mind, DeJon has been pretty lucky with the ladies, so he's an expert in this field!' Romeo adds as he proudly nods his head.

Nevaeh cannot help but burst out into laughter, even Sammy struggles to contain her mocking smile.

I force a fake smile but am eager to hear the rest of the events to understand how my Shayth fits into all of this.

DeJon shakes his head as he dismisses Romeo's comment. 'I'm telling you... it wasn't natural. It wasn't human! People can't move like that! The body structure, the joints, they were all dislocated as they twisted around each other!'

'Then what happened?' I ask to speed up his memories. 'Well, we didn't know what to think,' Tucker confirms.

'We all kinda just stopped in our tracks. And it's like, as soon as she realised we were there, she like, pulled her body back together, and was like crouched into a ball!

'She had her head tucked down, and we thought it was a little girl.'

'Yeah, so tucker tried being a hero!' Bazzer mocks as he pushes tuckers shoulders.

'We should have listened to Shayth man! I'm telling you…we'd be fine if we listened to him!' Tucker responds with regret.

'What…what do you mean? What did he say?' I ask as my heartbeat begins to rise.

'As soon as we saw it, he insisted that we turned back! He was pretty adamant about it till Tucker decided to become Superman!' Bazzer looks at Tucker shaking his head in disapproval.

'So we all slowly follow the footsteps of Tucker…and I don't know why coz it's something we never normally do!' DeJon adds in jest.

'Hey, you guys were just as curious as me!' Tucker insists in an attempt to defend himself.

'So then…as we approach her, she starts crying! I mean proper crying like a little girl you know! We thought maybe she's got lost trick or treating; I mean she sounded like a little kid!'

'What happened next?' Sammy asks, as she seems captivated by this incident.

'Well…we proceeded towards her to try and offer some help. But then, her cry became, I dunno, more sinister!'

We all stare with wide eyes. After a short pause, DeJon continues.

'She didn't sound like a little girl anymore… She sounded, fucking evil, as she rose to a stand with her cry turning into mocking laughter!'

'Where was Shayth?' I ask as you can hear the suspense in my voice.

'He was with us, staring, trying to figure out what the fuck!' Bazzer confirms.

DeJon leans further forward onto the tables as he looks around to make sure no one else is within hearing distance.

'So then…the crazy bitch stops crying and laughing and its silent. There's not a single car that drives past, not a single sound in the air at all! Obviously, at this point, we are all frozen in our positions. And then, the bitch takes a step forward towards us…

'We all shake on the spot and take a step back. It was so fucked up! We were just shocked and were trying to figure out what was going on.

'Her hair; it covered her face so you couldn't see anything! And she was wearing this white cloth; like a nighty or something. But it was all stained with blood and grime.

'She had no sleeves; you could see her pale skins and rashes and gashes across her.

'The psychotic bitch then takes another step towards us, and then another...'

'Then she starts growling like a fucking beast!' Bazzer adds as he seems a little agitated.

'Next thing you know, the bitch is running towards us! And she's fucking fast!' Tucker adds with a nervous yet hyper tone!

'Whaaat...' Nevaeh whisper's as she is engrossed in their events.

'I'm telling you... It was fucked up!' DeJon insists as he shakes his head.

'So what then?' I ask, desperate to hear of my Shayth!

'That's when we all shit a brick and ran for it! Bitch was chasing us! Like a fucking lunatic cannibal!'

'So...you ran away?' Sammy asks with a surprised tone.

'Sammy! At one point, the fucking beast was running on all fours!' DeJon answers to defend their actions.

'I'm telling you...whatever it was, it wasn't human!'

'But you ALL got away safe?' I add hoping that they will respond with "yes!".

'Yeah! Thank God we are fast! We got away, and then the next thing you know is that we turn back around... and the bitch is gone!' DeJon adds.

'What...just like that?' Nevaeh questions.

'Yeah! Just like that! Hey did you see where it went?' DeJon turns to ask Tucker.

'Nah bruv, I can't multitask! I was just focusing on putting one leg in front of the other!'

'So let me get this straight,' Nevaeh enquires. 'Four grown ass men... ran away, from a little girl that was probably running towards you to ask for help?'

'If she wanted help, why would she start laughing?' Bazzer counteracts to convince Nevaeh.

'Maybe her sugar rush kicked in from all the candy she ate from trick or treating?' Nevaeh adds in a mocking tone.

They shake their head at Nevaeh in disapproval as she giggles away at her joke.

'And so what then? Did you all get split up?' I ask still desperate to hear of when my Shayth was last seen.

'Kinda, I mean we re-grouped pretty quickly. But Shayth had long gone! To be fair, he is the fastest of us all.'

I stare at the ground as I begin to worry as to where Shayth may be.

'You've been really quiet. Is everything okay?' Nevaeh asks as we leave for the day.

'Yeah, I think I've just overdone it this week. Too many late nights, I suppose,' I try to keep the truth discreet, the worry I have for Shayth, knowing that the *shayateens*, the demons lurk among us.

'He's keeping you up till late is he!' Nevaeh teases.

'So you'll definitely be at the party tonight, right.' Nevaeh states more like a demand than a request.

'Yeah, I should be,' I respond sounding hesitant.

'No bailing on me, Liyana! Trust me; it will be a night to remember!' Nevaeh insists.

I offer a fake a smile, I fear Nevaeh may be right, but for all the wrong reasons.

'Aaarghh!' Micky shouts, trying hard to come across as a pirate.

'Wow! All you need now is a ship and a crew!' I add to encourage his excitement.

'Liyana it's probably best that you don't come trick or treating if you have a party to go to! We don't want you rushing and being late!' Aunt Liz adds in an apparent attempt to keep me away!

'A couple of rounds won't hurt!' Uncle Aidan insists as he struggles to put a costume on Diesel.

'Of course, it will!' Shouts Aunt Liz.

'We can't make her late! A girl needs her time to get ready!' Aunt Liz seems adamant for me to not join them!

'But we go together every year!!! Pleassssee, Aunt Liz!' Micky insists as he runs towards me and grips a hold of my hand!

'Liz!' Uncle Aidan shouts with a disapproving tone!

'Liyana, if you're happy to then you and Micky can go to a couple of houses now if you want?' Uncle Aidan gives me a warm, reassuring smile and Micky starts jumping with delight! I dare not look at Aunt Liz; I am sure she is scowling at us all!

As Micky and I drive to the closest neighbourhood, I notice how the leaves in the trees and bushes are slowly turning to an auburn shade.

I stare at the kids running around in their costumes holding their buckets of candy in their hands.

I think for a moment, why would a custom be created where it is encouraged to dress as ghouls while roaming the streets?

'This one, this one!' Micky shouts as we pass a house well decorated for this festive occasion.

I stop the car glancing towards him; I cannot help but to melt from the sight of his beautiful little face in the pirate costume.

Micky and I walk back towards the car. The neighbourhood becomes busies with teenage kids now roaming around for candy!

Micky and I talk about his big school party that Aunt Liz and Uncle Aidan will be attending alongside him. He seems excited and the joy on his face for a moment distracts me from the worry of Shayth.

As we arrive home, Aunt Liz and Uncle Aidan hurry to leave, leaving me in an empty house, the silence is eerie.

I jump out of the shower and put on a pair of jeans and a basic top.

I look through the recent messages on my phone and read of the excitement from my friends of their costumes and theatrical makeup.

As hard as I try to participate in the fun, my heart cannot stop worrying about my Shayth.

I sit on the edge of my bed, resting my face against the palms of my hands; the worry begins to consume me.

Has the event from last night got something to do with Shayth not coming to see me?

Have the guards of his dimension learned that he had defied their sacred laws?

My heartbeat rises from the sound of a tapping at the window! I turn to look up and find Shayth standing there, leaning his head against the glass.

He looks exhausted, shattered! But he holds a faint smile on his face from seeing me.

'Where have you been?' I shout as I throw my arms around him, squeezing him tight!

'I have missed you too!' he whispers as he kisses my neck and squeezes my body.

'I've been so worried,' I whisper in a shaky voice.

The sense of relief flowing through my body makes me realise just how much he means to me!

I didn't realise that I had been keeping myself so strong. But now that I am with him, now that I know he is safe, I struggle to compose myself.

'Please don't disappear like that,' I plea.

'Do not worry,' he whispers as he strokes the back of my head. As I sit beside him at the edge of my bed, I watch him sink his head down while looking at the ground.

He claws his fingers through his hair, in that moment, I know something is wrong.

'Shayth, are you in any danger?' I ask forcing a calm controlled tone.

He scoffs and offers a faint smile as he turns to look at me. He takes my hand and places a gentle kiss on the surface. 'You have no idea how much you mean to me,' he whispers.

I begin to feel sick in my stomach from anxiety. He's not answered my question; there must be something wrong!

'It's okay, you can tell me. What's happened?' I respond in a calm and caring tone.

I desperately try hard to stay in control, to stay strong for him! 'I need to ask of something from you,' he whispers in a soft tone.

'Anything!' I insist as I wrap both my hands around his.

'I do not want you attending the party tonight.'

He pauses as I stare at him with a confused expression.

I struggle to understand what this party has to do with his absence?

'I need you to trust me; I need you to stay home tonight.'

'Okay...' I confirm while looking puzzled.

'I don't understand, is everything ok Shayth?' I ask as I try to make sense of his request.

'Does this have something to do with what happened last night?' I ask in a desperate attempt to understand what it is that is making him react in this way.

'What do you know of last night?' he asks swiftly as his eyes lock onto mine, his demeanour becoming serious.

'Not much, just DeJon mentioned a crying girl that began to freak out.'

I feel somewhat nervous from Shayth's serious expression, almost a defensive, dominating expression.

He reduces the intensity of his stare as he rolls his head back and sighs.

I walk over to the cabinet to sip on my glass of water, feeling dehydrated from his tense expression.

'It's the strangest thing, the way DeJon had described the girl... I saw the same girl matching the same description in my dream last night. For a minute I thought it was you.'

I scoff at my own stupidity as I shake my head and look at the ground.

'LIYANA!' Shayth shouts in a stern voice.

'What did you just say?' he demands to know in an aggressive tone.

My heart spikes as I look across to him, I watch his body begin to vibrate while a faint glow radiates from him. Both his eyes and the lampshade begin to flicker, while his expression is stern and hard!

What have I done...?

'…It's a man's own darkness,
not his enemy or foe that lures him to evil ways …'

—   Buddha

29. Invitation to Evil

'As soon as I was out of their sight, from DeJon and the guys, I altered into my ethereal form. I could see everything that was happening, but they could not see me.

I ran towards the creature, but as soon as it saw me... I do not know if it sensed that I was from the spiritual world coming towards it at speed, but it began to run in the opposite direction!'

Shayth takes a deep breath as he recalls the events.

'I have not seen anything like that before; I have never witnessed the dwelling within a human form... I am not even sure if that was a person or a shape-shifting *shayateen*, or both?'

'But if it was to be a dwelling of a *shayateen*, a demon, that means it was a human body?' I question in confusion.

Shayth stares into the empty space in my room, a blank expression covers his face, as he looks deep in thought.

'I called upon my friends for their support, but it had disappeared. Long gone by the time they arrived.'

'So whatever it is, it's still out there,' I whisper under my breath.

'I need to keep you safe,' he whispers as he shakes his head in disbelief.

'But it was just a dream,' I state with a smile despite my heartbeat racing. My expression turns serious from Shayth's silence.

'But it was just a dream... right?' I ask again forcing a smile. Shayth stands and approaches me. He places both his palms across my cheeks.

'Whether it was a dream or not, I will never let any harm come to you Liyana...you are too precious to me.'

My eyes glaze over from shock!

'You are mine,' he whispers as he momentarily rests his forehead on mine.

Despite Shayth's subtlety, I understand exactly what he is saying. Whatever it was, it wasn't a dream.

'Okay, what's going to happen now?' I ask trying to remain calm and assertive despite my hands shaking with fear.

'Khallum, he will be attending the party. It took a lot of convincing, but I have another friend, Akheel, who has broken our sacred law to help determine what is happening.'

'What makes you think the *shayateen*, if it is dwelling within a human is going to be at the party of all places?' I ask feeling confused.

'I do not know when I lost track of it... I think it entered the dorms. It is a long shot, but we will scout around the grand park, dorms and anywhere else we might suspect.'

He looks deep in thought as he struggles to figure out what is happening. Suddenly the wildest thought hits me.

'Trixy... she wasn't in university today!'

'She is the least of my concerns Liyana!'

I pace along the room as I try to recall my last moments when I saw her.

'Shayth...' I whisper from which a frown grows on his face.

'What is it, what are you thinking?' he asks looking intrigued.

'Trixy... she threw DeJon across the stadium.

'Sammy, she spoke to Courtney who said Trixy was having vivid nightmares and ran out of her dorms in the middle of the night! And I don't think anyone has seen her since.'

'It... It could be nothing,' Shayth whispers while he contemplates the possibility of Trixy having been caught in this demonic battle.

He sits on the edge of the bed as he combs his fingers through his hair.

Shayth shakes his head as he frowns harder. Almost as if he is convincing himself that surely this cannot be possible. 'Liyana,' he whispers as his voice softens.

'Yes,' I respond as the tension slightly fades from within me. 'Can I hold you?' he asks as he looks up at me with his big grey eyes.

A soft smile appears on my face as Shayth stands to his feet. He wraps his arms around my waist as I lean my head against his broad shoulder.

'I just want to be with you,' he whispers in a defeated tone.

'You are with me,' I respond reassuringly as I comb my fingers through the back of his hair.

He takes a deep breath as he releases an emotional sigh. 'What was that for?' I whisper as I begin to frown.

'From the realisation and acceptance that this moment, is going to end soon.'

He squeezes me tighter as he places a kiss on the top of my head.

'I am sorry. I know it is awful to ask. But at least if I know you are here, I will know you are safe,' he whispers as an element of guilt flows through him.

'It's okay, don't worry,' I add reassuringly.

'Besides, I'm sure you will make it up to me,' I jest to lighten the mood and remove his guilt.

'I promise you!' he states in a stern tone as he takes me by the shoulders and looks deep into my eyes.

'I will come to you tonight. Regardless of what happens! Do not wait up for me, but sleep with a smile knowing that when your eyes awake, I will be by your side.'

He wraps me around his arms a final time before he walks to the balcony.

'Is there anything I can do?' I ask feeling helpless.

'Your prayers will help. Other than that, I just need you to stay safe. I will see you soon,' he promises.

The sound of a vibration within my room distracts my focus as I glance behind me to see my phone is bleeping.

I turn back to look at Shayth…he has already gone.

Nevaeh – *So excited! See you all in 30 minutes!*

Liyana – *Really sorry – can't make it tonight.*

Liyana – *Must have a 24-hour bug.*

Liyana – *Enjoy the party without me.*

Liyana – *And stay safe!*

I lay on my bed as I cuddle the teddy Shayth had gifted me, what seems so long ago.

I cannot help but worry about what may be happening out there. Fretting over what Trixy may be going through? That's if it is even Trixy, or someone or something else.

The more I think about it, the more I am convinced it must be her!

I lay in bed as I silently whisper prayers in my mind.

Please let no harm come to them; please let them conquer any evil they have to face, please bring them home safe, please keep my Shayth safe.

'Why the delayed arrival!'

I attempt to hide my frustration as Khallum and Akheel land beside me.

'Forgive me, brother. The opportune moment for discretion took longer than anticipated.'

Khallum greets me with our formal hug within our dimension. Our hands-on each other's shoulders as we stand inches apart while our auras reflect against each other.

'Where is our destination,' Akheel asks.

He seems hostile, from not wanting to be here of course.

Our sacred laws govern our existence, which he upholds and respects dearly.

I am grateful that he has made this sacrifice for me, despite it being apparent that he does not want to be here.

'We must search for the one named Trixy! She has dark hair and pale skin. I suspect it may be her body that the *shayateens* dwell within.'

Khallum and Akheel are dressed in our traditional attire. Hooded pale garments with slits across the back material, which allow for our wings to be exposed.

'We can remain in this form. The Halloween season will lead the humans to believe these are costumes we wear.'

Both Khallum and Akheel nod, demonstrating acknowledgment.

As we walk from out of the trees, I can see the herds of students gathered around the building from the depth of their auras vibrant against the dark night.

I turn to face Khallum and Akheel.

Khallum's expression shows one of excitement and eagerness whereas Akheel appears weary yet mildly appalled.

'You will witness impurities here. We must remain true to the cause and not focus on the judgment of the humans! We are here to find the *shayateen*,' I remind to ensure our objectives are at the forefront of our minds.

'I cannot recall when I last saw this bright redness in auras to this extent!' Khallum gasps in shock.

'The teachings here, the way of life here…it is different to our dimension. We may not like it, but we must respect it, we are only visitors of this dimension.'

The auras of deep orange and bright red flood the atmosphere, surrounding us with signs of lust, adrenaline, desire and vanity.

'Is there no purity, no innocence amongst them?' Akheel questions, with a look of disgust across his expression.

'Calm my dear brother. You will see goodness within them. But right now we must find the miscreant entity!'

We walk through the crowds, the women watch us in awe as we walk past. Their auras begin to burn a bright red with hints of orange indicating their desire and lust towards us.

My beautiful Liyana; with a constant glow of white, so rarely have I seen a continuous flow of purity and innocence within the human species.

I wish for this night to be over. Only so that I can accompany her, admire her…hold her.

'What is this!' Akheel shouts in disgust. I turn to see a young woman attempting to talk to him as he looks at her with horror.

She begins to stroke his wings, complimenting his costume. 'Ignore them!' I insist as we walk into the hall.

The base of the music vibrates the room while the flashing strobe lights make it difficult to focus on the individual's auras.

'Have you seen Trixy?' I ask an Aphrodite I find stood next to me.

She shakes her head as I watch her burning aura pulsate towards me.

The Aphrodite's wear thin white dresses fitted around their waists with slits all around. Their small-feathered wings and halos across their head help to determine what costume Trixy is likely to be wearing.

I continuously ask around yet Trixy is nowhere to be seen. 'We should go! We have tried and thus have done our part!' Akheel insists, desperate to leave the human world and re-join our dimension.

I sit in exasperation on an empty seat as I scan the room. 'What are we waiting for!' Akheel shouts in frustration.

'She will most likely be wearing a scanty angel dress with wings,' I respond with a stern tone.

'We must find her!' I insist, ensuring Akheel maintains his focus.

I shake my head as I look at the ground from irritation. An aura of deep red and smoky black flashes before me. 'I hear you are looking for me!'

Trixy spreads her legs as she sits on my lap and thrusts into me!

'I knew you would come round; I knew you would come to your senses,' she claims as she rubs her body against mine.

Her bridal veil attached to her halo and excessively sized angel wings take me by surprise.

I hold her shoulders back to increase the distance between us. She lifts the thin net veil from her face to reveal her gaunt facial structure and sunken eyes.

She flicks her tongue from out of her mouth as she proceeds to force it between my lips!

'Trixy STOP!' I shout with aggression as I grip her wrists tight in my hand.

'I know you want me, you dream about me, you can have me!' she insists with a malevolent tone.

She proceeds to grind against my body; I am forced to increase my strength as I push her further away by the wrists; it clearly puts her in pain!

'I'll give you everything if you just chose me Shayth!' For a moment I see a glimmer of an innocent being within her eyes, one full of pain. Anger and rage quickly shadow the glimmer! 'What the fuck does she have that I don't,' she screams in a tone deeper than her own.

I watch in disbelief as I witness her facial expression change. The colour of life in her skin is bled dry as she becomes pale. The lacerations across her body slowly become visible, revealing rashes and scars across her skin.

The gaunt depth of her facial structure renders her unrecognisable, as before my eyes, the skin across her lips and cheeks begin to split from dryness.

Her eyes instantly become deep and darkened as flashes of orange begin to rise to the surface of her iris.

The glow of darkness grows within her aura as she slowly bares her teeth with aggression.

At that moment Trixy stands to her feet and pushes me with force!

The unexpected force throws me off the chair and onto the ground.

Khallum and Akheel run towards me as they pick me from the ground, their expression appears shocked.

'That is not Trixy...' I whisper as I watch her disappear into the crowd. The *shayateen*, the demon, is within her!

....

...... LIYANA

The vibration from my phone wakes me from my light sleep. My phone is flooded with messages and Sammy has left a number of missed calls.

My phone begins to vibrate again as Sammy's name flashes on my screen.

'Sammy...' I clear my throat, which sounds choked from my sleepy state.

'Is everything okay,' I ask in a soft tone. The screaming in the background forces my eyes to open wide!

'Liyana!' she cries!

'Sammy! Sammy, what's happened? Are you okay?

'Liyana. No!! I can't find Nevaeh! She went looking for Trixy! She's gone mad!'

'Sammy where are you? What's happened!'

I sit up on my bed, I feel as if I am going to choke on my heartbeat pushing through my throat!

My breathing intensifies as my body begins to shake with panic!

'Trixy! Something's happened to her! She's throwing people across the room! And now Nevaeh's gone after Trixy, and I can't find her! Something's wrong with Trixy, it's not her!' Sammy cries throughout her hyperventilating.

'Okay, Sammy, listen to me,' I state in a calm yet stern voice. I grab my keys and run out of the house towards my car.

'Okay, listen; I need you to focus on you for a minute, okay. Now you need to go somewhere safe! Go somewhere well-lit with lots of people around! Do you understand me, Sammy!'

'Liyana, I'm scared!' She cries down the phone.

Her sobbing heart breaks mine, and I can think of nothing but to comfort her and shelter her from this fear as soon as I can! 'Sammy listen! I know you are scared but I'm in my car right now and I'm coming to get you okay! Together we will find Nevaeh! But right now, I NEED YOU to stay safe!

Can you do that for me?'

I put my foot down on the accelerator as the adrenaline pumps through my body.

'SAMMY!' I shout with anger.

'Yes, yes I will,' she cries in desperation.

'Listen! Go to the stores around the corner from the venue. I'm going to be there in 10 minutes, okay, and we will find Nevaeh, just get to safety first!'

'Liyana!' The phone crackles as I hear distorted screaming in the background.

The line cuts and I can no longer hear Sammy!

'Shayth,' I cry in a whisper as my hands shake on the steering wheel. I need to make sure everyone is okay. Sammy, Nevaeh, DeJon, my Shayth!

I drive recklessly to get closer to the party with no regards to the red lights or speed limits.

DeJon's name flashes across my phone.

'DeJon!' I shout as I press the caller button on my steering wheel.

'Liyana! What the fuck is going on?' The screaming in the background makes it difficult to hear DeJon clearly.

'Where are you? Where is Shayth? Are you both safe?' he shouts.

'DeJon I'm on my way!'

'What… you're not here? Liyana! Don't come here! It's not safe!'

'DeJon are you with Nevaeh or Shayth?' I shout in desperation to hear that they are both okay.

'Nevaeh? Where is she? Look, stay away from here Liyana! Oh, Fuck!'

He puts the phone down.

The car barely stands stationary as I run out to of the car looking for Sammy. I run into the store screaming Sammy's name.

'Liyana!' Sammy cries as she runs out from behind an aisle. For a moment I struggle to recognise her in an Adams Family Wednesday costume, with the wig and heavy pale makeup.

She wraps her arms around me and squeezes me tight as tears flood from her eyes!

Crowds of students begin to run past the store, fearing for their lives.

'What's happened? Where did you last see Nevaeh?'

'I don't know,' she cries.

'People are saying its Trixy, but it's not! It's not her! It looks nothing like her! It's an imposter!'

'Okay, okay, shhh,' I say as I hold her in my arms.

The fear has her voice shaking, as she breaths heavily while struggling to get her words out.

'Where did you last see Nevaeh?' I ask in a controlled calm tone.

She stares out of the window as the students run frantically while screaming and crying.

I put my palm on each side of Sammy's face forcing her to look directly at my eyes, ignoring everything happening outside. 'Sammy,' I call, to bring her focus back to me.

'Where did you last see Nevaeh?'

'We ran outside the venue and then one of the Aphrodite's came running out and told us Trixy has gone mad…and that she's thrown Bazzer across the room, through the glass fish tank.'

Sammy pauses; her eyes fill with even more tears.

'I wanted to run after her, but I was too scared…' she whispers as she begins to sob into her hands.

'Sammy, it's okay, you don't have to find her on your own. I'm here with you now. It's okay.'

I hold her tight in my arms for comfort as I look out the window to see the crowd running as if there is some kind of ambush.

'Come with me,' I whisper as I take Sammy by the hand and walk outside.

'Hey! Courtney!' I shout as I see Courtney with a couple of the Aphrodite's running past the store.

I release Sammy's hand as I grab Courtney by the arm, pulling her towards me.

She stares at me with a blank expression as she tries to make sense of what is happening.

'Courtney… I need you to tell me what you know! What's happening with Trixy!'

'I… I… I don't know anything,' she responds nervously.

The guilt is written across her face as she wriggles her arm to release it from my grip.

I pull her arm harder to stop her from wriggling, forcing her to look at me.

'Courtney… I don't care what it is that you guys have done! I just need to know so that we can figure out what is exactly happening!' I demand in an aggravated tone.

'It's not real…' she whispers as her eyes fill with fear.

'This can't be happening,' she whispers as she begins to shake and break down into tears.

'COURTNEY!' I shout to force her to snap out of her emotional breakdown.

'I'm sorry, Liyana! I thought it was bipolar or some kind of OCD, but it's not and…and… I'm so, so, sorry! I didn't realise this could happen!'

Courtney begins to sob as her knees weaken, and she loses balance.

'Courtney… Courtney it's okay! Just tell me what has happened!' I insist, desperate to get to the bottom of this.

'I didn't want to do it, but they were all going ahead with it. So I had no choice but to join them.'

'Join them? What did you all go ahead with?' I demand to know.

'I ran out as soon as the furniture started moving! I wanted nothing more to do with it after that…' she desperately insists.

'Courtney!' I shout to bring her focus to the point.

'Why was the furniture moving… what were you doing?'

'She wanted to get in between you and Shayth… She wants him to choose her over you.'

I release my grip from her arms as shock and confusion consume my expression.

'That's what she asked of them… When she invited them in. I thought it was just a game!'

'What GAME COURTNEY!'

She stutters before finally whispering the dreaded truth '…The Ouija Board…'

'…Hell is empty and all the Devils are here…'

— William Shakespeare

30. The Inferno

'The day you hit Trixy across the face…that's the night she insisted we all play!

'She had taken Shayth's pendant while dancing across him in the initiation party for us freshman.

'He was too busy staring at you to even notice!'

'What's that got to do with this?' I ask confused and feeling frustrated from the irrelevant information being shared.

'That's the pendant she took to Denise…you know the Goth!' I look to the ground as I recall a moment a few weeks back where I was leaving the university premises and noticed Trixy talking to Denise while they both stared at an object in Trixy's hand.

'Denise is the one who said the pendant is most likely a demonic symbol!

'I tried convincing Trixy that Denise was just being facetious, telling us what we would typically expect a Goth to say!

'But Trix, she was desperate! She's never been rejected.'

'My heart bleeds,' I snap with sarcasm while still trying to comprehend all this information.

'What happened the night you all decided to screw up?' I ask in a strong, stern tone.

'I don't know… Trixy was really into it. She was so excited! She welcomed the spirits and invited them to work through her to come in between you two; she was prepared to do whatever it takes.

At first, I thought the girls were moving the cursor. But as soon as the frames began falling off the walls and the candles and lights started blowing out; I ran… I left them all. I was so afraid. I sound crazy,' Courtney whispers in disbelief.

My mind frantically scrambles for ideas on what to do next, the feeling of hopelessness consumes me.

I turn to Sammy whose eyes are widened from the shock of the despicable actions of the Aphrodite's.

'Sammy... Sammy!' I shout to bring her back to focus. 'Go with Courtney; go back to your dorms!

'Do NOT wander off. Stay in well-populated and well-lit areas ONLY.

'Do you understand?'

'What about you...' Sammy whispers in fear.

'Don't worry about me, Sammy! I promise you; I will be fine. We just need to get you to safety and then at least I will not have to worry so much about you! Okay?'

She nods softly as tears flow down her cheeks.

She wraps her arms around me as she sobs against my shoulder.

'I don't know what I would do right now without you, Liyana,' she confesses in a vulnerable whisper.

'It's okay, that's why I'm here, okay. Just be strong for me, and I promise I will see you soon.'

She nods as we part our arms and part our ways.

I walk along the path towards the grand hall hosting the party. I watch in slow motion as witches, clowns, zombies and beasts roam the streets as they scream and cry in fear.

The sound of fear is sickening; its intensity increases as I approach closer to the hall.

'Stay in the light, don't wander alone! You need to stay with the crowd, stay in populated areas!' I insist to a young student who wanders off aimlessly on his own.

He nods as he frantically runs to safety.

'DeJon!' I shout as I run towards him!

He exists the grand hall as he and Tucker both carry Bazzer across their arms as they struggle down the stairs.

'Liyana!' he shouts back with a sense of relief! Romeo runs towards me and wraps me in his arms. 'Thank God you're safe!' he exclaims.

'What's happened! I blurt out as I look at the blood oozing from Bazzer heads.

'He's okay, he's had a fall that's all!' DeJon insists trying to convince himself.

Bazzer is dripping wet and seems somewhat semi-conscious, very disorientated!

'C'mon we need to get out of here!' Tucker insists, as they continue forward.

'Okay…just get to safety. Stay in well-lit areas and just stick together,' I gasp from shortness of breath.

'What!' DeJon shouts from shock!

'Liyana, you're coming with us. Let's move!' he insists in a stern, serious tone.

'No…no. I can't, I need to go in!' I insist as I take a few steps away increasing the distance between us.

'Liyana! The parties fucking over! Now you're comin' with us!' DeJon shouts in an aggressive, threatening manner.

His eyes widen as he stares at me in disbelief!

'DeJon, please…' I whisper in a plea as tears slowly fill my eyes. 'What the fuck am I supposed to tell Shayth when he asks me why I didn't take care of you?' he shouts barbarically.

'I need to help Nevaeh,' I whimper helplessly as tears slowly roll down from my eyes.

'Neva… Nevaeh!' Bazzer shouts in his disorientated state.

'Of fuck! Nevaeh!' DeJon repeats as his expression of anger turns to one of fear and guilt.

'Romeo!' DeJon shouts as he removes himself from under Bazzer's arm.

Romeo takes DeJon's place as he and Tucker continue to assist Bazzer forward.

I wipe the tears from my cheeks as I take a deep breath and maintain control over my fear.

'Please just trust me! Stay in well-lit and well-populated areas!' I state to DeJon and Tucker in a stern tone as I proceed forward towards the steep stairs leading into the hall.

'No! You need to go with them!' I shout as I turn behind me to see DeJon following me up the stairs.

'Liyana! I'm not letting you do this on your own! He shouts as he lowers his eyebrows.

'Look! You're the captain! You need to go and take care of your team! They need you right now!' I shout back trying hard to persuade him to turn back.

'Liyana!' DeJon shouts with wide eyes. He sighs as his eyes soften.

'You are part of the team,' he whispers with a hint of care and love in his tone.

'I won't be able to live with myself if I let you do this. If I leave Nevaeh behind...' he confesses.

We enter the hall, which looks like the aftermath of a violent riot, tables, chairs, glass, props all over the place, while the strobe lights dangle dangerously from the ceiling.

The broken music systems play on a repeat of the same note, as it vibrates the sounds of a deep base; it mimics the rhythm of my thumping heartbeat.

I can hear my heavy breathing amongst the vibrations of glass shattered beneath my shoes.

'Nevaeh,' I call in a controlled yet raised voice.

The base of the music in the background conjures a sickness in my stomach. With each step I take, I can feel my knees vibrate more and more. The fear begins to consume me slowly.

I gasp at the sudden silence.

I look towards the stage where DeJon stands behind the broken DJ booth.

'Nevaeh!' DeJon shouts as he jumps off from the stage and walks over towards me.

The flickering of live electrical wires throwing sparks within our vicinity can now be heard.

'Nevaeh!' I cry in desperation to find her.

The sound of electrical wires, falling props and the flapping of suffocating fish besides us is all we can hear.

Suddenly, a faint growl reaches our ears.

'What was that?' I ask DeJon as we slowly walk deeper into the hall.

'Don't think about it...let's just find her quick so we can get the hell out!' DeJon instructs in a quiet tone.

'Oh shit! We gotta be quick!' DeJon shouts as the sparks behind us develop into flames spreading wildly across the floor.

Within moments, the floor to ceiling drapes is caught alight as the flames burn with fury.

'Look over there!' I shout as I point towards the tables and chairs moving within the podium up on the balcony.

'Nevaeh,' I shout desperate to hear a response back. We rush towards the stairs leading to the balcony.

DeJon holds onto my elbow as I lose balance from the obstacles scattered across the floor.

As we run up the stairs, I slow my pace as I cannot help but feel we are being watched...

I look within the shadows above us in the ceilings. Something is watching us. I can feel it.

We approach the balcony podium; the pile-up of tables and debris begins to rustle.

DeJon and I pause for a moment, with caution not knowing what is buried beneath.

I grip my head with the tips of my fingers as the fear in my stomach enrages me with anger!

'I need to find Nevaeh,' I scream inside my head as I abruptly begin to throw the debris across from the mount!

DeJon mimics my actions as we toss away the tables and chairs! He grabs my arm and stops me in motion.

As we look down at the rubble we have cleared, we notice unusually large black feathers.

'Liyana,' he whispers.

'Stand back...' He slowly pushes me to the side and crouches to the ground.

The feathers begin to move; whatever it is beneath there, it knows we are here.

DeJon takes a deep breath and lifts the board covering the thing that lies beneath!

We both sigh with relief as we rush down to our knees. The Raven Mocker! Nevaeh!

DeJon lifts her head onto his forearms.

'Nevaeh!' he calls in a stern voice as he shakes her gently to awaken her senses.

She moans faintly as she slowly becomes aware of her surroundings.

'Nevaeh,' I cry as I place my palm across her cheek.

'My leg!!' she cries in pain.

'Oh Fuck!' DeJon exclaims!

'It's broken…' he whispers as he assesses the swollen damage.

'Liyana. I need you to grab that board there and find me something like a rope that I can use to tie the board against her leg!'

'Yes,' I affirm as I frantically search for something matching the description.

'What happened?' Nevaeh shouts in pain and confusion.

The ceiling lights fall to the ground crashing into the stacks of tables and chairs from the ferocious fire becoming intense.

The sudden crash makes us all jump as I hasten to find rope like material.

'Will this do?' I ask as I run over with what looks like a long shred of cloth from an Egyptian mummy outfit.

'Yeah, yeah! This is it!' DeJon shouts eagerly as he begins to tie the solid board against Nevaeh's thigh and shin.

'C'mon, I need you to focus!' he insists as Nevaeh slowly comes in and out of a conscious state.

Nevaeh moans in pain as we lift her off the ground, wrapping her arm around our shoulders as we begin to head towards the stairs.

'What the fuck is happening?' she shouts as she becomes more alert and observes her surroundings.

'We need to get out of here!' DeJon shouts as we pass the flying sparks of the live electrical wires resting on the debris.

'It's blocked! We can't go this way!' I shout over the roaring flames that barricade the main entrance we are heading towards.

'We gotta find another exit!' DeJon confirms as we turn back around and head towards the back of the room.

'Over there!' he shouts as he points towards a rear fire escape door.

The obstacles scattered across the ground make it difficult to manoeuvre while trying to be delicate with Nevaeh's broken leg. Hearing her scream in pain as her leg gets caught in cables and debris makes the environment sound even more hellish.

The flames begin to surround us as we approach the exit door. 'Its locked!' DeJon shouts as he desperately turns the handle trying to escape the inferno we are surrounded in.

'Take her,' he shouts across to me as he uses his broad shoulders to barge through the door.

The exit door shudders but remains closed.

'Hurry, DeJon,' I plea as I feel the heat from the flames penetrated through my body.

The sudden shriek of a demonic howl startles us all as we all turn behind us in fear.

Amongst the fierce roar of the flames, it's difficult to decipher from which direction the shriek came from.

DeJon takes a step back before stamping his foot against the door with all the force he has in him.

The exit door flies open as DeJon stumbles through from losing his balance.

'Here,' he shouts as he takes Nevaeh back under his arm as we all rush through the door.

As we all stumble from our speed through the corridor, it doesn't take long for the flames to light up the passage from behind us.

Seeing the fire door to exit the building gave us hope as we desperately pace along the long, narrow corridor.

A sudden flow of energy flows through me, a feeling of safety and relief.

Could it be because, we have found Nevaeh, the exit to safety lies ahead of us, or could it be Shayth? Is he around me; close to me right now? In his ethereal body? In a parallel dimension, watching over me?

The feeling soon disappears as we all shiver from the sound of another demonic shriek! The sense of safety disappears from within my soul.

As I turn to look behind me, at the far end of the long corridor stands a tall figure…

It blends within the shadows of the thick smoke hiding the flames of fire in the background. But its pale face is illuminated within the darkness. Its piercing orange eyes glare directly at us.

Its proceeds to step forward; slowly, towards us.

Its gaunt pale face focuses in our direction as its pace increases. It's dark scraggly hair frames its sickeningly evil face, which is covered with blisters and lacerations.

Its pale, translucent white skin flakes away from dryness, as it looks like a resurrected corpse… The look of death.

The lacerated scars are layered with thick dry blood, which has stained the white tunic.

'DeJon,' I whisper as the fear shakes my voice. 'What did this?'

'Some fucked up demonic animal!' He responds as he focuses on the exit.

'It...it's behind us...' I manage to whisper in a broken voice as I watch it close the distance between us.

Nevaeh and DeJon turn their head to the back of the corridor, their eyes widen in fear.

The demon beast jumps against the wall before beginning to crawl towards us! Its broken wings hang from its body and the glow within its eyes become fierce with rage and thirst.

Its pace increases as its double-jointed body crawls along the wall while it releases an unnatural growl, desperate to reach us!

'Oh Fuck!' Nevaeh shouts in fear, forcing us to increase our pace and drag Nevaeh with us!

The unearthly growling coming from the possessed beast, ripples through the hall as it drives a cold shiver of fear through us.

'It's fucking comin', it fucking coming!' Nevaeh screams as we all shake from fear while stumbling to maintain the strength from our quivering knees!

'Hurry the fuck up!' Nevaeh pleads as we reach the exit door! The sinister demon jumps to the ground while extending its hands towards us as the growling becomes more aggressive, more hellish; thirsting for our souls.

Its claws are covered with the blood of its victims and it shakes with intense hunger.

'Oh lord. Save our souls!' Nevaeh cries as the fear consumes her.

I gasp as it reaches out to grab me!

Its broken fingernails almost brush my face as its eyes light up with frenzy!

At that moment, a force drags the wickedness back into the darkness of the shadows while it howls and convulses from whatever it is that grips it.

The uncontrollable sigh of relief makes my head spin lightly. As we run through the exit door, a cold chilling breeze relieves us from the heat of the inferno we have escaped.

The clear air makes me realise how desperate my lungs are for oxygen from having been surrounded by the smoke of the burning flames.

We run around the perimeter of the building as we desperately seek for a path, which will take us as far away from this venue as possible.

We reach the front of the building, everything suddenly appears in slow motion.

The full moon shines down on us in the clear night sky, which carries the cry of students who watch the building engulfed in flames.

Our breathing shortens from the intense fear, my weak knees cannot help but collapse to the ground as we reach the bottom of the stairwell outside the venue.

Nevaeh almost follows, but DeJon with his broad shoulders manages to keep her balanced.

DeJon gently drops to the ground, making sure Nevaeh does not fall too hard as he coughs intensely from his smoke-filled lungs.

We all turn to look back towards the building as I scurry onto my feet from hearing the howling of the demonic beast as if it is being tortured.

We can see nothing within the darkness of the smoke and the fury of the flames through the arched entrance hall. We stare towards the top of the stairs as the sudden shriek terrifies us! We hasten to get away, desperately searching for safety.

Suddenly the window towering over the entrance archway comes crashing down as the satanic creature flies through the air while howling through the night. It lands ahead of us, flat on its feet, crouching down for balance before turning to face us.

The sound of crashing glass adds to the hellish tones of cries and raging flames that fill the air.

It crouches to the ground as it glares and growls in our direction.

We stand frozen in our position as the realisation hits us that the satanic *shayateen* barricades our path to safety.

We all shake within our skin as it stands to its feet displaying its filthy cannibalistic teeth.

It straightens its double-jointed limbs as it stands tall and breaths deep.

'YOU,' it growls slowly in a deep dual-toned voice as it extends its hand and points it claws towards me...

My eyes widen in fear that it knows me; it wants me.

It steps towards me as it tenses its body and arms preparing to come for me in speed.

'Go...' I whisper, as my body feels frozen from the shock of fear.

'Of fuck!' Nevaeh cries as we all exhale heavily.

'Go!' I shout as a glimmer of courage roots through me, *Never be afraid,* I whisper in my mind as I take a step forward.

'Liyana!' DeJon shouts with aggression to distract my focus.

The demonic creature begins to smirk as its eyes light with pleasure.

It's teeth displayed from the widening of its tight crackled lips. The teeth appear rotten and dirt stained with uneven surfaces and cracks.

It opens its jaws before slithering its tongue from between its teeth, its forked tongue waving to me as it growls with a sound of demonic pleasure.

My heart pounds through my chest, as I am no longer in control of my quivering body. Yet I have the strength to take the slightest step forward, despite not knowing where my fate now lies.

The *shayateen* releases a faint laugh before its face becomes twisted and devious.

Amongst the screaming of the crowd, the *shayateen* laughs with pleasure before it begins to pace towards me with its hands extended seeming desperate to get a hold of my soul!

My lungs tighten as I begin to hyperventilate from fear despite taking small steps forward, in desperation to save Nevaeh and DeJon.

The quivering of my knees leaves me frozen as I watch the *shayateen* close the gap between us.

A force of wind suddenly flows through me as more shattered glass from the arch top comes crashing down behind me.

My hair blows across my face, and my mysterious scent hypnotises me for a split moment. I close my eyes and inhale the essence of safety, the final reminder of my protector, my warrior.

My Shayth, I whisper in my mind as I open my eyes to face the *shayateen*, to meet my fate.

As my eyes focus on the creature, I watch the look of fear grow on the *shayateen's* expression as it crouches to the ground in a defensive instinct.

It releases a raw growl as it begins to bite away at the air.

The *shayateen* turns its back to us and runs through the path before picking up its speed while running on all fours; like a wild beast running away from its predators in a vicious battle. As a fire truck turns into the path, the demonic beast jumps onto its bonnet before leaping towards the trees, into the forest.

The night is filled with the ringing of the sirens and the screaming of the student who witnessed the vanishing of the demonic beast. The beast that has left a trail of blazing fire and frantic screams behind!

'…Whoever saves the life of one, it shall be as if they have saved the life of all mankind…'

– Quran 5.32 / Talmud

31. Desperate Reunion

I return home from the hospital.

I am thankful to God that everyone dear to me are okay, they are safe.

I sit in the shower, as I feel numb from the shock of the horrific events.

The warm water drips onto my bare skin, soothing my tense muscles. I sit in a daze, trying to make sense of everything that has happened, everything that I have witnessed.

I recall the screams of terror from the students petrified for their lives, the fear in their eyes as they crossed paths with a demonic being.

The *shayateens*, the demons had entered in multiple students, possessing them to behave in unnatural ways, torturing their souls and attacking the people surrounding them.

But the students know not the truth of the sinister encounter they have experienced. Of the battle they faced for their souls. I cannot help but burst into tears from recalling the memories of their pain, the fear in their eyes for their very own lives.

My heart breaks as I recall every vivid scream from each innocent soul, who are unaware of this invisible battle we face. I wish there was more I could have done to help them, to calm them.

The sickening feeling in my stomach grows, as I cannot help but shed tears driven by the fear of what may have happened to my Shayth.

He should have been here by now, I tell myself as I claw my hair, feeling distressed, unable to calm my pouring tears.

It's been hours since the *shayateen* disappeared from public. Surely if he was safe, if he was okay, he would have come back for us?

How can I get hold of him? How can I find him? How will I know he is safe?

My heart fears the worst, having seen the destruction the *shayateen* has caused. I cannot help but worry about the murder of my Shayth.

I slip into my nightdress and take deep controlled breaths to calm my palpitating heart from my overactive imagination.

As I open my en-suite door and enter my bedroom, my heartbeat rises from relief; I see Shayth sitting at the end of my bed.

I gasp in relief as my body begins to shake.

Shayth stands to his feet; I think of nothing but to run towards him, wrapping my arms as tightly around him as possible.

His deep, heavy breathing reflects one of relief as he holds me tight and places a kiss on the top of my head.

I can't control the tears; I begin to sob from relief that he is okay, that he is safe.

We share a warm, loving embrace before he loosens his grip on my back and places his hands on my waist.

I'm not ready to let go; I stand still, holding tight around him. He takes a small step back as he holds my waist in position. 'Please!' I whisper as I squeeze him even tighter while taking a step closer to close the gap between us! I snuffle away as I cry from the relief that he is okay, that he is here.

He holds me gently in his arms again, understanding that I am not yet ready to let go!

For the first time, I realise... I cannot live without him.

He is my world, my protector – my everything. Without him, my heart would be alone; my life truly would be incomplete.

He slowly lowers his hand to my waist as he attempts to take another step back.

'Please,' I whisper in a plea.

The thought of parting from his arms brings back my tears as I begin to sob even more.

I feel complete, in this very moment where I realise exactly how I feel for Shayth. I cannot let go.

Shayth begins to stoke the back of my hair as his breathing becomes heavy.

I guess that he can finally sense what I am feeling for him at this very moment, from the colours and vibrations of my aura.

Now than ever more so, he will understand, my world has become Shayth.

I refuse to release the tightness of my grip.

He bends down and takes me by surprise as he sweeps my legs off the ground.

I don't care what it is he is doing, so long as I can remain holding him tight!

He cradles me in his arms as he carries me across the room.

My head is buried in his neck as I inhale his masculine scent, never wanting it to leave me.

He lays me on my bed, but I still refuse to let him out of my arms.

I leave him with no choice, as he lies beside me, holding me tight.

I hold him close as I snuffle away my last tears.

We lay there, holding each other, not saying a single word. Simply allowing our emotions to tell each other exactly how we feel.

As I lay against his chest with my eyes closed, my heartbeat slowly mimics his pace. My breathing calms as his beating heart becomes less intense. I loosen my grip as we lay in silence, embracing each other.

'Liyana…' the faint whisper calls out to me.

'Liyana…' I slowly open my eyes as my blurred vision gradually becomes clear.

'Hey, kiddo! Just wanted to make sure you are okay?'

'Uncle Aidan,' I whisper as I slowly lift my head from off the pillow.

'Get back to sleep, I just wanted to check for myself that you're all right. That's all.

'Come down when you're ready, kiddo.' Uncle Aidan pulls his head away from the gap in the door as he closes it behind him.

I lay my head back on the pillow; my heavy eyes feel like I've barely had any sleep.

I turn to look at the clock on the bedside cabinet and see it's 09.30 am.

My eyes widen as reality hits me.

I sit up and look around for Shayth not knowing when it was he had left?

I comb my fingers through the top of my hair as I reach for my phone and find endless messages and missed calls.

My friends have sent multiple messages to thank me for my support last night.

I put on my gown and head downstairs for painkillers to soothe my splitting headache.

'Liyana!' Uncle Aidan calls out in relief.

'What time did you get home last night?' he asks in a concerned tone.

'Err... I'm sorry, Uncle. It was pretty late by the time I got home. Maybe 03.30,' I respond sounding distracted.

I cannot get my mind off Shayth. We barely spoke a word last night. I have no idea what happened to the *shayateen* when it ran off into the forests and whether or not it was in fact, Trixy. I run the tap to fill my glass and watch Micky playing in the garden with Diesel.

A smile grows on my face at the sight of my baby brother, safe and happy.

'Well is it true what they are saying?' Aunt Liz blurts out distracting me from adoring my brother.

'I'm sorry...is what true?' I whisper trying to focus on her question.

She nods her head towards the TV mounted on the wall.

The local news reports students carry out cruel and vicious hoax leaving many in hospital.

'Honestly! First, it's the crazy clowns, and now it's this!' Aunt Liz comments as she shakes her head.

'I'm glad you're safe, kiddo!' Uncle Aidan sighs as he sips his cup of tea.

'I should go and check on Nevaeh,' I whisper as I proceed to leave the room.

'Not without breakfast!' Uncle Aidan calls out in a stern tone. I turn back towards the table a n d t a k e a seat across them both.

'Hey, my hero!' Nevaeh whispers as she watches me enter the room.

'How are you feeling?' I ask as I hand her a bunch of flowers. 'Like I've been in the ring with AJ! You'd have thought I'd enjoy that, given how much I dream of him!' her humour puts a smile on my face; I stroke the hair away from her cheeks.

'I'm glad you're better,' I whisper as I give her a warm, loving smile.

'How is Bazzer?' I ask hoping she will have some information.

'He's good, he got discharged early this morning. Concussion. He just needs to take it easy for a few days.'

'I thought you weren't coming to the party?' Nevaeh asks with a frown.

'I wasn't...but Sammy called and said you're all in trouble. So I had no choice. I know you wanted me to come to the party, but to create all this to get me there Nevaeh!'

We both burst into a giggle as I sit by her side and take her hand into mine.

'So let me get this straight, while everyone else is running away from the party...you're the only fool that, then, decides to run towards the party?'

'Yeah, something like that,' I reply as I lower my head with a sheepish smile.

'That really is something, Liyana! I can't think of many people who would ever do that.

Thank you,' she whispers as she gives my hand a gentle squeeze.

'So how bad is it,' I ask as I look at the cast around her leg.

'It's broken! Will take weeks if not months to heal!'

'So, what do you think it was?' she asks with a serious, quiet tone.

'I dunno…maybe a bunch of freaks on drugs gate-crashing!' I respond with a smirk, trying not to give too much away.

'Yeah,' she scoffs in agreement. 'That's the only explanation there is!'

'I'm happy you're feeling better, Sammy.'

'I am so thankful to God that I have someone like you in my life, Liyana! I'm so sorry that I left you on your own.'

'Sammy, honestly! You have nothing to apologise for, okay! I'm here for you regardless.'

'I know, but I wasn't there for you, that's the point!'

'Sammy, you being safe was all that was important to me! If you were there by my side, who knows what could have happened to us! So please, everything worked out for the best, you really don't have to bear any guilt.'

'I wish there were more people like you out there, Liyana! I've never known someone to be so selfless.'

'That's really kind of you, Sammy, thank you.'

'I'll see you in university on Monday.'

'Yes, you too, Sammy. Take care of yourself.'

'You too, Liyana. Bye.'

'Bye.'

I place my phone beside my bed and walk out to the balcony. 'Where are you,' I cry in my head as I stare into the stars, longing for my Shayth.

'Hi…'

I gasp from shock and turn to look to my side.

'Shayth!' I gasp as I wrap my arms around him; I can't control the widening grin on my face.

I pull away as I look at his face and cannot help but to stoke his hair with my hands before cupping his cheeks in my palms.

He offers me a loving smile with wide eyes as he places his hands-on top of mine.

'I could not have even dreamt of you to feel for me the way you do,' he whispers, as his growing smile also seems to be uncontrollable.

'Shayth,' I whisper, as my expression turns serious.

'Are you okay, did you get hurt?' I ask as my hands begin to shake with panic.

I put my hands around his shoulders then reach them down to his elbows while my eyes scan his body to see if there is any sign of injury or pain.

'Liyana,' he whispers, forcing my glance to meet his.

'I am fine, nothing has happened to me, nothing has hurt me,' he whispers gently as he cups his fingers around my chin.

A wide grin reappears on my face as I have the sudden urge to hold him in my arms again!

I cannot help but giggle from my happiness. Shayth mimics my expression, which forces me to laugh even louder!

I sit up against the headboard whilst Shayth sits facing me. 'So what happened?' I ask bracing myself to hear how the horror ended.

'We followed it into the forests by the venue.'

'Was it really Trixy?' I ask hastily.

He nods his head as he looks down to the ground.

'She had invited them into her body, it was difficult to get them to leave,' he whispers as he shakes his head in disappointment.

'Where is she? Is she okay?'

'Yes, she will be,' he responds as sadness consumes his expressions.

'So what happened?'

'We battled with the *shayateens*.'

'Wait, shayateens? As in plural? As in more than one demon?'

'Yes…' he pauses while he sighs, then proceeds to explain.

'The three demons that came after you, they are the ones that answered Trixy's call, when she sought help from the spirit world.'

'How did you get them to leave?'

'It was difficult. But we finally managed.

'When we are in our form; dark matter, we can see the *shayateens* within her body.'

I look at him with a confused expression.

He looks around the room and takes my hand.

We walk towards my mirror, Shayth holds me while he stands behind me. I am staring at my reflection while he wraps his broad shoulders around me.

'See our reflection,' he whispers. 'Though you are standing in front of me, you can still see me behind you; I am taller and broader.'

'Yes,' I whisper as I nod.

'It is similar to this. We can see Trixy's physical body just as you are here. Whereas the *shayateens*, we can see them from within her, just as you can see my frame now, even though I am behind you.'

'Okay,' I whisper as I pay attention.

He takes my hand as we sit back on the bed.

'It is difficult, and we cannot conflict real damage to the *shayateens* while they dwell in Trixy's body as she would feel the pain, the injuries.

'But as soon as we pinned her down and were dragging at the *shayateens*, they jumped out willingly.

'You see, they are stronger when they are in their natural form rather than when they are in the body of a human.

'As soon as we had pinned her and thus trapped the *shayateens*, they broke out to conjure their strength to defeat us.'

'How come you couldn't see them before? When you went shopping and saw the woman in the park?' I question not fully understanding.

'I can only imagine at that time, perhaps, only one *shayateen*, only one demon dwelled within which is easier to conceal.'

'So what happened to Trixy?' I ask as worry begins to creep in.

'As soon as they released her body, Trixy fell unconscious. I am not sure how long her soul; her subconscious has been battling with the demons.'

'And what of the beasts?'

'We destroyed them; you will never see them again.' A shiver runs through my spine as my eyes glaze over.

Shayth takes my hand and offers me a gentle kiss on the surface.

'So where is Trixy now?' I eagerly ask, hoping to hear she is safe.

'Do not worry. She is at her parent's home.

'I dropped her off at the porch and waited till her parents opened the door and took her in.'

'So she saw you?'

'No, she was unconscious for most the time. She regained consciousness when her parents found her, woke her.'

'Well, is she okay now?' I ask as I begin to panic again.

'Do not worry. I visited her earlier today. She is fine. No severe injuries. Just bruising and a few minor cuts, nothing more.'

I pause as I think of the distress she must be in now.

'And what were you doing at the party?' Shayth asks with a serious tone as he raises an eyebrow.

'I... I'm sorry. I had no choice,' I explain in a pleading tone. 'Sammy called, and she was so afraid. I couldn't leave her in that state all lone. And then when I heard about Nevaeh... I had to find her!'

'You do not understand how much danger you put yourself under, Liyana. The shayateens, these demons were conjured to hunt you, to hurt you!'

'I'm sorry...' I whisper as a streak of fear runs through me. 'I just couldn't leave them,' I add as I lower my gaze down.

'You know...at one point it almost had you. And I didn't know if I could get to it in time before it...'

Shayth sighs as he shakes his head in relief.

'As we were leaving the hall?' I whisper in shock.

'Yes...' he affirms as he places his palm across my cheek.

'And what in God's name possessed you to proceed to walk towards the demons!' Shayth asks in a stern tone as he moves his palm from my cheek and places it firmly on my shoulder giving me a little shake.

'Oh... I...err... I was trying to get it away from Nevaeh and DeJon,' I whisper feeling sheepish at my foolish attempts.

'I couldn't bear the thought of them getting hurt when I knew all it wanted was me,' I add as I recall those terrifying moments.

'My heart jumped when I saw you take a step forward, Liyana... I thought I would lose you at that moment!

'I've never flown so fast before!' he adds as he shakes his head and places his hand on mine.

'I felt you fly past me...' I whisper as I lower my eyebrows and recall the sensation. The moment when my hair began to flow across my face, being surrounded by Shayth's scent.

'Liyana... I did not fly straight past you... I flew straight through you!' Shayth adds with wide eyes.

I reach for his hand and pull it towards me as I hold his palm in between mine.

I cannot help but smile lovingly towards him. My Shayth, my everything.

'You are certain Trixy will be okay?' I ask as I cannot help but feel concerned for her.

'Yes. She is with her parents who have already taken her to the doctors. She does not remember much. Trust me; she will be fine.'

'Okay,' I respond with a faint smile as I try hard to convince myself to no longer worry.

The mood feels lighter, less intense now that we know everyone is safe and the demons are no longer.

A thought suddenly hits me as I recall the events Shayth has explained.

'What is it?' he asks softly.

'So you left Trixy on the porch?'

'Yes...' he responds looking confused.

'And then what? Knocked on the door in your ethereal state while her parents came to open it.'

'Yes,' he answers as the confusion in his expression grows from my line of questioning.

I smirk for a moment as I recall the similar encounter Shayth must have experienced with me.

'You must be getting tired of picking up strays, having to hang around a porch, because we can't take care of ourselves.' I look up at him with big eyes as I offer a faint smile.

'And to think, no one was around when you knocked on my door, we must be such a nuisance to you!' I add as I scoff in jest.

'Liyana...' he whispers as a soft smile approaches his face.

He looks deep into my eyes as he leans forward and puts his palm softly around my neck.

'I did not knock on your door... I did not want anyone to take you away...

'You were in my arms the whole time. I watched you for hours that day, stroking your hair, stroking your cheeks. It's only when I saw your uncle driving up that I had no choice but to place you down on the porch.

'But even then, I sat there, right by your side...till your uncle took you inside the house and closed the door.

When the door closed, that's the moment I left...and the moment I realised...that I had to come back...for you.'

'…Appreciate the beauty of every moment, or forever will you live blind…'

— A.J. Missara

32. Cherished Moments

'Liyana!' DeJon shouts as he comes running towards me.

He wraps his broad shoulders around my tiny back and lifts me off the ground while swinging me around in joy.

'You are amazing!' he states as he finally decides to land me on my feet.

'Seriously, you're one top girl! I don't even know many men that would have the balls that you do!'

'Err...thanks... I think,' I respond slowly.

We both start laughing as he walks me to my class.

At lunch, Sammy and I sit on the benches of the stadium while we watch the boys practice amongst having our sandwiches. 'Liyana,' a voice calls out.

As I look behind me, I notice Courtney approach us.

'Hi, Courtney,' I greet with a warm smile.

'I just wanted to say thank you again...and sorry,' she offers, as she looks a little ashamed.

'Honestly, Courtney, it's all in the past. Let's all just learn from this and try to become stronger and wiser from everything we have been through,' I respond to help her defeat any guilt within her.

'I've quit the Aphrodite's! That's one thing I have learned,' she adds with a proud smile.

Courtney joins us for lunch, and the boys gather round while we all appreciate the company of each other.

The week flows by with no significant events, though it has been announced that no future Halloween parties will be permitted or hosted by the university!

'What is it?' I ask curiously as I watch Shayth stare at the ground appearing anxious.

I tuck my hair behind my ear as the night breeze picks up.

'May I...' he scoffs, as he looks somewhat sheepish.

'May I take you out tomorrow?' he asks as he turns to look into my eyes while leaning on the balcony.

I smile instantly and feel the butterflies awakening in my stomach.

'Err… Yes. I'd like that,' I respond as I feel my cheeks begin to blush.

He chuckles lightly at my reaction and walks towards me while placing his hands on my waist.

He looks into my eyes as he offers me his dazzling smile.

'May I meet…' he stops in mid-flow as my bedroom door slowly opens.

'Micky,' I whisper as I take a few steps forward to hide Shayth. Micky quickly closes the door behind him and tucks himself into the covers of my bed.

I turn to look at Shayth; he has gone…

'I've missed you, Micky,' I whisper as we cuddle in the duvet.

'I've missed you too, Liyana,' he whispers in a sleepy state.

'Can we do something this weekend, just you and me?' he asks with his innocent voice.

'We can do whatever you want,' I respond reassuringly.

'No one loves me like you,' he states as he dozes off.

'I will always love you, Micky,' I whisper as I kiss him goodnight.

Shayth and I sit together for lunch.

We laugh and jest and are shortly joined by Sammy and Courtney.

'Shayth, the jocks are searching for you,' Sammy informs. He sighs as he hangs his head down.

'I have been summoned,' he teases as he stands to his feet. 'How did you get on with your dark matter assignment and the theory of an alternate, parallel dimension?' Shayth asks Sammy before he leaves our table.

'Oh I've been meaning to tell you, to thank you!!' Sammy explains with excitement.

'I have got top marks for creativity and innovation!'

Shayth chuckles lightly and proceeds to congratulate Sammy. He offers me a sly wink accompanied with his gleaming smile before walking off towards the stadium.

As another week in university is complete, I walk to my car and am followed by Shayth.

'Liyana,' he calls out as he paces behind me.

I look to my side and smile at him as I bite my bottom lip.

'So,' he whispers; I can see the anxiousness growing in his expression.

'So, I wanted to make it up to you tonight.'

'Make what up?' I ask curiously.

'Well, I'd asked you not to come to the Halloween party, and you never got to dress as a…monster…'

We both begin to laugh lightly as I watch him with endearment.

'You have nothing to make-up, everything you have done has always been in my interest,' I reassure him.

I feel his hand at the base of my back as we walk through the small car park.

'Nevertheless, seeing as though the university has a ban on holding a firework display, I thought maybe we could spend this evening together?'

'I'd love that,' I whisper as I feel a little flush.

'So I was thinking maybe I could pick you up at 8 pm again?'

'That works well with me,' I confirm with a smile.

'And maybe, I could knock on your door…' he slowly whispers.

'Oh…' His suggestion takes me by surprise.

'Yes, of course. That would be nice,' I hastily add not to deter him.

He smiles nervously as I feel there is more he would like to ask.

'Okay. Great!' He pauses for a moment and then proceeds,

'And maybe I could finally get…get to meet Micky?' I am taken back by his suggestion.

My heart fills with joy at the very thought of the two most important people in my life meeting for the first time.

'I… I would love that…' I whisper in a choked voice. He sighs from relief!

'Great!' he exclaims!

Shayth leans into the car as I press down the window.

'I have put something in the boot. I hoped… maybe you could wear it tonight?'

I smile with a confused expression.

'It's something from my world,' he whispers. I'm speechless and not sure of how to react.

'I… I can't believe…' I begin to laugh feeling entirely thrown. 'Thank you!' I respond as I cannot help but smile at him.

My smile quickly disappears as I spot Romeo in the distance. 'Shayth… I have to go!'

'What has happened,' he asks with a slight frown.

'Nothing…yet,' I reply as I break a smile.

'Romeo's coming, and I don't think I can bear to live through what he is about to do…not again.'

I feel myself begin to blush as Shayth turns back to look at him.

'Liyana!' Romeo shouts as he proceeds to jog towards us.

'See you tonight,' I state as I reverse the car.

Romeo quickens his pace as he twirls to show me his back!

I look behind in the rear-view mirror as I drive off and can see his signature move of wriggling his body while caressing his back.

Shayth walks towards him with a smile as he shakes his head at his immaturity.

My heart begins to pound as I hear the doorbell ring. 'Ah, you must be Shayth!'

'Good evening, ma'am.'

'Oh please, call me Eliza! That's a lovely outfit you are wearing. I don't think I have seen anything quite like it before.'

'Thank you.'

'Please, please, come on in!'

I hear the footsteps as he steps into the hallway.

I cannot believe Shayth is in my house, downstairs, in the presence of my family!

'Ah. So you must be the one keeping a smile on my Liyana's face!' Uncle Aidan states.

'Good evening, sir,' Shayth responds with a polite tone.

I hear a patting, which I can only assume is Uncle Aidan welcoming Shayth with a friendly hug and a pat on the back. 'Come on through, young man, and please, call me Aidan.' Suddenly, Diesel breaks into a continuous bark.

'Diesel,' I hear Micky call out. No doubt he is trying to tame him. Diesel's bark surprisingly turns into whimpers, and I can hear his pitter patter head towards the kitchen.

I slowly walk down the stairs as I try hard to tame the butterflies within my stomach.

I stand in the doorway and watch Micky stare at Shayth while Shayth has a huge smile on his face.

'Have I met you before?' Micky asks Shayth in his innocent, childlike voice.

'Hi, Micky, I do not think we have met. My name is Shayth,' he responds as he leans down to Micky who is sitting on the rug close to the fireplace.

'Shayth. That's a beautiful name. Like my sister's name, Liyana. That's beautiful too! Hey, you have eyes like me!'

Shayth smiles and Micky mimics his expression.

'Maybe that's why your sister is my friend? Because my eyes remind her of you,' Shayth jests.

Micky looks at Shayth curiously.

'I have met you before!' Micky insists.

'I feel like I have met you lots of time. Do you work in my school?'

'No, Micky,' Shayth chuckles, 'I go to university with your sister. I have come to take her out today.'

'Are you taking her on a date? Liyana said she will tell me about a date when I am bigger.'

'Right, champ. Bedtime for you I think!' Uncle Aidan announces as everyone lightly chuckles from mild embarrassment.

'Liyanaaa,' Micky shouts as he turns and spots me in the doorway.

Everyone turns to look at me while Micky runs towards me and wraps his arms around me.

Shayth stands instantly and stares at me with a huge smile on his face.

'Liyana. I like Shayth; can he come out with us this weekend too? Just the three of us?' Micky asks with excitement.

'Let's talk about that tomorrow,' I respond to Micky as I kneel down to cuddle him.

'Come on now, Micky; I'll tuck you in,' Aunt Liz announces as she walks towards us.

'Goodnight, Liyana, Goodnight, Shayth,' Micky offers as he begins to run up the stairs with Diesel following behind.

'Have a lovely time Liyana…you really do look beautiful,' Aunt Liz compliments as she gives me a warm, proud smile.

I head towards the door with Shayth by my side.

'Make sure you both behave!' Uncle Aidan reminds us as we step out of the door.

'Of course, sir.'

'Aidan!' my Uncle reminds.

Shayth smiles. 'Of course, Aidan, thank you.'

As we close the door behind us, Shayth pulls out my Missara flower from within his jacket.

'You look beautiful, my Lady Liyana,' he whispers as I take the delicate flower in my hand.

'It's beautiful, this dress. You really shouldn't have.'

'You've enhanced its beauty,' he whispers as he leans forward and places a gentle kiss on my cheek.

'A princess, fit for a prince,' he whispers as he looks into my eyes. I smile sheepishly and cannot make sense of his witty comment.

He extends his arm, which I hold onto as we walk towards his car.

We arrive at a place where I have been before.

As he switches off the engine, Shayth walks around to open the passenger door.

He extends his hand to help me out of the low-seated car.

'I don't have to make you trawl through the forest now that you know who I am,' he whispers as he pulls me closer towards him and holds me tight by the waist.

Shayth slowly extends his wings from the slits at the back of his smart-hooded jacket as we levitate off the ground.

I cannot help but gasp, as I hold on tight to his shoulders. Shayth maintains a smooth pace as we continue to hover along the landscape with the forest trees beneath us.

As I look around, I see the reflection of the moonlight within the perfectly rounded lake.

My heart fills with joy as I recall our last perfect moments here. I notice the glass panel floating in the centre of the lake, which we head towards.

We land gently on the panel, and I cannot help but twirl once again.

I continuously laugh throughout my twirls, feeling mesmerised by the beauty and enchanting views.

The dress so similar to the one I wore last time, but far more elegant and lavish.

The multiple panels of white are coloured with hints of pinks and purples. Each of the panels decorated with sequins and rare stones; glistening in the moonlight from every twirl I make.

The cashmere-like sleeves are slit from shoulder to wrist, and the v-cut neckline maintains a level of modesty.

I look over at Shayth, who simply stands there with his head tilted as he stares at me with endearment.

I laugh as I cover my face from the embarrassment of my continuous twirling.

I run towards him, wrapping my arms around him tight.

'I love this,' I whisper with excitement as my chin rests on his shoulder.

As I pull my head back to face Shayth, my eyes meet his gaze. His eyes lightly sparkle; I can feel the excitement in my stomach becoming intense.

'Is there anything more that you could want in this moment?' he asks as he looks deep into my eyes.

'Nothing. This is perfect. This is beautiful,' I whisper with not a single worry or concern on my mind, simply the feeling of serenity.

'I have never known beauty like yours, Liyana,' he whispers with a serious tone to his voice.

'Your aura, your energy...it draws me to you. I could never be apart from you,' he whispers as he begins to frown.

'From the moment you reappeared into my life, you have become my pleasure, my pain, my only purpose.'

I lower my gaze as I recall how lonely I was only a few months ago, before I ever realised Shayth existed.

'There is nothing more to me, but you. We belong together, always,' he whispers as I raise my glance to reach his eyes.

A smile of love and excitement consumes me, which Shayth begins to mimic.

'This is it now, Shayth... This is us, forever,' I whisper with delight.

'And you are no longer afraid of what I am?' he questions with a frown.

'You are a *jinn*, but before that, you are my Shayth.'

In that moment, he squeezes me tight and begins to twirl us around.

I cannot help but to laugh out loud.

The skies are clear allowing every star above to twinkle down upon us!

'Are you ready?' Shayth asks as he puts me back down on my feet.

'Ready for what,' I whisper as I play with the back of his hair with my hands around his neck.

'There is nothing I would not do for you,' he whispers as he flashes me a wicked smile.

Instantly he spins me around, pulling me against him.

With my back pressed against his chest, he holds me firmly by the waist.

'Are you ready?' he whispers in my ear as his teeth softly bite against my earlobe.

'For what?' I whisper as my heart begins to pound.

'Tell me you are ready,' he insists.

'I'm ready.' I laugh out, not knowing what to expect.

'I want you to feel alive...' he whispers as he releases his grip from my waist and holds onto my hands.

Shayth raises my hands, placing them on the back of his neck. I cannot help but feel a little nervous as the motion seems to have awoken my senses.

I hold onto Shayth's neck as he returns his palms firmly around my waist.

'Ready,' he whispers as he brushes his lips along my neck offering me gentle kisses which send sparks throughout my body.

He begins to count down as I look into the sparkles of the sky. '5...4...3...2...'

With a loud bang, the fireworks light up the skies! I gasp as I hold tighter against Shayth's neck.

The skies fill with streaks of multi-coloured lights shooting through the night. The reflection from the lake intensifies each firework fighting with the other to be seen.

Shayth levitates slowly as we meet the height of the trees and are surrounded by the brightest of colours flowing around us; above us, beneath us, in every direction.

Our feet reach the glass panel; Shayth takes my hand and proceeds to twirl me amongst the flashes of lights.

His energy begins to flow through him, before he projects his energy towards me. I'm mesmerised as I watch the swirls of white and pale blue dance around us.

His eyes flicker with sparkles; we cannot help but laugh as we both twirl through the fireworks.

Life has never been so beautiful; life has never been so complete.

We pull close towards each other, as we cannot resist sharing a deep passionate kiss amongst the flashes of lights surrounding us in this perfect moment.

Shayth's warmth penetrates through me as I am hypnotised by our intense kiss.

The sound of the fireworks comes to an end and we slowly part, pulling away from each other's lips.

'Keep still,' he whispers with a wicked smile. 'The spin in your mind will pass in a few moments.'

I smile, as my eyes remain closed. I absorb every second of this perfect moment with my Shayth as for once; I feel like I have no care in the world.

I open my eyes slowly to find Shayth staring intensely at me with a tilted head and a dazzling smile.

I squeeze him tight in my arms in a warm embrace and close my eyes at the feeling of him kissing the side of my head.

I slowly open my eyes, wishing for this moment to never end. My eyes widen, as my body stiffens at the unexpected sight before me.

I release my tight grip from Shayth before leaning back. Shayth stares intensely at my unexpected expression, I look at him with concern before turning my glance back behind him.

Shayth turns to look in the direction of my gaze. 'Akheel!' he states in a tone of shock.

'What are you doing here?'

Akheel takes a step towards us. His posture and expression both registering signs of regret.

'Shayth,' the young man calls as he proceeds to take a few steps towards us.

'Our sacred laws are in place, which differentiates our species from the *shayateen*, the demons.

'Your actions have not gone unnoticed; our majesty demands your presence.

'You have been summoned…at once!'

- - - v- - - - -v- - - - -v- - - - -v- - - - -v- - - - -v- - -

Continue the Journey with Misanthropy – Dual Dimensions